SPIRAL OF NEED

SUZANNE WRIGHT

SPIRAL OF NEED

THE MERCURY PACK SERIES

Text copyright © 2015 Suzanne Wright

Published by Montlake Romance, Seattle

www.apub.com

Amazon, the Amazon logo, and Montlake Romance are trademarks of Amazon.com, Inc., or its affiliates.

ISBN-13: 9781503948068
ISBN-10: 1503948064

Cover design by Jason Blackburn

Printed in the United States of America

To all those who, like me, would probably fit in better among

mythological creatures than their own race.

You know who you are.

CHAPTER ONE

Nothing like being accused of attempted murder to complete a girl's Friday evening.

Alyssa "Ally" Marshall kept her expression carefully blank as she stared at the two wolf shifters sitting across from her. For at least an hour the enforcers had kept her detained in an empty room of the pack house before finally joining her, only to look at her as though she were a perfect stranger as opposed to one of their pack mates.

She knew why they had left her alone for so long. Shifters didn't do well with enclosed spaces. Placing her in a small room, bare except for three chairs and a desk, was obviously supposed to increase her discomfort and make her wolf feel trapped and isolated.

It worked, but Ally had fought hard not to show it. Fought hard to keep her pacing wolf from losing her shit. And fought hard to suppress the memories of the last time she'd felt so trapped.

Then the mind games had begun.

First Greg and Clint had tried the good cop/bad cop routine, which she'd found rather insulting to her intelligence. So while Good Cop Greg had done his best to convince her that he was her savior and Bad Cop Clint had been browbeating and antagonistic, Ally had remained calm as she firmly stated the facts.

Instead of listening to what she had to say and considering her side of the story, they had tried twisting her words. And she'd quickly realized that they hadn't brought her into this room to hear her version of the events. They had already made up their minds that she was guilty; what they wanted was a confession.

At that point, she'd demanded that they summon their Alpha but was told that Matt was talking with Ally's supposed victim and wouldn't be joining them. That was when Ally turned silent. She wasn't going to give them anything more to use against her.

No matter how much psychological pressure they put on her, Ally refused to crack. She didn't flinch, she didn't lose her temper, and she didn't evade eye contact. As they stared at her, she stared right back. Her wolf approved of her resilience, though the animal would find much more satisfaction in scalping the bastards with her claws. It wasn't a bad idea, really.

Greg had then turned from good cop into frustrated-as-all-shit cop, sighing and growling. And Clint had gone from bad cop to on-the-verge-of-snapping cop, slamming his hands on the table and aggressively invading her personal space. Ally was the only one in the room projecting an outward calm . . . and that was just irritating them even more. How grand.

"Do you have any idea how bad this could get for you, Ally?" Greg leaned forward. "Matt is going to be supremely pissed. You're facing an execution here. Tell us the truth, and we can help you. We'll reduce the penalty to banishment from the pack."

She snorted. Even if they did want to help her, they didn't have the authority to decide penalties.

"Continuing to maintain your innocence is pointless," stated Clint, rising from his seat. "We have evidence"—no, they didn't—"and we have witnesses."

What they had were the words of some asshole kids who had been detained in this room more times than anyone could count.

Greg folded his arms across his chest. "You said those boys approached you."

No, she hadn't. She'd said they surrounded her when she left her cabin mere seconds after she'd realized that not only had someone broken into the cabin while she was gone, but they had totally ransacked it.

Greg went on. "You also said you're certain that those boys made a mess in your home."

Personally, she wouldn't call breaking her furniture, slashing her clothes, spray-painting insults on her walls, smashing her TV, and slinging the contents of the refrigerator around her home a *mess*.

"But according to the eight youths, they were just hanging around, minding their own business, when you came at them and accused them of breaking into your cabin."

Which, of course, was a load of cock and bull.

"They claim that they assured you that they weren't responsible for the damage."

Another lie. In truth, they had delighted in confessing their involvement when they crowded her, laughingly informing her that Rachelle had put them up to it. And who was Rachelle? Only the delegate of Satan. She also happened to be the pack's Beta female.

"They insist that you refused to listen, that you persisted in accusing them of breaking into your home at Rachelle's request. Then you stated, 'I'm going to kill her!' before running off."

Had Ally *thought* the words? Multiple times. Had she spoken them aloud? Not even once, because Ally didn't bother with threats or warnings. She much preferred to challenge her foe, get the fight over with, and then go on about her day. But she'd resisted the urge to challenge Rachelle for several reasons— mostly because it was exactly what Rachelle wanted. Ally had no intention of giving that crazy heifer anything.

Clint came to Ally's side, resting his hands on the table. "*You* say that you headed for the pack house, looking for Matt, only to find that the place was empty. But, see, I don't buy that, sweetheart." His eyes drilled into her as his upper lip curled. "I think you knew that our Alpha would be of no help to you, knew that he would take Rachelle's side over yours."

Only one thing about his theory was true: Matt probably *would* take Rachelle's side.

"So then you decided to take the matter into your own hands, didn't you?" Clint's voice turned harder, louder, browbeating. "You did exactly as Rachelle claims: you tracked her down and attacked her from behind, slashing her back, giving her no chance to defend herself." He slowly stalked to Ally's other side as he continued, "She quickly righted herself and whirled on you, didn't she? That was when you sucker punched her, knocking her out, and ran like the coward you are."

Her wolf growled, insulted by the "coward" comment. Ally wanted to snort. If she'd wanted to kill Rachelle, she'd have gone at her from the front. And she'd have made sure she finished the job. Since she'd joined the Collingwood Pack two years ago, Ally had only been involved in two duels. Both times, Ally had won. She fought hard and dirty, but she did *not* attack from behind. And she did *not* run off like a coward. No self-respecting dominant wolf would.

"You were jealous because you lost Zeke to her," charged Clint with a taunting smirk, "and you thought that if she was out of the picture, you would get him back."

Even if she had wanted Zeke back, killing Rachelle wouldn't have achieved it. Since it was rare for shifters to survive the death of a mate, Zeke would most likely have died right along with her. As such, Clint's allegation couldn't be more pathetic. And because Ally had a terrible habit of accidentally speaking her thoughts aloud, she mocked, "Wow, you cracked this case *wide* open."

Clint flushed from the neck up, but after a moment he gave a careless shrug. "It's your word against Rachelle's." His tone made it clear that Ally's word meant jack shit. Unfortunately, that was true.

The past few months had sucked big-time. It had been a blow when her boyfriend found his true mate, but Ally was happy for Zeke. She had been nothing but welcoming and respectful to his mate, but the female had loathed her from minute one. Ally had felt the hate pouring from her in waves—literally. Being highly empathetic came with the Seer package.

Her intuition had told her that Rachelle Lavin was going to be trouble . . . and it had been right. Despite Zeke not hesitating to claim Rachelle as his mate, the female had immediately embarked on a hate campaign with Ally as the target.

Ally had been shocked when Zeke berated her a few months ago for supposedly insulting his mate. Confused and riled, she'd sought out Rachelle . . . playing right into the woman's hands, she later realized. Everyone had witnessed her yelling at her Beta female, who had remained calm and cool as she rebuked Ally and gave her pitying looks for her "jealousy."

That was when the "Ally's jealous" tripe had started. And she had quickly found that there wasn't a good defense against that seventh-grade insult. If Ally ignored it, she was jealous. If she responded with a smart comeback, she was jealous. If she got pissed and told them to go eat shit, she was not only jealous but bitter too.

Shortly after that incident, Rachelle had claimed that Ally was sending her hateful text messages. Again, Zeke had freaked at Ally. So again, she'd sought out Rachelle, demanding that she produce these fictional messages. To her utter shock and dismay, Rachelle had. Ally had adamantly and loudly denied sending them, insisted that Rachelle must have at some point taken Ally's cell phone and sent them to herself. Which, of course, sounded plain crazy—yet it was true. But no one other than Ally seemed to see that.

And so, her pack mates had slowly but surely pulled away from Ally. In the time she'd been part of the Collingwood Pack, she'd healed several of them and had twice saved the pack from conflict through her visions . . . but all of that had ceased to mean anything.

In their defense, Rachelle was a very convincing liar. She'd made Ally an outsider in her own pack. And thanks to the heifer's latest stunt, Ally might be cast out.

"No one's going to buy your story, Ally," Clint growled into her ear. Her wolf snapped her teeth at him. The guy certainly had the Prick Factor going on. "No one's going to believe you. We have a witness who claims they saw you attack Rachelle."

"I doubt that."

He straightened. "Oh, really? Why?"

"One, because the assault didn't happen. Two, because if you did have a witness, you wouldn't need a confession. As you said, it's currently my word against Rachelle's. People might trust her and like her, but that's not enough to justify an execution. Particularly since there are some gaping holes in Rachelle's little tale."

"Such as?"

"Why would someone who wanted to kill her run away while she was unconscious? Wouldn't they take advantage of that moment in which she was totally helpless and deliver a killing blow, considering they were a 'coward' and all?"

Clint was quiet for a moment. "Maybe you heard someone coming. Or maybe you noticed someone was watching."

"Or maybe Rachelle's just talking out of her ass." Again.

"You know what I think, Ally?" asked Greg.

"Oh, this is going to be good," she muttered sardonically.

"I think that you didn't really want to kill Rachelle. I think you just lost your temper at a weak moment. We've all acted impulsively with anger at some point, right?" His tone turned soft and understanding. More mind games. "I think that you might have genuinely believed Rachelle had ordered the boys to trash your cabin. You were already very upset with her for taking Zeke from you. You've been feeling lost and alone. Jealousy has often got the better of you lately, and who could blame you for that?" Greg actually patted her hand.

Oh, for Christ's sake, was she really supposed to buy this oh-so-caring act?

"When you walked into the cabin and saw the chaos, it was the icing on the cake. You did what anybody would do in that situation. You snapped, and you tracked down the person you convinced yourself was responsible. That was why you fled the scene after attacking Rachelle. Once you saw her unconscious on the ground, your anger dimmed and you felt bad for what you did."

"It's either that," began Clint, "or you went after Rachelle with the intention of killing her but then lost your confidence at the last moment. Which is it?"

"Do the right thing and tell us the truth," encouraged Greg. "Make things easier on yourself. As soon as you confess, this will all be over. Don't you want this to be over?"

Yeah, she damn well did. Frick and Frack had kept her in this tiny room for over two hours, and her wolf was at serious risk of losing it. But making a false confession wasn't on her list of things to do. "I've already told you what happened. I have nothing more to say."

Clint sighed. "Fine, if that's how you want to play it." He looked at Greg. "Call Matt. Maybe he'll do the execution right here, right now."

This was where she was obviously supposed to quiver in fear and finally confess. Instead, she gave a theatrical gasp. "What? Now? But the night is young, boys."

"*Ally*," Clint gritted out.

"Bring out the cuffs, let's have some fun."

"*Ally*."

She threw up her arms. "All right, I confess . . . I ransacked my apartment for fun, falsely accused a bunch of well-meaning youths, attacked my Beta female, and then stuck around long enough to be detained and possibly executed." She shrugged. "It seemed like a good idea at the time."

Clint's face flushed again—most likely because when she put it like that, it became clear just how pitiful their argument really was. "Don't get smart with me."

She snickered. "Are you sure you'd know if I did?"

"I'd say it's time we—" Greg paused as the door behind her swung open. "Zeke."

Oh, goody.

"She refuses to accept responsibility or—"

"I'll take it from here." Once the enforcers had left and closed the door behind them, Zeke took one of the seats opposite her, his blue eyes tired. He looked tortured, just as he had each time he'd stepped between Ally and Rachelle in the past few months.

She could *feel* how deeply it hurt him to choose sides; his pain chafed her nerve endings like sandpaper. That was what it was like for Seers: picking up positive emotions created pleasant, warm sensations. Negative emotions, however, could cause anything from mild discomfort to excruciating pain.

Despite Zeke's hurt, Ally couldn't muster any sympathy for him. They had been in a relationship for almost eighteen months. If there was one person in this pack who knew Ally well, it was Zeke. If there was one person who should have seen through all the lies, it was him. Yet even he had jumped on the "Ally can't be trusted" bandwagon.

It was hard to believe this male had once spoken of imprinting with her. Wolves who weren't true mates could still come together and mate through imprinting. It wasn't uncommon, since shifters knew it wasn't certain that they would find their true mates. But the process of imprinting hadn't happened for Ally and Zeke, and she knew why. Although she had cared for him, she'd never loved him.

Just the same, her wolf had been comfortable and content with Zeke, but she hadn't wanted him the way a wolf wanted its mate. Their inner wolves "felt" on a level that humans could never surpass: fiercely, wildly, ragingly, and ferociously. Her wolf's feelings for Zeke had never been that intense and all-consuming.

"What's my execution date?" Not that Ally honestly thought Matt would order that. He didn't have enough evidence to justify it, no matter how much he might wish differently.

"No one is going to execute you." Zeke sounded so tired that she almost felt bad for him. Almost.

"Well then, if you're going to banish me from the pack, get it over with." She could have left at any time, but she hadn't been prepared to let anyone drive her out of her own pack, particularly not some vindictive, unhinged skank. And she'd figured that everyone would see through Rachelle's act eventually, that because she was innocent the matter would soon fix itself.

"You're not going to be banished."

Well, that was a surprise. "Does this mean you doubt what your mate claimed I did?"

Zeke seemed to struggle for words. "I know that it doesn't sound like you, but you haven't been yourself lately. I believe you didn't set out to kill Rachelle, but the fact is that you did assault her. I've given you a lot of leeway, Ally. I've overlooked a lot of things, but I can't overlook this. I can't."

"So are Rachelle and I going to have a one-on-one instead?" How grand.

"No."

Of course not. Rachelle might be Beta female, but her level of dominance didn't exceed Ally's. Rachelle wouldn't want to chance being defeated by someone of lower rank. "I've apparently harassed and attacked her. Her wolf should be going crazy for vengeance. That alone should have caused her to challenge me."

He scrubbed a hand down his face. "A part of her feels sorry for you. She said she can understand why you're jealous. She admits that she'd feel just as devastated and bitter in your position.

She even argued to keep you in the pack when Matt was ready to banish you."

Ally double-blinked, shocked. "She did what?"

"She doesn't want you to be out there all alone. She told Matt and me that if you apologize and vow to end your jealous behavior, she'll even be happy for you to escape punishment."

And that was when Ally finally comprehended just what Rachelle had been trying to accomplish all along. Not drive Ally out of the pack. Not have her banished or executed—or at least not yet, anyway. No, Rachelle had been trying to isolate Ally. Trying to take away everything that was important to her. She wanted Ally to be miserable and alone, and she wanted a front-row seat to the show.

"All you have to do is apologize," Zeke repeated.

Laughing humorlessly, Ally leaned forward. "Apologize to her? I'd rather exfoliate my skin with barbed wire and then dive into a pool of chlorine." Something that Rachelle would know perfectly well. "Besides, I'm not in the habit of saying sorry for stuff I haven't done."

Zeke cursed under his breath. "Ally, she's trying to help you here."

Ally shook her head sadly. "I never thought you'd be so easily fooled." If his mating bond with Rachelle had fully developed, he would have sensed that she was lying. But still, he should have known that Ally was innocent. Should have known that even if Ally *had* attacked Rachelle in a moment of rage, she wouldn't have lied about it. Ally owned her shit. "So if you're not going to cast me out, and she's not going to challenge me, what's the punishment for my fictional crime?"

"If you don't apologize to Rachelle, we'll be forced to relieve you of your status."

The words were like a blow to the head. Status was everything to wolf shifters; it gave their wolves a clear purpose and stability. As such, to strip a wolf of their status was a very serious thing, designed to cut deep, to hurt both the wolf and the human side.

And it did. "I see." Her tone was flat, empty of any emotion, and gave away none of her wolf's righteous anger.

"Ally, look at me." Whatever Zeke saw in her expression made him stiffen, as if bracing himself for impact. "I didn't want things to be like this. Dammit, they don't *have* to be like this."

"You're right, they don't. But they are because your mate is a goddamn story spinner." Seeing that he was about to deny it, Ally quickly added, "Okay, explain to me why I would do these things she's accused me of."

"Jealousy makes people do things they wouldn't normally do," he mumbled as he averted his gaze. The words sounded rehearsed. Ally got the feeling they were Rachelle's words.

"You know me, Zeke. You *know* me. How could you believe this crap? How could you believe I'd begrudge you for mating? We both knew the score when we got together; we knew it would end if one of us found our mate. This shit happens to shifter couples all the time," she added with a nonchalant shrug.

A mixture of irritation and hurt flashed on his face. "Don't downplay what was between us, Ally. We came close to imprinting. Don't deny it." He raked a hand through his hair. "Look, I can understand if our abrupt separation and Rachelle's presence here hurts you. I sure as hell wouldn't have liked it if the situation were reversed, but I'd have respected it."

"I *do* respect your mating."

"Then why did you attack her?"

"Oh, for God's sake, *I did not touch her.*"

"Then how do you explain the injuries she's sporting?"

"She must have done it all to herself!" Yes, Ally knew how that sounded, and it made her cringe. It was like the more she denied the allegations, the worse she looked. "I know she's your mate, but I thought we were friends. You won't even *listen* to me, you won't even give me the benefit of the doubt!"

"Because the evidence is all there! Rachelle's got claw marks on her back, a bruised and swollen jaw, and the youths claim you left to pursue her. Then there are the text messages, the times you yelled at her, and the way you're constantly angry—"

"Wouldn't you be angry if false accusations were being slung at you, and no one believed a word you had to say?"

He pinched the bridge of his nose. "Why would she falsely accuse you of all these things?"

"Personally, I'm thinking it's to make you and the entire pack hate me, to leave me isolated and unhappy. But I'm open to the explanation that she grew up on a diet of paint chips and glue."

"I could never hate you." He released a tired sigh. "I care about you, Ally, and I always will. But Rachelle's my mate, and I can't let you target her like this. Regardless of what you think, I really don't want to ask you to step down from your position. But right now, the pack doesn't feel like they can trust you."

Which meant they didn't trust a word she said, and so any visions she claimed to have wouldn't be trusted either. There was literally no place for her here. "Get me a transfer."

"A transfer?" He looked genuinely shocked. Um, why?

"Yes, get me a place in another pack." Leaving did feel a little too close to fleeing, and her pride balked at that. But it was better to leave than to entertain Rachelle with her misery any longer. Of course, Ally could go back to her childhood pack. Her foster uncles would welcome her with open arms. But it wasn't a safe place for her; it would make her life more complicated and dangerous than it already was.

Zeke seemed to struggle with words for a moment. "That's not necessary. I know everyone's upset with you right now, but their anger will cool. Things will be back to normal within a month."

"We both know that's not true. I want a transfer."

His jaw hardened. "No."

"Why the hell not?"

Again he seemed to struggle. "Like I said, it's not necessary."

"It is to me. I want out of here."

"That won't be easy." He almost sounded pleased. "Any pack is going to be hesitant to take a wolf who was accused of attempting to kill their Beta female."

He was right, which meant she was stuck here unless she was prepared to choose the lone-wolf lifestyle—making her an easy target for the human anti-shifter extremists, not to mention other shifters. And Zeke didn't appear willing to help her.

She understood that Rachelle was his mate, and therefore his loyalty would be primarily to her; Ally wouldn't expect anything less. But he was also the pack Beta and had taken an oath to protect his Alphas and each wolf within the pack. It was an oath he was now violating.

"You've just lost what respect I had left for you." And now she had to get out of there.

"Ally, don't storm out."

As she reached the door, she glanced back at him over her shoulder. "If you truly believe I attacked your mate, you'd have your hand around my throat, shaking me like a goddamn rag doll. But you don't, because deep down you *know*, and your wolf knows, that *it didn't happen*." Ally swung the door open. "Anyway, there's no need for me to be envious of her claim on you—I always give my used stuff to the needy and disadvantaged."

With that, Ally waltzed out and slammed the door shut behind her. Then, cursing a blue streak, she stormed out of the pack house into the humid night. This was seriously turning out to be the shittiest day ever. On the upside, it couldn't get any worse, could it?

When she walked into her wrecked cabin, she realized that, yes, actually, it could. Sitting on her slashed leather sofa, draining one of Ally's Coke bottles, was the cause of all her problems. Everything in her wanted to lash out, to put this heifer through a world of never-ending pain . . . which was exactly what Rachelle wanted her to do. Then the bitch would have something else to complain to the pack about, wouldn't she?

"Well, hello there," greeted Rachelle, wearing a superior, ugly smile. As usual, her hatred gave Ally the sensation of having sharp shards of frost lodged in her chest. "I was just helping myself to what was left in your fridge. Hope you don't mind."

Now if she could just choke on the liquid, that would be great. Or maybe if she just went back to whatever asylum she crawled out of. "Ugly bruise you have there. Who gave you all the injuries?"

Rachelle delicately swept her finger over her swollen jaw. "One of the youths who did this lovely handiwork to your cabin. So, how did your meeting with Zeke go?" Rachelle's smile told Ally that she knew exactly how it had gone.

"Do you mean before or after we got down and dirty?"

Her smile faltered as her cheeks turned almost as red as the streaks in her bleach-blonde hair. "Must be hard losing your position in the pack. Embarrassing too. And to know that your own pack mates no longer trust you . . . Wow. Now that's gotta hurt."

It did, it burned like a motherfucker. But Ally wouldn't let her see that. Nor would she let her see just how defeated she felt right now. Why couldn't the woman just leave her the fuck alone? She had Zeke, she had the pack eating out of her hands, and she'd taken Ally's status away from her. There was nothing left for her to take. Except for her pulse, of course. But Ally strongly doubted that Rachelle wanted her dead. Not just yet.

"Would you like to see what I have?" Rachelle rose to her feet and approached her.

"Is it infectious?" Ally asked dryly. When the skank reached into the neck of her T-shirt and dug out a gold chain with a wolf pendant, Ally's stomach knotted.

"I still can't believe he gave it to me."

Neither could Ally. She had bought that for Zeke last Christmas, had done a lot of searching before she'd found the perfect present. And now *she* had it. "Why would you want to wear something that *I* gave him? If there's logic in that, it's escaping me."

"Giving it to me proves that you no longer matter to him. That this chain no longer means anything to him. It's proof of his devotion to me."

Nope, Ally still didn't see the logic there. It was clear that this woman's antenna didn't pick up all the channels. "I have to wonder if things could have been different if you hadn't been deprived of oxygen at birth. Just a thought."

Rachelle planted her hands on her hips. "You're just jealous. Admit it."

Oh, this was getting old. "Careful. You're confusing sheer loathing with jealousy."

"You are, you're jealous!"

"Of what exactly? Your manipulative streak? Your distance from reality? The voices in your head that tell you you're pretty?" She shook her head, done with this bitch. "I don't have the patience to deal with you right now." Ally opened her front door and swept out a hand.

"You can't throw me out! I'm Beta female of this pack! I'm of superior rank!"

"You're also neurotic and have cancer of the soul. And I have better things to do with my time than listen to your shit."

"Fine." She literally marched to the door, pouting. "I have to go meet Zeke anyway."

Watching as the blonde stomped outside, Ally called out, "Before you go, I was just wondering . . . do you like how I taste?"

Rachelle's eyes bugged, and her cheeks turned purple. "You bitch!"

Laughing more than she'd laughed in a long time, Ally slammed the door shut.

CHAPTER TWO

I'm calling in a favor."

That was all the message had said.

The sooner Derren Hudson found out what his friend meant by that, the better. Because, despite being on the visitor's side of the protective glass, Derren wanted nothing more than to get the fuck out of there. Being in this place, surrounded by guards; bare walls; the bleak atmosphere; and the scents of fear, oppression, and dejection . . . it all brought back memories that he didn't want to think about. Memories that had his wolf pacing with angst.

A door far behind the glass opened, and a number of shifters in orange jumpsuits began to file out, each heading to their visitors. Derren straightened in his seat when a wolf he hadn't seen in five years came striding toward him wearing a crooked grin.

It was never good to owe a sociopath a favor, and there was no doubting that Cain Holt had become exactly that. Bearing in mind the things that had happened to him long ago in a juvenile detention at the hands of abusive human guards, it was no real surprise that the guy had shut off emotionally. Derren and Cain had watched each other's backs in that hellhole, which was why

Derren would always consider him a friend . . . even if the guy had lost his moral compass.

Cain's hatred and disgust of prejudiced humans had led him to join The Movement—a band of shifters that worked to protect their kind from human anti-shifter extremists who attempted to introduce laws such as sequestering shifters to their own territories, inhibiting them from mating with humans, placing each one on a register, and limiting shifter couples to one child.

These extremists argued that shifters were too dangerous, violent, and animalistic to be around humans. Some of those laws might have come to pass—thus starting a war—if the extremists hadn't been exposed for running a hunting preserve that allowed them to hunt, brutalize, and ultimately kill shifters, including their pups. The brutality had shocked the nation and, as such, discredited the extremists' argument.

However, that hadn't stopped the extremists from continuing to press for restrictive laws and committing random acts of violence, and so The Movement had been formed and was growing in power each day. It wasn't what anyone would call "subtle;" they liked to make public statements to convey that prejudice and violence wouldn't be tolerated.

In sum, shifters were doing exactly what all predators did when under attack: they were fighting back. If the extremists had expected shifters to be victims, that was their mistake.

The human law enforcement agencies *thought* they'd identified the key players within The Movement. In truth, they didn't have a damn clue. Shifters like Cain acted as a front, a face for people to point at, which placed Cain and others like him under the constant watch of law enforcement . . . thus enabling the true key players to remain under the radar.

Although Cain and others acted as faces of The Movement, they never did anything that would enable the humans to pin serious charges on them. As such, the humans had arrested Cain and a few other shifters on minor charges, determined to have them serve *some* time in confinement. Derren honestly didn't know how Cain was coping with being cooped up all over again. He had to give the guy credit where it was due.

As Cain took the seat behind the glass and put the telephone receiver to his ear, his guard backed away—fear shimmering in his eyes. Yeah, Cain's reputation had a way of inspiring fear in people. Lifting his own receiver, Derren greeted him simply: "Cain."

The wolf nodded. "Been a long time." Although they had remained in contact over the last five years, they hadn't spoken in person. "We can talk freely. My guard kindly removed the bug from this phone."

Most likely out of blind terror, thought Derren.

Cain glanced around. "Brings back a lot of memories for you, doesn't it?"

Too many.

"Heard you were made Beta of the Mercury Pack. I'd say congratulations, but I'm doubting you're happy about it."

Cain was right. Derren disliked responsibilities. Why? Because responsibilities meant being committed to something, and being committed to something meant losing freedom and choices. If there was one thing that Derren wasn't good with— thanks to spending much of his youth in juvie—it was being trapped or hemmed in. And that was exactly how his position made him feel.

So many responsibilities came with being Beta, including advising his Alpha on important issues and acting as a negotiator when dealing with other packs. Derren's average day involved patrolling the border of pack territory, helping to train and lead the enforcers, spending time in his office doing paperwork, and dealing with any grievances from the pack. In a nutshell, his job was to sustain the emotional and physical protection of each and every one of his twelve pack mates.

It was a lot to take on for someone who was particularly averse to responsibilities. He would have turned the job down if his Alpha, Nick Axton, hadn't been one of the people who watched his back in juvie. Derren owed him. He supposed he should be thankful the pack was relatively small. Many of his pack mates had commented on how well he "fit" the role, given his personality and temperament.

"It takes a particular kind of wolf to be Beta," his Alpha female, Shaya, had said. *"Someone who's observant, good at giving advice, and commands obedience; someone who'll confront issues head-on, who's extremely protective by nature, and who is perfectly in tune with the Alpha male. That's you, sweetie."*

Yeah, but being "suited" to the role and being "content" in the role were two very different things. And how was a person supposed to deserve the trust of others when he couldn't offer the same in return?

Derren had been stripped of the ability to trust a long time ago. But he didn't lament it, didn't view it as a weakness. Being wary of others, reminding himself that even the people closest to him could be capable of betrayal, would ensure he was never taken off guard again. Nick was the only person in whom he'd invested any real degree of trust, but the guy had earned it.

Still, confiding in people wasn't Derren's style, so he stuck to the subject at hand. "I got your message." He'd received it via a mutual contact. Cain might be in jail, but he still had enough influence to pass on messages to the outside world.

"You always pay your debts, which is why I knew getting you here wouldn't be a waste of my time." Cain leaned forward, resting his elbows on the table. "You remember I told you my pack was slain when I was eight?" At Derren's nod, he continued. "There were only two survivors—me and one pup; she was just six. I took her with me to stay with my uncles in the Brookwell Pack. You probably saw her when she visited me in juvie. Brown hair, huge eyes."

Derren remembered a pair of mesmerizing emerald eyes. Remembered his wolf's curiosity, how the animal had wanted to take a closer look.

"Anyway, my Ally likes pack-trotting. Doesn't stay in one place for more than a few years. But we've always kept in touch. And even though I got my ass dumped in here, I've had people check on her. I got word that her pack's giving her a hard time."

"Hard time?"

"It turns out she was seeing some guy—the Beta." Cain didn't sound too happy about it. "Then, a few months ago—*bam*—he found his mate. The female's been making things difficult for Ally. Two nights ago, she actually accused Ally of coming at her from behind and trying to kill her."

"*Did* she try to kill her?" Derren was expecting Cain to bristle, but the guy smiled. It was strange what Cain would be offended by and what he'd find amusing.

"Look, my Ally's a fierce little thing—I should know, I taught her every combat move she knows. But she wouldn't attack from behind. That's not who she is."

"Did her Alpha cast her out?"

"No. Maybe he doesn't believe the Beta female's account, or maybe it's something else. I don't know."

"Who is her Alpha?"

"Matt Ward. He leads the Collingwood Pack."

Derren knew Matt well enough, since the guy's land bordered the territory of Derren's old pack, where Nick had once been Alpha before forming the Mercury Pack. Although Derren didn't know the Beta as well as he knew Matt, Derren had judged Zeke to be good at his position. "If you're right and Ally is innocent, then what's happening is a shame. But I don't see what it has to do with me, in any case."

"It didn't have anything to do with you before, but it does now." Cain's tone turned grave. "I want you to help her."

"Why? Even though she left your pack, I'm pretty sure the Brookwell wolves would still be willing to help her."

"Of course they would. My uncles raised Ally—they adore her, think of her as family. But my pack has been under the scrutiny of extremists and human law enforcement ever since I joined The Movement. I've kept my connection to Ally quiet. Otherwise, she could be used against me."

It was a wise decision. "And if you send anyone from your pack or The Movement to help her, she'll come under the scrutiny of the humans too," Derren concluded. Still . . . "Cain, you've got a lot of contacts." Scary, dangerous, and equally sociopathic contacts. "Why come to me with this?"

"I could send some people to 'take care' of the situation, sure. But that would end in violence. Ally and I lost our parents when our entire pack was slain because of what a couple of assholes did. I won't do the same, and Ally would never forgive me if I did. Besides, I only trust a handful of people in this world. You're one of them."

Derren snorted. "You don't trust me, you just trust that I'll keep my word."

Cain shrugged. "Same difference. The point is I trust that you'll keep my Ally safe."

It was odd to see his friend care about anything other than The Movement. The more time Cain had spent in juvie, the more he'd changed, grown indifferent and hard. He didn't see people as "people" anymore. To Cain, those he kept in his life were either associates or accomplices—things he could use. Yet, this female was obviously very important to him, which could only mean that she was his mate. A mate Cain didn't intend to claim, for whatever reason, or she wouldn't have been dating Zeke.

"What is it exactly that you want me to do?"

"I want you to take her to stay with your pack for a while. I'll be out of here in four months. I'll take matters from there."

21

Sighing, Derren leaned back in his seat. Doing what Cain had asked wouldn't be easy, since Nick hated outsiders around his pack. "You should have gone to Nick with this. He's the Alpha."

"Yeah, but he doesn't owe me a favor." Anger thickened Cain's voice as he continued. "She's not safe there with those fuckers, Derren."

"It's possible that she wouldn't be any safer at the Mercury Pack right now." A week ago, one of the enforcers, Jesse, had become ill after hunting an animal on their territory that they later discovered had been poisoned. After further investigation, the pack found other animals on their land had been poisoned as well. "There's been a minor attack on the pack."

Cain didn't ask Derren to elaborate, aware that pack business wasn't shared with outsiders. "If you need the matter taken care of, I can arrange that."

"We don't even know who's responsible. It could be an isolated incident." Though Derren doubted it.

"Could be." Cain didn't seem any more convinced of that than Derren. "Nonetheless, it changes nothing. Your pack might not be the safest place to be, but Ally's in more danger where she is. Even if she wasn't, I won't tolerate people making false accusations against her."

"That's why you came to me with this," Derren discerned. "Kind of sneaky of you." Not that Derren was surprised. Cain was manipulative and self-serving.

Cain shrugged, unrepentant. "I want Ally safe. If playing someone's conscience will make that happen, I won't hesitate."

"You're forgetting that I don't have much of a conscience."

"Then do it because you owe me."

And Derren really did owe him. If it hadn't been for Cain, he would never have tracked down the lying bastard who had put the nail in Derren's metaphorical coffin and sent his fourteen-year-old ass to juvie. "Fine. I'll do it."

Cain gave a satisfied nod. "When I get out of here, I'll deal with her pack. Until then, I need to know she's away from them. Understand?"

Since Derren didn't really have any choice in the matter . . . "Yeah. Tell me what I need to know about her."

"Her full name is Alyssa Marshall. She's twenty-six years old. And she's a Seer."

Derren's spine locked. "A Seer?" It came out a growl.

"I know how you feel about Seers, Derren, and I get it. I do. But Ally is *not* that son of a bitch. She's a good girl."

Derren placed one hand on the table, ready to push out of his seat. "Find someone else to help her. Trust me, Cain, you do not want me around her." His distaste for Seers ran too deep.

Rather than reacting in anger, Cain sank into his chair. "And here I thought you were a man of your word."

He *was* a man of his word, dammit. Derren's one redeeming quality was that he was loyal to the bone once that loyalty was earned. "This is not me going against my word—"

"Oh, but it is, Derren." Leaning forward once more, Cain spoke in a low voice. "I tracked that fucker for you, I handed him to you and Nick on a silver platter, I helped you bury him, and I kept my mouth shut about it. All I asked for in return was one favor. *One.* Am I asking you to find, kill, or bury someone for me? No. I'm asking you to protect someone very important to me. Someone who's being held responsible for things she hasn't fuck-ing done . . . just like you were."

If Derren was another guy, a decent guy, those words might have given his conscience—stunted though it was—a twinge. But what made him hesitate to reject Cain's request wasn't a sense of guilt, it was the reminder of exactly how much Cain had done and risked for Derren, and how little Cain was asking for in payment. There was a big issue at play, though. "Nick will never go for it. He has a hard-on for Seers too."

"Then convince him."

Like it would be that simple. And taking into account that the rest of the pack wasn't too fond of Seers either, one word came to mind: "Fuck."

This was one of the reasons Derren highly respected his Alpha female: she had the singular ability to make Nick reconsider his decisions. Oh, Nick listened to Derren, respected his advice, and trusted his judgment. But only Shaya's opinion truly mattered to Nick.

When they had first met, Derren hadn't been too sure about her—having watched as she rejected Nick over and over. She'd had every reason to push Nick away, considering he'd failed to claim her when he had the chance. But Derren hadn't liked seeing his friend so cut up. And since Nick had left his pack to track her down, Derren figured she should have at least given Nick a chance. Eventually she had, and Derren had quickly learned that Shaya Critchley was strong, wise, and had a huge heart.

They had formed their own pack, thanks to Derren's meddling, and Nick had purchased a chunk of land where a number of hunting lodges were situated. The main lodge looked like a rustic mansion and had been refurbished with Shaya's tastes in mind. Despite Nick's reluctance to be an Alpha again, it had all worked out pretty well . . . except for the part where he'd withdrawn Derren's self-appointed bodyguard position and made him his Beta.

Derren could have refused, but that would have called into question his loyalty to Nick. Still, loyal to his Alpha or not, the subject of Ally Marshall wasn't something Derren could afford to drop.

As Derren had expected, Nick had freaked at the idea of having a Seer in his pack, even if it were only temporary. Shaya hadn't been any happier about bringing in an outsider . . . right up until Derren had explained Ally's sad situation, which had appealed to Shaya's compassionate nature. If someone had a problem, she would do what she could to fix it—and she would make sure that Nick helped.

So now the Alpha female was doing her best to convince Nick that they should give Ally sanctuary. Although Nick appeared to be stubbornly sticking to his decision, Derren could sense that the guy was wavering, hating the idea of upsetting his mate.

"We shouldn't get involved; this is none of our business," insisted Nick from the sofa, cuddling their infant daughter and plucking at her short, blonde, corkscrew curls. Like her mother, Willow had a pixie look about her, but she had Nick's green eyes. She was also Derren's goddaughter.

Staring down at Nick, arms folded, Shaya frowned. "It is your business if Cain is your friend."

"I don't have friends."

She rolled her eyes. "Of course, my mistake: you have 'contacts,'" she said dryly. "But you like Cain, right?"

Nick grimaced. "I don't *dis*like him."

Eli, Nick's younger brother and the pack's Head Enforcer, laughed. "Which basically makes him your BFF."

It was true that Nick did his best to alienate the majority of the population, being strongly averse to company. The guy was a born leader, an alpha by nature. But he didn't like having lots of people around him, which was unfortunately for him one of the trimmings that came with the Alpha role.

"This is your friend's mate, Nick," stressed Shaya. "Even if he has no intention of claiming her, she's still his mate. Doesn't that mean anything to you?"

Derren wondered if much of Shaya's compassion came from knowing what it was like to have her mate choose not to claim her.

Caleb pursed his lips. "I wonder why Cain hasn't mated her." The submissive male belonged to the same pack as Shaya growing up and was a lifelong friend of hers. Caleb was also genuine, smart, and had recently mated another submissive male within the pack, Kent.

"Maybe it's to keep Ally safe," Shaya theorized. She looked at Derren. "You said Cain told you he keeps their connection quiet to keep her off the humans' radar."

"Yeah," confirmed Derren, "but he also said he's known her since she was six and he was eight. He could have claimed her after he left juvie when he was eighteen. Instead, he let her go pack-trotting."

As such, Derren wasn't quite sure why Cain had refrained from claiming her. In fact, he wasn't sure how Cain was managing to ignore the mating urge either. It was supposedly painful. But then, Cain didn't *feel* the way others did. Not anymore. Maybe that had stopped the mating urge from coming into play.

"It doesn't matter," maintained Nick. "It's none of our business. Besides, this could blow over soon. It's natural for the Beta female to be jealous of her mate's ex-partners—mates are possessive like that."

"Yes," Shaya allowed, "but if the Beta's so jealous that she's bitter, spiteful, and targeting Ally to this extent, that's not good. I don't believe the Beta will let this go."

"I agree." Kathy, Nick's mother, reached for a babbling Willow, but Nick was having none of it. He was just as possessive and protective of his daughter as he was of his mate. "*But* the fact remains that this Ally person is a Seer." The latter word dripped with disgust.

Nick spoke then. "I don't like Seers. I don't trust them. And I don't want one around my pack." His expression said: *end of story.*

Shaya seemed baffled. "Why? What's so bad about them?"

For a moment, Derren wondered if Nick would mention what had happened all those years ago—a story only very few knew. But, as it turned out, Nick didn't have to mention Derren's past to make his point.

Nick arched a brow at Shaya. "Have you forgotten what happened with Roni and Marcus?"

Roni, Nick's younger sister and an enforcer, had mated with

an enforcer from the Phoenix Pack. Rather than asking either of the couple to switch packs, Nick and the Phoenix Alpha male had blooded so that the mated couple now belonged to both. It hadn't made the packs into one, but it had united them on a psychic level, making each one an extension of the other.

Nick continued, "They almost didn't mate because a Seer fed them bullshit about Marcus's mate being someone else."

It was yet another example of Seers misusing their gifts. As Derren considered Roni a good friend, it had pissed him the fuck off—adding to his loathing for Seers.

Shaya waved a dismissive hand. "That's because Kerrie is an evil bitch. It doesn't automatically make Ally one."

Marcus tilted his head, conceding that. "How would you feel about Ally being here, sweetheart?" he asked Roni, while lounging on the other sofa with his arm draped over her shoulders. The two were an unlikely pair in that he was a dominant, very sociable, easygoing charmer, while Roni was a socially inept, intimidatingly intelligent, and seriously lethal tomboy.

"I'll only have a problem with her if she turns out to be anything like Kerrie," replied Roni. "Honestly, though, I can't see anyone being more evil than that bitch."

Eli's eyes narrowed at Roni. "Not sure *you're* in a position to call anyone evil." He ran his tongue along his teeth, which still had a slight pink tint thanks to Roni's latest prank. The two siblings insisted on playing pranks on each other on a regular basis, merely for their own entertainment.

Roni rolled her eyes. "Are you still holding on to that?"

"You put red food coloring on my toothbrush! I looked like a damn vampire after I brushed my teeth this morning!"

"Well, if you hadn't poured baby oil into my shampoo bottle, it would never have happened, would it?"

"So," began Marcus before the siblings could argue any further, "you're saying you're okay with Ally being given sanctuary here?"

Roni shrugged. "I'll support whatever decision Shaya makes. You?"

Marcus thought about it for a second. "I won't have a problem with Ally being here, as long as she doesn't share her visions with me. In my opinion, it's best not to know the future anyway. It can just fuck up the present."

Derren couldn't have said it better himself.

"If you're referring to what happened to Trey," began Shaya, "that wasn't the Seer's fault—the blame belongs to Trey's father." Trey Coleman was the Phoenix Pack Alpha male.

Kent looked at Marcus. "What happened to Trey?"

"It's Trey's story to tell," replied Marcus. "All I'll say on the matter is that when he was a kid, the Seer of his pack told his dad he'd usurp his position one day."

As everyone knew all about the deceased, violent, and totally fucked-up Rick Coleman, it was easy enough to conclude that the old bastard had punished Trey during his entire upbringing for something he hadn't even done yet.

Cutting off whatever Nick was about to say next, the front door opened and there was a cacophony of exasperated voices. Three Mercury enforcers strolled into the living area, arguing. More accurately, Jesse and Zander were berating an eye-rolling Bracken.

Derren immediately summed up the situation, sighing tiredly at Bracken. "What did you and Dominic do this time?"

Dominic was a Phoenix Pack enforcer, who seemed to have no self-control and would probably fuck any female who stood still long enough. Though flirty and just as fond of sex as the average shifter, Bracken was a big gamer and preferred technology to people. It surprised everyone when the two enforcers became friends. Together, they had a talent for getting themselves in deep shit.

It was Jesse who responded. "Oh, they only had a threesome with an Alpha's mate."

"*Intended* mate, *intended* mate," Bracken stressed. "Her father has arranged for her to mate some guy, but they're not true mates. She wanted one last fling before the ceremony." He looked at Jesse. "You've seen her—was I supposed to refuse?"

Jesse nodded. "Yes. That was exactly what you were supposed to do."

"You're lucky," Zander told Bracken. "If the Alpha wasn't absolutely terrified of Nick and our pack, he would have challenged you." Nick had quite a reputation.

"We'll discuss this later," Shaya told the enforcers, gesturing for them to sit. "Right now, there's a more important issue to discuss."

"There's nothing to discuss," corrected Nick. "We've said all there is to say."

As if Nick hadn't spoken, Shaya informed Jesse, Zander, and Bracken of the Ally Marshall situation. Derren and Nick had first met the three enforcers in Arizona, where Nick had tracked down Shaya to claim her as his mate. The enforcers had separated from their old pack and, basically, followed Nick around until he agreed to form a pack and accept them as part of it.

Derren liked the three wolves. Jesse was the most practical of the trio, very circumspect and composed. He was also so serious that he made Derren seem fun. Bracken was a joker and not what anyone would call "deep." Emotionally, he could be as equally affected by a hurtful insult as he could be by the discovery of a stain on his clothes. Zander wasn't the most sensitive or empathetic of people. But he was sharp-witted and so intrepid that Derren would be surprised if the guy's heart rate ever went up, no matter the situation.

When Shaya finished telling Ally's story, Bracken puffed out a breath. "I've heard of that kind of thing happening before. A guy meeting his mate while in a relationship, I mean. His ex-girlfriend couldn't handle it and killed herself."

Shaya's face crumpled. "Ally is probably in similar pain."

"You should be more worried about the safety of the Beta female than her," said Kathy with a huff. "Trust me, you never want to upset a Seer. No. They can hold a grudge."

Shaya's gaze sharpened on Kathy. "Why do I have a feeling you've had a run-in with a Seer?"

The woman evaded the question. "Have you ever met one?"

Frowning thoughtfully, Shaya replied, "I don't think so."

"Then that means you haven't. Seers aren't people you forget." Kathy sneered as she elaborated, "They're all the same: kooky, whimsical, gaga, think everything's a spiritual quest, and believe they're attuned to nature." Her expression said *pathetic*. "And they think they're much more important than they are. In their view, the pack wouldn't be so safe without their visions, so they're owed obedience and reverence."

"You talk about them like they're separate creatures." Shaya sighed. "They're just shifters who happen to have visions."

"It's more than that. They can feel people's emotions. And they can heal."

"Isn't that a good thing?" Kent frowned.

Ignoring that, Kathy went on. "The point is, it's not natural. They're not *just shifters*. Their 'gift' didn't appear in wolf shifter lines until a wolf imprinted on a voodoo priestess centuries ago."

Eli's brow furrowed. "I thought he imprinted on a white witch."

"I thought it was a dark witch," said Bracken.

Caleb shrugged. "I thought a female wolf imprinted on a shaman."

Shaya exhaled a heavy breath, impatient. "So . . . if no one really knows, it's safe to say it could be none of those things."

"Believe what you want." Kathy shook her head. "But this isn't the place for her."

Shaya danced her disappointed gaze around the room. "You're going to refuse to help Ally just because of a gift she has?"

"Seer thing aside, we should probably consider something else." Jesse rubbed a hand over his military haircut. "Just because the Beta female's jealous of Ally doesn't mean she's not telling the truth."

Eli turned to Derren, his analytical brown-eyed gaze narrowed. "Are you *sure* Ally was falsely accused?"

Everyone's eyes honed in on Derren. "I believe that Cain thinks she's innocent."

"The guy's a cool liar," Nick reminded him as he placed a wiggling Willow on the floor, who then crawled over to her mother.

Shaya looked as though she were seriously contemplating hitting her mate. "That doesn't mean he *was* lying. And Derren said Cain told him that if he sent people to destroy the Collingwood Pack, she'd never forgive him. That says a lot about her character."

"But so does the fact that she's the true mate of an insane wolf." Kathy crossed one leg over the other. "She could be just like him."

"Mates are often opposites, they balance each other out," Shaya pointed out. "Look at me and Nick. And Roni and Marcus."

Zander began tapping his fingers on the arm of the sofa. "Wouldn't the Beta male of the pack know through his mating link if his mate was lying?"

Marcus nuzzled Roni's neck. "Not if the bond's not fully developed."

"If the Beta female really does have it out for Ally, she'll keep on going," stated Shaya, picking up Willow. "We need to help her. We need to get her away before the Beta female finally succeeds in getting her cast out or worse."

Nick met his mate's glare. "I don't want a Seer in my home."

She sighed, exasperated. "You're being ridiculous."

"I'm looking out for my pack, *that's* what I'm doing."

Shaya sniffed haughtily, planting a kiss on Willow's cheek. "Fine. If you won't do it for Ally, you could consider doing it for Derren. Cain isn't going to like it if Derren doesn't live up to his word."

"Yeah," agreed Zander. "I've heard plenty about Cain Holt. Apart from the fact that he joined The Movement, none of it was good."

"That's because he's mentally disturbed," spat Nick.

Shaya's brow slowly slid up as she stared at her mate. "Then I'll bet you and he get along quite well."

Ignoring Eli's chuckle, Nick slashed a hand in the air. "I'm not having a Seer in my home."

"If Cain's part of The Movement, he must know a lot of people," mused Jesse. "*Dangerous* people who could easily deal with this for him."

"He does," verified Derren. "But we all know how The Movement 'deals' with things." It involved blood and death. They'd simply go in there, destroy the pack, and then go out for pancakes or something. "Cain doesn't want them involved. They'd lead the humans right to Ally."

"How long before Cain's out?" Zander asked.

"Four months," replied Derren.

"I tell ya," began Eli, "I wouldn't like to be the Beta pair of the Collingwood Pack when Cain gets out."

"Why?" asked Kent.

Eli arched a brow. "How, exactly, do you think a sociopath will protect and avenge his mate, whether he's claimed her or not?"

"He'll go after the people who hurt her," deduced Bracken.

Shaya nodded. "And how, exactly, do you think said sociopath will react if Derren doesn't live up to his word and keep the guy's mate safe—especially if something happens to her in the meantime?"

Bracken looked at Derren. "He'll go after you. Maybe even punish our entire pack because we all refused to help her."

Shaya nodded again. "And all because some jealous heifer decided to make life hell for her mate's ex." Softening her expression, she sat next to Nick. "If this happened to Willow, and she needed help, wouldn't you want someone to be there for her?"

Nick growled. "No one will ever lay a fucking finger on her."

"Yes, we all know that if anyone even *thought* something offensive about your baby girl, you would disembowel them before they could blink. But what if she didn't have any of us to protect her, if she was pretty much all alone in the world . . . wouldn't you like to think that someone else would protect her?"

He narrowed his eyes. "Playing the Willow card is below the belt."

"Ally would only be staying here for four months. That's not long. And unless you want Derren and Cain having serious problems, you don't have much of a choice anyway."

After a long moment, Nick sighed. "You sure about this, Derren?" Translation: *Are you sure you want to be around a Seer, considering how you feel about them?*

"I'm sure." Being a man of his word sucked.

Nick sighed again. "Fine. We'll help her. But, Derren, she's your responsibility while she's here."

Despite being relieved that he wouldn't find himself at loggerheads with Cain, he couldn't help resenting the situation. Even if he didn't have very personal issues with Seers, he wouldn't be looking forward to watching over a flaky, free-spirited wacko with a sense of entitlement.

After the evening meal, Derren and Eli headed for Collingwood territory. Soon enough, they were sitting in Matt Ward's office. The guy had happily welcomed them, wanting news on how Nick and the rest of the Mercury Pack were doing.

Once the chitchat was over, Matt asked, "So, what can I do for you?"

From the chair opposite the Alpha, Derren shrugged carelessly. "Well, it's simple, really. You and I both have a problem, and I figure we can help each other."

Matt's brow crinkled. "Oh? And what problem is that?"

"Alyssa Marshall."

The Alpha stiffened, but he didn't speak, just moved his startled gaze from Derren to Eli.

"She's a member of your pack, correct?" prodded Derren.

"Yes." The answer was hesitant.

"I have it on good authority that she's having a hard time here at the moment. That she and your Betas are having some ... issues."

Matt's eyes narrowed. "Where did you hear that?" He was clearly affronted at the idea of outsiders knowing his pack's personal business.

Derren waved away the question. "The good news, Matt, is that I can help you with this."

"How so?"

"I can take her with me."

Matt looked wary, most likely expecting Derren would want something in return. "Why would you do that?"

"Let's just say that her safety and happiness is very important to someone you do not want to fuck with. Here in your pack, she's neither safe nor happy. And that's a problem for him, because it's a problem for Ally. That makes it a problem for you."

Panic flitted across Matt's face. "Who is this person you're referring to?"

"That's not important."

"I protect all my wolves," insisted Matt defensively, "including Ally. Why would you want her?"

"The person who wants her protected trusts me to ensure that that's exactly what she'll be." Derren held Matt's gaze with a determined look. "Give her to me, and the current issue in your pack will be gone."

Matt swallowed nervously. "Who wants her?"

"I told you, that's not important."

"I will not hand over one of my wolves without knowing where they'll be going."

"She's coming with me to my pack."

Matt was quiet for a moment. "What have you heard?" In other words, how much did Ally's protector know?

"I've been told that your Beta female is giving Ally problems, that she accused Ally of trying to kill her."

"I haven't cast Ally out. I doubt her guilt." Matt was likely saying that *now*, since he was anxious that he might have offended someone who would seek vengeance. He had every reason to be anxious.

"Of course you do. And my friend will be happy to hear that. Just as he'll be happy to hear that you didn't cause any fuss about this." Derren leaned forward. "Give her to me."

Another nervous gulp. "I'll send for her."

CHAPTER THREE

E yes had been glued to Ally as she made her way to the pack house. Most held hatred and accusation, while others held pity and disappointment. With those emotions battering her, the journey felt like walking through a cold mist. As usual, no one had said a single word to her. It was perfectly clear that, although she was still in the pack, she remained a social outcast.

Ally wondered if Matt had summoned her because Rachelle had laid more accusations at her door. Or maybe her punishment was about to increase. Zeke had told her that Matt didn't want to banish her, but that didn't mean he wouldn't change his mind. Well, there was really only one way to find out.

Inside the pack house, she knocked on Matt's office door, and quickly received a "Come in!"

Refusing to show any panic or anxiety, she straightened her shoulders and entered. And stopped dead in her tracks at the sight of two unfamiliar wolves. She studied the powerfully built male with the short bronze hair and indomitable look and her voice of intuition whispered, *merciless.* Yeah, Ally could see he was some-one to be wary of. The blend of impatience, dubiousness, and dis-trust that seeped from him caused her scalp to prickle and itch.

Moving her attention to the dark, supremely masculine male beside him, Ally realized he wasn't so unfamiliar after all. She'd seen him before in a juvenile detention facility long ago. His body had changed since then; he was taller, his shoulders had broadened, and his build was solid and defined. He was currently watchful, tense, and still; those brooding pools of dark velvet stared too hard, saw too much. His sensual mouth was set in a harsh line; it had a cruel edge to it that hadn't been there years ago.

Back then, the teenage Ally had felt curious when she saw him. Now, a crushing carnal hunger licked over her skin, heated her blood, and pooled low in her stomach—it was instant, elemental, and made no sense.

Unlike his friend, he didn't radiate emotion. He was so guarded that only brief flashes broke through that cool surface. Those flashes of suspiciousness, rancor, scorn, and confusion were enough to chill her skin. But that chill was eased by the sparks of a sensual hunger that made warmth bloom in places it had no right being.

It was a hunger she could see he resented.

He might be attracted to her, but he didn't like it. That irritated her wolf, who—also having recognized him—had sat up, rapt by his dominance and self-assurance.

Suddenly his dark eyes slowly raked over her, lingering a little too long on her mouth. She refused to blush under his intense inspection. "He sent you," she guessed. *Cain.* She doubted it was pure coincidence that a wolf who served time in juvie with Cain had come here.

A curt nod was all she received in response—the guy clearly wasn't happy about it. Neither was she. Ally had been hoping that Cain wouldn't hear about what had happened, given his violent way of handling things. He must have her more closely watched than she'd thought.

"I'm Derren Hudson." His silky smooth voice slid over her, teasing her senses. "This is Eli Axton. We're from the Mercury Pack."

She'd heard a little about the pack—mostly that the Alpha

was very powerful and very dangerous. "How much does . . . our mutual friend . . . know?"

"Everything."

Shit. "I take it he relayed my story to you?"

Another sharp nod. "I'm here to take you with me."

Yeah, she'd gathered that. "Where to?"

"My pack. Temporarily."

And no doubt, Cain would deal with everything when he was released from jail.

Matt cleared his throat. "Ally, I just wanted to say that I always believed you were innocent. And I certainly don't believe you attacked Rachelle last night."

"Really?" she drawled, skeptical. Fear wafted from him, sending a crawling sensation down her arms.

"Yes, but I have no proof," stressed Matt. "Rachelle's accusation is very serious. As Beta female, she should protect her pack mates. If her accusations are false, she has violated her oath and placed you in danger. She would have to be severely punished, and I would have to replace her as Beta, which would mean Zeke would also have to step down. Without solid proof of her guilt, I cannot justify making such a decision. Just the same, I cannot execute or banish you without solid proof of your guilt. I want to be clear that I am not casting you out." Matt's voice was both firm and reassuring. "There is really no need for you to leave. I can guarantee your safety here."

"No, you can't," Derren told him.

The wolf was right; Matt couldn't. Ally knew that Rachelle wouldn't stop. The pack was so certain of Ally's guilt, and she had no supporters. She had no one who would defend her against any future allegations. No one who would ensure there were consequences if her cabin was again vandalized.

Still, leaving with two perfect strangers, neither of whom wanted to be in her company, wasn't all that appealing either. Sometimes it was a case of "better the devil you know."

As if Derren sensed her hesitance, he narrowed his eyes. "Matt, could you leave us alone a minute?"

She was kind of surprised that he would ask an Alpha to leave his own office. She was even more surprised when said Alpha did as requested.

Derren stepped forward. "I can't let you stay here. Cain wants you away from this place."

And Cain would flip on Derren if he didn't take her away— yeah, she got that. But . . . "I'll find a way to contact Cain, explain it's my decision to remain here."

"Why would you want to stay? From what I've heard, they don't want you here."

"And you don't want me to go with you."

He inclined his head. "I won't deny that. But here you're around people who might physically hurt you. That wouldn't be the case if you came with me." When she didn't speak, he added, "Cain wouldn't have sent me if he wasn't positive that you'd come to no harm with me."

That was true. The fact that he had told Derren of their connection showed just how much he trusted him—or, at least, how much Cain trusted him to maintain his silence on the subject. And she had faith in Cain's judgment. Still . . . "You say you won't harm me, but there's so much bitterness and hostility when you look at me." It left a sour taste on her tongue. "Why?"

Derren ground his teeth. "I don't like Seers."

And she didn't like being surrounded by prejudice, but, hey, life was full of disappointments. "I'm pretty sure 'don't like' is an understatement." When he didn't deny it, she asked, "Yet I'm supposed to trust you?"

"No, you shouldn't trust me. I'm only loyal to those who've earned it. But I *will* do what Cain's asked of me."

"Why?"

"I owe him a favor."

"Very noble, but I have a feeling my phone battery will last longer than your attempt at tolerance." She would bet it wasn't a quality he could ever claim to have. Surprisingly, his mouth twitched in amusement. "Why in the world would Cain send you, of all people, to help me when you so obviously despise Seers?"

"He knows I'll keep you safe."

Yeah? Ally wasn't all that convinced. But the fact was that she didn't need Derren or anyone else to shield her; she was a strong, dominant female. All she really needed was to get the hell away from the Collingwood wolves. Strong or not, she couldn't fight an entire pack. Derren was her ticket out. In that sense, the Mercury Pack was the lesser evil.

She sighed, resigned. "I need to get my stuff."

Derren's wide shoulders relaxed slightly. "I'll come with you."

"That's really not necessary."

"I've been charged with keeping you safe. That's exactly what I'm going to do."

And there would be consequences for him if he failed, she knew. "All right."

When he crossed the room to her, she realized that actually it wasn't "all right" at all. Because as his delicious scent slithered over her—Brazilian coffee beans, oak bark, and hot sex—Ally's wolf's interest was replaced by arousal. And that was just the last thing that Ally needed.

It wasn't often that Derren and his wolf were in accord on things. It wasn't that their natures were very different, it was that they were so similar—hard, pushy, stubborn, and mostly serious. They both had such strong, forceful personalities that they clashed a lot. But they had one very big difference: their taste in females.

Derren was attracted to confident, bold females who took life as seriously as he did. His wolf, on the other hand, was so easily bored that he tended to like playful, defiant females that would present a challenge.

This difference in tastes could be problematic. His wolf didn't fight Derren's choices in females, but he also didn't invest any interest in the relationships, which the females would sense and resent. Just the same, Derren would find himself grinding his teeth whenever his wolf was driving him to pursue a female that Derren wasn't attracted to in any sense.

For once, though, they were in total agreement when it came to a woman: Alyssa Marshall was fucking captivating.

Her almond green eyes, framed by thick coal-black lashes, were just as mesmerizing as he remembered. The very second they had met his gaze, it had felt like every ounce of blood in his body had rushed to his cock. Lust had blasted through him with an alarming force, leaving him a little shaken. He wanted to lap at that smooth olive skin. Wanted to cup those high, perky breasts in his hands. Wanted to wrap that sleek mocha-brown curtain around his fist while he ate at that full mouth. And his wolf was urging him on.

Never had Derren had such a visceral reaction to a female. It was unexpected, and he didn't trust it. Nor did he trust that the attention of his easily distracted wolf was absolutely consumed by her. Was she doing some weird Seer thing? Using her gift to attract him and his wolf?

The truth was that it didn't truly matter, because never in a million years would he get involved with a Seer. Never. Since she was his friend's mate, she was off-limits, in any case. Whether Cain intended to claim her or not, it was doubtful he'd like it much if a friend was sniffing around his mate. Derren's wolf, however, was no more affected by that than he was by Derren's distrust of her. The animal wanted her. Simple.

Glancing at the female walking beside him, Derren had a hard time believing she was a Seer. He'd been expecting a colorful, loud woman with crimped wavy hair, too much eyeliner, and hippy-like clothes. Instead, he was looking at a slender, self-composed, casually dressed female wearing a minimum amount of makeup.

Even with her dressed in tight-fitting jeans and a simple

long-sleeved T-shirt with a scarf loosely hanging around her neck, Derren wanted to back her against one of the trees, strip her naked, and explore every delectable inch of her. He'd let her keep the black midcalf boots on, though.

Cursing inwardly, he shook his head to clear the image from his mind.

Not a lot surprised Derren—maybe because he was simply too jaded. But Ally Marshall . . . she wasn't at all what he'd expected. Still, whether or not she looked and acted like a Seer, that was exactly what she was. And he'd remember that, because he knew better than most that Seers could be corrupt, self-righteous, and misuse their gifts.

As they traipsed through the woods, heading for her cabin, they saw members of her pack here and there. Most of them ignored her, and she ignored them right back. One or two glared, and she pointedly ignored them too.

"Are you . . . in business with Cain?"

Knowing she was asking if he was part of The Movement too, Derren shook his head. "I'm just an old friend. You remember me." He'd seen recognition flash across her face in Matt's office.

"And you remember me."

A guy didn't forget eyes like hers.

She pointed at a cabin a few feet away. "We're here."

He frowned at the collection of garbage bags and broken furniture on the porch. Paint had been splattered all over the front of the cabin, and one of the windows had weblike cracks running through it. "What happened?" His wolf growled, flexing his claws.

She shrugged. "Kids."

Kids wouldn't be inspired to do this kind of damage unless their issue with Ally was extremely personal, or unless . . . "Was the Beta female behind it?"

"So you believe my story?"

She looked pretty surprised that he might believe in her innocence. Understandable, since nobody else had. Although he doubted that she was guilty, he wasn't convinced she was definitely innocent. His hesitation apparently answered for him, because she sighed, regarding him with disappointment. Like she'd expected more—better—of him. To his total irritation, he found himself strangely feeling both shitty and defensive.

Rather than voice that disappointment, she blanked her expression, shutting him out—which his wolf seriously didn't like—and turned away. As she headed inside, her heart-shaped ass swayed in a way that seemed unintentionally provocative. "Give me ten minutes."

The moment Derren stepped inside her small cabin, he knew it was a mistake. It had been bad enough breathing in her enticing scent as they walked. Here, it filled the air and wrapped around him. Fuck, she smelled like wild berries, grapefruit, and sin. The combination was heady.

He was tempted to return outside, but there was always a possibility that someone could sneak in the back door; he needed to cover both entrances. After all, if she truly was being targeted by the Beta female, said female might not appreciate Ally getting away from her.

As he waited, he took in the interior of the cabin. There was none of the quirky, whimsical décor that Seers were known for. In fact, she didn't seem to have put her own stamp on the place at all. It was plain and basic, like a rental home.

Soon enough, she reappeared with one suitcase and a bag. His wolf wanted to rub up against her, wanted her scent on his fur. This could get annoying real quick. "Why didn't you foresee how the Beta female would react?" Assuming Ally was telling the truth, of course.

"Seers don't have visions about their own future, just as healers can't heal themselves. Our gifts are supposed to help us serve others, not ourselves."

"But that's not the way your kind often works."

"No, it's not."

He blinked, startled by her honesty. He'd expected her to bristle, become defensive on behalf of her kind. When he just stared at her, she arched an impatient brow. Abandoning his thoughts, Derren took the suitcase. "You good to go?"

She inhaled deeply. "I'm ready."

As they strode through the woods, they again passed the occasional shifter. Spotting Ally's luggage, the wolves snickered, sending her *good riddance* looks. They obviously thought she'd been banished and that Derren was escorting her off the land. Ally seemed indifferent to it all, but he wasn't buying it. He decided it was more likely that she was refusing to give them the satisfaction of seeing how much it hurt.

Derren found Eli waiting near their SUV, talking with a still-nervous Matt.

The Alpha turned to Ally with a shaky smile. "It feels wrong to watch you go. Stay, Ally."

Derren stiffened. "She's not safe here." Cain had been right about that. Derren had seen how these wolves were giving her an ice-cold shoulder, and he didn't like it. It made him remember a time when he too had been isolated, cast aside, and then betrayed by those he should have been able to trust.

Seer or not, guilty or not, she was now under Derren's protection. He wasn't happy about it, and he didn't welcome yet *another* responsibility. But he'd take it as seriously as he took his Beta duties, because that was who he was.

Movement in his peripheral vision made Derren's head whip to the side. A tall male was fast approaching, tension in every line of his body. *Zeke.* When his eyes slid to Ally and then down to her luggage, a series of emotions flickered across his face—predominantly rage.

"What's going on?" Zeke demanded.

Matt took a step toward his Beta. "Ally's leaving the pack."

"*What?* Why?"

As the Beta and Alpha proceeded to argue, Eli looked at Ally. "Now that you're packed, we can go." He took her suitcase and bag and put them in the trunk of the SUV.

When Derren began to lead Ally to the backseat, Zeke made a beeline for her. "Ally, wait."

Instinctively, Derren obstructed his path. "Don't even think it." His wolf curled back his upper lip in a fierce snarl as the animal dropped into a fighting stance, rearing to pounce. His wolf had a black, vicious temper. Right then, he was eager to rake his claws across the Beta's abdomen, to warn the male away from Ally.

Zeke said through his teeth, "I want to talk to Ally."

The expectation of obedience in his tone rubbed Derren's fur the wrong way. "You can do it from here. Though you should probably make it quick."

"Ally, you don't have to go."

"You believe I attacked your mate," she said. "Surely you'd feel a whole lot better knowing she's safe from my evil clutches."

A muscle in Zeke's jaw ticked. Again he moved toward her, and again Derren blocked his path. "What the fuck is your problem, Derren?" Zeke growled.

Simple: like his wolf, Derren didn't want Zeke within reach of Ally. "She's under my protection."

Fury flared in Zeke's eyes. "No, she's under *my* protection. *I'm* her Beta."

Hearing the heavy dose of possessiveness in that statement, it was clear to Derren just how close Zeke had come to imprinting on Ally. Bonding with his mate would naturally have dulled his feelings for any other female, but it was apparent that Zeke still hadn't quite let go of Ally.

"Not anymore," Derren firmly stated, a slight taunt in his tone.

"Ally, you don't need to leave."

"Zeke?" asked a new voice filled with uncertainty. Then a blonde sidled up to Zeke, taking in the scene with a perplexed expression.

"They want to take Ally," Zeke told her.

The blonde's eyes bulged in anger as she glared at Derren. "You can't do that! She's ours! Ally, do *not* get in that SUV!"

Totally straight-faced, Ally replied, "Sorry, I don't take orders unless I'm naked."

Derren was *not* going to entertain the thoughts and images that her comment sent raging through his mind.

"Get over here now!" shouted Rachelle. But Ally just blinked at her. Rachelle's voice dropped a level as she growled, "You need to seriously rethink defying me."

"And guys need to stop shoving their hands down their pants to play with their balls in public." Ally shook her head. "Some things will never change."

If Derren hadn't been so preoccupied keeping Zeke back, he might have been able to stop Rachelle before she got anywhere near Ally. As it was, he barely reached her in time . . . but by then, Ally was slamming Rachelle facedown over the bonnet of the car next to the SUV, her hand gripping Rachelle's nape, dominant vibes radiating from her . . . which had his wolf falling head over heels in lust.

"This, here, is why you never challenged me, Rachelle. You knew you couldn't take me. You knew I'd humiliate you in front of the entire pack and put your suitability as Beta under question. Embarrassment-wise, this has to rank high."

"Ally . . ." It was a plea from Zeke to release his mate.

After a long moment, Ally pushed away from her. "She's all yours, Zeke. I can only pity you."

Dismissing the Beta pair, Derren opened the rear door of the SUV while Eli jumped into the front passenger seat. "Get in, Ally." Once she was inside the vehicle, his wolf settled a little. Without another look at the pathetic excuses for shifters, Derren hopped into the driver's seat and drove off.

Ignoring the sound of Zeke calling her name once more, Ally settled into the backseat while the Mercury males sat up front. As the SUV crossed the border of Collingwood Pack territory, some of the tension left her. She was now away from Rachelle, from the wolves that had betrayed her, and from the danger that the false accusations presented. And it was hopefully the last Ally would ever see of Zeke, Rachelle, and Matt.

Switching on her iPod and inserting her earbuds, she smiled inwardly at how satisfying it had been to watch their reactions as they realized that, hey, they couldn't keep her trapped there; she wasn't all alone in the world, despite Rachelle's best efforts; and there was someone out there who would look out for her. If Matt told the Beta couple about Ally's mysterious protector, they might even become as nervous as their Alpha. How grand.

But as much as Ally found the idea of their anxiety rather amusing, she very much doubted she'd find Cain's reaction fun. Although she was pissed with the Collingwood wolves, she didn't want them all badly hurt. She could never predict what Cain would do, only that it would be bad. He hadn't always been so angry and detached, hadn't always been so violent. But the longer he'd stayed in juvie, the more he'd lost of himself—she'd seen it each time she'd visited him there.

Cain's reaction wasn't the only thing she worried about. Despite Eli accompanying Derren to collect her, it was clear that he was just as distrustful of her as Derren. As such, it was likely that the rest of his pack felt the same. There was a lot of prejudice against Seers, thanks to the misdeeds of some.

In any case, no pack would welcome the eyes and ears of an outsider—particularly if said outsider "saw" more than others.

Yeah, her time with the Mercury wolves wasn't going to be easy or peaceful. Particularly since her wolf was most fascinated by Derren, despite his dislike of her. The animal was drawn to his strength, his scent, and how sure and confident he was. Not that, in spite of how uncomfortable Ally was around Derren, she blamed her wolf for that. No, Derren wouldn't be an easy guy for any woman to resist.

As it was, Ally wouldn't have to worry about resisting him, since he resented her very presence. And that was an extremely good thing, because Ally had never been good at resisting temptation. And the very last thing she wanted right now was to get involved with another wolf after her disastrous experience with Zeke.

It was beginning to darken when they finally crossed the border of Mercury Pack territory. Still, her night vision allowed her to see her surroundings clearly. Leaves littered the dirt path that lay amid a forest of regal, towering trees—many of which displayed typical territorial animal markings.

There was an impressive hunting lodge in the near distance; while the base of the lodge was constructed of large stone, the upper levels had timber frames. The place was illuminated by fairy lights that decorated the trees surrounding it, making it seem cozy and almost magical.

Derren pulled to a stop in the center of a row of all-terrain vehicles, a Winnebago, and a Mercedes. Well, someone had varied tastes. Returning her iPod and earbuds to her pocket, Ally was out of the SUV before Derren could open her door, which seemed to aggravate him for some reason. Her wolf was enjoying the scents of sun-warmed earth, moss, and pine; basking in the peaceful yet untamed atmosphere.

Carrying her suitcase, Derren tipped his chin toward Eli, indicating for her to follow him into the lodge. Inside the living area, three wolves waited on the luxurious sofas, while an adorable pup was playing with some toys on an oval rug. There was a real rustic tone to the homey, spacious lodge, which was complemented by the stone fireplace.

Two of the wolves got to their feet. *Mates,* Ally sensed.

The ethereally beautiful redhead was, to Ally's total surprise, smiling in welcome. The imposing blond male at her side, however, was making his suspiciousness of Ally perfectly open in his piercing eyes—it was a look she'd seen many times before. Yep, prejudice against Seers existed in this pack all right. Great.

"Ally," began Derren, "these are my Alphas, Nick and Shaya."

Ally knew that although it was important that she was respectful, despite being there under sufferance, it was also important that she didn't appear weak. That meant not cowering under the force of the Alpha male's disapproval and vexation, even though it felt like hundreds of wasps were stinging her body. Head held high, voice steady and strong, she said, "Ally Marshall. I appreciate you giving me sanctuary."

"It's nice to meet you, Ally," said Shaya. Both Ally and her wolf could sense that, although the Alpha female was submissive, she was strong in her own way.

When Nick didn't greet Ally, Shaya rolled her eyes. "Don't take it personally. He's one of the most antisocial people you'll ever meet. Over there is Nick's mom, Kathy."

The small brunette just stared, her dislike of Ally evident in both her expression and the distaste that was like the slash of a razor on Ally's flesh.

"And this . . ." Shaya picked up the infant. "This is my baby girl, Willow."

Ally smiled at the pup. "Good Lord, aren't you just adorable."

For a short moment, Willow looked at Ally . . . almost as if assessing her. Then she flashed her a wide smile, reaching out to touch her cheek.

"And obviously you've met Derren and Eli, our Beta and Head Enforcer." Shaya cocked her head. "Should I call you Alyssa or Ally?"

"Ally's fine."

"Have you eaten?"

"Yeah, I'm good."

"Well, if you get a little hungry, there's some food in the guest lodge you'll be using."

They were putting her in a guest lodge? Ally had been expecting them to order her to stay with Derren, given how unwelcome she was here. This was a huge relief. Ally liked space and privacy, and she certainly didn't want to constantly be in close proximity to him all the time.

"You can meet the rest of the pack in the morning when you come here for breakfast. After that, I'll give you a tour, since it's a little too late for that now." Shaya turned to Derren. "We've put Ally in the guest lodge nearest to yours. Can you escort her there?"

He gave Shaya a nod before signaling for Ally to follow. Giving the Mercury wolves a brief good night, she followed him through an archway that led to a dining area and kitchen, liking that it was all one open space. Outside, a Labrador was wagging his tail excitedly.

"That's Bruce," said Derren, watching as the dog rubbed his body all over Ally's legs and butted her hand for a stroke. His wolf was jealous, wanted the same attention, which was just plain pathetic. "Let's go." Bruce stayed at her side as Derren escorted her to the guest lodge, irritating his wolf and pricking at his jealousy. *Pitiful.*

Feeling his negative emotions slap at her as they walked in silence, Ally wondered how she could possibly be attracted to someone who not only disliked her so much but caused her such physical discomfort. Yet, the hunger was there all the same, taunting her and making her feel edgy. Her wolf's fascination with him wasn't helping matters at all. Nor were his flashes of raw need that were like fingers teasingly trailing down the length of her spine.

Oh, help.

As the lodge came into view, Ally halted with a gasp. She hadn't envisioned this at all. It was just . . . beautiful. The timber L-shaped lodge had a wraparound porch, which would no doubt overlook the lake she could see just beyond the building. The front of the lodge was glazed glass, allowing plenty of natural light to fill the space. Situated on a rise, it was perfectly positioned for her to spot anyone approaching. "It's . . . Wow. Just wow."

Derren smiled a little. "If you like the outside, you'll love the inside."

It turned out that he was right. The two-story den was gorgeous with its stone fireplace, corner sofa, chest-like coffee table, and a massive TV on the wall. From there, it was easy to see the lofted bedroom, which was located above the small dining area and kitchen, overlooking the den.

The oak flooring continued through the entire space, matching the oak kitchen. At the rear of the lodge was a staircase that led to the bedroom and bathroom. The right wall of the bedroom was all glass, giving the space plenty of light. But . . . "This glass is reflective, right?" she asked Derren, who was placing her luggage at the foot of her bed.

Amused, Derren assured her, "Yes. No one can see inside." He pointed to his own lodge, which was bigger than hers but simpler in its design. "I live across the lake." Then he found himself blurting out, "Why was your childhood pack assassinated?" Just like that, her expression shuttered. "Don't do that," he said. For some reason, the idea of her closing down on him . . . it offended him.

Memories smacked into Ally. Screaming. Howling. Her nails snapping as she clawed at the—

Ally slammed a door on the memories. When she finally spoke, her tone was flat. "I don't talk about it. Ever."

As she headed for the stairs, Derren realized he'd been effectively dismissed. He didn't like that. And if she thought he was so easily handled, she was in for a big surprise. He followed her into the kitchen, where she switched on the coffeepot. "I won't press you on that." For now. "But there is something else I need to know."

Finally finding the cupboard where mugs were kept, she grabbed only one to make a statement to the persistent asshole that he wasn't welcome to stay. Annoyingly, that seemed to amuse him. "What's that?" she said.

He leaned against the counter, intensely aware of this female in a way that unnerved him. His eyes settled on her luscious mouth; images of just what he could do with that mouth flickered through his brain. "What really happened in the Collingwood Pack? I've heard a little from Cain, and I've heard Matt's version, but I haven't heard yours." And when he'd watched her overpower Rachelle, it had become blindingly clear that Ally wouldn't have needed to attack her from behind. So just maybe Ally had been wrongly accused after all.

"You know all you need to know. She said I tried to kill her. I didn't."

"There's more." Cain had said the pack had been giving her a hard time. "I've been charged with protecting you. I can't do that if I don't know everything." And, yeah, he was being nosy too. His smile widened as he watched her pour more milk in her mug than coffee.

Turning away, she headed outside with her drink. "I'm away from the Collingwood wolves now—that's all that matters." Seeing a hammock on the porch, Ally knew she'd be spending a lot of time out here, relaxing.

Derren followed her, coming to stand in front of where she sat on the porch step. Bruce settled beside her, his wagging tail tapping the deck. "You really think they'll leave you alone? Obviously you didn't see the possessiveness on Zeke's face when he looked at you." Derren's wolf growled at the memory. "He still considers you his, and neither he nor his wolf is going to like that someone took you away."

She believed Zeke still cared for her, but not that he'd had any trouble letting go—particularly since he'd bought Rachelle's lies and refused to get Ally a transfer. "If that were true, he wouldn't have turned on me the way he did."

"Trust me, he hasn't let you go yet. As for his mate, she was genuinely angry that you left." He took a single step toward Ally, compelled by the wicked urge to touch her that he very barely resisted. It didn't help that he took her enticing scent inside him on every inhale. "Tell me."

Caught in the power of his dark gaze, Ally did. She gave him the entire story, beginning when Zeke met Rachelle and ending with the things Zeke had said after the interrogation. "I think she wanted me executed eventually. But not yet. What she was doing wasn't really much different from someone physically torturing their captive as they lead up to the main event." She sighed, getting to her feet. "Well, it's late. Good night."

Dismissed again. Derren went to grab her wrist but she jerked away, avoiding his touch like it was a poisonous snake. It shouldn't have bothered him. Not a tiny, little bit. But a growl seeped out of him just as his wolf tugged at the reins, offended and angered by the rejection. "Problem?" he rumbled.

"There won't be as long as you don't touch me."

He stepped right into her personal space, leaving only inches between them. "Oh? And why is that?" And why did he care?

"It'll hurt."

Both he and his wolf stilled. "My touch will hurt you?"

"If someone's emotions are strong enough, they can bleed into my system through touch. You're so angry at me, so bitter. It's uncomfortable enough to just be around you. If you touch me while those emotions are running through you, it'll hurt." And having his need pour through her body, adding to her own, would have Ally so turned on she'd be shaking with it. But he didn't need to know that.

Derren had heard that picking up the emotions of others caused physical sensations for Seers, but he hadn't known it could be painful. "I'll keep my hands to myself." Why a part of him balked at that idea, he didn't know. His wolf viciously clawed at his gut, enraged by it. "One last thing. Don't think about running."

Startled that he'd suspect she would do anything of the sort, she asked, "Why would I run?"

"I think you may have figured out that not everyone here is going to be as welcoming as Shaya. I don't want you fleeing."

Affronted, she sniped, "I don't flee. And I may not trust you, and I may not be convinced you have any interest in whether or not I'm safe, but I do trust Cain and his judgment."

The faith and affection in the latter words added to the jealousy that was already riding his wolf. Not a jealous person, Derren had always been able to roll his eyes at his wolf's envy. But right now, he shared it. This female messed with his fucking head just as much as she messed with his senses.

"If you both trust and care for each other so damn much, why hasn't he claimed you? Why would he overlook his mate dating other guys? And why would you *want* to?" An emotion flickered across her face, but it was gone too quickly for Derren to identify it.

"Why do you have so much rage and pain inside you that it's a total wonder you haven't gone insane with it?" she shot back. As she'd known he would, he closed down. Her laugh was empty of humor. "Unless you're willing to share your own business, don't ask me about mine."

Perversely, her defiance entertained him as much as it did his wolf. This was a female who could hold her own, who brooked no bullshit. Derren could respect that, even as it irritated him that he had no answers to his questions. "Remember: don't think about running. You wouldn't get far anyway. I have your scent." A scent that seemed designed to fucking tantalize him, his cock, and his wolf.

Her voice hardened. "Let me assure you that if at any point I do decide to leave here, that's exactly what I'll do. But I won't run. I'll walk right on out of here *while you watch.*"

"I'd stop you before you got anywhere near the border."

Ally knew her smile was a little feral. "You could try."

Derren's mouth curved. "You should know better than to challenge a Beta." With that, he spun on his heel and strode away, taking Bruce with him.

Once he was out of sight, Ally exhaled a heavy sigh. Being so close to Derren was hard on her composure. Not just because his emotions battered at her, but because he pulled sexual reactions from her body that alarmed her.

She hadn't realized that he assumed Cain was her mate, though she supposed it was an easy leap for him to make since Cain was so protective. For a single moment, she'd thought of correcting him. But instinct had made her stop. While the Mercury wolves thought Cain was her mate, they would be more inclined to let her be. After all, shifters would launch full-scale wars over their mates.

She didn't like to lie, but this was just a teeny-weeny lie of omission that wouldn't hurt anyone but might keep her safe from these people who didn't like outsiders, didn't like Seers, and didn't want her here.

Sure, it was hiding behind Cain, in a sense. Her pride—as strong as that of any dominant female wolf—bristled at that. But her pride had also balked when she'd considered leaving the Collingwood Pack months ago, and look where that had gotten her. So if hiding behind Cain's reputation would keep her safe, so be it.

CHAPTER FOUR

Ally kept her head held high as she walked into the main lodge the next morning. Any other time, she would have had a small breakfast in her own lodge. For one, she was very far from a morning person. And two, if the shifters were as unwelcoming as Derren predicted, it was going to be physically uncomfortable to be around them all. However, to turn down Shaya's invitation would not only be seen as rude but as if she was scared to face the pack. Although Ally wasn't interested in pointlessly striving to earn their approval or respect, she wasn't going to have them thinking she was spineless. Shifters pounced on weaknesses.

In the kitchen, Shaya, Eli, and two males were seated at the long table, while Kathy was at the stove. Shaya beamed. "Morning! Come sit!" She patted the seat beside hers. "Guys, this is Ally."

Instantly, Ally sensed that the two submissive males were mates. "Nice to meet you," she said as she sat, wincing internally at her gruff tone. "I'll seem friendlier when I've had coffee." Reaching for the coffeepot on the table, she then poured some into the mug that had been left on a coaster in front of her.

The dark wolf tipped his chin, a slight curve to his mouth. "I'm Caleb. This is Kent." Neither exuded any unwelcoming vibes. Instead, they appeared to be neutral on the subject of her presence.

The spiky-haired male's words were unexpected. "I love all that long, silky hair."

"Um, thanks." Feeling something rub against her legs, she peeked under the table. *Bruce.* He'd settled at her feet, chewing on a slice of bacon.

"Like me, Kent used to be a hairstylist. Seeing such healthy, gorgeous hair is like a stroke to his senses." Shaya took a sip of her own coffee. "How do you like your lodge?"

Ally smiled, knowing her delight was evident. "I love it." After unpacking the night before, she had shifted forms and done a quick scout of the area to assure and calm her wolf, who had been going crazy at all the new scents and had wanted to explore. After that, both Ally and her wolf had felt calmer, lighter. And Ally knew that for as long as she stayed here—unwelcome or not—the lodge would be her haven.

Shaya's next words were low. "Has Derren been okay with you?"

Apart from the fact that he made her want to do wicked things to his body? "Yeah, why?"

"He doesn't always make the best first impression."

Recalling his pushy, tenacious behavior, she said, "You're right, he doesn't."

Shaya chuckled. "He's a good guy. One of the most decent guys I've ever met, even if he is hard in many ways. Nick would never have chosen him as Willow's godfather if that wasn't the case. Derren adores her, just as she adores him. And he looks out for his pack, dutifully fills a role he doesn't even want. But . . . he has a thing about Seers. It's a blind spot for him. What I'm trying to say is: don't take his sullenness personally."

But how could Ally not take it personally? The Seer side of her nature wasn't separate. If he had something against what she was, then it was most certainly personal. Instead of voicing that thought, she said, "Thanks for letting me stay here."

Kathy plonked an empty plate in front of Ally, snatching her attention. "So . . . you're a Seer." Kathy had said "Seer" in the same tone one might use for "serial killer." Again, the woman's antipathy was like the slash of a razor.

And so it begins. "I am."

A haughty sniff from Kathy. "You don't get a lot of dominant Seers. They're mostly submissive."

"Are dominant Seers more powerful than submissive ones?" Eli spooned some cereal into his mouth. His dubiousness and distrust hadn't left him, making her scalp prickle again.

"Not that I know of." Ally piled some food onto her plate. "I think it just depends on the individual." She hadn't spent enough time around other Seers to really know for sure. It was difficult for two Seers to exist in one pack unless one of those Seers was a child. Adult Seers tended to clash and battle for the position, much like two alpha males would fight for the position of pack Alpha.

"You don't look or act at all like a Seer." Caleb nudged his mate with his elbow. "Does she?"

Kent shook his head. "I would never have guessed."

Three males entered, laughing among themselves. Shaya gave them a smile as she said, "Ally, this is Bracken, Jesse, and Zander. They're three of our enforcers."

They were also totally hot, but since all three were oozing so much wariness that her skin itched, Ally wasn't enamored. Her "Hi" was met with stiff nods.

"We also have two other enforcers, Roni and Marcus," added Shaya, "but they're not here this morning. You'll meet them in a few days."

Apparently not done, Kathy planted one hand on her hip as she glared down at Ally. "I'm a straight shooter, so I'll tell you right now that I'm not convinced you didn't try to kill your Beta female."

Ally shrugged. "That's all right. I'm not convinced I care." She had to show these people she had claws, that no bullshit would be tolerated.

"At least you have spine. But that won't earn you any respect here. Not when you are what you are."

"You mean bored?" Ally's wolf bared her teeth at the older female, but her anger was quickly replaced by anticipation as the scent of Brazilian coffee beans, oak bark, and hot sex tickled her senses. A moment later, Derren was striding into the kitchen. He walked with a sense of purpose that had her wolf growling with arousal. It flustered Ally a little too, if she were being honest.

Flashes of his usual negative emotions slammed into her, chilling her body. Again, though, the chill was alleviated by the need she felt pulsing through him—acting as a stroke to her inner thighs. It took everything she had not to squirm in her seat. Settling into the chair next to her, he exchanged greetings with everyone before looking at her. Eyes of dark velvet drank her in.

He said quietly, "I went to your lodge to walk you here."

It was an admonishment . . . as if she should have been waiting for him like a good little girl. "Huh. Not sure why you think I need you to hold my hand."

The comment should have irritated Derren, but he found himself wanting to smile at her prickly manner. Noticing that Kathy was snarling at her, he arched a brow. "Problem?"

Kathy shrugged. "I was just about to tell Ally here that if she has any visions while she's with us, we don't want to hear about them."

"Just to clarify"—Ally sat back in her seat, arms folded—"if I was to have a vision warning me that one of you was in danger, you wouldn't want to know? You'd prefer I kept that information to myself?" She wasn't surprised when Kathy hesitated to answer or when the other wolves shifted restlessly. They might not like what she was, but they'd have no problem using her if it really came down to it. *Nice to know.*

Finally, Kathy replied, "We're a strong pack. We don't need help from outsiders."

Shaya sighed tiredly. "Kathy, I know you mean well. And I know you're just looking out for us. But it seems you're forgetting who is Alpha female around here." The reprimand was gently delivered, but it still rang with Shaya's strength.

Straightening to her full height, Kathy flicked her short brown hair away from her face. "I haven't forgotten." Her gaze returned to Ally. "But I also haven't forgotten that my daughter almost lost her mate because of a Seer. The bitch lied to him, told him that his true mate was a whole other female—gave him a false description of everything. She did it so she could have Marcus for herself. Luckily for Roni, it didn't work. Are you even listening to me?"

Ally double-blinked. "I was. A little. But then I got distracted by the hairs on your chin." Hearing choking noises, she noticed that Kent was patting a coughing Eli's back pretty hard.

Kathy pointed at her. "Don't think it's okay for you to insult me just because you're under Derren's protection. My Roni won't stand for it, and she could easily take you any day of the week."

Derren wasn't too sure of that. Roni was lethal, but he'd seen how fast Ally moved. She had seriously good reflexes. If nothing else, she would be able to hold off Roni. He'd thought Ally would bristle at Kathy's words—it was not only an insult but an oblique threat. Instead, she seemed mildly amused yet also on the verge of boredom. He was quickly learning that he should never "expect" anything when it came to Ally. She wasn't easy to read or predict. "Enough, Kathy," he told her firmly.

The woman ignored his warning. "I'm just making my point that I don't trust Seers."

Ally smiled gently. "Admitting your problem is the first step to recovery."

For a moment, Kathy said nothing—apparently words had failed her. Derren could attest to the fact that that didn't happen often. Then, muttering under her breath, Kathy took her seat. Derren turned to Ally. "You won that round."

Ally simply shrugged, hiding her frustration. She should be used to the prejudice by now, but it never ceased to grate on her nerves. In between bites of breakfast, the Mercury wolves talked between themselves. Everyone but Shaya purposely excluded Ally from the conversation. Their collective rejection was causing her head to pound.

She had just finished eating when Nick walked in with Willow in his arms. His stride faltered at the sight of Ally, but he gave a slight nod—it was one of acknowledgment as opposed to one of greeting. Still, Ally returned it. To offend Nick would be to offend Shaya, and Ally liked the Alpha female.

Taking the infant from Nick, Shaya cuddled her. "Feeling any better, angel?"

That was when Ally noticed how pale and tired the little girl looked as she chewed hard on a toy. "What's wrong with her?"

"She's just teething, but it's not a pleasant time for babies."

"Let me help." Ally gently cradled Willow's face, pushing some healing energy into the infant. Through the same link Ally had just opened, Willow's pain traveled to her. "There." Drawing back, Ally smiled at the baby, who tugged on her hair with a chuckle.

"What did you do?" There was no tension in Shaya . . . unlike the others, who had turned stiff as boards the moment Ally had touched Willow. Like she'd ever hurt a child.

"Took the pain away." Ally cupped her own jaw then, wincing. "It really does hurt."

Derren spoke then. "So, whenever you heal someone, their pain becomes yours?" His wolf didn't like the idea of her in pain.

"Yes, but it eases off pretty quickly. There. It's already gone."

Bracken put down his fork. "Okay, I gotta ask . . . what's it like having a sociopath for a mate?"

"And now we're done." Shaya rose to her feet. "How about a tour, Ally?" The Alpha female shot Bracken a withering look.

The enforcer raised his hands. "It was just a question."

Derren asked Shaya, "Can the tour wait till after lunch? I have some things to do this morning."

"You don't need to come with us." Shaya gently handed Willow back to Nick.

"Ally's under my protection while she's here."

"She's not going to come to any harm with me. And I'm pretty sure she can take care of herself anyway."

Pushing to her feet, Ally smiled at Shaya, thankful for the vote of confidence. "I'm ready when you are." Derren looked as though he might object again, so Ally rolled her eyes—earning herself a growl. How grand.

"Wait," said Derren. "Give me your cell."

Ally frowned. "Why?"

"Because I need to put my number in it." She was under his protection now, and that meant he'd have to be there if she needed him. With a shrug, she handed him her phone. He keyed in his number, then used her cell to call his phone, which effectively gave him her number. "Done." She was careful not to touch him as she took the phone from his hand, and that had his wolf baring his teeth in annoyance. "If there's a problem, call me."

If there were a problem, Ally would take care of it herself. Dominant females always dealt with their own shit. Rather than argue, she said, "Sure."

First, Shaya gave Ally a tour of the main lodge, showing her the bedrooms, the game room, the luxurious bathroom, and finally the basement—which had an indoor swimming pool and bar.

"No one's used it since Roni almost drowned," said Shaya. "It's a long story. To sum it up, we had some trouble with a jackal pack; they invaded our territory, and Roni battled with the Alpha. He tried to drown her. Marcus still hasn't quite gotten over it."

"And I'll meet them in a few days?"

"Yes, they split their time between here and my best friend's pack, since that's where Marcus is from. We share him and Roni with the Phoenix Pack. You heard of it?"

"I've heard of the Alphas. The Alpha female was latent for most of her life, wasn't she?" It was unheard of.

"That's right. Taryn's wolf surfaced later." It was said with utter pride. "Do you think the Collingwood Betas will give you any more problems?"

"No." Unfortunately, she didn't sound totally convinced, and Shaya picked up on it.

"But?"

"But Derren does."

"Let's hope he's wrong. Though Derren rarely ever is. It's kind of annoying. Come on, there's more to see."

Shaya guided Ally around Mercury Pack territory, showing her the land, the borders, where each of the lodges were, and the gorgeous waterfall. As they walked, Shaya told her all about the roots of the pack, where each of the members came from, and how Nick had come to blood with the Phoenix Alpha male.

Just before lunch, they came upon Derren training the enforcers—all five of the males were wearing only their jeans, revealing sets of very impressive abs.

"They sure are easy on the eyes," commented Ally with a sigh.

Shaya smiled. "Yeah. Don't get me wrong, I would never be attracted to another guy now that I'm mated. But that doesn't mean I'm blind."

Her wolf watched, curious and impressed, as Derren dueled with Zander. Although Zander was incredibly fast, he couldn't evade Derren's reach. Still, it wasn't an easy win for Derren, who then took a quick break to take a drink from one of the water bottles on the ground. At that moment, his gaze—dark, heated, and brooding—landed on Ally. Her skin burned under the weight of that gaze, her insides twisted with need, and her mouth dried up.

Oh, help. It simply wasn't fair.

"Ah, shit!" cursed someone, his voice nasal. It was Bracken, Ally quickly realized—she was glad for the distraction.

Laughing, Shaya said to Eli, "You broke his nose *again*?"

Eli didn't look the least bit repentant. "He was irritating me."

With a sigh, Ally approached. "Let me help." Bracken regarded her like she was a ticking bomb. She arched a challenging brow, poking at his pride, daring him to back away.

The enforcer rolled his shoulders, rising to the challenge. "All right."

She gripped his nose . . . and then snapped it back into place.

He stumbled backward, shouting, *"Fuck!"* Stunned, he glared at Ally.

She shrugged one shoulder. "I said I'd help. I didn't say I'd heal you."

Eli laughed. "She got you there, Bracken."

Realizing he'd been had, Bracken . . . smiled at her. Smiled? Weird. But then, dominant male wolves often were.

"Come on," Shaya chuckled, nudging Ally gently with her elbow. She didn't mind the touch. Shaya was a soothing, calming person to be around. But Ally sensed that the Alpha could be dangerous if the situation called for it.

Resisting the urge to take one last look at Derren, Ally turned and followed Shaya. "Tour done?"

"Yes, and I have to get back to Willow. It's almost time for lunch anyway. You coming?"

Ally gave her a wan smile. "I'll be honest with you, Shaya, it's unlikely I'll spend much time at your lodge."

The Alpha female practically pouted. "Why? Is it because the pack was so shitty toward you this morning? I would have interfered, but I didn't think you'd appreciate it—that would have made you look weak."

"It would have, and I'm glad you let me deal with it myself. But it's not about their behavior. This is their pack, their home, and they have every right to feel how they feel." Even if it did offend and frustrate her. "Part of being a Seer is being highly empathetic. Having all those negative emotions streaming at me physically hurt—not to mention pissed off my wolf."

Shaya's shoulders sagged. "I'm sorry."

"You have nothing to apologize for. You've been great, and I'm really thankful that you've been so welcoming. But I can't spend much time around the pack without hurting. And it's not fair to them either. They shouldn't have to feel so uncomfortable in their own home."

"They'll come around."

Doubtful. "Until then, I'll be mostly at my lodge, which is no hardship at all. I really do love it."

"Okay. But I'll come by every day. I'll need to bring fresh stock for your fridge anyway."

Ally smiled. "Be sure to bring Willow."

"I will."

"Now go see your beautiful baby girl."

As they parted ways, Ally headed back to her lodge. Well, it wasn't *her* lodge, it was just her designated guest lodge but, hey, it was a conversation she was having with herself, so she could be as possessive of the place as she wanted.

Finally there, she did what she often did when she had lots of crap on her mind: she cooked. It relaxed her, was a creative outlet that soothed all her senses and took her away from her worries.

It was Cain's youngest uncle, Sam, who had taught Ally how to cook. And how to hotwire a car and escape zip ties. Cain's uncles, all four still unmated . . . well, they hadn't really known what to do with a little girl. Their version of raising her had been to teach her "important life skills."

By the time she was eleven, she knew how to drive, how to skin animals, how to pick a lock, and how to brew beer. She could also reel off the military alphabet and speak Russian, Spanish, Italian, German, and Mandarin. Surprisingly enough, most of it had come in handy at some point.

Once her beef stir-fry was done, Ally took her meal outside and settled on the porch step that overlooked the lake. At total contrast to her morning meal, the atmosphere was calm and peaceful, with only the sounds of the forest to break up the silence.

After a few minutes, there was rustling in the grass. She couldn't help frowning at the sight of a large gray wolf cautiously approaching, nostrils flaring. Taking in his scent, she realized it was Bracken. Stopping a few feet away, his eyes glued to her plate, he licked his lips.

She rolled her eyes. "Typical male." She flung him a chunk of beef. "Now go." He did, but only moments later another gray wolf appeared, this one broader. Jesse, her senses told her. She grumbled, "You're all the same." She threw him a chunk of meat, and he snapped his jaws around it before running off. That was when a third wolf appeared; he was a mix of brown and gray. Zander. "Do you guys have no shame?" With a growl, she threw him a piece of beef too. "No more. Go."

Done with her lunch, she went inside to fetch the plate of cookies she'd baked. It was as she resettled on the step that the three wolves reappeared, side by side. "Oh, for God's sake."

When Derren arrived at the main lodge for lunch, he was surprised to find no sign of Ally. He'd figured she'd accompany Shaya there after the tour. When he was halfway through his lunch and she still hadn't appeared, he was about to call her cell. But then Shaya suddenly spoke.

"Ally's not coming."

Confused, Derren echoed, "She's not coming?"

"She said she probably won't spend much time over here."

Bracken stopped with his glass halfway to his mouth. "Why?"

"Because you're all so cold and mean that it physically hurts to be around you." Shaya shot them all disappointed looks.

Swallowing hard, Bracken looked kind of guilty. "It hurts her?"

"Negative emotions cause Seers pain," explained Shaya.

"Wow." Jesse blinked. "I didn't know that."

"It's for the best that she sticks to the guest lodge," said Kathy, refilling Zander's glass. "Something wrong with your food?" She glanced at Bracken and Jesse. "You two haven't eaten much either."

Scratching the back of his neck, Bracken admitted, "We might have binged on beef and cookies before we got here."

"Ally makes these giant chocolate chip cookies and, good God, they almost brought tears to my eyes." Jesse's groan was close to orgasmic.

Zander nodded slowly, smiling almost dreamily. "They were really good."

"The beef was cooked to perfection," proclaimed Bracken, a faraway look in his eyes.

"So she's handy in the kitchen, is she?" asked Kathy sharply.

Wide-eyed, Bracken spluttered. "Of course she's not as good as you." Kathy just huffed. The moment the woman had turned around, he mouthed, "Ally's cooking is *way* better."

"I heard that, Bracken!"

He gaped at Kathy's back. "I didn't say anything!"

Eli chuckled. "Mom has eyes in the front, back, and sides of her head."

Shaya looked at Nick, who was feeding Willow some kind of disgusting mush that she shockingly appeared to be enjoying. "Don't you care that your attitude put Ally in pain?"

Nick glanced at her sideways. "I didn't know it would hurt her, but I can't help how I feel."

"She healed our daughter. Doesn't that count for anything?"

"Yeah, it does. And I'm grateful, Shay. But one little deed isn't going to change how I feel about Seers."

Leaving the Alpha pair to dispute the matter while the rest of the pack offered their opinions here and there, Derren finished his meal and headed for Ally's lodge. Just to check on her, he told himself. It had nothing to do with the fact that his wolf was hounding him to go to her. Nothing to do with the fact that Derren himself wanted to see her . . . just because.

When his knock on the front door went unanswered, he rounded the lodge and found her lounging in the hammock listening to her iPod. Tuning everything out? Her scent twined around him, making his cock twitch to life.

Turning off the music, she asked, "Everything okay?"

Since her T-shirt had ridden up a little, flashing him a view of the swirly tattoo on her navel—no, it wasn't okay at all. He found himself wanting to trace it with his tongue. "Shaya told me you plan to hole up here."

"I figure that'll make it easier for everyone."

Derren knew it wouldn't be easy for her at all. Shifters were tactile creatures; social and sexual touch was important to them. Going without it wasn't good for their mental state, particularly that of their animals. "That'll be tough on you, and you know it."

Her tone dry, she said with a sweet smile, "Yeah, life will be so very hard and depressing without you . . . it will be almost the same as having you around." His eyes narrowed dangerously, but his mouth curved in amusement. "It's not like I'll be totally alone all the time. Shaya will come see me. Being around her doesn't hurt."

Guilt began to bloom inside him. He didn't want to hurt her. In fact, everything in him recoiled at the idea. And knowing that just being in close proximity caused her pain . . . it made him feel like a bastard.

"Tell me why you hate me, Derren."

The words shocked him. He liked hearing her say his name, which made absolutely no sense. "I don't hate you." He *wanted* to, because it would mean he could shake off his attraction to her.

"I'll rephrase: Why do you hate my kind?"

He didn't want to talk about it, but he found himself explaining, "Let's just say I never would have ended up in juvie if my old pack's Seer hadn't lied about a vision, turned my entire pack against me, and then stood up in a human court and testified against me."

So much pain and anger—it was like ice picks embedded in her lungs, and it made Ally's wolf whine to see him that way. Although she didn't know just what lie the Seer had told, Ally could understand the depth of Derren's rage. She'd heard from Cain exactly what juvie was like.

"You have no rights in there," Cain had told her. *"No say in your life, no privacy, no place to run as a wolf, no one to care if you live or die. If you can't defend yourself, if you can't fight, you'll never survive it. If the guards don't get ahold of you and have their sick idea of fun with you, the other prisoners might, especially if you break the 'prisoner code.' No one gets out of there whole, Ally. No one."*

Who wouldn't be angry to have been through that, to have lost so much of their youth? To have been trapped in a place where they were always watching over their shoulder, where they'd been hurt over and over by the guards who were supposed to maintain order? Add in that Derren hadn't deserved any of it, had carried the blame for something he hadn't done, and it was no wonder there was so much pain, anger, and darkness in him.

Ally might not be able to relate to his experiences in juvie, but she did know how much it hurt to be blamed for a crime she'd played no part in, to have everyone turn against her. If she were to come across someone who made her think of Rachelle, who brought back those memories, Ally couldn't say she'd be all that happy to be around that person. And if she'd been charged with protecting them, Ally definitely wouldn't have liked it very much. So, yes, she could understand Derren's reaction to her.

Careful not to unbalance the hammock, she sat upright. "I'm sorry for what happened to you—"

"I don't want pity," he snapped.

"Good, 'cause I'm not giving you any." Anyone who could survive juvie was worthy of respect and admiration, not pity. "It's true that power corrupts, and some Seers abuse their gifts. But the same could be said for Alphas. How many times have you heard of Alphas abusing their position and power? Or dominant wolves using their vibes to suppress and force less powerful wolves to submit against their will? You can't tell me you haven't known at least one person guilty of that."

Derren wanted to object, but he knew she was right. He simply hadn't thought of it that way before.

"People do shit like that because they're assholes, Derren. Not because they're Seers, or Alphas, or dominants. It's all about the individual."

He wanted to dispute it, wanted to hold on to his anger . . . but he couldn't. She was right again.

Even though it wouldn't be easy and her wolf wouldn't like it, Ally proposed without heat, "Look, how about I stay out of your way, and you stay out of mine?"

It would probably be for the best, but Derren knew he wouldn't manage for long. This female drew him, was like a magnet to his wolf. He'd dreamed about her the night before, dreamed he was balls deep in her, his teeth piercing her neck, his hand clutching her breast. Just the memory had his cock hardening. Suddenly she inhaled sharply, and a flush crept up her neck and face. He knew then that she could sense his arousal.

Ally cleared her throat. "I think you should go."

She was right once again; he really should. But Derren had always been a person who did what he wanted as opposed to what he should. "What does it feel like?"

Perplexed, she asked, "What?"

"Emotions cause physical sensations for you, right? I know you can sense that I want you." He took a few steps toward her. "What does it feel like to you?" He knew what it felt like for him. His hunger for her wasn't soft or tame or romantic. It was vicious, sharp-edged, and biting. It was raw desperation that had teeth and claws, and it had him in a tight grip. "What does it feel like?" he repeated.

Like teeth plucking at her nipples, but she wasn't about to tell him that. Then a crooked, satisfied smile surfaced on his face, and she winced. "I said that out loud, didn't I?" His chuckle answered that. "Bye, Derren." She thought he'd taunt her, but he turned and strode away, disappearing into the trees.

Her wolf lay down with a snarl, no doubt intending to sulk at his absence. But even the animal understood that there was too much darkness in Derren for him to ever accept her. He wasn't a bad person, though he seemed to believe he was. But he was misguided in many ways, broken on some level. And even if she hadn't been a Seer, he could never have trusted her. Trust and acceptance was important to Ally.

Derren could give her neither.

CHAPTER FIVE

*I*t was dark. So dark. She hated the dark.

Shivering with cold and fear, she shoved at the huge rocks that had tumbled down in front of her. They didn't budge an inch. She was trapped.

"It's okay, Ally, we're going to be okay."

No, they wouldn't be. He didn't understand. He hadn't seen what she had. "We have to get out." She pushed harder at the rocks with her small hands, but they still didn't move. Panic filled her, and she clawed at them as she began to shiver so hard her teeth chattered.

A hand on her arm pulled her back. "Ally, stop, you're going to hurt yourself."

"We have to get out! We have to warn them or they'll die!"

As something wet and rough grazed her cheek, Ally jerked awake with a gasp—and realized a large black wolf was nuzzling her. Before she had the chance to push him away, he backed off. It wasn't the first time over the past week that she had snapped awake in the hammock, haunted by a bad dream, to find the black wolf standing there. Watching over her? Being nosy? She didn't know.

As if satisfied that she was now fine, he loped away just as he usually did. Although she was grateful to Derren for pulling her out of the dark, she hated that he knew how damaged she was. Didn't like that he'd seen her vulnerable.

Although sometimes Ally managed to fall back asleep after a nightmare, she sadly didn't manage to do so that morning. Getting up with a sigh, she filled her system with caffeine and a small breakfast.

The past week had gone pretty much the same for Ally. After breakfast, she'd go for a run in her wolf form. Shortly after that, Shaya would visit with Willow for a few hours. At lunchtime, Bracken, Jesse, and Zander's wolves would appear, begging for scraps. Ally would then spend the rest of the day either reading, baking, or watching TV. Then she'd have dinner before lounging in her hammock on her porch, listening to her iPod, where she'd eventually fall asleep.

She'd often see glimpses of Derren going to and from his lodge, but he'd never spoken to her. The small amount of company hadn't bothered her. Being mostly alone had stopped her from being bombarded by other people's shit. It almost made her feel like a normal person. Seers would often have sensory overload, and they each had ways of blocking the world out when necessary. Listening to music helped Ally with that.

She was so used to having only Shaya and Willow as visitors that she was shocked when Kent and Caleb accompanied them that morning. Both males were polite and friendly. Maybe because Ally relieved Willow of any discomfort each day, and they appreciated that. Or maybe because Shaya had bullied them into it—Ally really had no idea.

In any case, the mated males then invited Ally to their lodge so that Kent could show her how beautifully he'd styled the interior. He was horrified that Ally hadn't added any personal touches to her lodge. The fact that she was only a *guest* was irrelevant to Kent. In his mind, she should have put some kind of stamp on the place, marked her territory in some way. Surprisingly, Shaya agreed. But when Ally explained that interior design wasn't really her thing, Kent begged her to allow him to do the task for her.

So after Shaya dropped Willow off at home for her midday nap, Ally was ushered by Shaya, Kent, and Caleb to the males' lodge to see how great Kent was at interior design. When they were almost there, they stumbled across Derren having a training session with the enforcers in a clearing. She and the others paused to watch, and Ally had to admit that the enforcers had very good techniques. When Jesse put Bracken flat on his ass, Shaya, Kent, and Caleb all winced.

Ally, on the other hand, wanted to ask why the hell Bracken had let Jesse win. When all eyes zoomed in on her, she smiled weakly. "I said that out loud, huh."

"He didn't *let* me win," Jesse growled at her, rotating one shoulder.

"What makes you think Bracken did that?" Derren's tone was curious, not doubtful.

"Jesse has clear tells," replied Ally. "It was obvious by the way Bracken watched for them that he knows what they are. But sometimes he didn't dodge Jesse's moves, even though he's fast enough to do it." Recalling Shaya informing her that Jesse was still recovering from a recent illness after his wolf had hunted a poisoned animal, Ally wondered if Bracken had therefore taken it easy on his pack mate.

"Very good," Derren commended, sounding genuinely impressed.

Jesse whirled on his Beta. "I won that round fair and square." His glare returned to Ally as he sniped, "You've watched me fight a couple of times and now you think you know my technique well enough to see if I have any tells?"

"Yeah, I do," Ally said simply.

Jesse sniggered. "Well, if I'm really easy pickings—"

"That's not what I said," interrupted Ally with a bored sigh.

"—why don't you come over here and we'll have a little one-on-one."

"Jesse, leave it," Derren bit out.

But the enforcer didn't. He shrugged innocently. "It'll just be a friendly spar."

"I don't spar," Ally told him. "I fight—no rules, no limits, no holding back."

A smirk from Jesse. "Then this will be fun."

Derren put a hand on Jesse's chest to stay him. "Drop it." The words came out guttural as his wolf lunged for supremacy, wanting to protect Ally. If the guy harmed her, Derren would have to harm him in turn. Since the night Ally had given him some home truths, he'd chewed on the things she'd said, and he'd had to face that he'd unfairly been an ass to her. He knew he was irrational when it came to Seers, but it was no excuse. Like she'd said, power corrupted, but it depended on the individual and not their status.

"Don't worry, I'm not going to leave her banged up." Jesse's smile was all teeth. "I don't abuse women. But I can tell that she's strong. I want to know how strong."

Shaya turned to her. "Ally, are you sure about this?"

"He's not going to back down. And neither am I." That wasn't who Ally was. She took Bracken's place opposite Jesse, her feet braced shoulder-width apart. "Normally, I don't give warnings. But you really don't want to fight me, Jesse."

"Why is that?"

"Because I *will* defeat you. I *will* enjoy it. And I *will* crush your pride, which has already taken a beating this morning."

His smirk widened. "Take your best shot, little Seer." He took on a fighting stance, his eyes twinkling with excitement.

Fighting to keep his prowling wolf from surfacing, Derren went to stand by Shaya, asking, "You're not going to stop this?"

She looked as anxious as him. "If I interfere, it would be the same as saying I don't trust her to protect herself. Things are tough enough for her here as it is. She'd be respected more for rising to the challenge and losing than she would be for backing down."

He knew Shaya was right, knew that any interference would only serve to undermine Ally and piss her off. Even his wolf understood that, though he was too angry to settle down.

Derren watched as Ally kicked off her shoes and stood still, alert, her eyes glued to Jesse. Then the enforcer moved, his fist flying toward Ally's jaw as he went for a knockout punch. The move was fast and hard . . . but Ally sidestepped him, twisted her upper body, and stabbed her claws into his side. There were no fancy, practiced moves with Ally. Every punch was dirty and pitiless, and Derren saw Cain's influence in each one. She didn't claw at Jesse as he aimed blow after blow at her; she used her claws like they were knives—slicing, stabbing, and carving without mercy.

A bleeding Jesse repeatedly came at her with uppercuts and impressive kicks, but she evaded most of them . . . letting Jesse tire himself out, become weaker with lethargy and blood loss.

Derren was impressed. His wolf? Not so much. The animal was livid with Jesse, which worsened when the male delivered a hard kick to her ribs. It was—

"Holy Mother of all that's blue, how the fuck did she do that?" exclaimed Bracken.

Derren had no idea, but she'd just done it again. He wouldn't have thought it was possible if he hadn't seen it for himself. In the matter of a single second, Ally had shifted into her wolf form, bit deep into Jesse's shoulder, and then shifted back into her human form just as quickly. It had happened so damn fast that it hadn't affected her clothing other than to slightly tear her T-shirt and shorts.

In between stabbing and striking Jesse, she repeatedly switched forms for just a fleeting moment, enabling her to use her wolf's strength, speed, and fangs. It was so shocking and distracting that it caused Jesse to make mistakes. That, together with her brutal hits and sharp reflexes, was enough to earn her dominance within the fight.

It was only a matter of time before Jesse was pinned to the ground by a white wolf, jaws clamped around his shoulder. A second later, it was Ally leaning over Jesse. "You should have listened to me," she told him as she rose to her feet.

Jesse seemed to be in too much shock to feel a dent in his already wounded pride. "How can you do that?"

"Cain said he taught you combat," said Derren as everyone gathered closer to her, "but he can't switch from form to form like that." It should not be possible. Her animal shouldn't have been prepared to pull back repeatedly from a battle like that. The wolf should have fought Ally for supremacy, wanting to deal with the challenge and danger herself. Instead, she'd worked so in sync with Ally that she shifted forms like water.

"It works because my wolf and I are completely at peace," explained Ally. "We trust one another. We're a team."

"And your wolf respects that, and she feels respected enough to pull back when you want her to because she knows you won't cut her out of a fight," deduced Zander, to which Ally nodded.

Eli puffed out a long breath, looking impressed. "Nick's in tune with his wolf, but not to that extent."

"I didn't think it was possible." Shaya smiled at Ally. "Roni would have loved to watch that."

Hearing Jesse wince slightly, Ally felt bad. "I'll heal you."

He shook his head. "No, I deserved that. I was arrogant, and I taunted you. But thanks for the offer. You fought well." The other enforcers nodded in agreement.

As their respect slid over her skin like lotion, she smiled inwardly. "If you change your mind, Jesse, I'll be at my lodge." She turned to face Shaya . . . only to find her way obstructed by a powerful, solid, and way-too-alluring body.

Noticing the blood in her hair, Derren said, "You must have a bad cut on your head. Let me see."

She stepped back. "It's fine."

"Let me see," Derren insisted without raising his voice. "I need to check the injury. I won't touch your skin." No matter how badly he wanted to know how it would feel under his hands.

Swallowing hard, she nodded. "Just my hair." As long as he didn't touch her skin, his emotions wouldn't seep inside her. Although . . . she couldn't help but notice that the brief flashes weren't so sharp and biting today. Apparently he was in a good mood.

As his fingers gently parted her hair, Ally's stomach clenched as a fierce need slithered through her. It didn't matter that he was only touching her hair. Having his body eating up her space, his hot breath on her forehead, his brooding eyes focused solely on her . . . There was an intensity and intimacy to the moment that took her by surprise.

Derren released her hair, but he didn't step back. He breathed her in, letting that luscious scent settle in his lungs. "It's stopped bleeding, but it's deep. You'll need to clean it."

That was gonna sting like a bitch. "I'm going to my lodge to take a shower."

"I'll walk you back."

"It's okay." She stepped away, intending to leave. "I'm—" She broke off as a strange, ominous sound whooshed through the air. "What—" A deafening, piercing boom shocked the breath from her lungs, and she was suddenly encased in heat. Flames grazed her skin as she was propelled through the air and crashed to the hard ground. She heard a crack, and quickly realized it was her skull.

The adrenaline rushing through her helped her ignore the ringing in her ears, the disorientation clouding her reasoning, and the agony attempting to take hold of her. Her instincts told her to get up and *move*.

She crawled away from the corroding heat at her back and the trees that were collapsing around her. A hand suddenly snatched her arm and dragged her forward, urging her to move faster.

When the hand released her, she collapsed on her front. A face was staring into hers. A face she knew. *Derren.*

He cast a nauseated glance at her back, and she wondered what he saw there. "Wait here, I'll be right back."

Wait there? Her instincts didn't think that was a good idea. She should keep moving, get as far away from the danger as possible. And she would have done exactly that if Caleb hadn't crouched in front of her, asking her questions she didn't understand—the pain at her back was so consuming she couldn't think.

A chorus of curses and grunts of pain was quickly followed by the appearance of several others. They were heaving two wolves along with them, one of whom was a coughing and badly injured Eli. Ally double-blinked in surprise as a body was dumped at her side.

"Do something!" ordered a harsh male voice. Jesse. "You can save her!"

But she couldn't. Shaya—her body unmoving, her eyes open wide, her skin scorched and red and blistered—was already gone.

"Help her!"

"I can't! She's dead." It was too late. Ally closed her eyes against the emotional and physical blow to her system. Feeling hands pulling on her upper arms, making frost jab her bare skin, Ally opened her eyes with a gasp . . . and found Derren standing in front of her, the image of concern.

"Ally! Ally, answer me!"

Instinctively, she shrugged out of his hold, escaping the chill and hunger coming from his touch. Glancing around, she saw that there was no fire. No heat. No fallen trees. The male eyes around her regarded her curiously.

"Are you okay?"

Hearing that familiar voice, Ally glanced at the redheaded female beside her. Not dead but alive. At once, realization hit Ally, and horror slammed into her. "Move! We have to fucking move *now!*" She grabbed Shaya's arm and pulled hard as she turned and ran.

"Where are you going?" demanded Zander.

Without breaking stride, she very briefly glanced at him over her shoulder. "Unless you want to burn, *run!*" Footsteps thudded behind her as the males kept pace with her and—

A blast of fire. A rumble through the ground. Heat racing along her back. Trees crashing.

She wasn't sure what sent her sprawling to the ground. The impact of the explosion? The reverberations in the ground? Her own instinct to dive away from the danger? She didn't care, was simply glad of two things: One, she didn't feel the same pain as she had in the vision. Two, Shaya was alive, albeit shocked and scared.

"Fuck!"

Hearing a harsh exclamation, Ally looked to see Eli and Caleb supporting Derren's weight as they lowered him to the ground at her side. Resting on his front, he hissed out a breath. Bile rose in her throat as she got a look at his legs, the denim torn and sticking to the badly burned skin.

"He shielded me," said Kent as his mate called Nick on his cell phone. "Derren shoved me to the ground and covered me." And took the injuries intended for Kent.

"You can heal him, right?" Bracken asked Ally.

She struggled to a sitting position, startled by Derren's harsh *"No."*

"Derren, let her help you," encouraged Eli.

"No," he again ground out, looking close to blacking out. His eyes blazed into hers. "It'll hurt you. It already hurts when I touch you."

Yes, and feeling the agony of his injuries would make it worse, but . . . "This is what I do, Derren. Now shut the fuck up and keep still."

She gently laid her hands on his legs, over the charred denim. A contrary combination of frost, heat, and pain invaded her system, prickled her nerve endings. Ignoring the agony, she pushed healing energy into his body. The moment the loop between them opened, his pain flowed into her. The more soothing energy she gave him, the more it felt like her skin was blazing, tightening, and eating away at itself.

A soft hand landed on her shoulder. "Ally, you can stop now." Oh, good. Then she collapsed.

Derren ignored the knock on the door of the guest bedroom, just as he'd ignored the others. Instead, he lazed in the chair beside the bed on which he'd laid an unconscious Ally three hours ago. The sight of her ashen face and the dark smudges under her eyes was making his wolf frantic. She hadn't tossed or turned even once. She'd remained so still that if it weren't for the subtle rise and fall of her chest, he would have worried that she was dead.

Another knock; this one louder, harder, impatient. "Derren, open up!" *Shaya.*

Although it was the Alpha pair's lodge, he hadn't let them or anyone else inside the room, mindful of how vulnerable Ally was at the moment. Having her lying there, out cold, while under the same roof as people who might mean her harm . . . it nettled both Derren and his wolf. The animal was very much on edge, pacing and anxious for Ally to wake up.

"She's my friend, Derren, I want to see her! I'm worried about her!"

If his conscience wasn't so undeveloped, he might have felt bad for Shaya. Right now, though, he was only interested in Ally. He didn't truly believe any of his pack would harm her, but his protective instincts wouldn't allow him to take the chance. While she was vulnerable, he'd watch over her.

A feminine huff traveled through the door. "Taryn's on her way here. If she thinks that Ally might potentially need her healing skills, she's going to come up here and there'll be no stopping her. Unless, of course, I can assure her that I've seen Ally for myself and she's fine."

Cursing, Derren stalked to the door and yanked it open, finding most of the pack gathered behind a smug-looking Shaya. He knew that she'd played him, but he also knew she was right. Taryn, a powerful healer, would demand to check on Ally if Shaya couldn't assure her that it wasn't necessary. He moved aside for Shaya. "Just you." Ignoring the complaints coming from the others, he shut the door.

The redhead's expression crumpled into one of concern as she approached the bed. "Has she flitted in and out of consciousness?"

"No. She hasn't moved an inch." At least the wound on her head from her fight with Jesse had healed.

Shaya gently took hold of her wrist. "Her pulse is strong. I'm guessing her system has shut down while she recovers. She used up a lot of strength."

He was thinking the same thing. "Why is Taryn on her way here?"

"We called Roni, told her what happened. When Taryn heard, she insisted on coming along with Roni and Marcus."

"Is she bringing Trey?" If so, that would be a problem. As Marcus had told them, Trey despised Seers. Derren was resolute that Ally would be spared the prejudice from now on.

"I don't know, Roni didn't say."

Another knock on the door had Derren sighing. *"Go away."*

"Let us in, we just want to see her," groused Kent.

Derren grumbled to Shaya, "I should have taken her to her own lodge." Or his. Somewhere she'd have space and privacy. Noticing the smile on his Alpha female's face, he frowned. "What?"

"I see your attitude toward her has done a one-eighty. It's 'bout time."

Coming to stand at Ally's side, he smoothed a strand of her hair between his fingers. "She healed me."

"You sound mystified."

"After the way I acted, I wouldn't have blamed her if she sat back and watched with glee while I writhed in agony."

"Ally's prickly and she doesn't take too kindly to bullshit, but she's also moral and fair."

Yeah, he got that. "She foresaw the explosion."

"I'm guessing so. One second she was fine, the next she was staring into space and her pupils had turned white."

"Did you see the way she looked at you when she snapped out of it and saw you were beside her?"

Shaya swallowed hard. "Like she'd seen a ghost."

And that spoke volumes about just what Ally had seen in her vision. And just how much they owed her.

"Shaya!" called Caleb. "Roni and Marcus are here with some of the Phoenix Pack!"

"I'm coming!" Shaya gave Derren a weak smile. "If she wakes up, send for me."

Once she'd left, he returned to his seat and clasped his hands beneath his chin as he continued to watch over Ally. Some of the color was coming back to her cheeks, but not enough for his liking. What worried him most was that she was so still. He'd seen her sleeping many times in her hammock, noticed that she fidgeted something awful in her sleep—especially when she was having nightmares.

He wasn't sure what those nightmares were about, and he didn't have the right to ask. But it both interested and concerned him that she suffered from them so regularly. The fact that she wasn't his concern didn't seem to matter to his instincts or to his wolf. And it was slowly not coming to matter to Derren either.

His thoughts cut off as her eyelids fluttered and one leg straightened. Then those almond green eyes met his. Confusion, wariness, and surprise fought for supremacy in her expression as she glanced around. "You're all right," he assured her. "You're in Nick and Shaya's lodge."

Her gaze returned to his as she licked her lips, seemingly more alert now.

"How are you feeling?"

It was a long moment before she answered. "Okay."

"Do you remember what happened? Do you remember the explosion?"

After another moment, she nodded. "What was it?"

"We think it was a rifle grenade of some kind." He hadn't made much of a contribution to Nick's investigation, wanting to stay with Ally instead. "You healed me. It was hurting you. I could feel it." He'd hated that. He was a dominant wolf shifter; it was in his makeup to protect females and children, especially those directly under his protection. But whether he'd wanted to or not, he'd caused her pain. And she'd still willingly taken his. "But you didn't pull away. You took my pain and added it to your own. Why?"

She swallowed. "Because it was the right thing to do."

"I didn't deserve your help."

"Oh, I know that."

His mouth twitched into a smile. "Thank you for what you did."

"Don't thank me. It's what I do."

Apparently praise made his Seer feel uncomfortable. "I'm still grateful."

Sitting upright, she threaded a hand through her hair. "How long was I out?"

"A little over three hours. You don't seem surprised. Is that normal?"

"Only if the injuries I've healed are extensive."

It was safe to say that third-degree burns counted as serious. "Do your eyes always turn white when you have a vision?" Although he'd met several Seers, he'd never been present while one had a vision.

"As far as I know, yeah."

"I didn't like seeing you like that. It was like you were somewhere else." Like her soul had vacated her body, left it cold. His wolf had panicked. "Shaya died in the vision, didn't she? You saved her." Ally opened her mouth to speak, but then there was a familiar loud, rhythmic knock at the door that told him it was his Alpha male. "It's Nick. You up for visitors?"

Ally shrugged. "Sure." What she really wanted was to leave and get back to her lodge. She was feeling groggy and irritable, which wouldn't make her good company for anyone. She watched as Derren opened the door, allowing Nick to enter, and then closed it on the faces grouped there. She was sure she'd seen Kent, Caleb, and Bracken—all of whom had been scowling at Derren.

Ally swung her legs off the bed to better sit up. Derren returned to her side, his stance oddly protective.

Nick noted it with a raised eyebrow before turning to Ally. "How do you feel?" His condemnation and annoyance seemed to have melted away, replaced by an appreciation that warmed her skin.

"Okay."

"From what the others told me, it sounds like you had a vision. Is that right?"

She nodded, barely managing to repress a shudder as the sight of Shaya's dead body flashed in her mind.

"Can you tell me what you saw?"

"I saw exactly what happened out there. An explosion."

"But you were all hurt pretty badly in the vision," he assumed.

"She saved Shaya's life," said Derren, wanting his Alpha male and friend to fully appreciate and acknowledge just what he could have lost today if it hadn't been for Ally.

Nick only briefly flicked his gaze to Derren. "I'm in your debt, Ally. And I won't forget that."

She would have told him that there was no debt, that she owed him for letting her stay with his pack temporarily. But he was already leaving, ushering the wolves that stood outside the door into moving along.

"Ready to go back to your own lodge?" asked Derren once they were alone again.

She closed her eyes, holding up a hand. "Stop."

"What?"

"Being nice. It's weird."

His mouth curved slightly. "You like me better when I'm a bastard?"

She pinned his gaze with hers. "I'm still a Seer, Derren. Yes, I healed you. And yes, I saved Shaya's life. But I'm no different than I was before that happened."

"I know." Derren sighed. "Everything you said when we last talked . . . You were right. I've been shitty toward you, and it's going to stop."

"So you no longer hate me, just like that?" Doubt was heavy in her tone.

"I never hated you." He squatted in front of her. "You can't *feel* that something's different?"

"You're always hard to gauge." Admittedly, though, the fleeting emotions she was sensing were predominantly appreciativeness, regret, and a strong protectiveness—all of which felt like the softest fur brushing against her.

"Then let me prove it. Don't jerk away." Derren traced the black shadow under her eye with his index finger. "Did that hurt?"

Shockingly . . . "No." Not even a little. Quite the opposite, actually. It didn't matter that the touch had been featherlight and far from seductive. The heat of his body had been like a brand on her flesh, making need begin to curdle low in her stomach. And she had to get out of there before he sensed it. She got to her feet . . . and then blushed when she realized he was now eye level with her crotch. Sensing he was about to tease her for what he could no doubt very easily scent, she bit out, "Don't."

Standing upright, he raised his hands. "I didn't say anything."

"You didn't have to." It was obvious he was stifling a smile. Silent but amused, he led her out of the room and along the landing to a flight of stairs. From there, Ally could hear multiple voices coming from downstairs—some of which were unfamiliar. It was clearly packed with people. How *not* grand.

"I know you probably want to go straight back to your lodge," said Derren, "but these people are nosy fuckers, and they want to get a look at the person who saved Shaya's life. Just come say hi, and then I'll get you out of here."

To her surprise, Derren remained slightly in front of Ally in what seemed to be a protective move as he led her into the kitchen. Instantly, a hush fell upon the room, and several emotions crashed into her, primarily curiosity.

Relief washed over Shaya's face. "You're awake." She headed straight for Ally and greeted her with a tight hug that made gratitude and affection seep into Ally's system. "You look much better." With a smile, Shaya turned to the others—most of whom were seated at the table. "Everyone, this is Ally. Ally, this is Roni and Marcus."

The slender female gave her a small nod, while her dark, incredibly hot mate offered Ally a quiet "Hey." Ally gave them both a small wave.

Shaya continued, "And these wolves are from the Phoenix Pack." She gestured to two males. The burly one had a real grumpy air about him while the athletically built male regarded her warily. "That's Ryan, a Phoenix enforcer, and Tao, who's their Head Enforcer. The scowling, totally ripped guy leaning against the wall is their Alpha, Trey." Whereas the enforcers appeared mostly neutral, the Alpha's aversion to her—or, more likely, to what she was—made her skin itch.

At that moment, the back door opened and two wolves entered. Shaya said, "This gorgeous woman here is their Beta, Ja—"

"Oh my God, Ally!" The familiar tall female with long sable hair came flying at her, eyes wide in both shock and recognition. "Hey, how are you?"

Ally gladly accepted Jaime's hug. "I'm great. You?"

Pulling back, she said, "They kept referring to you as 'the Seer,' but it never occurred to me that it could be you!"

"So," interrupted the brown-eyed tower of muscle that appeared at Jaime's side, "you two know each other?"

Jaime replied, "Ally was with our old pack for, like, eighteen months." She returned her gaze to Ally. "That was almost six years ago, right?"

Ally nodded. "You're part of the Phoenix Pack now?"

Jaime smiled proudly and leaned into the brown-eyed male. "This is my mate, Dante."

Ally wanted to ask if he was *the* Dante—the guy Jaime had talked about many times. Although he'd left Jaime's old pack when he was just a teenager, Jaime had never gotten over her crush. If the fact that they were now mated was anything to go by, it must have been because they were true mates but hadn't known back then.

"Ally once had a vision that Gabe was going to be attacked by a group of falcon shifters," Jaime told Dante, referring to her brother. "It saved him."

"Really?" Dante's frown gradually slipped away. "It's good to meet you, Ally."

Shaya released a sigh of relief. But then her entire body froze as a tiny blonde with sharp charcoal-gray eyes planted herself in front of Ally. Shaya cleared her throat. "Ally, this is Taryn, Alpha female of the Phoenix Pack." Taryn's shrewd gaze assessed her from head to toe and back again.

"Taryn," drawled Derren, knowing there was every chance Taryn would carry the same prejudice toward Seers that her mate did, given the pain it had caused him.

She waved a hand at Derren. "Oh, cool it, Hudson. I'm not gonna give her shit. She saved my best friend's life and healed my goddaughter. As far as I'm concerned, she walks on water." Taryn gave her a respectful nod. "If you ever need anything, just ask." Her stamp of approval must have been what her enforcers had been waiting for, because then Tao and Ryan nodded at Ally in greeting, along with the seriously hot blond, who was grinning impishly.

Shaya gestured at the blond, seeming reluctant to introduce him. "This is another Phoenix enforcer, Dominic."

His grin widened. "Hi, I have big feet." Everyone groaned, other than Jaime, who laughed, and Derren, who growled.

"Dominic, I really wouldn't exercise your habit of dishing out cheesy chat lines on Ally," Shaya advised him. "Derren's kind of . . . protective."

The Phoenix enforcer was the image of innocence. "It's just that she looks a lot like my next girlfriend."

Derren growled again. "Take Shaya's advice and leave Ally be."

Dominic just grinned at him before winking at Ally, and she couldn't help but smile. He was obviously a world of trouble.

"Now you've all seen her, so back off," ordered Derren. "She's leaving."

Ally pointed to the blood matting her hair. "I kind of need a shower."

Jaime hugged her once more. "Expect plenty of visits from me while you're here." Ally smiled at that. Jaime was always good company.

Shaya said, "I'll come see you when everyone's gone home."

As Ally followed Derren out of the kitchen, the Mercury wolves either offered her a "hey" or a nod of thanks—none of which were begrudging or had hints of wariness. It satisfied her wolf, who'd found it difficult being part of a pack, even temporarily, that didn't accept or include her.

As her lodge came into view, Ally inwardly sighed in relief. Now all she needed to do was get rid of the persistent, indomitable, and annoyingly hot male at her side. But since she got the feeling he didn't intend to go anywhere, and he was a guy who didn't seem to pay attention to what other people wanted, she doubted it would be easy.

CHAPTER SIX

Entering her lodge, Ally slung her jacket onto the sofa and headed for the stairs. Sensing that Derren had expectedly followed her inside, she said, "You can go now."

"Not until you're steady on your feet." Derren wanted to go upstairs with her, help her get clean, take care of her—an odd feeling that was made stronger by his wolf's urge to do the same. But he hadn't earned that level of intimacy with her, and it was best for everyone if he ignored the urge in any case.

Ally couldn't deny that she was still a little weak, but she'd be damned if she'd admit it out loud. "I don't need a nursemaid."

"Good. I'd just send her away anyway."

Knowing he'd purposely misunderstood what she'd said, Ally just rolled her eyes. Not interested in wasting what little strength she had on arguing with him, she left him in the kitchen while she took her shower. Since her head wound had healed, it barely stung when she shampooed her hair. She wanted to linger, to let the hot spray wash away her tension, but she was too tired.

Dressed in her sweats, she made her way downstairs. Derren was still in the kitchen, and he'd apparently made himself a sandwich. "Feel free to make yourself at home." The bite of sarcasm in her words actually made him smile.

He plonked the sandwich on her dining table. "Sit. Eat."

Well, that made her bristle, even as her stomach rumbled. "I don't respond well to orders."

"Yeah, I'm learning that." He moved closer, breathing in her delicious scent mingled with her coconut soap. "You need to eat something. You missed lunch, and you used up a lot of energy. Eat."

Although his Beta tone was irritating as shit, she wasn't the type to cut her nose off to spite her face. So with a huff, she took a seat and dug into her sandwich, which was actually pretty good. She purposely gave her full attention to the sandwich, disregarding the wolf opposite her. But it was hard to ignore a six-foot-plus male who was packed with hard muscle and armed with an unrefined sexuality. Especially when said male wanted her attention.

"Is it always like that?" Derren asked. At her questioning look, he added, "The visions. Do they always seem real?"

"Yes." Even when she was sleeping, they were never unclear or dreamlike.

"Must be hard, scary, watching people you know—maybe even care about—be seriously hurt or die." He deliberately brushed his foot against hers beneath the table, almost smiling at her reproachful narrow-eyed look. "I guess the flip side is that you get to save them."

"Not all of them." At his speculative look, she cursed. She hadn't meant to say that out loud.

"Who didn't you manage to save?"

She *so* wasn't going there. Done with her sandwich, she got to her feet. "You know what, I think I'll go relax in the hammock for a while. I'm tired."

"I'm not so easy to dismiss, Ally. Surely you've figured that out by now."

She had. It was a frustrating quality that part of her admired. "Look, I'm grateful that you watched over me while I was unconscious. But I'm fine now. You don't need to stay."

"I know." But he was still going to stay; his expression made that clear.

"Fine. Do what you like."

"I will." He always did. It had made him a difficult son to raise, since his parents were—

Instantly, Derren shoved the memory of them and their betrayal from his mind before it had the chance to darken his mood.

Stepping out onto the porch, he had to smile at the sight of Ally lounging in the hammock, eyes closed, listening to her iPod. And effectively dismissing him once again. She was a stubborn, prickly little thing intent on holding the world at a distance. Why that intrigued him, he really couldn't say. But very little intrigued Derren, and the fact that she *could* do that drew him as surely as her scent and delectable body.

He could fully admit that to himself now that he was no longer looking at her through a dark cloud of resentment and suspiciousness. He was no longer knotted up inside, no longer unreasonably angry with her or himself for how badly he wanted her. It made him able to see her more clearly—see the sharp, strong-willed, wounded female who possessed a dangerous edge and who could show loyalty and kindness to a pack that hadn't given her the same.

With that one deed, she'd earned not only his respect but his loyalty. Maybe even a piece of his trust. That pleased and relieved his wolf.

Hearing footsteps, he turned just as Shaya and Nick rounded the corner. Derren gently tugged on Ally's hair, gaining her attention. She scowled until she noticed her new visitors.

Switching off her iPod and pulling out her earbuds, Ally sat up. "Hey. What's this?" She eyed the plate in Shaya's hands that was covered with tinfoil.

Shaya smiled. "Kathy knew you'd missed lunch, and she didn't think you'd feel like cooking."

Surprised, Ally raised her brow. "A peace offering?"

"No, this is what packs do. We take care of our own."

"She's already eaten," Derren told her, irrationally offended by another wolf taking care of Ally. "I made her a sandwich."

"Which he bullied me into eating," grumbled Ally, carefully taking the plate from Shaya. Peeling back a little of the foil, revealing pasta and salad, she sniffed.

Nick's brow furrowed. "What are you doing?"

"Checking for poison."

Shaya rolled her eyes, snatching back the plate. "I'll put it in the fridge. Take it out when you're hungry."

Ally thought it was kind of ironic that saving Shaya's life through the use of her gift had earned her acceptance, when the very reason the pack had initially been so unwelcoming was because of said gift. It would no doubt gall Kathy on some level, since she'd been clear that she didn't want Ally to share her visions. To be fair to the woman, though, she'd backed right down and owned up to her mistake by offering her acceptance. Ally could respect that.

When she reappeared on the porch, Shaya told Ally, "Kathy will never be fond of Seers, but you're now the exception. And please know that I'll love you forever. To think that I might have missed my daughter growing up, that Nick might have died right along with me . . ." She shuddered, eyes glistening.

Cuddling his mate close, Nick pressed a soft kiss to her temple. He then spoke to Ally. "We won't forget what you did."

"Do you have any idea who caused the explosion?" Ally asked him.

"Eli and the enforcers scouted the direction from which the grenade was fired," Nick replied. "They came across a spot that smelled strongly of foxes, but there were no tracks."

Derren blinked. "Foxes?" He hadn't received an update before now, since he'd stuck with Ally as opposed to joining the enforcers.

Nick nodded. "The trail went stale after a hundred feet. It took everything I had not to keep going to hunt them down and rip them to pieces," he rumbled.

Ally frowned. "Why didn't you?"

"The last time someone crossed our border was to lure away the males from the main lodge so the females were vulnerable. That was the night Roni almost died." A muscle in Nick's jaw ticked. "I won't make that mistake again, no matter how badly I want blood. Especially not when every instinct I have tells me to stick close to my mate and child."

"The poisoned animals and rifle grenade have to be related in some way." Shaya rubbed her temple. "I find it too hard to believe that two attacks could happen so close together unless they were related."

Derren agreed, but . . . "Using two different forms of attack makes no sense, though. Hell, using a human weapon makes no sense." Shifters fought with tooth and claw—even foxes, though they could be sneaky, cheating fuckers.

"Unless it's the extremists." Shaya shrugged. The leader of a particular group of extremists had also happened to have been a guard in the shifter juvenile detention where Nick and Derren had been incarcerated. Hating Nick for badly injuring him when he'd fought off the bastard's attempts to abuse him back then, the guard's group of extremists had targeted Nick—which had simply led to the bastards' deaths.

To the outside world, the group had mysteriously "disappeared." Of course the other anti-shifter extremists groups speculated that Nick was responsible, and it was that fear of him that kept the other groups from retaliating. But just maybe their fear wasn't getting in the way anymore.

"I'm not convinced it's the extremists," said Nick. "I think someone's playing with us. That they want us to be confused about who we're facing."

Shaya pursed her lips. "If so, it's working."

"Which side of the border did Eli and the enforcers find the foxes' scents?" Derren asked Nick.

"The side that flows into Miranda's territory." Nick skimmed his hand up and down Shaya's arm. "Which will mean she'll also try hunting the trespassers."

"Miranda Whitney is Alpha female of the Sutherland Pack," Shaya told Ally.

"I've heard about her." Ally swatted away a mosquito. "She runs the pack alone, right?" It wasn't common for an unmated female wolf to run a pack.

"Yep," confirmed Shaya, her mouth tightening in distaste. "I don't like her. But we're cordial and civil because she's our closest neighbor."

Ally understood that. Neighbors often watched out for each other, chased away trespassers, and informed each other of any suspicious activity. Hearing her cell phone ringing, she excused herself and went into the lodge. Retrieving her cell from the pocket of her jacket, she tensed when she saw "Zeke" flashing on the screen. It wasn't the first time he'd tried calling her since she'd left the Collingwood Pack. Unfortunately, he wasn't deterred by her ignoring those attempts. Finally the cell ceased ringing, and she exhaled heavily.

"Who was that?"

Spinning on her heel, she found Derren staring hard at her. "Nosy little bastard, aren't you?"

With two purposeful strides, he closed the small distance between them. "Who was it?" When she didn't answer, Derren snatched the phone from her hand, unsurprised to see there was a missed call from Zeke. She might not realize it, but the same expression always took over her face whenever the subject was the Collingwood Beta—one that contained betrayal, hurt, and weariness. It never failed to prickle the protective instincts of Derren and his wolf.

Ally held out her hand. "Give."

He might have, but then a beeping sound was quickly followed by "1 New Message" flashing on the screen. Before she could seize the phone, he opened the message and read it aloud. "Ally, why won't you talk to me? I just want to know that you're okay." Derren met her pissed, narrow-eyed gaze as she yanked the cell from his hand. "You've been ignoring his calls. Good. Keep it that way."

Her spine locked. "Who I speak to is *my* business. Should I grab a ladder so you can step out of it?"

"I don't want him contacting you." He didn't want a single ounce of her time spent on the fucker.

"And you think I do?"

No, he didn't. She looked more pissed about it than he was. Maybe it was time he had a little chat with the Beta—his wolf fully supported that idea. Derren's intention must have been right there on his face, because she shook her head.

"Don't, Derren. If he thinks bugging me will get him any kind of a reaction, he'll keep doing it."

Derren's wolf snarled. "I should just overlook that he's harassing you?"

Confused by his implication that it would be an unreasonable request, Ally snickered. "Yes, you should. I'm no one to you."

His hand snapped around her wrist in a proprietary hold. "Wrong." He didn't know what she was to him, but it wasn't "no one."

She tensed as his expression blackened and possessiveness oozed from his skin to hers. It slithered over her like demanding, territorial hands. As his eyes fell to Ally's mouth, his need punched its way inside her—filled her, taunted her, and acted as a flick to her clit. Her knees buckled. Oh, help. "Tone it down," she ground out.

Scenting her heat, Derren smiled inwardly. "Now we're even. I'll check on you later."

And he did, to the delight of Ally's wolf. When he couldn't coax Ally to come with him for dinner at the main lodge, he stayed with her. The little shit also ate half of her meal. Then he rose from the porch step and held out his hand. "Come with me."

Ally narrowed her eyes. "Where?"

"I want to show you something."

"What?" Wariness coated the word.

"Stop being so suspicious. Come with me," Derren repeated.

There was a dare in his eyes that made Ally's shoulders stiffen. She'd be damned if she'd show any weakness. "Fine." She placed her hand in his, swallowing hard as his hunger and satisfaction seemed to invade her pores, and he pulled her to her feet. "Let me just put this inside." Once she'd set the empty plate in the sink, she returned to the porch. "Where are we going?" She tried to sound vaguely annoyed, but she was actually curious. And his smile said he knew it.

"You'll see."

As he led her into the forest, she quickly realized they were headed in the direction of his lodge. But he didn't take her inside. He led her deeper into Mercury territory. When they reached a small clearing, he urged her to squat beside him.

"Look."

"What am I supposed to be looking at?" She didn't see anything. She could smell plenty of wildlife, but she couldn't see anything.

"See the small rock overhang over there? Watch closely."

Moments went by, and she still didn't see anything. "There's nothing—"

"Shush. Give them a minute."

Them? She went to question him again, and that was when she noticed a little movement. Something was crawling out from under the rock . . . something small with black fur. And then, with a brief struggle, it was out. Another one joined it. And another one. "How adorable are they," she whispered with total awe. Ally guessed the little wolf pups were around four weeks old.

Moments later, a mature female wolf followed them out of the hole. Fuck, it was a wolf den. "Derren, we really shouldn't be here."

Full-blooded wolves weren't bothered much by shifters, but they didn't like them around their pups.

"It's okay," he assured her.

No, it wasn't—especially since four more adult wolves had approached the den. "We should go." She exhaled a relieved sigh when Derren stood. But then the apparently suicidal shithead moved toward the wolves.

She grabbed his hand to stay him. "What are you doing?"

"Come on."

"What?" Her voice was a strangled squeak.

"Don't you want a closer look?"

"No. The adult wolves will totally freak out." She didn't relish the idea of scaring them. Or pissing them off and being attacked. Derren just gave her one of his silky smiles.

"Stop being a chickenshit."

"I am *not*."

"Then come on," he dared. Although he knew never to expect anything when it came to Ally, Derren had come to learn that she always responded to a challenge. As he'd expected, she straightened her shoulders and stood.

"If I get pounced on by a pack of wolves, and you put me in a position where I have to hurt them to defend myself, I'll slice your throat."

His smile widened. "You might give it your best shot."

Against her better judgment, Ally followed Derren out of the trees. The wolves looked up and extended their noses. Their nostrils flared as they took in the scents of the two shifters, and a large black male slowly padded to Derren. Instead of growling a warning, the male rubbed against Derren's leg. "You've been around them before," she realized.

Derren nodded. "They come to the river at a spot pretty close to my lodge. Hold out your hand." Before she could hesitate, he took one of her hands and held it toward the Alpha male. The wolf took a long sniff before letting out a soft snort. "My scent is on you, so you have his stamp of approval."

When Derren tugged her toward the pups, Ally dug in her heels. "That would be pushing the adults too hard." He ignored her, yanking her to his side. To her total amazement, none of the wolves protested when Derren crouched a few feet away from the pups. She gaped at him. "They let you near their pups?"

"They see me as part of their pack. It's why they keep pissing on my porch." The pup in front sniffed the air and took a step toward Derren. Gradually, the pup moved closer and closer until he butted Derren's hand. The other two pups followed their littermate's lead, and soon they were all nibbling on Derren's hand and pawing his thigh.

Unable to resist the cute little buggers, Ally squatted next to Derren. At first, the pups backed up a little—unnerved by the new presence. But, just as they had with Derren, they soon came close to investigate . . . looking up at her through blue eyes. They played with her, batting at her offered hand. "I want one."

Derren chuckled quietly, happy to see Ally smile.

"Thank you for bringing me here." She understood why he had. It was an apology, of sorts. His response was a short nod.

Despite her protests, Derren walked her back to her lodge. He'd be a damn liar if he claimed it was simply a protective act. The truth was that he was buying some time with her. He might have delayed having to leave her, but . . . "You look tired." There were still dark smudges under her eyes, and her olive skin lacked its usual healthy glow.

"It's been a long day. I'll be fine by morning."

"Good." She turned to go inside, and Derren found that he couldn't just let her go—not without tasting her just once. His hand shot out, grabbed her shoulder, and twirled her around. Then he was on her. His hands fisted in her hair as his mouth devoured hers. His tongue plundered her mouth, sweeping against her own.

She tasted just as she smelled: exotic and sweet. And nothing had ever tasted better.

Shocked, Ally stiffened against him. A part of her—the part that was wounded by her experience with Zeke—wanted to push him away and maintain a distance between them. Another part of her wanted to thrust her fingers through his dark hair and meet his kiss.

The latter part won, and Ally's body burst to life. A satisfied growl rumbled up Derren's chest, vibrating against her nipples, as one strong hand collared her throat. Bristling at the possessive move, she scratched his scalp with her claws. Snarling, he tightened his hold and—

Their mouths broke apart, panting, as a howl split the air. Her thought processes like mush, it took Ally a moment to discern it was the howl of a full-blooded wolf; it wasn't one of alarm. Forcing herself to release Derren's hair, she let her arms fall to her sides. But she didn't back up—that required more strength than she had.

Derren wanted nothing more than to back her into the lodge and taste and explore every inch of her, to drive deep inside her as he'd dreamed of doing every damn night since he brought her here. But she was tired, and what she needed was rest. If he followed her inside, it would be the last thing she'd get. Besides, although she wanted him, he could see she was still wary of him. He wanted there to be nothing but need in her eyes when he finally had her.

He brushed his thumb over her mouth. "You taste better than anything else I've ever tasted." And he wanted more. He'd have more. Just not right now. "Get some sleep." With a restraint he hadn't known he possessed, Derren walked away.

CHAPTER SEVEN

Receiving a text message from Nick summoning him to his office, Derren abandoned his paperwork—gladly, since it was past eight o'clock in the evening—and immediately headed there. He found Nick, Shaya, Eli, and the enforcers waiting inside. The dark energy radiating from Nick was enough to make Derren stiffen. "Something else happened?"

Standing behind his desk with Shaya at his side, Nick sighed. "The day after the grenade incident, I contacted Donovan, asked him to look into whether any other packs are having the same kind of trouble. My theory was that if our culprit's style is to use various forms of attack, it would be something they have done before. He contacted me ten minutes ago. There's no indication that any other packs have undergone the same experience. But he found something else." Nick paused, seeming to take strength from the hand Shaya was rubbing up and down his arm. "We're on a hit list."

A boom of stunned silence followed that announcement. Derren had thought of many different possibilities that might account for what was happening, but he hadn't considered this.

It was Roni who finally spoke. "Could you repeat that?"

"A hit list." Nick's voice hardened. "Someone wants us dead. And not just us. There's also a hit out on the Phoenix Pack."

Curses rang throughout the office.

"Does Trey know?" Marcus rumbled.

Nick shook his head. "Not yet. I'll call him once our meeting is over."

"It explains everything." Eli seemed to be talking more to himself than anyone else. "It wasn't one person using different forms of attack. It was different people trying to cash in on the bounty. Hyenas *were* responsible for the poisoned animals, and foxes really *did* attack."

"It even explains the use of the rifle grenade," stated Zander. "Most hits are taken care of with firearms."

"The hyenas and foxes who attacked were all probably lone shifters." Marcus fingered one of Roni's ash-blonde curls, as if touching her calmed him. "They often become guns for hire."

Anger mixed with Derren's shock, making his voice a growl. "Who put the hit out on us?"

"That's just it, we don't know." Nick's jaw hardened.

Derren blinked. "You don't know?"

"There's a website that provides a list of people or packs that have bounties on their heads," explained Nick. "Anyone interested in collecting on any of those bounties simply has to do the deed and prove it afterward. The problem is that whoever runs the website protects the identities of the people who submit requests for a name to be placed on the list. Only the person behind the website knows their identities."

"So we need to find this person," said Bracken.

"Donovan tried." Nick leaned back against his desk. "There's actually a group of shifters already working on it. But the site is run on some kind of high-tech, super-fucking-advanced anonymity network that protects the creator's identity. To make matters even harder, the site also has all kinds of 'trip wires' that sense anyone trying to hack into it and immediately delivers viruses that crash whatever computer is being used."

"Shit," Eli bit out. "This isn't going to be like the problem we had finding the jackals; we can't rely on hackers to trace the servers or IP addresses." At his brother's nod of agreement, Eli asked, "So what now?"

"Donovan said he'd keep trying, but his opinion is that it would take him years to get past those trip wires—mostly because the trip wires keep changing, like a moving labyrinth. He said he's never seen anything like this before. The hit on us could have been placed by one shifter, an entire pack, or some kind of organization. All he knows at this point is that they're also responsible for the hit on the Phoenix Pack."

Bracken scratched his nape. "They want every single member of both packs dead?"

Nick nodded. "Every single last one."

Jesse whistled. "Then this is very personal."

Eli folded his arms across his chest. "So the question is . . . who hates both packs so damn much?"

"Someone who both packs thoroughly pissed off." Marcus exhaled heavily. "That should make it easier to work out who it is."

"It could still be hyenas," mused Bracken. "I mean, plenty of them died here at our hands after they accompanied the jackals in the recent battle. The Phoenix Pack joined us for the fight, and they killed plenty of hyenas too."

Roni inclined her head, but she didn't appear convinced. "Who else could be responsible?"

"The extremists." At the skeptical expressions directed his way, Jesse added, "Think about it. Who better to use to kill shifters than *other* shifters? Especially when no one would expect the extremists to do it."

Frowning, Shaya shook her head. "The extremists like the violence, they enjoy hurting us. They wouldn't have someone else do it for them."

"We should consider the council," Derren claimed. "We know too much. We have evidence that one of their members was using the jackals as their very own attack dogs."

Shaya nodded. "The council doesn't like to get their hands dirty. Putting a hit out on us—that's their style."

Nick sighed. "Until we find out who this is and eliminate them, we need to step up security and defend our territory rather than disperse to go hunting the culprits."

"We can't afford to separate," said Shaya, her worry reflected in her voice. "Especially when our pack is so small."

"And if we leave our territory to go hunting, it makes us easier targets." Nick curled an arm around Shaya. "On our own territory, we're more powerful. So we don't make it easy for anyone hoping to collect on the bounty by separating. We make them come to us. And then we kill each and every person who tries to come at us. Word will soon get out that anyone who attempts to collect on the bounty will disappear."

"The Phoenix Pack will probably do the same," Marcus told them.

"I'll notify Trey of what's happening," said Nick. "After that, we need to inform the rest of our pack. We need them to be vigilant."

So, having called everyone into the kitchen of the main lodge for a meeting, they did just that. Kathy, Kent, and Caleb were clearly worried. To Derren, Ally seemed more pissed than anything else. When he saw her pinch the bridge of her nose while her brow creased in pain, he cursed himself for not considering that being around a bunch of shifters who were currently vibrating with rage would be hard on her.

Leaning into her, Derren asked in a low voice, "Need to get out of here?"

"I'm fine." Her expression smoothed out as she strived to hide her pain, but she didn't fully manage it.

"Come on." He cupped her elbow as he rose, bringing her to her feet. "I'm taking Ally back to her lodge," he told Shaya.

Realization crossed the Alpha female's expression as she took in the lines of strain on Ally's face. Shaya gave her a sympathetic smile. "Go before your head bursts."

Frustrated at being literally dragged out of the lodge, Ally huffed at Derren. "I was handling it just fine." He simply snorted at her. "And I don't need anyone to walk me home." She'd told him that plenty of times, but he always did it anyway, ignoring her mutterings. She'd like to say she was annoyed at having him insist on escorting her home, but she'd actually come to enjoy his company. Yeah, he'd initially been a misguided ass. But there was a lot to him that she admired and respected—especially that once his loyalty was given, it was absolute. After the betrayal of the Collingwood wolves, particularly that of Zeke, she appreciated just how important a quality that was.

As if thinking about him tempted fate, she received a text message from Zeke just as she reached her lodge. It was the same ol' spiel he'd spouted in several of his other messages, and the whole thing was getting tedious.

Noticing that Ally's expression had morphed into one that he hadn't seen for a couple of days, Derren guessed, "Zeke?"

Her head shot up. "How did you know?"

"You only get that look on your face when it's him."

"Huh. Well, good night." She had no wish to discuss Zeke. But Derren being Derren, he followed her inside the lodge and into the kitchen. Persistent little bastard.

She ignored his powerful body leaning against the counter as she made a single cup of coffee, communicating that his time was up. Not that she expected it to bother him. In fact, the harder she tried to get rid of him, the more determined he became to stick around. Derren wasn't a person who could be handled.

He invaded her personal space, and Ally couldn't help but tense. Not because she didn't want him close, but because she did. And that wasn't at all good, because he had the ability to reduce her body to a puddle of need. Each and every time his skin came into contact with hers—no matter how brief the contact was—his arousal snaked into her system and served to increase her own.

"Let me guess," Derren drawled, barely holding back a growl at the idea of Zeke refusing to leave her alone. "He wants you to go back to the pack and he promises it will be different this time and that he's willing to listen to what you have to say."

She blinked. "Wow. That was good. Do something else. What am I thinking right now?"

"You're picturing me naked." Unable to help himself, Derren crowded her and skimmed his nose over the crook of her neck like he'd been aching to do all fucking day. "Your scent . . . It makes me want to bite you." A voice in his mind told him to pull back, reminded him that she was another guy's mate. His wolf growled at that, opposed to the idea of any other male possessing her. But it wasn't just any male, dammit, it was Cain. And Cain was his friend and . . . "Fuck it, I can make new friends."

Ally gasped in surprise as Derren's mouth slammed down on hers, his tongue thrusting into her mouth and stroking her own. One hand fisted in her hair while the other gripped her hip, keeping her body aligned to his as he crammed her against the counter. He was all she could see, feel, taste, and smell. Her body instantly responded to him; her mouth met his demanding kiss, her hands threaded through his hair, and she began grinding against his hard cock.

It was frantic, rough, and desperate; she'd never experienced anything like it. That scared her enough to make her shove him away—something that only worked because she'd caught him by surprise—and put some distance between them.

"Come here, Ally. I want you."

Those words made her stomach clench. "Yeah? Well, after what happened with Zeke, the last thing I'm interested in is getting involved with anyone." She wouldn't set herself up for more pain.

"It doesn't have to be more than sex." But even as he said that,

Derren knew it wouldn't be an emotionless fuck. She was someone he'd come to respect, who'd earned his loyalty, and who even had some of his trust. None of that was minor for him.

She scoffed. "That's what Zeke said in the beginning."

Covering the space between them in one stride, Derren put a finger to her lips. "Don't say his name."

When he would have kissed her again, she planted a restraining hand on his chest. "You hate my kind, remember."

He cupped her jaw. "I told you that I don't feel that way anymore." She'd changed the way he saw things. "I meant it."

Ally believed him. How could she not, when his sincerity smoothed over her like the softest silk? Those eyes of dark velvet were glittering with a raw, vicious need—one that she could *feel* as surely as she could feel her own. She closed her eyes against the dangerous temptation of him, because one thing she'd never been good at was resisting temptation.

Derren licked along her throat and swirled his tongue around her pulse. "I want to see my cock in you. Want to watch it moving in and out. Taking you." Finally.

She wanted the same. No, she *craved* it. And that was the problem. Ally wanted him with a desperation that was unlike anything she'd ever felt for another guy. That spooked her, especially since her wolf's hunger for him was just as intense. Add in that Cain, who thought of her as a little sister, would go ballistic that his friend had "used her" and . . . "It's not a good idea," Ally whispered, her eyes still closed.

Derren nipped her pulse. "No, it's an amazing fucking idea."

"But Cain—"

He bit her bottom lip hard. "This is about you and me, Ally. No one else. Look at me." Finally, she opened her eyes. "Just us. Got me?"

The intensity and heat in his eyes trapped her, demanded what he wanted. Could she just forget everyone else, forget all the reasons why she shouldn't do this? Maybe, maybe not. But she damn well wanted to. "One night." That was all she would allow herself.

"One night," Derren agreed. He gripped her chin, warning her, "But don't think I'll only have you once tonight." He took her mouth again, needing her taste, needing every single response she had to give.

Ally hissed as the tips of his claws dug into her hip through her shorts. Their clothes were quickly removed as they feasted on each other's mouths—licking, sucking, biting, and giving no reprieve. He kept her so flush against him, it was almost hard to breathe. His hands were firm, purposeful, and possessive as they roved and clutched her hard enough to bruise.

She raked her claws down his solid abs, feeling the urge to trace the dips and hollows with her tongue. She felt hot, restless, and empty. Flames of need were licking over her, building the tension. A hand fisted in her hair and arched her body so he could suck a nipple into his mouth; every tug was so hard it was painful. There was an urgency to his every movement, as if he'd waited too long for this. They were out of control, and she knew it.

Ally drew back, trying to gain some balance. "Wait—" He didn't; he snarled and took her mouth again—this time harder, rougher, and more insistently. With one swift move, he had her flat on her back on the oak floor, his powerful body covering her. Not at all gentle, he shoved his finger inside her.

"Fuck, you're so wet for me." Derren thrust another finger inside her, groaning. It was going to be a tight fit. He pumped his fingers in and out of her, scissoring them, stretching her. When her pussy began to tighten around them, he knew she was about to come. "That's it, baby. Come. Give me what I want." He curled his tongue around her nipple and suckled hard. Moments later, she cried out as she came.

Shit, he wanted to taste her, but he didn't have the control to hold back any longer. "I need to be in you." Needed it so badly he practically shook with it. Gripping her wrists, he pinned her hands above her head. "Look at me." The second her eyes met his, he slammed into her. He groaned as her pussy clamped around him. Tight. Slick. Hot. Perfect. He watched where their bodies were joined as he withdrew from her pussy before then driving himself balls deep inside her. "I like seeing my cock in you."

Ally struggled against his restraining hands as he frantically pounded in and out of her. But even as both she and her wolf balked at being dominated that way, Ally was curling her legs around his hips and arching into his fevered thrusts. "Let go of my hands," she snarled.

His upper lip curled, and his grip on her wrists tightened. "No."

"*Now*, Derren." Instead, he upped his pace. She snapped her teeth, grazing his chin. "I said *let go*." He didn't.

As Ally kicked at him, cursing and growling, Derren found that he didn't mind the challenge, didn't mind if she fought his dominance. "No. You *like* me pinning you down." It was a taunt that made her growl. "And you like me fucking you hard, don't you, baby? You like having my cock in you."

As his mouth clamped around her pulse and sucked hard enough to mark, she growled, "Don't you dare brand me!" The bastard bit her. Worse, his teeth didn't release her as he hammered into her. But the fight left Ally as her orgasm barreled into her with such force that she thought she'd black out.

As she screamed, and her pussy rippled around his cock, Derren cursed against her neck. Driving his cock as deep as he could go, he exploded inside her. Filled her. And a deep sense of masculine satisfaction settled into both Derren and his wolf.

For long moments, neither he nor Ally spoke. It was Ally who broke the silence. "You bit me." And her wolf *liked* it, the traitor.

"So I did." He started to withdraw . . . but Derren found he couldn't leave her body yet. He smoothly plunged back inside with a groan. "Again."

Derren shouldn't have been at all surprised to wake up and find himself alone. After another round on the kitchen floor, he and Ally had migrated to the bedroom, where he'd made her come all over his tongue before they'd crashed. Sometime later, he'd woken up and taken her again. He'd intended to reach for her yet again, but she was gone.

Seeing that it was still dark out, he made his way to the kitchen, where he pulled on his jeans before going in search of her. He found her exactly where he knew he would: in the hammock. Her face was scrunched up in pain, and she was squirming restlessly. It was something he'd seen her do in her sleep many times before.

Protectiveness surged through him, and his wolf whined in concern. Derren crouched before her and pressed a light kiss to her mouth. Her eyelids flickered open, but her gaze was cloudy and faraway. He had the feeling she wasn't properly awake, wasn't really seeing him. "You're safe, baby," he murmured. Wherever she went in her sleep, it wasn't safe.

"I couldn't get out," she muttered so quietly it was a wonder he heard her. "I couldn't get out to warn them." Then her eyelids closed once more.

He didn't know what the hell that meant, but he did know he wasn't leaving her out here alone. Scooping her into his arms, he settled into the hammock with her draped over him. He played his fingers through her hair and smoothed his other hand down her back, relishing that he could touch her as he pleased. It . . . steadied him, soothed him somehow.

All the time he'd spent holding back, resisting the urge to touch her, had been agonizing in a way that made no damn sense. It had left him mentally and physically on edge . . . as if he'd been suffering from a lack of skin-to-skin contact for years. But the only touch he'd been starved of was hers. And he'd felt it acutely.

If he didn't know for a fact that she was someone else's mate, Derren would have wondered if she was his. It would have explained the hint of possessiveness that had been there from the beginning. Would have explained his wolf's obsession with her. Would have explained the depth of Derren's hunger for her.

He'd never wanted any female—hell, any*thing*—the way he wanted Ally Marshall. Had never before felt like he'd go insane if he didn't have this one thing.

Now that Derren had finally had her, now that he knew what it was like to be in her and have her come apart around him, his hunger should have technically eased. It hadn't. The raw, razor-sharp need was still as overpowering as before. One night with her wasn't enough.

Derren's eyes fell on a bite mark—*his* mark—on her neck, and his wolf growled with satisfaction. A brand was a symbol of possession, and for a shifter to leave a brand on another was, in effect, a temporary claim. On some level, Derren had known from the very first thrust that he'd need more than one night. And just maybe the brands she'd left on him indicated that she felt the same. But shifters were known to leave brands if the sex was wild enough, and there was no denying that what had happened between them had been wild and primal.

Whatever the motivation behind Ally marking him, she wasn't getting away from him. He needed more than one night. Of course she'd object to that, whether she wanted the same or not, because Ally was skittish. But he knew he wouldn't behave and leave her alone . . . even if she did have the potential to fast become an addiction.

CHAPTER EIGHT

The smell of coffee woke Ally . . . which was odd, since she was sure she'd switched it off—

Derren's mouth on hers. His fingers threading through her hair. His cock thrusting inside her. His teeth grazing and biting.

As the entirety of last night's events crashed into her mind, she moaned. Although she didn't regret any of it, she still cursed herself for being weak and giving in to him. Or, more accurately, for giving in to herself. Her wolf was extremely smug about it.

Ally was surprised he'd lingered. She'd pegged him for the type to scamper while she was sleeping and escape any morning-after awkwardness. She should have known better. Derren didn't flee from anything. He faced everything in life head-on, almost daring the world to come at him.

She, on the other hand, would have been happy to avoid any post-one-night-stand discomfort. As a shifter, she had no hang-ups about casual sex. After all, a girl had to eat. Still, a one-night stand was new territory for her. She didn't know the morning-after etiquette.

Did she say thanks and hint for him to leave?

Was she supposed to make him breakfast?

Were they meant to discuss it? She didn't really see the point in postmortems.

Getting it right was important, because she'd have to see this guy every day for the next few months. She didn't want things to be weird and uncomfortable between them from this point on.

Hoping she didn't make an idiot out of herself by drowning in an ocean of unnecessary embarrassment, she headed inside the lodge. Fully dressed and looking unfairly presentable for a guy who had spent a huge portion of the night fucking her into oblivion, Derren was in the kitchen. His gaze met hers, filled with heat and awareness, as he offered her a mug of coffee.

"Morning," he greeted, twirling a strand of her hair around his finger. "I'm not good in the kitchen, so I didn't even bother attempting to cook."

No awkward vibes, no uneasy silence. Surprised, Ally took the mug. The weight of his intense gaze made a blush unexpectedly stain her cheeks. She felt . . . vulnerable, but she couldn't explain why. She cleared her throat. "I thought you'd have left."

His eyes narrowed slightly. "Did you now?"

As his gaze dropped to her neck, she remembered how he'd bitten her there. "I told you not to mark me."

"I carry your mark too." Derren rolled back his shoulder, reminding her how she'd dug her claws so deep in his flesh that she'd drawn blood.

Her face heated even more. "That was my wolf." The animal had lunged for him, wanted to brand him as he'd branded her.

A smile curved his mouth. "Blaming your wolf? Tut, tut, tut."

Yeah, that was low. And yeah, okay, it would be fair to say that she hadn't fought her wolf's urge to brand him. That simply pissed her off, because, dammit . . . "I'm not a possessive person."

"Neither am I." He skimmed his fingers along her collarbone. "But you . . . it's different with you."

Seeing the flare of determination in his eyes, she swallowed hard. "We agreed that it would be just one night, Derren."

"We did. But I've changed my mind. I want more."

She sighed. "Look, I'm not saying last night wasn't good. It was—"

"Fucking amazing. And it will happen again."

"We need to forget it ever happened. Cain will flip if he—"

"What have I told you?" He gripped her jaw. "This is about you and me. No one else." Neither Derren nor his wolf wanted her thinking of any other guy, particularly the one who was her intended mate. Jealousy slithered through Derren every time she even said Cain's name. "What he'll think or feel about us makes no fucking difference to me."

She pulled out of his hold. "It should. He's your friend, and you'd be risking that friendship." Cain would be pissed that his friend had "used" the girl he viewed as his little sister—that was how he'd see it.

"Yes, so that has to show you how badly I want you."

She closed her eyes as she sifted a hand through her hair. The guy was so unbelievably stubborn it drove her crazy.

"Look at me, Ally. Be honest, this isn't about Cain. You're hesitating because you don't want a repeat of what happened with Zeke. I get it. But I'm not him. I would never turn on you like that."

"No, you wouldn't," she conceded. He was too loyal for that. In such a situation, he would claim his mate, yes, but he wouldn't treat Ally like she was a stranger. He would support and defend Ally if she needed it. "But I have no wish to lose someone else to their mate. To be put aside again."

Derren laughed, but it had a bitter edge to it. "The likelihood of me recognizing my mate is practically nonexistent." He'd once heard a mating bond be compared to a frequency. If it were jammed by such things as doubts, fears, or an imprinting bond, the shifters would be unable to pick it up. Derren was too damn messed up inside to be able to sense his mate.

Ally didn't need to ask why he'd assume that. "You have issues with trust." Not to mention that he was so preoccupied with serving Nick that he wasn't fully living his own life. She didn't bother asking why he felt so indebted to his Alpha. Derren shared only what he chose to share when he chose to share it, and she respected that, because she didn't like confiding in others either.

"My point is there can't be a repeat of what happened with Zeke," said Derren, the latter word a growl.

Maybe, but what he didn't realize was that it wasn't just about how she'd lost Zeke to his mate. Ally had also lost her life the way it was. She'd suddenly found herself living alone, was more pitied than respected, and had eventually lost everything—including her status.

"Stop overthinking it, Ally. This doesn't have to be complicated; we're not talking permanence here. But we're not talking some kind of empty fling either. I like you, I respect you."

In other words, while this would be casual and temporary, it also wouldn't be meaningless sex to him. That idea made Ally hesitate to rebuff him again. Emotionless flings weren't something she was capable of; she wasn't one of those people who could separate sex from feelings. If she hadn't come to like Derren, she could never have slept with him. She could only agree to this if their temporary relationship wouldn't be impersonal and cold.

Derren's cell phone ringing cut off what he would have said next. He knew by the ringtone that it was Nick. Without losing eye contact with Ally, Derren dug his cell out of his jeans pocket. "Yeah?"

"Come to the main lodge."

Hearing the urgency in his Alpha's tone, Derren stiffened as his wolf shot to alertness. "Problem?"

"There could be." Nick hung up.

"I have to go," Derren told Ally, returning his phone to his pocket. He cupped her nape, pinning her gaze with his. "Understand this, Ally. There is very little I consider an obstacle when I want something. And when I want something as badly as I want you, I won't let anything or anyone keep me from it. I marked you, and I don't consider that a small thing. Do you? Is branding a guy something you do often?" he rumbled.

After a long moment, she confessed, "No."

That was what he'd thought. "We both want this, Ally. Don't we?" He needed her to admit it to both of them.

His eyes dared her to lie, but she didn't. "Yes."

Derren smiled. "Good girl." He kissed her hard, pouring every bit of his hunger and resolve into it. When he finally pulled back, he brushed his thumb over the mark he'd left on her neck. "Don't cover it up."

Minutes later, Derren was striding into the living area of the main lodge, where most of the pack stood around. He frowned. "What's going on?" he asked Nick.

"Fifteen minutes ago, a car pulled up outside the road leading to the main lodge," replied his Alpha. "It didn't cross into our territory, but it isn't showing any signs of moving. Eli and Bracken took a closer look without approaching the vehicle. There's one guy inside, and he's not only covered in injuries but he's unconscious."

"He's also in the passenger seat," added Eli, "which means someone drove him there and then deserted him."

"You're certain he's not dead?" Derren asked Eli.

It was Bracken who answered. "His chest is rising and falling. It's a small movement, but it's there."

Shaya cuddled Willow close. "Knowing there's a wounded guy so close who might need our help isn't sitting well with me. I don't like the idea of just leaving him there. But the whole thing seems . . . off to me."

Zander nodded. "Like a trap."

"Or a distraction," mused Derren, his instincts stabbing at him. "Something to make us look one way while someone comes at us from another angle."

Nick's eyes widened. "Fuck."

This doesn't have to be complicated.

Derren was right, Ally told herself as she poured more coffee into her mug. She never would have expected it when they'd first met, but they had become friends. Not the type of friends who shared secrets or memories—their friendship wasn't intimate like what he had with Nick and Roni; like what Ally had with Cain. But the interactions between her and Derren had evolved into a casual friendship where there was a mutual respect and regard.

A fling based on this kind of friendship could work for Ally. There would be no laying demands on each other, there would be no expectations, and there would be no need to confide about emotions, fears, ideas, or hopes. Yes, this could work out fine for both of them. Because as much as Ally was more of a commitment kind of girl, she didn't have the emotional ability to give that to anyone right now.

However, there was no denying that there were plenty of reasons to not get involved with Derren. For one thing, Cain would go apeshit; he was very protective of her, considered her his baby sister, and wanted her to have a mate and family of her own. He knew that Ally wasn't the casual sex type, and he'd see this situation as Derren using her. But it was impossible to explain all of that to Derren since he didn't want to hear it.

Another reason to steer clear of a temporary relationship with Derren was the not-so-simple fact that she hadn't been able to fight her wolf's desire to brand him. Not when Ally herself had wanted to leave a mark of possession on him to make it clear to other females, to him, and to his wolf that she didn't share.

Ally sighed at the beeping of her cell phone. No doubt it was Zeke again. And that right there was yet another reason to avoid a fling with Derren: it could end very fucking badly. Ignoring the beep, she took her mug and settled on the porch step. Zeke had also sent her a message around midnight, which she'd only noticed after Derren had left. It wasn't until she'd read that message, wherein Zeke had claimed to miss her, that she'd begun to wonder if just maybe Derren was right. Maybe Zeke was finding it hard to let go.

Shifter males were possessive. Dominant males were even more so. Zeke had almost been as possessive of her as Derren was growing to be. Although Zeke would choose his mate over Ally any day of the week, he and his wolf could still be finding his abrupt separation with Ally hard to adjust to.

That would explain why he hadn't wanted to get her a transfer from the pack when she'd asked. If that were the case, the best thing she could do was continue to ignore his attempts to speak to her. What worried her was that it might drive him to come and see her.

Snapped out of her musings by a loud high-pitched sound, Ally put down her mug and jumped to her feet. It was a cry . . . a baby's cry. *Willow.* Without thought or hesitation, she sprinted into the forest, tracking the frightened cry. Her mind distantly registered that she was heading in the direction of Kent and Caleb's lodge, but Ally's focus was solely on getting to the baby. Willow's wails got louder and louder as Ally came closer to the opening in the trees she could see up ahead. Ally burst into the small clearing and—

"Ally, no!" The choked-out warning came from Caleb, who was sprawled on the ground with Kent. Both were badly injured, and both were covered in blood. *What the fuck?*

Ally's head snapped in the direction of Willow's cry . . . only to find that there was no Willow there, and a fucking cougar shifter was leaping off a tree branch, its feline gaze trained on Ally with—

Flinching as heat scalded her fingers, Ally dropped the coffeepot back onto the counter. Understanding quickly dawned. "Fuck!" Snatching her cell from the end of the counter, she dialed Caleb's number.

He answered after only two rings. "Hey, Ally, how's—"

"Don't leave your lodge! Whatever happens, whatever you think you hear, *do not leave your lodge.* It's not Willow, it's a trap." Ending the call, she quickly called Derren. The phone kept ringing and ringing, and she cursed. "Come on, come on."

Then there was his voice. "Baby, I can't talk right now—"

"Cougars."

"What?"

"There are cougar shifters on our territory!" Cougar screams could often sound like babies wailing or women screaming. "I had a vision! They're near Kent and Caleb's lodge!" The predator in her wanted to track the felines and rip them all a new asshole for trespassing on Mercury territory with the intention to kill.

"Ally, don't move. Don't go after them alone."

She wouldn't, because that would give the cougars what they wanted. But she wasn't going to hole up at her lodge either.

"I mean it, Ally. I need you to stay there. We're bringing Shaya and Willow to you."

"What? Why?" But he'd already hung up. By the time she'd quickly washed and replaced her long shirt with a white, long-sleeved T-shirt and her faded blue jeans, the pack arrived at the lodge. Only Derren, Bracken, Kathy, and Shaya with Willow in her arms filed inside.

"What's happening?" Ally asked them.

"We weren't prepared to leave anyone at the main lodge, considering what's parked outside the border," replied Derren.

That didn't make a lick of sense to Ally.

Derren pinned her with a determined look. "Lock the doors and stay inside. Don't split up—not for anything." His wolf didn't want to leave her, but even the animal understood that the need to protect the pack was vital. Wanting his head firmly on the threat on their territory, Derren ignored the urge to kiss her and forced his mind to the current issue.

Ally watched as Derren joined the rest of the pack outside. As one, they all shifted into their wolf forms and charged into the forest. Confused, she turned to Shaya. "What was he talking about?" As Derren requested, Ally secured the locks.

"Someone parked a car outside the road leading to the main lodge." The Alpha female was slowly pacing, her daughter balanced on her hip. "There was an injured, unconscious guy in the passenger seat."

"Decoy," Ally guessed.

"I called an ambulance," interjected Kathy from the sofa. "EMTs were taking him away when we left the lodge."

"My guess is the cougars were using the vehicle as a distraction." Bracken's gaze was scanning his surroundings through the windows. "They had to know that Nick would summon his Beta and enforcers to the main lodge to tell them what's going on."

Shaya nodded. "The cougars were able to cross the border without being noticed, and it left the other members of our pack who were scattered around our territory vulnerable to them."

"They were mimicking Willow's cry," Ally told them. "In the vision, I mean."

Bracken briefly glanced at her. "Smart. It's a trick cougar shifters sometimes use. No shifter—submissive or dominant—would ignore the cry of an infant. They'd rush right in to help."

That was exactly what Ally had done. "In my vision, I didn't even think to call for help. All I could think about was getting to Willow."

Bracken didn't appear surprised. "When they use this particular lure, that's what they count on. If their intention was to mimic Willow's cries, they were probably hoping to draw any of the pack members that weren't in the main lodge to them."

"Getting rid of the pack, little by little." Cougar shifters really were tricky fuckers. "Kent and Caleb were dying in my vision. I would have been next."

A muscle in Bracken's jaw ticked. "When you have a small pack, the loss of three members makes a big difference in a battle."

"And it's an emotional blow that can make you act out in rage," Shaya pointed out.

"How many cougars are out there?" Bracken asked Ally as she came to stand next to him, watching for any threats.

Ally shrugged. "I only saw one in my vision." But she highly doubted one cougar was working alone, given that Caleb and

Kent had been so brutally attacked. They could have held their own against one cougar.

Bracken shot her an odd look before asking quietly, "So, want to tell me why this place smells of you, Derren, and sex?" At her scowl, his expression turned innocent. "It was just a question."

When his Alpha male halted a safe distance away from the clearing, the black wolf did the same. It had been easy for the pack to track the cougars. They had simply followed the fake cries. His Alpha looked at the black wolf and jerked his head to the left before then going in the opposite direction. The black wolf understood the order. He led half of the wolves one way, while his Alpha led the others another. Stealthily and silently, the pack moved to loosely circle the clearing. Surrounding and trapping their prey was a tactic they had used before.

The black wolf sensed the presence of five cougar shifters. The felines were not on the ground. Each one was positioned on a tree branch.

As his Alpha shifted before him, and the gray-white wolf—Eli—flanked him, the black wolf sensed that Derren wanted dominance. He drew back and gave his human half control.

"One of us needs to lure them out of the trees," Nick whispered to Derren and Eli when they shifted. "If we don't, they'll just climb as high as they can and hop from tree to fucking tree."

Derren agreed. Keeping his voice low, he said, "Me and Eli will drop back and then noisily bolt into the clearing, as if in a panic."

Eli nodded. "I counted five of them. There are eight of us. The odds are in our favor."

Cougar shifters had the advantage in a one-to-one fight, as they were much stronger than wolves. But a pack of eight against a pride of five could potentially win, but not without serious injuries.

"Everyone but me will pair up," said Nick. "Two wolves versus one cougar should come out on top." Not prepared to waste any time, Derren shifted. Eli followed his lead.

The black wolf and the gray-white wolf ran a distance away before loudly rushing through the forest. They burst into the clearing, instantly going back-to-back as they scanned the trees. Ambushes were typical of cougar shifters.

The fake cries stopped instantly. Five cougars leaped out of the trees, hissing and snarling. All were males, and all were dominant. The black wolf curled back his lips, exposing fangs and gums, as he growled in warning at the trespassers that wanted to hurt his pack. The cougar before him, bulkier than the others, took a single step forward. The wolf's hackles rose, and his ears flattened as he again bared his teeth with a growl. Each of the cougars snarled in response.

A howl split the air, making the cougars freeze. The rest of the pack hiding in the trees rushed into the clearing. They attacked without hesitation. Four of the cougars twisted to defend themselves. But the fifth was focused on the black wolf.

The gray-white wolf lightly brushed his body against the black wolf. Growling, the two wolves circled the hissing cougar. Then the wolves lunged and slammed into the cougar's sides. A heavy paw batted the black wolf's muzzle, raking him with sharp claws. The scent of blood filled the air. The black wolf jerked back, shaking his head.

The cougar twisted and pounced on the other wolf, snapping his jaws. The Head Enforcer yelped, and blood sprayed on the ground. Anger surged through the black wolf, and he leaped onto the cougar's back. The feline shrieked as claws and teeth sank into him. The gray-white wolf mercilessly ripped off the cougar's ear. Another shriek.

A heavy weight suddenly crashed into the black wolf, making him lose his purchase on the cougar and slam into the ground.

Then a second cougar was standing over him, snarling. He went to slice open the wolf's exposed stomach, but a blur of dark gray barreled into the cougar, knocking him aside.

Quickly the black wolf righted himself and moved to aid the female—Roni—who had helped him. But her mate had now reached her side. Confident the female didn't need his aid, the black wolf turned back to his initial opponent. The cougar was trying to wrap his jaws around the gray-white wolf's head. The black wolf knew that such a move could crush his pack mate's skull. Just in time, the Head Enforcer jerked back and avoided the jaws. Then both wolves slammed into the cougar again.

The feline shrieked as two sets of teeth and claws sank into him. He turned just enough to swipe the black wolf's flank, claws tearing away fur and skin. But neither wolf released him. Together, they wrestled the feline to the ground and onto his back. Straddling the cougar, the black wolf tore out his throat as he slashed open his stomach with his claws. Both wolves howled their victory.

As the black wolf turned, he saw his pack mates stood around, their sides heaving as blood oozed from several wounds. He too was bleeding and panting. In pain. Tired.

Four maimed, lifeless cougars were sprawled on the ground. The fifth was back in his human form, as was the black wolf's Alpha. Sensing that Derren wanted dominance, the black wolf ceded control.

Derren hissed through gritted teeth as he stood upright. He was bleeding and aching like a son of a bitch—especially with the fucking slashes on his face and down his sides—but he shelved the pain. Approaching Nick, Derren realized that the fifth cougar was dying; blood poured from several wounds and trickled from his mouth.

"Who was it?" Nick demanded, crouched beside the shifter.

The shifter's upper lip curled. "I wouldn't tell you even if I knew," he wheezed angrily.

"You don't like that your friends here are dead? Then you shouldn't have come after me and my pack. You should have known better."

"He doesn't know who put the hit out on us?" asked Derren.

"So he says."

"Do you think he's telling the truth?" panted Jesse. With the harsh bite mark on his ear and the very deep gashes on his chest and back, he'd suffered the worst injuries.

Nick nodded. "Whoever's behind all this wants to remain anonymous. If they didn't, we'd know who it is by now. But Donovan still can't find out. And Donovan can find out *anything.*"

"People will keep coming," the cougar wheezed, an ugly smirk surfacing on his sweating face. "They have a hundred thousand reasons to do it."

Nick glanced down at him. "But now you know it wasn't worth the risk, don't you? And so will anyone else who comes." He turned to the pack. "Let's go. My mate is going insane with worry." Nick would be able to feel it through their mating bond.

When they were near Ally's lodge, Shaya came racing out and threw herself at Nick. He held her tight, whispering in her ear. Derren pulled on the clothes he'd left on the porch—which hurt like a motherfucker as the material rubbed against his wounds— and headed inside. His gaze went helplessly to Ally, whose eyes widened at the sight of him. Yeah, he knew his face had to look a mess. She made a beeline for him, and he knew she was about to heal him. "Don't." She halted, looking . . . hurt. As if he'd rejected her. "I'm not the one who needs your help."

At that moment, Zander supported Jesse's weight as they both stumbled inside.

Bracken blinked at his fellow enforcer and friend. "Shit, Jesse."

Ally winced, no doubt in sympathy at how deep the enforcer's wounds were. "Sit him down, Zander."

When Ally moved to sit in front of a naked Jesse, Derren grabbed her arm. "Wait." He whipped off his own T-shirt and threw it at the enforcer. Understanding, Jesse covered his groin, a small smile on his face. Rolling her eyes, Ally knelt in front of Jesse and placed her hands over his chest. Derren couldn't help but tense at the sight. He didn't like her touching another guy—especially a naked guy—but Derren wouldn't begrudge his pack mate a healing. Not totally, anyway.

Seeing her face pinch in pain as Jesse's agony flowed into her, Derren placed his hands on her shoulders to comfort and steady her. His wolf hated that she was hurting, wanted to shift and soothe her somehow.

Kathy laid out drinks and sandwiches. "All of you eat. You need your strength." She gave her daughter a pointed look. "Roni, sandwich. Marcus, leave some for the others."

Flashing a charming smile at Kathy, Marcus took three sandwiches for himself while his mate called Caleb and Kent with her cell phone, summoning them to Ally's lodge. It took the males a mere minute to arrive.

"So what happened out there?" Bracken asked Nick.

Ally only half listened to Nick's recounting of the tale, most of her concentration on healing Jesse. How the guy smiled in that kind of agony, she'd never understand. Once she was done, she turned to Zander, ready to offer her help. But then Derren was tugging her away.

"They're all fine, Ally," insisted Derren, knowing she was weak from their pain. "Their wounds are already healing."

"Yeah, and I can speed up the process. Jesse's injuries were deep but not extensive. I've got enough energy to offer more help."

Driving Derren slowly insane, the stubborn female then went on to heal Zander, Roni, and Eli. As Marcus and Nick were well on their way to being fully healed, they politely declined her offer to heal them. That was when Ally turned back to Derren, her pale face a mask of resolve. Even tired from healing the others, she was still determined to help him. "Save your strength, Ally, I'm fine."

Her gaze studied the slashes on his face that had torn into his lips. "No, you're not." And he'd scar badly if he was left to heal on his own. She also didn't miss the claw marks on his sides.

"It looks worse than it is."

"Then it won't take much energy for me to heal you, will it?" Ally frowned as a sandwich was suddenly stuffed into her hand.

"You have to eat," stated Kathy before stalking off.

"I was thinking," began Shaya, garnering everyone's attention. "It's not good that everyone lives so far apart. Caleb, Kent, Roni, and Marcus should move into the main lodge for a while. Their lodges are the farthest away from there, which makes them the most vulnerable against any kind of attack."

Roni seemed about to object, but then she sighed in resignation. "And if we *were* attacked, the pack would have to separate to get to us."

"Exactly. We have plenty of guest rooms." Shaya pursed her lips. "It might actually be a good idea for everyone to either stay there temporarily or share the lodges that are closest to the main one. For Willow's sake, if nothing else. I want her surrounded by people who will protect her."

"Zander can bunk in my lodge," said Eli. "Bracken can stay with Jesse."

Jesse scowled at Eli. "You're sticking him with me?" Bracken seemed to find Jesse's frustration funny.

Eli shrugged. "You're the only one he doesn't constantly irritate."

Derren offered, "I'll move into Ally's lodge so she's not alone."

Beside him, she stiffened. "That's okay, I'm—"

"Or you could just stay at the main lodge," Derren proposed. "With all these people. With all the noise and a constant bombardment of emotions. I'm sure you'd love sharing space and having a total lack of privacy, so—"

"Fine," Ally bit out. "Derren will stay with me."

Shaya smiled. "Excellent. That means no one's ever alone."

So low that only Derren heard, Ally whispered, "You can have my bed, since I never use it."

"Oh, we'll be using it," he said with a smile.

"I don't like to sleep inside."

"Who said we'd be sleeping?"

She shook her head at him. "You're such an asshole."

"Derren," Nick called out. "Can we talk a minute?" It wasn't a request.

Derren followed his Alpha outside onto the porch. He knew Nick well enough to know what this was about, so he didn't bother playing dumb.

"You slept with Ally."

"Yes." Even if he'd wanted to deny it, he couldn't. His scent and the smell of sex was all over the damn lodge. His wolf liked it, considered it a territorial marking.

"Do you really think it was the best idea to fuck Cain's mate?"

"She's not his." The denial was sharp and instant. "If he doesn't want to claim her that makes her free."

Nick scrubbed a hand down his face. "It's not that simple, Derren." No, it wasn't. "Cain will see this as a betrayal, especially since he entrusted her safety to you. He'll think you took advantage of that trust."

"Are you telling me not to touch her again?"

"There's no point," said Nick. "No one can get you to do anything you don't want to. But think about what you'll be risking. Cain's been a good friend to you, in the only way a sociopath can be. Do you really want to fuck up that friendship? Do you really want to find yourself on the receiving end of his fury?"

"This isn't about him. It's about me and Ally."

"Yeah, you and *his mate*."

His wolf growled. "She's not his mate."

"In another life, where Cain was normal, she might have been. And that's close enough to count."

"She's been dating other guys for years."

"Yeah, but you're not dating her. You're fucking her. That's different. And it will make a world of difference to Cain. Just think about whether sleeping with her is worth the storm that will head your way if you don't put an end to it now."

At least twenty minutes went by before everybody left. Twenty minutes in which Derren chewed on what Nick had said. Cain *would* see him being with Ally as a betrayal. Derren prided himself on being loyal, especially to those who'd earned that loyalty. Cain was one of those people.

Ally approached him, eyes narrowed. "You're thinking pretty hard over here. There are so many emotions tormenting you right now." Her hands cupped his face, and then a loop between them opened as she pushed healing energy into him.

"Ally," he admonished.

"Shut the fuck up." There was no heat in the words. "I can't kiss you if it'll hurt, can I?"

Derren snaked his arms around her, pulling her tight against him. And he knew that, yes, being with her *was* worth whatever trouble it might cause him. He needed her on a level he didn't understand, couldn't begin to explain, and chose not to overthink.

His wounds tingled as they healed—a soothing hum in his bones. She then used a wet cloth to gently clean his face. "Thank you, baby." His mouth devoured hers, licking, biting, and sucking on her bottom lip. Sliding his hands under her thighs, he lifted her; she curled her limbs around him. "Shower."

She smiled, flashing a dimple he hadn't before noticed. "Any excuse to get me naked."

He returned the smile. "Of course."

After taking her against the shower wall, her legs locked around his waist, he left to go join Nick and the others to discuss how best to tighten the pack's security measures. As such, it wasn't until Ally arrived at the main lodge much later to watch a football game in Nick's game room that she saw Derren again.

She'd literally taken three steps inside the main lodge when he appeared before her, his expression strained. She was about to ask him what was wrong—particularly since his hands landed on her hips and literally began urging her backward—when he forced a smile and said, "Maybe you should go back to the lodge."

Ally frowned. "Why? What's wrong?" She inhaled deeply, picking up a collection of scents: Roni, Marcus, Jaime, Dante, Dominic, Tao, and . . . someone else. Someone unfamiliar.

"Is that *her*?" a loud, witchy voice shouted.

Derren sighed. Dropping a kiss on Ally's mouth, he said, "Brace yourself."

To Ally's confusion, he turned to stand protectively in front of her. Rolling her eyes, she moved to his side . . . and that was when an old female wolf came out of the living area into the hallway, a snarl fixed on her face. The other six wolves followed. Roni and Jaime looked frustrated, but Marcus, Dante, Tao, and Dominic seemed amused.

The old woman huffed. "This must be the infamous Ally," she mocked. Hostility, sourness, and indignation flowed from her, leaving a tart taste in Ally's mouth.

Jaime smiled apologetically at Ally. "This is Greta. She's Trey's grandmother." Ah. Jaime had mentioned Greta during their Skype conversations. Apparently she was very antisocial, a little psychotic, extremely prudish, and very possessive of "her boys"—otherwise known as Trey, Dante, Tao, and the Phoenix enforcers. She also had a serious problem with Seers, because Trey had had a bad upbringing, thanks to a particular premonition.

Greta's upper lip curled briefly. "I'd thank you for healing my Roni, but I know Seers—you have an agenda."

Ally arched a brow. "An agenda?"

"Seers always do," she spat.

"Really?"

"Your kind can't be trusted. It's a well-known fact."

129

"Greta, Ally's visions and healing skills have been invaluable," maintained Derren, a growl seeping into his voice.

Greta looked at him. "Oh, I'll bet they have. She's helping because she's trying to win you all over so you'll let her stay here. Can't you see she's manipulating all of you?"

"That's not what's happening." Roni sighed tiredly. "There's no agenda. No manipulation. No conspiracy."

"Yes, there is, sweetheart." Greta's tone didn't invite argument. "You just can't see it yet. I've warned Shaya and Nick, but have they listened to me? *Noooo.* She's still here. You've all got enough trouble to deal with right now. This little hussy will make that worse!"

"Hussy?" echoed Ally. Should she be entertained by this? She figured she should be offended, but instead Ally strangely found herself wanting to laugh.

Ignoring her, Greta went on, "In my opinion, you're all mad to let her stay. You don't owe her anything just because she healed you and had some visions. I'll bet she's made no other contribution to the pack."

"That's not true. She makes the best chocolate cake ever," stressed Roni.

An exasperated flush crept up Greta's neck and face. "She's a Seer!"

"Who makes the best chocolate cake ever," repeated Roni. "You're missing what's important." Marcus and Dominic chuckled.

"You didn't even tell me you had one staying with you! How could you keep this from me, Roni?"

Dante spoke then, his voice dry. "I think Roni was worried you'd overreact; clearly it was a pointless concern." Tao snickered.

Marching up to Derren, Greta told him, after shooting a withering scowl at Ally, "*She* doesn't belong here! And I don't want her around my Roni!"

"And I just don't care, Greta." Derren's tone wasn't harsh, but it was firm. "Ally's staying. That's it. Now stop with all this, because she's done nothing to deserve it."

"He's right," said Jaime, but Greta ignored her and spoke again to Derren.

"I'm not surprised *you're* defending her. I can smell her on you. I thought you had more sense than to get involved with a Seer."

Ally smiled, leaning into Derren. "Once you've had a Seer, you'll never go back." There was an amused snort that might have come from Dominic.

"No wonder Taryn likes you." Wearing a superior look, Greta studied Ally from head to toe. "You're just like her—common, disrespectful, slutty."

"They're some of my best qualities." It was taking everything Ally had not to laugh her ass off. The old dragon was priceless.

Greta humphed. "Well, Taryn, Jaime, and my Roni might like you, but *I* don't."

"And that's supposed to make me feel, what? Devastated?"

Eyes practically swirling with anger, Greta turned back to Derren. "See, she has no respect for her elders!"

"Respect has to be earned," he said simply, "And it's not like you're being respectful to her, is it?"

"Why would I respect her? She's a Seer!"

"*And she's staying.* Let it go," Derren ordered.

Straightening, Greta inhaled deeply—her chest seemed to puff up. "If you want to have her here, fine. But mark my words, you're making a mistake." Her face twisted into a fierce scowl that locked on Ally as she continued, "You might have them fooled, hussy, but *I* can see right through you. So I'll warn you now, your cards are marked."

Ally smiled. "*So* happy we're not letting this fester." With another humph, the old dragon stormed out of the lodge. Looking at Jaime, Ally raised her brows. "Wow."

The Beta female sighed. "Yeah."

Derren spoke to Dante. "I'm surprised you left your territory."

"We caught her trying to sneak out to see for herself that Roni was fine." Dante shook his head in exasperation. "It was either bring her here or watch her attempt to sneak away again. If she'd gone out alone, she could have been hurt or taken."

"They'd have brought her back within the hour," mumbled Jaime. "She'd have made them crazy."

Dominic took a step toward Ally with a roguish smile—only to be halted when Tao grabbed him and Derren released a warning growl. "What?" the blond asked innocently.

"Dom, no," said Dante.

"I was just going to—"

"No."

Catching Ally's confused expression, Tao explained, "He was going to use a cheesy line on you."

"I was not." Dominic sounded appropriately offended. "I was just going to—"

"*No,*" Dante again burst out.

The blond enforcer sighed. "Fine, Jaime, I'll ask you."

Dante got in his face. "You will fucking not." Dominic just laughed, looking delighted by his Beta's frustration.

"So, basically, he just likes to drive his friends insane?" guessed Ally.

Smiling, Jaime nodded. "Trick, another of our enforcers, is the worst tease ever. But Dominic takes supreme joy in winding up males—especially mated ones—by flirting with their females. So, either he has the IQ of a Cheerio or some kind of death wish. We're not yet sure."

"We'd better go, we shouldn't stay away from our territory too long." Jaime gave Ally a tight hug. "Take care, sweetie."

Ally patted her back gently. "You too." She thought Derren was going to lunge at Dominic when the blond stepped forward to hug her. "Ignore him," Ally advised Derren, chuckling.

"Don't test me, blondie," drawled Derren, glaring. The threat didn't seem to bother Dominic one little bit.

Derren and Ally walked the Phoenix wolves to the parking lot. Dominic was just about to get into the Chevy when he shouted, "Hey, Ally, do you know the difference between a hamburger and a blow job?" At her frown, he asked, "No? Wanna have lunch sometime?"

"Oh my God." Dante shoved him into the vehicle before shooting an apologetic glance at a laughing Ally and a homicidal-looking Derren. "I wish I had an excuse for him, but I don't."

Watching the Phoenix wolves drive away, Derren growled at the sight of Dominic waving out of the window. "You know," he said to Ally conversationally, "one day I might just kill him." She laughed again.

CHAPTER NINE

W ill you stop throwing my baby!"
Ally entered the living area to find Shaya scowling at
Derren, who was holding Willow high in the air while Bruce
stood at his feet, wagging his tail excitedly.

"She loves it." As if to prove it, Derren threw Willow once
more and easily caught her. The baby giggled, kicking her legs like
crazy. Bruce gave a playful bark.

Shaya put her hands on her hips. "Yes, I'm well aware that my
daughter has no fear. But *I* do. And you make me nervous when
you do that."

Derren's gaze whipped to Ally when she advanced farther
into the room. "Hey. Have you come for dinner?"

"Yup." She'd been coming to the main lodge more and more
since the pack's acceptance. She still spent most of her time at
her own lodge, but she joined the pack for at least *one* meal a day.

Shaya sighed, shoving a hand through her curls. "Ally, you
deal with him. He listens to you."

Uh, no, he didn't—to Ally's utter exasperation. Derren didn't
listen to anyone. She knew he wasn't the real source of Shaya's

irritation. "You're not doing too well with being restricted to your territory, are you?"

Six weeks had gone by without incident, but no one believed for a second that the danger had passed. Donovan had sent a security team out to install all kinds of high-tech gadgets, including discreet yet high-quality cameras that were now scattered around the perimeter of Mercury territory. In addition, everyone's cell phones had been fitted with GPS trackers. The same had also been done for the Phoenix Pack at Nick's request.

Even so, people were conscious that gadgets weren't going to keep them safe, only help them. However, not leaving pack territory was driving people crazy.

"No, I'm not doing well with it at all," admitted Shaya. "I badly want to visit Taryn. It's not the same, talking on Skype."

From the sofa, Eli spoke up. His voice was gentle but firm. "You know why you can't go visit. The Phoenix Pack is in as much danger as we are. You wouldn't be any safer there than you are here."

So far, there had been two unsuccessful attacks on the Phoenix Pack—one of which had been an electronic wipeout to help the culprits get through the security, but their resident hacker, Rhett, had quickly countered the attack. Like Donovan, the talented hacker was having no luck with discovering the identity of the person behind the hits, though.

"Remember what happened the last time you left our territory against Nick's wishes?" Eli asked Shaya.

Ally guessed he was referring to the time that Shaya had been targeted by jackals.

"I'm not going to sneak off," Shaya snapped. "I'm not stupid."

"I know how you're feeling," Bracken said to the Alpha female, looking just as glum.

Roni snorted. "The only reason you're unhappy is that you're horny."

"Death by blue balls." Bracken shook his head. "I never thought I'd go out this way."

Derren winced as Willow got a firm grip on his hair, making Ally smile. Since much of his time was taken up by his job, living with him had been easier than Ally had expected. She still had plenty of space and time alone. She also had sex on tap, which was really good.

He didn't complain when she often left him in the middle of the night in favor of sleeping in the hammock. He accepted that she preferred to sleep outside, and she'd often wake up in the morning to find that he'd joined her at some point.

Her wolf loved having him around, having his scent everywhere. The animal was becoming more attached to Derren than Ally was comfortable with. The animal thought of him as *hers*, and she growled whenever Ally thought about how she'd be leaving him in the near future. If Ally was honest, the idea of leaving the Mercury Pack—leaving Derren—wasn't one she relished much either. But Ally was careful not to allow herself to get too settled.

"*Oh my God.*" Eli's gaze shot from his cell phone to his sister. "You are fucking unreal!" Obviously more pranks were being played.

"What did she do?" Marcus chuckled. Roni was studying her chipped nails, looking suspiciously innocent.

"She hacked into my Twitter account *again!*" Eli was glaring at her as he continued explaining to Marcus. "She tweeted, 'My jaw is killing me. I'm never wearing a ball gag again!'" The muffled laughs coming from his pack mates made his flush deepen. "I'll get you back for this, Roni."

"So you always say." She was totally unconcerned.

Long after dinner, when most of the pack was relaxing in the living area, Zander called Nick with news that they had visitors. The identities of the visitors had everyone groaning in annoyance.

"Why do you think Miranda's come?" asked Caleb.

Shaya shrugged. "Guess we'll soon find out."

"How did she become a lone Alpha female?" Ally asked Shaya.

"She rose to the position when her boyfriend was made Alpha male, even though they hadn't imprinted. But then her boyfriend met a mysterious death. Plenty of guys have attempted to get close enough to her to become Alpha male, but none of them have stuck around long." Shaya fought a smile as she added, "She's also quite the cougar, goes for guys who are at least a decade younger. She has a thing for Derren."

"She has a thing for Betas," he corrected. "Males who she thinks aren't interested in being Alpha and won't threaten her position of lone ruler but are also strong enough to appeal to her."

Neither Ally nor her wolf liked the idea of anyone but her finding Derren appealing.

"Do you think you could try not irritating her for once?" Kathy asked her daughter. "Since she's our neighbor and all."

"Only if she leaves Derren alone," said Roni, who was leaning into Marcus. "It's just creepy watching a woman who's at least a decade older than him eyeing him like he's candy. It's one thing if an older female likes a younger male—I can accept that and I won't judge it. But it's another thing altogether if she's some kind of predatory seductress that preys on younger guys and wants them wrapped around her little finger."

Yeah, Ally didn't think she was going to like this woman *at all.*

"Besides," added Roni, "it's always her who starts it."

Marcus began massaging his mate's hand. "That's because she feels threatened by your level of dominance, sweetheart." Roni was very dominant—so much so that she could quite easily be an Alpha of her own pack if she wished to be. The same could be said of her mate. He was charming and seemed very laid-back, but Ally could sense that there was a dark and dangerous side to him lurking beneath all that charm.

Shaya sighed. "Let's hope Miranda doesn't stick around long."

Derren did his best not to stiffen as Miranda and two of her enforcers entered the living area a few minutes later. Honestly, he didn't understand why he was suddenly so tense. She'd been on his territory a number of times, and although he'd been irritated by her presence, he'd never felt . . . threatened.

"Miranda, what a surprise," drawled Shaya, her smile deceptively pleasant, gesturing for the female to sit on the sofa opposite of her. Miranda's enforcers stood behind her, on guard. To Ally's annoyance, there was no denying that the Alpha female was beautiful with her flawless face and wicked curves. She'd gone a bit heavy on the eye makeup, though; she looked like a damn panda.

"Shaya, it's always a pleasure," replied the brunette. She swept her gaze around the room, offering a smile of greeting to everyone. Once that gaze landed on Roni, it hardened. "Still a tomboy, I see."

Roni cocked her head. "Did you know that a certain study found that seventy-nine percent of mascara contained staph infection? Just watch out for impetigo, food poisoning, boils, and cellulitis—they're some of the symptoms."

"*Roni.*" Marcus's admonishment was amused as opposed to stern.

She blinked innocently. "What? What did I say?" The female enforcer often spouted out useless and totally random facts to either repel or irritate people. It actually worked. Like now with Miranda, people regarded Roni as if she was weird or annoying and so, as such, not worth talking to.

Moving her attention from Roni, Miranda then spotted Derren. She gave him her usual wide, sultry smile—an invitation that he had never responded to. "Derren." There was both delight and enticement in the sensual purr. "How nice to see you."

Derren would bet she wouldn't be so interested if he weren't a Beta. She knew the effect she had on males; she relished it, used it, and believed it gave her some dominion over men. Derren wasn't so easily led. Beautiful or not, she held no appeal at all for him. She was sly, manipulative, egocentric, and liked to lead men around on a leash—as if that in itself was a symbol of power. He had no intention of being on anyone's leash. He again ignored the invitation in her smile but, being civil, tipped his chin at her and her enforcers in greeting.

"Why are you here?" asked Nick abruptly. Trust him to cut right through any small talk.

Miranda chuckled. "I find that I like your directness, Nick. As for why I've come . . . I wanted to know if you've had any luck in tracking the foxes who fired the grenade on your territory. I've had some of my own men attempt to find them—I don't allow intruders on my territory, least of all to attack my neighbors. But we haven't been able to track them."

"Neither have we," admitted Shaya.

"It seems so strange. I would have thought that if a grouping of foxes had a grudge against you, they would have challenged you by now."

But this wasn't about grudges or challengers, it was about cashing in on a bounty, so the situation was very different. Derren didn't say that aloud, though.

"Have there been any further attacks?"

Shaya shook her head, clearly intending to ignore Miranda's attempt to fish for information. "None."

Miranda shrugged. "Perhaps it was a few drifters acting alone."

"Maybe," said Shaya.

Miranda sighed. "I'm glad to hear there has been no more trouble."

As Miranda's gaze returned to him, Derren followed his wolf's instinct and protectively shifted a little closer to Ally. And that was when he understood the cause of his tension. It wasn't that he felt personally threatened by Miranda; it was that he viewed her as a potential danger to Ally. It was a supposition that was nothing more than paranoia, really, and it reminded him of the way Nick acted when outsiders were around Shaya. Clearly his Alpha male was rubbing off on him.

Obviously identifying the move as a protective gesture, Miranda's azure-blue eyes took in Ally, sizing her up. "And who is this, Derren?"

Well, that made Ally and her wolf bristle. Failing to address her directly was an insult. She spoke before Derren could respond. "I'm Ally."

Miranda stared at her, waiting for her to elaborate. Ally didn't. "Friend of yours?" the Alpha female asked Derren.

Surprising Ally, it was Roni who answered. "A *very* good friend." The implication that the relationship was sexual was right there in the enforcer's tone. Oh, that evoked strong emotions from Miranda. Up until then, no real emotion had tainted the air around Miranda. But now, malice and spite slithered over Ally, making her skin feel raw like she'd been scratching at it for days. Miranda's lust for Derren was dark with greed. It wasn't so much Derren that she wanted but the opportunity to rule and possess him. Her wolf snarled, ears flattening.

Miranda arched a brow at Ally. "Is that so?"

Ally thought about simply ignoring the question. After all, getting involved in Roni's "let's annoy the creepy bitch" game might not be the wisest idea, since conflict between neighbors never ended well; she didn't want to cause trouble for the Mercury wolves. But what came out of Ally's mouth was: "Yes, it is." And Roni couldn't have looked any happier.

Those words surprised Derren and brought a satisfied growl from his wolf. Ally publicly admitting their relationship was a claim of sorts. Derren wondered, however, if Ally even realized what she'd done. Since the first night he'd taken her, she'd been very careful not to mark him again, which pissed off his wolf. Derren didn't like it much either—particularly since the drive to brand her over and over was like a fever in his veins.

Feeling the urge to push Ally, to see how far she'd go to reinforce her claim, Derren began to possessively play his fingers through Ally's hair as Shaya distracted Miranda with a conversation about shoes.

Sensing the silent challenge, his expectation that she would back down, Ally slipped her hand onto his thigh instead. As she'd told Shaya, Ally never backed down. His response was to nip her earlobe. She rubbed her cheek against his jaw, smiling at the low rumble that vibrated in his chest. That rumble snatched Miranda's attention, and her eyes slammed on them. Malice once again crawled over Ally.

"It's a relief to hear that everything's fine." Miranda looked from Nick to Shaya. "I don't expect you to confide in me, but I'd just like to reiterate that if you decide you need my backing against an enemy, I am willing to give you my support."

Most likely at the cost of their souls, thought Derren.

Rising, Miranda shot Derren another sultry smile. "Maybe you could escort me and my enforcers to the border of your territory."

"Nick and I will do that," Shaya quickly offered. "I know Derren is busy."

The moment Miranda left, Ally's wolf settled down. Although Ally bristled at the idea of another female having any interest in Derren, she was slightly amused by the discomfort she'd sensed it caused him. "So. Miranda . . . Little old for you, Derren, isn't she?" Ally teased. The others chuckled.

His nostrils flared. He was really tired of taking shit about it. "You think this is funny?"

Ally's chuckle burst free. "Oh, come on. *You* would if the situation was reversed."

Wrong. He'd be pissed. He didn't like even the *thought* of anyone else wanting her. His wolf became infuriated at the idea of anyone coveting Ally.

Resisting the temptation to tease him further, Ally said, "I'm heading back to my lodge. You coming, or do you have more work to do?"

In actuality, Derren had plenty of work to do. But he wanted time with Ally. More specifically, he wanted time *alone* with

Ally. "I'm done for today." Having said good-bye to everyone, they strolled out into the warm evening. "Let's take a little detour before we head back."

"Where are we going?" she asked curiously. He didn't answer. After a reasonably short walk through the forest, they neared a clearing Ally didn't recognize. She could hear the river close by. "Seriously, where are we going?"

Derren chuckled. He'd fast learned she wasn't the most patient of people. Stepping into the clearing, he pointed. "There. See."

Yes, Ally did see. Her mouth dropped open. "It's . . . wow." Adjacent to the river were three hot springs framed by a formation of rocks. "Are they natural?"

"Yep. The third one is the coolest. Come on, strip."

They both kicked off their shoes and shed their clothes before sinking into the water. It was just the right temperature, and Ally sighed in pleasure.

"You can't make that noise right now," Derren told her as he draped his arms over the rocks behind him.

"Why?"

"It makes me hard." It was the same sound she made when he was tasting her.

Ally chuckled. "You're already hard."

"Of course I am. You're naked." If he was honest, his cock went hard at just her scent. "Come here. Straddle me."

Eyes narrowed, she wagged a finger playfully. "Nu-uh. We can't have sex here."

He snorted. "Obviously." It was important to keep the springs clean. "But I want to touch you." He wanted her close. "*Ally.*" Rolling her eyes, she shuffled closer to him. He curled his hands around her hips, lifted her, and brought her to straddle him.

"Happy now?"

"Very." He sucked her lower lip into his mouth; a growl of approval rumbled up his chest when her body relaxed into his. Meeting her captivating emerald gaze, he tilted his head. "So many secrets in those eyes." Ally Marshall was one big mystery. In the beginning, he hadn't minded that. Now, it bugged him that there were so many things about her that he didn't know. "Tell me one."

She blinked in surprise. "Tell you a secret?"

"Yes." His interest in her had shifted a fraction in the past six weeks. Become something else. Something more. Something that might threaten their agreement that what was between them didn't have to be complicated. Yet, he wasn't fighting it. "Tell me why you like to sleep outside." He skimmed his hands up her arms. "I know you have nightmares. Where do you go?"

She swallowed. "The dark."

"You said you couldn't get out to warn them. What did you mean?"

Ally tensed. "What?"

"Once when you were having a nightmare, I tried to wake you, and you said you couldn't get out to warn them." Instead of elaborating, she pulled back, averting her gaze, which was clouded with uncertainty. "One time when I was in juvie, six human guards beat me up and tortured me with electrical rods and Taser guns." Her eyes whipped back to his, fury replacing the uncertainty. "I knew they were going to kill me, and I knew they were going to rape me first. I'm sure Cain's told you enough about juvie that you know that's not uncommon. The only reason I'm alive is that Nick intervened."

That was why he felt so indebted to Nick, Ally now understood. She wanted to tell Derren she was sorry for what had happened to him, but she knew that would be the last thing he'd want to hear. He was frustratingly too macho to accept compassion. "Why did you share that with me?" It was a memory that was personal, private, and painful.

"Because this isn't a one-way thing. I'll share with you, and you'll share with me." He brushed his thumb along her cheekbone. "Tell me why you sleep outside."

"It's not a pretty story."

"Neither are any of mine, baby."

Because Ally figured honesty deserved honesty, she explained. "My childhood pack wasn't much bigger than this. We all lived together in one huge house. There were only five kids in total. Me and Cain were best friends, and we used to play together in a fort that we set up with the help of our parents. Anyway, one night Cain was chasing me out of the fort, and as we reached the pack house a large pack of wolves invaded our territory." An ache began to build in her chest as she remembered the screams, the blood, and the chaos. "Our pack didn't stand a chance."

"That was the night it was slain?"

She nodded.

"You and Cain got away?"

"There wasn't a chance in hell that we'd have gotten away . . . but then the battle around me suddenly ended and I was back in the fort with Cain. I realized I'd had a vision. The trouble was that as I tried to get out in a panic to warn my pack, I dislodged one of the rocks. The front of the fort collapsed."

"That was what you meant when you said you couldn't get out to warn them," Derren deduced.

"Yes." She'd clawed at the rocks, tried her best to dig her way out. "We were trapped there for hours, and it was so dark." It didn't matter that her shifter night vision had allowed her to see clearly; Ally had never liked the dark as a kid. "We could hear them screaming and howling. By the time we got out, they were all dead." Maimed bodies of adults and pups had lain all around the pack house.

Slipping his hand to the back of her head, Derren tugged her close and kissed her lightly. "Did you ever find out why they were all killed?"

She inhaled deeply. "Apparently one of the enforcers raped a mated female wolf. Shifters will burn down whole countries to avenge their mates. The guy was never going to let that go. But instead of killing the bastard responsible, he killed our entire pack in a rage. He must have felt bad about it later, because he didn't come for me or Cain when he found out two pups had survived; he didn't try to finish the job." Cain's uncles had understood the guy's rage, but they had still gone after him to avenge the death of their brother.

"I'd say there's no excuse for what he did. But I know that if my mate was hurt, the last thing I'd be is rational. I'd want to destroy the fucking world." He'd eviscerate anyone who threatened Ally, whether their relationship was temporary or not. As usual, his wolf snarled at the idea of her leaving. "No wonder you have nightmares. I'm sorry you lost your family, baby."

So was she. "I lost them when I was too young to really appreciate them."

"Then you went with Cain to live with the Brookwell Pack?"

She nodded. "His uncles pretty much adopted me."

"What's the pack like?"

"Large, boisterous, would use any excuse to throw a celebration to get blind drunk."

"Do you keep in touch with any of the Brookwell wolves?"

"I talk to my uncles by phone. And they visit me when they can."

"I thought Cain kept them away from you so that you stay off the humans' radar."

"No, leaving the pack kept me off the radar. But my uncles still slip away and meet me sometimes, just like Cain does. I'll never forget how they took me in and accepted me." Still, she'd always felt like she was leeching off someone else's family. Although she adored her uncles, Ally had never felt settled there. Never found her place. And so she'd flitted from pack to pack over the years, searching for it. But she never found it.

For a short while, she'd thought she'd found it in the Collingwood Pack. She'd let her guard down a little, but that had come back to bite her on the ass when Zeke—

"Don't think about him." Derren cupped her face, trapping her gaze with his. "He's not worth an ounce of your time."

SUZANNE WRIGHT

It freaked her out that Derren could read her so well. "It's not that I'm dwelling or anything. It's that—"

"You trusted him not to hurt you, but he did. And now you wonder if you can trust your own judgment anymore." Derren understood that well.

She nodded. "If you can't trust yourself, who can you trust?"

Derren curled his arms tight around her. "You can trust me." She'd no doubt find that difficult to believe, considering he'd been a total ass in the beginning. But it was true.

"And you can trust me, but you don't."

He tapped her nose. "That's where you're wrong. I was a complete bastard to you, but you healed me—even though the burns were severe, and even though you knew my agony would then become yours, you did it. You had to have known that using that much energy would knock you unconscious; that it would put your safety in the hands of people who hadn't exactly been welcoming to you. But despite all that, despite all the prejudice you received because of your gift, you used that gift to heal me. You have my trust."

Ally understood that wasn't something she should overlook or take lightly. Having someone have such faith in her—especially after her previous pack had withdrawn their trust—healed a little rift inside her. Ally rested her forehead against his. "I'm honored to have it." And she wanted to keep it, but she might just lose it when he realized she hadn't corrected his assumption that Cain was her mate. "Derren, there's something you should know. About Cain—"

Derren cut her off with a kiss. "I don't want to hear about him."

"But—"

"No."

"This is important."

"Cain's got nothing to do with us." Derren bit her bottom lip when she would have spoken again. "I don't want him here."

Between us, he didn't say but she clearly heard. Not wanting his mood to turn sour by pushing him, Ally sighed. "Fine. But you can't say I didn't try to tell you."

"I don't want to know."

Maybe it really wouldn't be important to him, thought Ally. After all, they had agreed their relationship would be temporary, so whether or not Cain was her mate wasn't relevant.

Derren nipped her neck, wanting her attention solely on him. "I have another question. Who taught you to shift so easily between forms?"

"My mom taught me how to be at peace with my wolf. Without that, it isn't possible. But if someone can manage that, it's easy for them to do what I do."

"So it's not a Seer thing?" he asked. She shook her head. "When did you have your first vision?"

"I don't know. I've been having them for as long as I can remember."

"They must have been hard to handle when you were a kid." They seemed hard enough to handle *now.*

"They could be scary. But even back then it bothered me more when something happened and I didn't see it coming. People don't understand that Seers don't 'see' everything." She shook her head as she added, "You wouldn't believe the amount of times someone blamed me when something bad happened. Some even accused me of having a vision but not warning them. Even when I was a kid."

He double-blinked with astonishment. "You were advising a pack when you were a kid?"

"My grandmother—who sadly died with my parents—was considered Seer of the pack, but, yes, if I had a vision that needed to be shared, then I was naturally expected to share it."

Derren traced her collarbone with his finger. "So you got the gift from your grandmother?"

"Yes, it skips a generation. The eldest Seer always trains and guides the child until they hit at least eighteen. At that point, the eldest Seer will either 'retire,' or one of them will move to another pack. Two adult Seers can't exist in one pack without being at each other's throats."

"A little like two Alpha males or two Beta males."

"Exactly."

Unable to resist that mouth, Derren flicked his tongue over her upper lip. "So your grandmother trained you?"

"Right up until she died that night the pack was slain, yeah."

Not liking the sadness in her voice, Derren smoothed his hands up and down her back. "Who guided you when you moved with Cain to his uncles' pack?"

"No one. They didn't have a Seer there."

"And I'll bet they expected you to act as the pack's Seer." He didn't like that.

"If I had a vision, I shared it."

Protectiveness surged through him at the idea of a six-year-old Ally being held partly responsible for her pack's safety. She didn't sound at all angry or resentful of that or anything else that had happened to her; he admired that. "It's a shitload of responsibility to put on a kid."

Ally tilted her head. "You despise responsibilities, don't you?"

Ah, so she'd picked up on that. "Much like you, I don't like feeling trapped." He couldn't like anything that made him feel confined, which was why he strongly doubted he'd ever mate. Even if he somehow recognized his true mate, his reluctance to be part of anything that took away his choices or freedom could prevent the mating bond from ever fully developing.

"You know, feeling trapped doesn't *mean* you're trapped. It's just what you feel. I know I'm damn weird for sleeping most of the night outside—"

"Waking up to find it's dark after just having a nightmare where you were trapped in the dark is bound to make it hard to fall back asleep. A lot of people stay awake after nightmares. You've found an alternative—albeit uncommon—way to cope with it. That doesn't make you weird."

"And feeling the weight of responsibilities isn't weird either—especially when you're responsible for the well-being of an entire pack." She ran her fingers through his hair. "I think you worry you'll let them all down."

His smile was stilted. "My conscience isn't developed enough for that."

"And I think you don't believe you deserve their faith in you."

"I don't. They've given me their trust. But I can't give it back." Not to all of them.

"You don't *want* to trust. It's a self-preservation thing for you. I'm not being judgmental, just making a point."

He swirled his tongue inside the hollow of her throat. "What's that point?"

"That your responsibilities aren't trapping you." Her words came out a little breathless, since what he was doing felt too good. "Taking on responsibilities means taking charge of your life. It's your own personal shit that's trapping you."

Maybe. But while he was hard as a rock, the only thing he could really think about was being inside her. "Finished preaching?"

She sniffed. "For today."

"Good. I want to be in you."

"You'll have to catch me first." Then she fled, laughing as she heard him cursing behind her as he rushed to follow.

CHAPTER TEN

The chiming of his cell phone pulled Derren from his paperwork. He frowned at the unfamiliar number. "Hello."

"Derren?"

His entire body stiffened as shock locked his muscles. He recognized the female voice. It was older, harder, than when he'd last heard it.

"It's Roxanne." His older sister. "Mom and Dad . . . they died last night."

Died? He probably shouldn't care. Had always assumed he wouldn't. But he had to ask . . . "How?"

"Dad had a heart attack. And Mom," choked Roxanne, "didn't last long after the mating bond broke." She cleared her throat before continuing, her voice now stiff and formal. "The funeral is tomorrow morning at ten, if you want to attend." She hung up before he could respond.

For a moment, Derren just sat there, unmoving. Then came the sudden urge to bolt, to get outside and inhale the fresh air. Without a word to anyone, Derren barged out of his office and out of the main lodge. He didn't give a thought to which direction he was heading, he just walked. He waited for some kind of emotion to hit him.

Something.

Anything.

But there was nothing.

He wasn't sure how long he wandered aimlessly, but he realized that at some point he'd subconsciously made his way to the lodge he shared with Ally. He found her drinking coffee at the dining table wrapped in a terry robe, her hair damp. She looked up at him with a smile. That smile quickly faded.

"Derren." Rising, Ally slowly moved to him, alarmed by the numbness coming from him, causing one continuous drone to ring in her ear. Something was very wrong. "Derren, what is it?" He didn't respond. He just stood there, his expression blank and his eyes cold. She fisted her hands in his T-shirt. "Has there been another attack?"

"No." His tone was flat, emotionless. "I had a call I wasn't expecting."

"Who called?"

"My sister."

Okay, well, that had been the last thing she'd been expecting to hear—particularly since she hadn't even known he *had* a sister. Since that day at the hot springs, he'd shared more and more with Ally. But the subject of his old pack had always remained untouched, and she'd respected his wish to keep it private.

"My parents are dead."

Ally rocked back on her heels. "Oh God." She didn't know what to say to him. "I'm sorry" didn't seem like enough. Instead of speaking, she slipped her arms around his waist and hugged him. His skin was cold beneath his T-shirt. "I should be good at comforting people who are grieving, considering I lost my family." But she'd been too young to grieve in the same way adults might.

Loosely curling his arms around her, Derren rubbed his cheek against hers. "I'm not going through the same grief that you went through, baby. I haven't spoken to my parents since before I was sentenced to juvie. They believed I was guilty." And they'd died still believing it.

"That's why your sister didn't come and tell you to your face," she realized. Even so, telling someone that their parents were dead over the phone was a shitty thing to do unless it simply couldn't be helped.

"I'm surprised she even bothered to tell me." His sister had disowned him as openly and easily as his parents had. "It's even more surprising that she told me about the funeral."

"When is it?"

"Tomorrow morning."

Ally met his empty gaze. "Do you want to go?"

"I don't know."

"Don't think you *have* to go, that you owe it to them," insisted Ally. "I don't know what happened in your old pack, but if your parents turned their backs on you, then you owe them nothing. Only go if you *want* to. And if you do, I'll be with you."

Derren cocked his head. "Why would you do that?"

"I don't want you to be alone."

Her words warmed him. This thing between them might have started out casual and easy, but it was becoming increasingly far from it. "A funeral isn't a good place for you, baby. All that grief . . . it'll hurt you."

Like she cared about that. "I'm not letting you go alone." Her wolf hated seeing him this way, wanted to rub up against him to offer comfort. Ally felt so freaking helpless. Physical pain she could take away with her gift. Emotional pain wasn't something she could heal. "How can I help? What can I do?" In a mere moment, his dark gaze went from cold to feverish with need.

Derren answered her question with a hard kiss, ravaging her mouth with his lips, tongue, and teeth. He wanted to lose himself in her, *feel* something. When he was with her, all he did was feel. Everything about Ally incited his senses. He drove his tongue deep into her mouth, just as he wanted to drive his cock deep into her pussy.

Drawing back, Derren skimmed the pad of his thumb along her bottom lip. "One day, I'm going to have this pretty little mouth on my cock." Her eyes narrowed in defiance, so he bit her lip. "Because it's mine." With one tug, the belt of her robe was undone. He pushed it off her shoulders, letting it fall to the floor, revealing every perfect inch of her. "I want to fuck you hard and deep. But not yet."

His hunger called to hers, brought her body to life; that was how it always was between them. Ally moaned when a hand knotted in her hair and arched her back slightly. He swooped down to suck a nipple into his mouth. His hot breath seemed to burn her flesh, sending sparks of fire through her body. A strong, calloused, confident hand cupped her neglected breast. He knew exactly what she liked and exactly how she liked it, and he always gave it to her.

She loved the way he touched and licked her as if he'd never get enough of her; he was aggressive and desperate yet careful not to use his strength against her. The hand in her hair moved down to clutch her ass and yank her against his cock. Ally shivered as he ground against her clit through the denim of his jeans, needing more. The abundance of raw sexual energy that always hummed beneath his skin beat at Ally's control. She clawed at his T-shirt, tearing it from his body, smoothing her hands over sleek, hard muscle.

"I need your taste in my mouth." The scent of her pussy was driving Derren insane. "Don't move." He kicked her legs apart and dropped to his knees. He gently parted her slick folds with his thumbs and slid his tongue between them, groaning at her taste. As his tongue lapped and teased, she whimpered and moaned; her claws dug into his shoulders hard enough to draw blood. "That's it, Ally, scratch me." *Mark me.* He flicked her clit with the tip of his tongue before suckling on it just hard enough to push her over the edge.

Panting, Ally watched as he shot to his feet; his face was a mask of raw hunger, and there was a merciless glint to his dark eyes. For an instant, those eyes flashed wolf, making her own wolf try to lunge to the fore.

"I want you bent over that table with my dick in you." Spinning her, Derren placed a hand on her lower back and shoved her forward. She slapped her hands on the table to brace herself, but she growled over her shoulder—a warning that he'd gone too far. She was a dominant female wolf, so of course she didn't like being manhandled. When Ally would have reared up, he curved his body over hers, caging her.

Knowing it was a weak spot for her, he hummed against the hollow below her ear. "I'm going to fuck you until you scream for me, Ally. I'm going to shove my cock so deep in your pussy, you'll feel me for days."

She struggled against the hands that shackled her wrists. "Get off me."

"No. You're strong, baby, I get that. I'm not dismissing it. But both of us can't be dominant in bed." He didn't mind that she battled his dominance. But the more their relationship had crossed the realm of "casual," the harder Ally had fought his dominance—as if she was also fighting what their relationship could become. Derren wouldn't allow that.

He needed her to acknowledge what pulsed between them, needed some level of submission. "You have to trust me enough to let me lead." There couldn't be a power exchange without that trust. He licked over a brand he'd left on her shoulder. "I'll take care of you, make you come so damn hard. But you have to let me lead."

Guys had tried to dominate Ally before, tried to show her *who was in charge*. But that wasn't what Derren was doing, wasn't what he ever did. Oh, he dominated her as best he could, sure. But he never did it in a way that disrespected her. He battled her dominance, acknowledged it was there. *But he'd never bent her over a freaking table before.*

The submissive position prickled at her dominant instincts, making her wolf bristle. Ceding all control—it required strength and trust. She had the strength, but her trust? She didn't think she could give him that. It wasn't that she didn't feel she could trust Derren. It was that she didn't know if she could trust herself to make good judgments.

Sensing her struggle, Derren pressed a kiss to her throat. "You can trust me." He rocked his hips forward, making her clit grind against the table. Her gasp made him smile inwardly. "Let me ask you something. Do you think I'd ever harm you?"

"No."

"Good girl." Another kiss to her neck. "You know I'll always keep you safe. Don't you?"

Ally did believe that. He was honest, reliable, and he'd protected her from day one—even when he'd thought she was someone he could never trust. "Yes."

With that one word, a slight fissure in Derren's defences repaired itself. "I'll never hurt you. And I'll never let anyone else hurt you. You can trust me." He traced the shell of her ear with his tongue. "Trust me enough to let me lead, Ally."

It was so easy to say, yet not so easy to do. If he'd demanded her complete trust, she would have fought him. But he was simply asking her to trust him enough to submit in bed. She could give him that much. So she let her body go lax against the cool surface of the table. A growl of approval rumbled out of Derren. The stubble on his jaw grazed her cheek as he again spoke into her ear.

"That's my girl." His voice was thick, possessive. Ever so slowly, Derren eased his weight off her upper body, loving the sight of her there like that, submitting to him—just how he wanted her. He skimmed a finger between her folds, finding her slick and ready. She squirmed against his finger. "Tell me what you want, baby."

"You know." She gasped as two fingers slipped into her pussy. He slowly pumped them in and out of her. It was bliss, but it was also torture because it wasn't enough.

"So fucking hot and tight." He withdrew his fingers. "I think you're ready for me."

The sound of a zipper slowly opening sent a tremor down the length of Ally's spine. The anticipation that had built inside her was now agonizing. She *ached* for him, for the carnal release her body knew he could give her. When the head of his cock bumped her folds, she arched back, trying to take his cock inside her. A strong hand on her lower back flattened her against the table once more. "Derren . . ."

Jaw clenched, he smoothly thrust himself balls deep inside her. Her pussy quivered and tightened around his cock, wrenching a guttural groan from him. "I love sliding my cock in you."

The tips of his claws dug into Ally's hip as he fucked in and out of her with rough, branding, powerful strokes. All the while, one hand remained splayed on her back, pinning her in place. She had to fight her instinct to buck against his hand, and he rewarded her by upping his pace. Her body wound tighter and tighter, and her claws sliced out, leaving deep grooves in the table.

He roughly tangled his fingers in her hair and yanked her head up. "Fucking come, Ally. Do it." Then he lunged down and sank his teeth into the crook of her neck. She fragmented, and her pussy contracted around him as she screamed his name. Derren reared back and jammed his cock deep as he exploded. *"Fuck."*

It was as if he'd poured every ounce of his strength inside her along with every bit of his come, because he had to brace his elbows on the table so he didn't collapse on top of her. When he could finally move, he placed a kiss between her shoulder blades and slipped out of her.

Ally's postclimax cloud began to disperse as she felt strong arms lift her and cradle her against a solid chest. Derren took her straight upstairs and laid her on the bed, and she let her eyes slide shut. He disappeared into the bathroom, only to come back moments later with a wet cloth to gently clean her. When he finally lay beside her, he pulled her flush against him.

"Have I fucked you to sleep?"

"No," she mumbled, forcing her eyes open to find a glint of amusement in his own. "But it was close."

Derren laved a brand on her neck before inhaling deeply. "You smell so good." He sucked at the hollow beneath her ear, and her blissful sigh was his reward. "My wolf loves your scent."

"The feeling is mutual."

His wolf's ears pricked up at that. "For you or your wolf?"

"Both."

That answer satisfied both sides of his nature. "Good."

As hints of his frustration and indecision flashed at Ally, her skin began to itch. "The shock's beginning to wear off, huh."

Derren sighed. "They were good to me when I was a kid. I never would have seen their betrayal coming."

She wanted to ask what had happened, but she didn't want to poke at a wound that had barely scabbed over. So instead, she gave a little of her own past, leaving the decision of whether to share his in return up to him. "I don't remember a lot about my parents. My mom . . . she was always smiling, always on the move. My dad was a very active person, a very dominant wolf. I remember the Alpha wanted him to be Beta, but he refused because my mom didn't want to be Beta female or to share so much of him with a job."

Derren knew it wasn't uncommon for females to resent their mate being Beta, since the position took up a great deal of their time and energy. "My parents were both submissive."

Ally gaped. "Really?"

He nodded, a slight smile tugging at his mouth. "Extremely submissive. Having a son as dominant as me was a shock. My mom spent a lot of time in her greenhouse—she loved growing things. My dad was a total nerd with a *Star Wars* fetish."

"Seriously?"

Nodding, Derren began threading his fingers through her hair. "As you can imagine, I didn't have much in common with either of my parents. But they were good people."

Not good enough. "What about your sister?"

"She's submissive, though not as submissive as they were. Roxanne is what you might call a 'follower'—she goes with the crowd, doesn't always think for herself." It wasn't because she was submissive. Whether dominant or submissive, a shifter could be strong-willed, feisty, and decisive.

In a nutshell, there were only two differences between dominant and submissive wolves: dominants were always physically stronger, and dominants could release heavy vibes that would force the submission of *any* wolf less powerful than them, which therefore made all submissive wolves vulnerable to dominants.

"That's why I'm shocked she contacted me," he continued. "The rest of the pack wouldn't want me at the funeral. I would have thought she'd do what they expect and not tell me."

"It was way over a decade ago that you lost your family. A lot can change in that time. Maybe she's not so easily led anymore. Maybe she even doubts your guilt."

Derren snorted inwardly. "None of them doubted my guilt, Ally." His tone turned grave. "Trust me on that."

Ally doodled circles on his shoulder with the tip of her finger. "I take it the Seer was a damn good liar then. Maybe he was related to Rachelle."

"What makes you so positive I'm not guilty? You don't even know what I was accused of, yet you believe I was innocent of it."

"Then tell me about it." Hastily, she added, "Only if you want to. No pressure. I won't be offended if you'd rather not talk about it."

He'd definitely prefer not to talk about it, but he wanted to see Ally's reaction, wanted to know if she'd doubt him. "I was accused of raping a human girl."

Totally stunned, Ally just gawked.

"One of my friends from the pack, Wayne, was dating her friend, and that was how I met Julia. I only saw her a couple of times. Nothing at all happened between us. She had a human boyfriend—who hadn't liked me one bit, paranoid that I wanted his girl. A couple of weeks after I last saw Julia, she was raped."

"She told the police it was you?"

"She told the police she was followed home by a wolf. That as she was walking down an alley, someone then jumped her from behind, forced her onto her hands and knees, and raped her. It was her boyfriend who first mentioned me; he told the police I was jealous of him, that I wanted her. Unfortunately, those cops had a hate-on for shifters, so they immediately considered me the prime suspect, even though there wasn't an ounce of evidence. Apparently Julia had washed it all away."

"And your pack's Seer told them you were guilty?" Ally asked. At his nod, she added, "Why?"

"His son, Wayne, was the one who raped her. Wayne broke down and confessed to me and his father. The next day, cops turned up at our territory. The Seer, Neil, had called them; told them he'd had a vision that it was *me* who'd raped her. He said that I'd forced him to keep it quiet by threatening to accuse his son, but that Neil didn't feel he could hold his silence any longer." Derren smiled bitterly. "He was a convincing liar, I'll give him that."

"And, what, the police were happy to accept that?"

"They hated shifters, and they wanted justice for Julia. They wanted someone to blame more than they wanted the truth."

That made Ally think of how Greg and Clint had interrogated her; having already made up their minds on the matter of her guilt, they'd simply wanted a confession—not the truth.

"I was banished from the pack, so I didn't have shifter legal representation. I had a human attorney who also happened to hate shifters. Neil stood up in court and testified against me. When your own pack stands against you, that's enough to send you to prison."

Because packs stuck together, protected each other from

outsiders. Turning their back on Derren was as good as announcing he was guilty. "Did you tell your pack you were innocent?"

"Of course. But Neil had already told everyone that the only reason he'd kept his silence was that I'd threatened to accuse his son of the crime if he told anyone. So when I spoke up against Wayne, no one was surprised. If anything, it gave further weight to Neil's account."

Anger and sadness rose up in Ally. "No one from your pack doubted the Seer?"

"If they did, they kept that to themselves."

"Your parents accepted the Seer's tale, just like that?"

"I think they didn't *want* to believe it, but then Wayne said I'd confessed the crime to him. The girl had either convinced herself it was me or she was coached by the cops, because she said in court that she remembered my voice telling her to 'shut up and take it.'" Derren had almost fucking lost it that day. Being accused of something so distasteful had made him feel sick and enraged.

"So, not only were you wrongly prosecuted, but the girl didn't really get justice at all, did she?" Ally inhaled a calming breath, knowing Derren didn't need her anger right now. "And Wayne got to walk free and rape more people."

"I heard he killed himself a couple of months after I was sent to juvie." It hadn't particularly surprised Derren. Wayne had never been mentally strong.

"And that didn't make people wonder if just maybe you were telling the truth?"

"If it did, nobody came to see me in juvie to say any such thing."

"Assholes," Ally bit out. Because she'd come to know Derren in ways she hadn't anticipated, she knew something else. "You killed the Seer, didn't you?" For a moment, he didn't say anything. Then he nodded, his eyes searching hers for condemnation. She sighed. "Good."

Derren stared at her curiously. "You don't have any doubts about my innocence at all, do you?"

Realization hit her. "You didn't tell me before now because you worried I might suspect you raped her."

Sensing she was offended, Derren said, "Let me ask you something: if someone were to ask you what happened with Rachelle, would you quite easily tell them?"

No, she'd think they would disbelieve her just like almost everyone else had. "Point taken." Ally idly petted his chest. "I know this is going to sound shitty, but I'm surprised you're even considering going to the funeral after what they did."

"Part of me thinks 'fuck them.' But another part of me wants to pay my respects to the parents they were before the pack Seer fucked everything up."

He was a better person than she was. "Does Nick think you should go?"

"He doesn't know about it yet. I haven't told anyone but you."

That touched her. He'd needed something to fight the numbness, and he'd gone to her. Not his Alpha and best, most trusted friend, but *her.*

"He might insist I don't leave our territory. It's a dangerous time for our pack right now."

"He knows you well enough to know you'll do whatever it is you want to do. And if you're going, I'm coming with you. I told you, I don't want you being alone."

Derren swallowed, more affected by her support than he would have expected. "Nick will probably send some of the enforcers with me."

"That's not the same as having support. It's possible to be surrounded by people and still feel alone."

She was right. And the truth was that Derren wanted her with him. She had a way of calming him, of restoring his balance. Like then. She'd melted that icy numbness, helped him face the situation and think it through. Moreover, she'd believed in him. She hadn't doubted his innocence for even a second. She hadn't pulled away or looked at him any differently. "I need you again." He was coming to suspect he always would.

It was dark. Too dark.

Worse, she was cold and trapped. "We have to get out." She shoved the wall of rocks as hard as she could, but they just wouldn't move. Fear and panic whirled through her, making her shiver and claw at the rocks.

"It's okay, Ally, we're going to be okay."

Not if she didn't tell everyone what she'd seen. She clawed harder at the rocks, and Cain's hand suddenly yanked her away.

"Ally, stop, you're going to hurt yourself."

"We have to get out! We have to warn them or they'll die!"

"What do you mean, they'll die?"

"Ally," another voice interrupted. "Ally, wake up, baby."

She shrugged free of his hand and again went at the rocks. Her claws snapped and her fingers bled as she tried to find a way out. The scent of blood filled the air.

"No, Ally, we can't get out that way."

"We have to!" Because the intruders were coming. They would kill them all.

"Ally, it's just a nightmare, baby. Open your eyes."

She froze as several loud, challenging howls split the air. "They're here."

"Ally, wake the fuck up!" That demanding, authoritative voice was too powerful to ignore.

Ally burst out of the dream, and found herself looking into familiar pools of dark velvet. *Another damn nightmare, on schedule.* It was like they waited for her.

Derren cupped her neck. "It's okay, baby." Her mouth crashed on his just as her arms locked around his neck, as if he could anchor her where she was. Like a cat, she rubbed her body against his, bringing his cock to life.

He didn't usually sense when she was having a nightmare, but he'd been wide-awake—his mind latched on the news he'd received from his sister. Ally had done no more than squirm and scowl, but he'd instantly understood she was trapped in the dark again.

He grunted as her hand curled around his cock and began to pump. Her mouth was desperate, hot, and seeking—he knew what she was looking for from him: to forget. If that was what she wanted, he'd give it to her.

Derren rolled her onto her back. "Shush. You're not there anymore. The dark doesn't have you now." He slipped a hand under her ass and tilted her hips. "I do." He thrust hard and deep, groaning as her pussy clamped around him. *So fucking good.* Her legs wrapped around his hips and her claws dug into his back as he plunged in and out of her. Her hard nipples stabbed into his chest, making him remember just how sweet they tasted.

"Harder," she rasped, her eyes glazed with lust.

"I'll give you what you need. I'll always give you what you need." His pace furious, he fucked her into the mattress. The headboard slammed against the wall but he didn't give a shit. If this was what she needed, she'd have it. Her pussy began to flutter around his cock. "Ready to come for me?" He slipped a hand between their bodies and strummed his fingers over her clit.

She bit him. Reared up and bit him right on the shoulder as her pussy clenched and milked his cock.

"Son of a bitch," he growled, slamming home one last time as he emptied himself inside her. Panting and shaking, he stared down at her—shocked and gratified that she'd marked him. A dreamy smile tugged at the corner of her mouth, and then she fell asleep. Derren wondered if she'd even been truly awake to begin with. He snickered. "Little minx."

CHAPTER ELEVEN

G rief was such a complicated package of emotions. Anger, hopelessness, disbelief, regret, fear, guilt, loneliness—it all flowed from the people around Ally and battered at her, giving her a sharp, pounding headache.

Watching as the coffins were lowered into the ground, she stood beside Derren while Nick and Roni flanked them. Despite the dangers that came with leaving pack territory, Nick and Roni had both been adamant that they would be present at the funeral with Derren. Apparently, they were the only two people in the pack other than Ally who knew everything that had happened to him. Bracken and Marcus had also come along, but remained outside the border of the territory. In case Nick's SUV was targeted, he'd ordered the enforcers to follow in a separate vehicle. It was a good thing, since Marcus had refused to let Roni leave pack territory without him anyway.

Shocked, nervous, and fearful, Derren's old Alphas had tried turning him away when he appeared on their territory. But when Nick had pointed out that he could—and absolutely would—make life difficult for them if they didn't grant Derren the simple right to be present at his own parents' funeral, the Alphas had folded. Nobody with a brain wanted Nick Axton as an enemy.

Since they had arrived, Derren had avoided touching Ally, as if worried that his emotions would bleed into her and increase the pain she was already feeling. While she was grateful, she also wanted to touch him and soothe him—especially since his old pack was behaving atrociously.

The adults kept their pups shielded, hiding Derren from their view . . . like he was a sick predator, and the mere sight of him would traumatize the kids. Their suspiciousness, disgust, and fear felt like acid on her tongue. It was pathetic, unfair, and maddening.

There was only one adult who had made proper eye contact with Derren: a petite female with eyes and hair as dark as his. Ally guessed it was his sister. Whenever her mate caught her casting glances at Derren, the guy would nudge her with his elbow; she would then instantly lower her gaze. No, Ally didn't like him at all.

She didn't like any of them, and she didn't like them being near Derren. He'd been through enough. Had been unjustly punished for something he hadn't done, had spent most of his youth in juvie, and had suffered greatly in that fucked-up place. And these people—who had let down a fourteen-year-old boy so badly, who could have prevented all of it if they had just been willing to listen to his account—thought it was okay to treat him this way? Nu-uh.

Her heart had ached for him the night before when she'd seen just how shocked he was that she believed he was innocent. The extent of the damage and pain his old pack's betrayal had caused him had become extremely clear to her. Even if she didn't know him well enough to know he wasn't capable of harming a female that way, she only had to consider that Derren wasn't a guy who made excuses for himself. Like Ally, he believed in owning his shit, in taking responsibility for his actions.

If he said he didn't do it, she believed him.

As the service ended, the crowd began to disperse. The grievers all gave Derren plenty of space as they passed—their eyes wide with fright and their mouths flat with distaste. A growl seeped out of Ally before she could stop it, making a few of them jump. Ha.

"It's okay," Derren told her, his voice low.

Ally looked at him. "No, actually, it's not."

Okay, no, it wasn't. Derren loathed that he'd been branded a rapist—a creature that should be fucking killed on sight. Roni had almost been raped as a teenager, and the shifters here had lumped Derren in the same category as the fuckers who had attacked her. But he refused to get worked up about it right now; he had enough shit going on in his head. "Had you expected anything different?" He hadn't.

"I'd hoped that maybe they'd developed a bit of sense at some point in the last decade and a half."

Derren forced himself to resist the urge to touch her, not wanting to worsen her pain. "To admit that they were wrong, even to admit it to themselves, would mean accepting they're exactly what you called them on the way here this morning—'ignorant, easily led, thoughtless bastards.' No one would want that title." She just humphed, which pulled a weak smile from him. "Snippier than usual this morning, aren't you?"

Yeah, as it happened, she was. In truth, Ally was feeling a little off-balance today. As usual, she had woken up wrapped in strong arms. What wasn't at all usual, however, was that she'd woken up *in her bed*. Yep, she'd spent the whole night in bed. That hadn't happened since . . . well, since before her childhood pack was slain. She didn't know what that meant. Did it even mean anything? Was she overthinking it? Probably.

Nick, looking as pissed with these wolves as Ally was, turned to Derren. "Ready to go?"

Derren nodded. He'd paid his respects to the parents he'd once had as a kid. There was no longer any reason to—

"Shit, what the fuck does this asshole want?"

Roni's words had Derren tracking her gaze to find a stout, elderly male shifter pausing a short distance away. Derren realized it was an old friend of his father's.

"You shouldn't have come," the man stated firmly.

Ally waved a hand. "Yeah, yeah, keep walking." The aging shifter blinked at her, clearly surprised. "You get to feel how you feel. You don't get to offload those feelings on other people." She ushered him away with her hands. "Shoo." The male actually did.

Unable to help it, Derren pressed a kiss to her temple. "Thanks, baby."

"Here we go again," grumbled Roni.

Another shifter stopped close to them. It was a female this time, and Derren easily recognized her. He nodded stiffly. "Roxanne."

"Derren." She cleared her throat, and a brief smile flickered on her face. "A lot taller than when I last saw you." Seeing that her mate was fast approaching, she quickly continued. "Mom and Dad . . . they had a will and—"

"I don't want anything from them, Roxanne." Derren didn't speak with bitterness or anger. He was simply stating a fact. "I just came here to pay my respects."

Her mate placed a hand on her shoulder. "Honey, it's time we left."

Roxanne bowed her head. "Yes, Warren."

Warren eyed Derren suspiciously. "I've heard a lot about you." Derren would bet he had.

"I don't know how you heard about your parents' death or the funeral"—so Roxanne *had* gone against the crowd for once in her life—"but you had no right to come here."

Derren tilted his head, his tone steady and calm. "What makes you think your opinion has any relevance whatsoever to me?"

"It *is* kind of odd that he expects you to care," agreed Roni.

"They were my parents," Derren said to Warren. "I have every right to attend their funeral. The fact that you're shitting all over this day by causing a fuss at their graveside . . . Not sure they would thank you for that."

Roxanne tugged on her mate's arm. "We should leave."

Warren sneered at Derren. "Do these wolves here with you know what you did?"

Ally spoke up. "Know that he was prosecuted for a crime he didn't commit? Yes, we do." She gave him a bright smile. "So you can run right along."

Warren narrowed his eyes at her. "Blind faith can be a dangerous thing."

"Yeah, I know." Ally shot Roxanne a meaningful look, and she actually flushed. Apparently the female *did* in fact wonder if she'd done wrong by her brother. "Wondering" wasn't enough, in Ally's book. Roxanne should have acted on that sliver of doubt. He was her baby brother, for God's sake.

"Let's just leave," Roxanne told her mate.

"Yes, let's." Warren straightened his shoulders. "I have no wish to be in the presence of these people."

Ally smiled at him again. "How awesome for you. Bye now."

Warren looked to the two bulky, blank-faced wolves that the Alphas had assigned to "escort" Derren. Translation: they were there to watch him closely. "Escort them off our territory." The wolves didn't appear impressed to be receiving an order from a male who was barely dominant and, as such, had no authority over them. They dismissed him with a look.

Derren was more than happy to leave. "Let's get out of here." He took Ally's hand in his as they all made their way to the SUV that was waiting outside the pack's territory. He paid close attention to their "escorts." One walked in front of them while the other walked behind them.

There were also other wolves—who apparently thought he wouldn't sense them—padding through the forest to their right and keeping pace with them. Noting that Nick, Roni, and Ally occasionally flicked their gaze in the direction of the forest, Derren knew his pack mates had also sensed them.

When he finally crossed the border, Derren's wolf stopped prowling in apprehension—though he remained watchful and on guard.

"What a pack of utter assholes," remarked Roni. "You know, Derren, if your sister hadn't been so disloyal to you, I'd feel sorry for her for having that pompous bastard as her—"

The breath left Ally's lungs as Derren's body crashed into her, and she hit the ground hard behind the SUV as he yelled, "Down!"

There was swearing, grunting, loud snaps cracking the air, and the sound of tires screeching away. It took her a few seconds to process what had happened. *Someone had fucking shot at them.*

"Ally, are you all right?" Derren asked, frantic as he searched her body for injuries.

"Yes, but you're not." Dread filled the pit of Ally's stomach as a red stain began to bloom over the shoulder of his shirt.

"We need to get in the SUV *now*." He pulled her to her feet as he looked at Nick and a hobbling Roni. Yes, Derren's first concern should have been for his Alpha. But when he'd caught a glint of silver hanging out of the passenger window of a black van, his primal instincts had urged him to protect Ally.

Nick carefully placed a cursing Roni into the rear of the SUV. "She took a bullet to the thigh."

"It went straight through, I'll be fine." But there was pain in Roni's voice.

Derren held the rear door open for Ally. "Get in, baby."

She didn't; her eyes were on the red stain that had spread way too far for her peace of mind. "Derren, let me see."

"Help Roni first." Derren practically shoved her inside before hopping into the passenger seat. Immediately, Nick sped off.

Roni jerked in her seat and then cradled her leg. "Motherfucker! Jaime's right. Getting shot isn't fun."

That did sound like something Jaime would say. Ally laid her hands near the wound. "It's okay. Just be still."

"You didn't foresee this?" Nick's voice was like a whip.

Without moving her gaze from Roni's injury, Ally told him, "Seers don't see everything. That's not how it works."

"Nick, lay off," Derren ground out before swerving to face her. "Baby, it's not your fault." He knew she'd feel guilty.

"We've grown complacent because of Ally's visions," said Roni as the wound finally closed over. She gave Ally a nod of thanks. "You're handy to have around." At that moment, Roni's cell phone rang. Marcus's frantic voice made her wince. "I'm fine. Really. Ally healed me, I'm fine. Just get the fuckers for me." With that, she hung up.

"Are Bracken and Marcus following the van?" Ally asked.

"Yes." Roni returned her cell to her pocket. "They'd better catch the bastards."

Derren snorted. "Marcus is driving. He just watched his mate get shot, so, yeah, he'll catch them."

Ally leaned forward in her seat. Derren caught her hand before she could touch him.

"No, baby, you can't heal me yet."

Her wolf growled. "Why?"

"The bullet isn't out."

"Fuck," Ally snapped. The skin was probably already beginning to heal over it.

"I'll dig it out when we get back," growled Nick, enraged.

When they got back to the main lodge, Nick did exactly that using a sterilized pair of tweezers, and, although Derren hadn't made a single sound, Ally knew he was in agony. After healing him, she cleaned him up, and he put on one of Nick's shirts—refusing point-blank to have a shower until he'd seen the trigger-happy bastards that Marcus and Bracken did in fact capture.

"I'll be back soon." Derren gave a pale Ally, who was nibbling on a sandwich that Kathy had made her, a quick kiss. "Eat all of it." She'd used up more energy than he was comfortable with. He turned to Shaya, who apparently read his mind.

"I'll take care of her," vowed his Alpha female.

Satisfied, Derren accompanied Nick and Eli to the toolshed where their captives were being held. The small building wasn't far from the main lodge.

Bracken and Marcus met them outside. Marcus, his eyes repeatedly flashing wolf, looked ready to explode with rage. It was understandable.

"We have a problem." Bracken's scowl was dark with anger. "They're speaking in Russian."

Nick frowned. "Russian?"

"At first I thought they were American but communicating in a different language to throw us off. But we checked their IDs. They're polar bear shifters from Moscow."

"They have to speak at least a little English," said Eli.

"I would think so," agreed Bracken. "They're acting like they don't understand us, but my guess is they're playing dumb."

"They're chatting plenty in Russian to each other," interjected Marcus, his voice barely human, "but I don't know what the fuck they're saying."

"That's all right." Nick straightened his shoulders. "Once we've had a little quality time with them, they'll speak plenty of English."

"These guys don't look like the type to easily give up information," said Bracken. "Both of them are covered in enough scars to suggest they've been captives before. And polar bears are tough, tenacious fuckers." Which meant that Bracken was right: they did indeed have a problem.

As something suddenly occurred to Derren, he said, "Hang on a second." He returned to the main lodge, finding Ally still picking at her sandwich like a bird. "Baby, you speak Russian, right?" He recalled her telling him how her foster uncles had taught her several languages.

Her brows drew together. "Yeah."

"Come with me." Keeping her hand in his and ignoring her questions, Derren guided her to the toolshed.

Roni had joined the others outside the small building, trying desperately to calm her pacing mate.

When Marcus's manic gaze locked on Ally, he nodded at her. "Thank you for healing Roni. Again."

Ally gave him a half smile before turning to Derren. "Okay, why am I here?"

"The captives are Russian," Derren replied. "We need you to translate for us. I'd rather you weren't here to see this—interrogations aren't pretty. But they might be able to tell us who put out the hit on us, and we need to know."

Eli looked at Ally curiously. "You speak Russian?"

"She speaks five languages," Derren told him, proud. "And that's not including English."

Bracken's brows flew up. "Impressive."

"Let's get started." Nick went to move but stopped as Derren spoke.

"Wait, I have an idea." Once Nick heard and approved the idea, the Alpha led all six of them inside the shed. Derren guessed that Roni was only there to keep Marcus from slitting the polar bears' throats before Nick was done questioning them.

Ally studied the heavily built shifters, who were each secured to a chair. They appeared bored as opposed to afraid, but their unease gave her pins and needles in her fingers.

Bracken broke the silence, pointing to the one on the left. "That over there is Andrei. Next to him is Misha."

With a predator's grace, Nick slowly walked to stand directly in front of them. "I don't think I need to introduce myself." The bears just stared at him. "As you can imagine, I have a simple question for you. Why did you shoot at us?"

Neither answered; both looked confused, as if unable to understand Nick. But Ally sensed no such confusion from them at all.

"I'll ask one more time," rumbled Nick. "Why did you shoot at us?"

Andrei flicked a look at Misha and said in Russian, *"It would seem he doesn't know about the hit."*

Amusement briefly glinted in Misha's eyes. He replied in Russian, *"The Alpha's not so smart after all."*

Nick growled, his voice a crack of thunder. "I know you speak English, so don't fuck with me. *Answer my question."*

"And I suppose he'll kill us if we don't." Andrei oozed exasperation. *"Does he think we'd be stupid enough to believe that he'll let us live if we talk?"*

Misha shrugged one shoulder very slightly. *"We can handle whatever he does to us. Not like we haven't been sliced before."*

Nick began to very slowly pace in front of them. "Did you ever hear of a form of torture called 'The Water Cure'?"

Andrei's exasperation increased. *"How can a cure be torture? This shifter makes no sense to me."*

Misha briefly glanced at his friend. *"Like I said, he's not smart."*

His tone that of a professor, Nick elaborated. "The torturers would secure their captive's nose and then stick a tube down their throat. Then the torturers would pour either vomit or piss down the tube. Their captive wouldn't be able to hold their breath for long, so they'd have to ingest what was in the tube."

Ally almost smiled as both Misha and Andrei tensed.

Nick continued. "The torturers would do it over and over, only stopping when the captive was full. Like that's not bad enough, the torturers would then use a stick to hit the captive's stomach until he vomited. Worse, the torturers would then do it again. And again. And again."

Andrei's mouth twisted. His exasperation was replaced by apprehension. His eyes momentarily slid to Misha as he said— still speaking in Russian, *"I must admit, I have not heard of that."*

Nick smiled at the polar bears. "Merciless, right? But then—as I'm sure you've heard—so am I, especially when my pack's safety is threatened. You shot my sister and my Beta. For that alone, you *will* die here today. It can happen in two ways. You can tell us what we want to know, and I'll hand your punishment over to one of my enforcers. As you can see, he's raring to fucking destroy you since you shot his mate. He'll make it quick."

Andrei and Misha cast Marcus a wary glance.

"But if you don't answer our questions, *I'll* deal with your punishment. And I will keep hurting you over and over again. Don't doubt that for a second. And in the end, you'd eventually tell me what I want to know anyway. In my opinion, it makes sense to just get it out of the way and die quickly. But, of course, the choice is yours. To tell you the truth, I'm more eager to make you suffer than to get answers straightaway."

Andrei looked at Misha. *"Do you think he's bluffing?"*

"I think he'd do it and enjoy it." Misha didn't look nervous, but his unease chafed Ally's skin.

"I suppose the question you have to ask yourselves is this," began Nick. "Is the person who put out the hit on us worth the torture?"

Misha stiffened. *"He knows about the hit."*

Andrei eyed Nick warily. *"Not so stupid after all. How unfortunate."*

Nick danced his gaze from one to the other. "All we want is his name."

"Sadly for the Alpha," said Misha, *"we plan to escape and kill them all. Do you still have the knife in your boot?"*

"No, the rabid-looking one took it." Andrei shot a glare at Marcus, who did in fact look a little rabid at that moment.

Misha didn't seem fazed. *"No matter, Andrei. We have other ways."*

After a long moment of silence, when it was clear that the bears intended to keep up the "we don't understand English" pretense, Nick inclined his head. "All right. If that's how you want to play it. Can't say I'm all that disappointed."

"Maybe they really *don't* understand English," suggested Eli, though Ally was pretty sure he didn't believe that.

Bracken nodded. "Only someone amazingly dense would choose the water cure over a swift death."

Derren sidled up to Nick. "You know, we could always contact Maxim Barinov and ask if he's heard of these guys." Maxim was a Russian polar bear they'd met in juvie.

Misha's eyes widened. *"They know The Sniper."*

Derren continued speaking to Nick. "I talked to him a few days ago. He said he'd try to find out who sent out the hit. Bet he'll be pissed when he finds out two of his own kind tried to cash in on it." As Derren had hoped, the Russians looked suitably afraid. Maxim's reputation as a professional sniper and all-around unforgiving bastard was well known.

"Yeah," agreed Nick. "Wouldn't surprise me if he came here to join in on the fun."

Wincing, Derren said, "He can be a sick bastard when it comes to torture."

"Maybe we should give them what they want," Andrei quickly proposed to his friend. *"I would rather die at their hands than face Maxim Barinov. He would threaten to go after our families. And, truth be told, I would rather avoid The Water Cure. Something tells me that if the Alpha gets started, he will not stop whether we give him a name or not. Look at the bloodlust in his eyes."*

"But if we give them a name, they will find a way to cancel out the hit," Misha pointed out. *"Then no one will avenge our deaths."*

"That is true. We could give them a false name," suggested Andrei. *"A masculine name. Maybe someone who we'd like to see dead. These wolves would easily buy the lie, as they would never imagine a woman is responsible. I was surprised myself—until I heard it was a Seer. They can be vengeful creatures. We'll tell them it was the Russian polar who—"*

That was all Ally needed to hear. "It's a woman. She's a Seer."

Roni blinked. "A Seer?"

Ally nodded. "They didn't say her name; they intended to give you a false name—pin it all on some guy they hate."

Andrei and Misha gaped at Ally, who shrugged at them and said, "What, you think you're the only ones who speak other languages?"

"You tricked us," accused Misha, switching to English, looking weirdly impressed.

Yes, they had been tricked. Derren had suggested not revealing that Ally could speak Russian; to let them think they could speak freely to each other because no one understood them. "Not so smart, are you?" she asked them in English, paraphrasing their remarks about Nick. They narrowed their eyes.

"Roni, get me the tubes," ordered Nick. Roni obligingly retrieved two tubes from a tool bench. Ally had no idea if they were props or if Nick truly intended to use them. Given that she wasn't sure if Nick was totally sane, and his sister had just been shot, it was possible that it was the latter.

Misha and Andrei both stiffened.

Nick glared at them. "I warned you that if I didn't get a name your punishment would be mine."

"You have the truth." Andrei spoke in English. "The female told you."

"Exactly, *she* told me. You intended to lie to me." Nick gave them a disapproving look. "That's very disappointing."

"They don't want a quick death," Ally told the Alpha. "They plan to escape."

Derren arched a brow. "Do they now?"

"That won't be happening," Nick stated. He turned to Eli and Bracken. "Secure their noses. Marcus, hang back until their stomachs are full. Then you can hit them as hard as you want."

"Wait," said Misha desperately in English, "we will give you a name." Andrei nodded, just as desperate.

"Why would you suddenly want to do that?" Ally tilted her

head. "Before, you said you *didn't* want to, because if the hit was canceled there would be no one to avenge your deaths."

"That sadly means I can't trust a word you say." Nick shrugged. "Besides, I don't need a name. There's only one female Seer who hates both my pack and the Phoenix Pack badly enough to put out a hit on both."

"I'll find her, and I'll kill her," vowed Roni.

Beside her, Marcus clenched his fists as he growled. "But first, we take care of these two bastards who dared to shoot my mate."

Eli strolled toward the bears, obviously eager for vengeance on behalf of his sister. "With. Fucking. Pleasure."

CHAPTER TWELVE

She either thought he was dumb or she believed that he didn't know her well.

She'd be wrong on both counts. Derren would wager he understood Ally better than most people did, despite only having known her a short time. You could have someone in your life for years but never really know them; others you could come to know in a matter of weeks.

It would be fair to say that Ally wasn't an easy person to read. She didn't wear her emotions on her face. But Derren had come to know her so well that, with a single glance, he could tell if she was tired or hungry or pissed or had something on her mind.

Right now, as he leaned against the counter watching her prepare them lunch, he could sense that something was wrong. "What's eating at you?"

Her almond eyes landed on him for a mere moment. "Nothing."

"When you lie, you shrug your left shoulder."

Ally's shoulders suddenly locked in place. "If you're going to bug me while I'm cooking, get out of my kitchen."

Instead, Derren took a sip from his mug. The woman made excellent coffee. "You've been *off* since yesterday." After the interrogation, she'd turned uncharacteristically quiet and pensive. When he'd questioned her, she had assured him that she was fine. Of course he'd been fully aware that she was lying, but he'd given her the emotional space she needed, trusting that she'd talk when she was ready. But . . . "I gave you time. That time is up, baby."

"Time to do what?"

"Time to share with me of your own accord." He moved to her as she was plating their chicken-fried steaks and mashed potatoes. Not prepared to let her go on hurting, he pressed, "What's bothering you?"

She swallowed. "My kind caused your pack pain again."

He cupped her chin and turned her face to his. "Hey, that's not on you. Kerrie didn't do it because she's a Seer. She did it because she's jealous, bitter, and apparently suicidal. It's all about the individual, remember?"

Ally was conscious of that. But she was also mindful that it had taken a lot of time to make the Mercury wolves see that. She worried that Kerrie's actions would undo what Ally had done and would make these people she'd come to respect and care for turn away from her. It would hurt a lot more than she was comfortable admitting even to herself.

"No one is going to blame *you* for this, Ally. Things aren't going to go back to the way they were at the beginning," Derren wouldn't allow it.

She narrowed her eyes. "For the record, I don't like how easily you read me." She comforted herself with the knowledge that he simply had a talent for reading people in general; it wasn't that she had become an open book to the world around her. Hopefully.

His mouth curved. "Trust me on this: no one in the pack will think any differently of you now than they did before they learned about Kerrie's involvement. Trust me," he repeated.

"I do."

Hearing her say that without missing a beat, having someone in his life who had such total faith in him, was both heady and comforting. And Derren had no intention of giving that up, of giving Ally up. His original curiosity in her had later became fascination, but that fascination had shifted and become an addiction. She was an obsession he couldn't shake off. She dominated his thoughts, consumed his wolf. Derren found himself hurrying to finish his Beta duties to spend more time with her each evening.

Ridiculous as it was, he didn't like sharing her with others in the pack. The scent, sight, or thought of her made his cock begin to harden. He wanted her constantly, couldn't get enough of her—if he was able to, he'd be in her twenty-four/seven. He wanted to be in her right now.

Sensing his intense need for her, Ally shook her head with a smile. "Later. First we eat."

As usual, they sat on the porch to have their meal. "Have Roni and Marcus located Kerrie?" Ally asked Derren. She knew the mated pair had ventured to Kerrie's pack that morning, where one of Marcus's sisters was also a member. Apparently, Kerrie hadn't been seen by her pack for a few months. Her parents claimed she was going to visit friends in another pack but that she hadn't been specific as to whom she was visiting.

"Marcus has called every one of Kerrie's friends that were on the list his sister gave him," he replied. "They all said they haven't had contact with her in months."

"They could be lying."

"Of course they could, but Nick can't afford to separate our pack to go hunting. So, instead, he's done something quite cunning."

"What?" Ally shoved a forkful of chicken in her mouth.

"An hour ago, he put out a reward for either Kerrie's capture—making it clear he wants her brought in alive—or for any information that leads to her whereabouts."

Clever. "Do you think it'll work?"

"I think there are plenty of people who would want to gain favor with Nick, so it's very possible that someone could come forward."

Halfway through her lunch, Ally said, "Tell me a little about the Kerrie situation. I know she lied about Marcus's mate being someone else because she wanted him for herself. But why would she take the rejection and his mating to Roni so badly?"

"Before Roni, Marcus's relationships were short and simple. But he didn't lead females on—he always made it clear that he wasn't looking for anything permanent. Outwardly, Kerrie didn't seem to take it badly when he ended things. They even remained casual friends. She told him that she'd had a vision of his mate; she gave him a false description, told him that the female needed him and was a lot like his mother—which scared the shit out of Marcus."

"Why?"

"I don't know exactly. All he's told me on the matter is that he doesn't have contact with her for a damn good reason." Derren sipped his Coke. "So by telling him that his mate was someone he so obviously wouldn't want to accept, Kerrie made him opposed to mating with his true mate."

"Probably hoping that it would make him open to imprinting with another female," Ally surmised. "Like Kerrie."

"Yes. And by giving him a false description of his true mate, Kerrie was no doubt doing her best to make it extremely difficult for him to recognize his true mate when he found her."

"Did Kerrie lie about the fact that she'd had a vision of him with his true mate, or did she truly have a vision and it was *Roni* she saw with him?"

Derren finished chewing his chicken before answering. "Roni believes it's the latter. When she and Kerrie first met, the Seer froze at the sight of her and acted weird. She tried coming between Roni and Marcus. She first warned Roni away by saying that Marcus's mate needed him. Later she told tales to Marcus's father, who turned up to see him and berated him for choosing Roni over his mate. At that point, Roni and Marcus had already realized they were mates and had claimed each other. Kerrie was too late."

"Did Kerrie admit she'd been talking out of her ass?"

"No. She insisted she was telling the truth about her vision, and she claimed that Roni had turned Marcus against her." Done with his lunch, Derren put the plate aside.

"So she hates Roni for that, and she most likely hates Marcus for not choosing her over Roni. She's angry her plan didn't work." Ally took a swig of her drink. "I'd say it seems unlikely that someone would go so far as to wipe out two packs for what two people did, but I've seen firsthand that there are people who would see an entire pack killed for vengeance." Her wolf growled at the memories of that night. "And they say that hell hath no fury like a woman scorned."

Derren nodded. "They're right." A series of beeps came from inside the lodge. Recalling that he'd left his cell phone on the counter, he picked up his empty plate and rose. "I'll be right back."

Hearing rustles in the grass, Ally rolled her eyes at the three wolves lingering nearby—on schedule. Evidently, Derren was right; the pack didn't intend to treat her any differently than before. Or, at least, these three scavengers didn't. She flung them the three extra chicken-fried steaks she'd made. Since the three enforcers never failed to make a brief visit at lunchtime, she'd taken to cooking extra food for them every day.

When Derren reappeared, flashes of aggravation and antipathy came from him—the combination was like spikes digging into her skin. Alarmed, she stood upright, and her wolf was equally anxious. "What is it?"

A muscle in Derren's jaw ticked. "I just received a text from Nick. You have visitors."

"*I* have visitors?"

"Matt, Zeke, and Rachelle are here."

Oh, goody.

A few minutes later, all of Ally's fears that the Mercury wolves would go back to hating her were completely eradicated. As she and Derren sat at the table in the main lodge opposite her visitors, most of the pack gathered behind Ally both supportively and protectively. The only shifters absent were Zander and Jesse—since they were on perimeter duty—and Kathy, who had taken Willow upstairs, away from the outsiders.

Ally's wolf growled at the visitors, baring her teeth. She wasn't at all pleased to see the Collingwood wolves; she remembered their betrayal, how they had withdrawn from her. The animal no longer had any respect for Matt or any regard whatsoever for Zeke. As for Rachelle . . . her wolf wanted to lunge at her and rip out her throat. It was an appealing idea.

Matt's smile was shaky. "It's very good to see you, Ally. You've been missed."

There was a snort of disbelief, and Ally thought it might have come from Shaya.

Matt cleared his throat, his smile faltering slightly. "How have you been?"

"I've been fine." Ally sank into her seat as she studied each of them closely and sifted through their emotions. Matt was feeling as nervous as he looked. Although Zeke appeared deceptively calm, he was seeping both tension and . . . longing? Rachelle, on the other hand, gave off waves of hostility and loathing—though she was the picture of pleasantness. What was new there?

Zeke nodded at Ally, wearing a bland smile. "Glad to hear it."

"You look good, Ally," complimented Rachelle, sounding very sweet and sincere. It made Ally grind her teeth so hard, her jaw ached.

Ally ran her gaze over the three of them as she asked, "Why are you here?"

It was Matt who answered. "We hoped that, if nothing else, we could mend bridges." In other words, Matt was still panicking that Ally's protector would seek retribution and, as such, he wanted to make nice with her.

Derren arched a brow as he drawled, "Did you now?"

Rachelle's devious eyes took in the Mercury wolves—you didn't need to be empathetic to sense that these shifters didn't consider the three visitors to be in the least bit welcome. "Ally, could we talk alone?"

Derren responded for Ally without missing a beat. "No."

Zeke's smile turned bitter as his focus switched to Derren. "Oh, that's right, you consider yourself her protector."

"She doesn't need protecting from us," stated Rachelle, "we're her pack." Her expression very sad, Rachelle sighed heavily—as if the whole thing weighed heavily on her shoulders. Oh, she was a super-good actress. Ally just hoped the Mercury wolves saw the lying skank for what she truly was. "There have been some issues between Ally and me, granted, but that's all. We're pack, and that means something to me."

"It's not my pack anymore," said Ally flatly. "I'm not planning to return."

"I understand why you might feel wary of coming home," interjected Matt, "but I can swear to you now that things will be different this time round."

Like she'd ever believe that. Her voice harder, she repeated, "I'm not planning to return."

"You don't belong here, Ally," Zeke stated. "You belong with us, your pack."

"Like she already told you repeatedly," began Derren, his voice close to a growl, "she's not part of your pack anymore."

Clenching his fists, Zeke narrowed his eyes at Ally. "I don't know what Derren's told you, Ally. I don't know if he's filled your head with crap about letting you join his pack. But he told Matt that your stay here would be temporary."

"It will be," confirmed Ally, "but then I'll be joining another pack." Her wolf snapped her teeth at that comment—her frustration was directed at Ally this time. The animal didn't want to be anywhere but there with Derren.

Rachelle took Ally's hand in hers, looking appropriately hurt when Ally immediately snatched it back. "Ally, please reconsider leaving the Collingwood Pack. I know you and I didn't get off to a great start. You despised me on sight. But that's hardly surprising, given the way your world fell apart when Zeke left you. It had to have been so hard for your wolf too."

Currently, Ally's wolf was flexing her claws, wanting to take a swipe at Rachelle. The Beta female looked and sounded so understanding and mature—nothing in her expression gave away the hatred that flowed from her and sliced at Ally's skin like a steel blade.

"Admittedly, I wasn't comfortable being around someone who had been in a serious relationship with my mate. My wolf certainly didn't like it." Rachelle raised her hands as she added, "I can hold my hands up and be honest here: I wasn't the nicest person to you in the beginning. Betas have responsibilities to their pack mates, and I wasn't there for you like a Beta female should have been. It was petty of me to disregard you that way, and I apologize for that."

"I owe you an apology too," said Zeke. "I knew you were hurting when I claimed Rachelle, but I didn't check up on you. As Beta, your well being was my responsibility, and I neglected it. Maybe if I hadn't, things would have been different."

Rachelle nodded. "Zeke and I are partly to blame for everything. I don't think that things would ever have escalated the way they did if we had just been there for you." Her eyes actually got all teary. She blinked away the tears and sniffed. "I just feel so bad about it. That petty, mean, inattentive person—that's not me, and I'm ashamed of how low I stooped."

God, the woman was good. Zeke and Matt totally bought it. And Ally began to seriously panic that just maybe the rest of the room would buy it too. Rachelle had certainly been able to fool everyone else. Ally honestly wouldn't blame the Mercury wolves for falling for Rachelle's act. Her wolf would, though. Too elemental in her way of thinking, her wolf wouldn't account for all the complications in this situation. If the Mercury Pack believed Rachelle, she'd see it as yet another betrayal.

Rachelle gave Ally a pleading look. "I want to know if we

can please put the past behind us. I understand why you did the things you did to me, I do. I can only *imagine* how it must have felt for you to lose Zeke and watch him claim me. Not that I'm saying it excuses that you attacked me, of course, but—"

Ally had had enough. "Shock me, Rachelle; say something true." That had the crazy heifer gaping. "We both know why you're really here," Ally added calmly. "You're trying to turn this pack against me too. You're trying to isolate me again." She tilted her head. "Not getting bored with this at all?"

To Rachelle's credit, she quickly recovered from her surprise and continued with her act. "Ally, please be assured that that isn't my intention. I do not want—and never have wanted—to turn anyone against you."

Ally scoffed. "Woman, don't make me hit you with your own broom. Just cut the crap, be a big girl, and give me some honesty." *Show everyone the* real *Rachelle.* "You loathe me."

Anger flared in Rachelle's eyes for the briefest moment. "That's not true."

"You're sure about that?"

"I could never loathe someone who's important to Zeke."

Ally smiled tauntingly. "Not even when I tell you I taught him that little thing you like?" Rage blasted out of Rachelle, hitting Ally's head like a hammer. Ho, ho, ho—taunting her was working. And Ally's wolf fully approved.

"That was immature and uncalled for, Ally. I'm doing my best to mend things here. I'm taking responsibility for my part in how awful things became for you." Rachelle was still saying all the right things, but she wasn't sounding so convincing anymore—not when her voice quavered, her face had hardened, and her eyes blazed. "Can we not try and get past all this? Can we not start again? That's all I want: to fix this, to make it right, and to do better by you this time around."

"Is it my turn to talk utter bullshit yet?"

Zeke put a calming hand on Rachelle's arm, so presumably

he could sense his mate's anger growing and bubbling just as Ally did. "We don't want to argue with you, Ally. We just want—"

"You know, Ally," interrupted Rachelle, "Mia told me that this would be pointless."

Oh, Rachelle was playing ball now. Why else would she point out the betrayal of Mia, a female wolf who had once been a close friend of Ally's? Zeke and Ally had often gone on double dates with Mia and her mate. Needless to say, when Rachelle joined the pack, the Beta female took Ally's place on those dates. She had also taken her place as Mia's friend, and it had hurt to be so utterly ditched that way.

"She told me there was no way you would apologize, that you're too envious and bitter," continued Rachelle. "But I didn't want to believe that."

"What a coincidence, I don't believe it either."

Ignoring that, Rachelle went on. "I was hoping Mia was wrong. But everyone here can see the truth, Ally. They can see how sour, offensive, hateful, unforgiving, and remorseless you really are."

"Coming from a demented, poisonous, mind-numbing, substandard intelligence . . . that means absolutely jack shit." Ally shrugged. "But, hey, if believing all that crap about me makes you feel good about yourself . . . well, all the power to you, I guess."

Rachelle's upper lip curled. "You're jealous."

"Here we go again." Ally rolled her eyes. "Get a life, Rachelle. I'm too busy to deal with your insecurities."

"You're jealous, *just say it!*"

"Yes, I want to slide into your skin and become you," said Ally dryly.

"You can't stand that I have Zeke! You can't stand that he wants me, not you!"

Ally could see that Rachelle either truly believed that or *wanted* to believe it—like it boosted her teensy-weensy ego or something. "Don't you see you're so deluded and crazy that it goes totally beyond crazy and enters a completely new dimension of crazy?"

Rachelle pounded her fist on the table. *"Admit it. You're jealous!"*

"Go home, Rachelle. I'm sick and tired of riding your crack-brained roller coaster."

That was when the dumb heifer lunged. Before Ally could do anything more than jump to her feet, Roni's hand snapped around Rachelle's throat and dragged the skank to stand in front of her.

Then several things happened at once.

Zeke flew across the table, ready to defend his mate, but had his path blocked by Derren and Marcus.

As Matt stood, Nick dived over the table and planted himself in front of the Alpha before he could move to help either Rachelle or Zeke.

Growling and snarling, the other Mercury males placed Ally and Shaya behind them and formed a protective wall.

"Don't fucking move," Roni growled into Rachelle's face. "You might be a Beta, but I'm more dominant than you are. You can sense it, can't you?" When Rachelle struggled and clawed at Roni's hands, the female enforcer just tightened her hold. "Fighting me would be stupid and pointless. Trust me when I say I've taken down tougher shifters than you."

"Let her go," growled Zeke, pointlessly attempting to get to the females.

Roni spared him a brief, uninterested glance. "Nah, I don't think I'm going to do that."

Again Zeke tried to shoulder his way past Derren and Marcus, so Derren shoved him back hard enough to make him almost lose his footing. "Your mate started this," growled Derren, "and now the other females will finish it."

Until then, Derren hadn't interfered—despite his protective instincts going crazy—because it wouldn't have been good for Ally. When a dominant wolf had their enemy right in front of them, they didn't ask someone else to defend them. They faced that enemy down or they submitted. Derren had had no intention whatsoever of making Ally seem weak.

"Nick . . ." Matt's voice was calming. "There doesn't need to be any violence here."

Nick bared his teeth at the other Alpha. "Tell that to your wolves."

Rachelle's voice was unsteady as she addressed the female collaring her. "This is between Ally and me."

"Then challenge me," dared Ally tauntingly, skirting around the wall of protective males. Shaya followed her, ignoring Nick's disapproving growl.

Instead of reacting to Ally's dare, Rachelle spoke again to Roni. "Ally's not even your pack mate."

Roni raised a brow. "Do I look affected by this?"

"Let her go," Zeke ordered.

"Ooh, will you stamp your feet if I don't?" Roni quipped.

When Zeke tried to reach his mate yet again, Derren spoke through his teeth, "Get back." Since Zeke was obviously a fucking idiot, he took a swing at Derren. Without so much as flinching, Derren caught Zeke's fist in his hand. "Wrong thing to do." Derren crushed the Beta's fist so hard bones cracked—forcing the wolf to understand who was more dominant. Only when Zeke's body lost some of its tension did Derren release him. "This is for the females to deal with."

"You expect me to watch them harm my mate?" demanded Zeke, cradling his injured fist with the other hand.

Marcus snorted. "Roni's not harming her; she's restraining her. My mate's version of 'harming' goes something like hanging her opponent by their own intestines."

Shaya sidled up next to Roni, glaring at Rachelle through eyes flashing wolf. "You don't come into *my* home and attack *my* friend. We gave you permission to step onto our territory provided there would be no violence. Yet, you dared to violate that promise—not to mention the rules of hospitality."

"Ally provoked me," accused Rachelle.

Shaya smiled. "No, she hit you with reality while you persisted in entertaining us with your bullshit story. You're good, but we *know* Ally. We know she's not the person you described."

Ally's entire being warmed at Shaya's faith and trust. Her wolf too basked in it.

"You *think* you know her." Rachelle licked her bottom lip nervously. "She's just fooling you."

Shaya gave her a pitiful look. "If you actually believe that, you're just fooling yourself."

"You don't know her!" shouted Rachelle.

"Oh, but we do."

Seeing how pissed Rachelle was that none of the Mercury wolves were buying her act, Ally smiled at her. "It's a bummer when no one believes you, isn't it?"

"Now, this is what's about to happen, Rachelle. Roni will release you." Ignoring Roni's pout, Shaya continued. "Two of my enforcers will escort you to your vehicle. Matt and Zeke will be close behind you with their own escorts. Then you'll leave here. You'll never, ever come back. And you'll never bother Ally again."

Roni went nose to nose with Rachelle. "If you do, I'll come for you. Whether Ally's staying with our pack or not, I'll come for you. I'm the last person you want tracking you down."

Fear oozed from Rachelle and slithered over Ally. She couldn't blame Rachelle for being afraid. She *should* be, since Roni was absolutely lethal and meant every word. Ally often sparred with the female enforcer, so she knew exactly how tough and brutal she could be. Not to mention vengeful.

Only once Rachelle had nodded as much as Roni's grip would allow did the female enforcer release her. Instantly, Roni and Marcus escorted a panting, red-faced Rachelle outside.

As Eli and Bracken began to lead Zeke away, Derren glared at the Beta. "Same goes for you. *Stay away from Ally.*"

"We wanted to make things right," swore Matt, shaking his head sadly.

"Maybe *you* did," allowed Nick, who was acting as Matt's escort. "But your Beta female didn't. She's made things even worse for you." And Cain would most likely go apeshit.

"Ally, I'm truly sorry for what happened today." Matt held up his hands when Nick growled. "All right, I'm leaving."

Derren went to Ally's side and tucked her hair behind her ear. "You okay, baby?"

Hearing that, Zeke's head whipped to face them. "Is *he* the reason why you haven't been answering my calls?"

Ally replied tonelessly, "I've been ignoring them because we have nothing at all to say to each other."

"And *you*"—Shaya jabbed her finger into Zeke's chest as she planted herself in front of him—"you're even worse than your mate. You think it's not obvious why you came here today? You miss Ally. You want her back in your pack because you want to keep her close to you all the time. You can't let go of her, even though you're mated and your feelings for Ally have dulled. When you care for someone, it's hard to switch it off—I get that. But trying to keep her near when you're mated to someone else is selfish and cruel."

Zeke didn't say anything, but his shoulders sagged slightly.

"Stop calling Ally," Derren rumbled. "She isn't yours anymore. Got me?"

The Collingwood Beta didn't answer, just let Eli and Bracken take him outside. Needing to *see* the threats to Ally leave their territory, needing that assurance they were no longer in close proximity to her, Derren followed them and sidled up to Nick. Only once the Collingwood wolves drove over the border did Derren's wolf settle.

Eli and the enforcers returned to the main lodge. Derren was just about to follow when Nick's voice stopped him.

"This isn't just fucking to you. Possessiveness is stamped all over your face whenever you look at Ally. You care about her, don't you?"

Yeah, Derren did. It was unexpected, since he wasn't the type to connect with people. But what was more unexpected was that he didn't regret or fear it. She was prickly, defensive, very cautious, and had a smart mouth—all of which he found kind of cute. Making her more appealing to him, she was strong, dependable, trustworthy, dangerous, brooked no bullshit, and helped others with no strings attached. It was a complex combination that fascinated him. "I'm keeping her."

Nick didn't seem surprised. "Does she know this?"

"After what happened at the Collingwood Pack, she's a little skittish." She didn't want to watch her partner find his true mate and leave her again. What Ally didn't understand was that Derren couldn't let her go, not for anyone. He'd chosen her. Marked her. She was his now. He'd need to make it clear he was serious without piling too much pressure on her. The problem was that Derren was too possessive of her to be subtle.

"So you want her to stay, be part of the pack?"

Derren arched a brow. "Is that a problem?"

"After what she did for Shaya and Roni, of course not. I owe her. Besides, I like Ally. She makes you live your own life. You've been my shadow for too damn long. Just because I saved your life doesn't mean you owe me yours. Being my Beta and protecting my family is enough."

"I didn't protect you at the funeral." He'd only thought of Ally.

"Because your loyalties are divided now. That's not a bad thing, Derren. A guy's female should always come first to him." Nick folded his arms across his chest. "Cain isn't going to like you being with Ally, whether he wants to claim her or not."

"He'll just have to fucking deal with it." Derren's wolf growled his agreement. Cain had an attachment to Ally and cared for her in his way, but that was all Cain was capable of feeling. Derren could give her more than Cain ever could. "The main problem won't be him, it'll be convincing Ally to stay. She likes to pack-trot." She'd obviously never felt truly settled anywhere. He'd have to work on changing that.

Nick snorted. "While you have Shaya on your side, it shouldn't be as hard as you think. Shaya adores her, and she doesn't want her to leave. Do you think Ally will be open to imprinting?"

"Maybe." But maybe not. He wasn't exactly a prince fucking charming. Wasn't smooth or easy to be around like Marcus. He doubted there was a person on the planet who could love him as he was. Also, being Beta meant that a lot of his time was taken up by his job, which was something that could make a female feel neglected.

Yeah, the chances of Ally choosing to imprint with him were slim. But those chances were still there. And he'd damn well take them.

"What if Cain gets here and says he's changed his mind and decides to claim her?" asked Nick.

"I won't step aside." There was no going back for either him or Ally. As far as Derren was concerned, Cain had missed his chance. Derren wasn't noble enough to give him another shot with Ally.

"Not even if she wants you to?"

"Not even then."

So when she woke up that night, fear in her eyes, Derren was there for her again, making her forget her nightmare and cry out his name. Afterward, he brushed his thumb along her jaw. "I'm keeping you, Ally Marshall." And she'd just have to accept it, because he wouldn't let her go. "You're mine."

Startled and spooked by that very sincere announcement that almost sounded . . . binding, Ally didn't speak for a moment. "Yours?"

"All mine. You got under my skin, became my obsession. There's no going back."

She swallowed nervously. "What do you want from me?"

"Everything you have to give. And I'll get it."

CHAPTER THIRTEEN

C ain's not your mate, is he?"

Ally froze at Shaya's words. It hadn't been a question; it had been a sure statement. Sitting on the rug of Ally's living area with Willow, Ally peered up at Shaya, who was lounging on the sofa. "How did you find out?"

"I've suspected it for a while now. See, Nick didn't claim me straightaway. The sexual cravings nearly drove me insane, and it was physically painful for him to resist the urge to mate. Even from day one, you never seemed to be suffering from any of that. Still, I wondered if the reason the mating urge hadn't come into place for you and Cain was that he's just not capable of any kind of connection. But if nothing else, you should have lamented that you'd never have your true mate. Believing Nick would never claim me made me feel dead inside. You never gave any indication that you were hurting."

"Derren assumed Cain was my mate, and I didn't correct him," Ally confessed. "I figured I'd be less likely to be targeted by members of your pack if people thought Cain was my mate."

There was no judgment on Shaya's face. "Understandable. Does Derren know the truth now?"

"No." Ally flinched as Willow whacked her leg with a rattle—apparently the pup didn't feel that Ally was paying her enough attention.

Shaya chuckled at Willow's antics before continuing. "You should tell him. You don't need to keep up the pretense now. The entire pack accepts you. They'll protect you with their lives after all you've done for us."

"I've tried to tell him." Ally pressed a button on the baby's wolf toy, making it howl. Willow chuckled in delight. "He cuts me off whenever I even mention Cain."

"That's probably because he's so possessive and determined to keep you."

"Yeah. I figured that. That's something I never saw coming." She hadn't thought he would ever feel that way about her. Although it had spooked her, it didn't scare her to the extent that she wanted to end the relationship. Self-preservation dictated that she leave him, but an ache built in her chest whenever she envisioned doing so. Her wolf went batshit crazy at the idea of leaving.

"How do you feel about it?" asked Shaya.

"Torn. A big part of me wants to see where things can go, but there's the problem that I don't know how *he* feels. I know he wants me to be with him, I know he's possessive. But he's never given me any indication that he cares for me."

Ever since his "I want everything from you and will get it" declaration a few weeks ago, he'd been focused on Ally so intensely and overwhelmingly that it was enough to unbalance her. But it was also a little heady having someone's complete attention on her. Still, being "obsessed" with her and caring for her were two different things.

Shaya snorted softly. "It's obvious that he cares for you. Derren's possessive of you to an extent that I didn't think he was capable of. He never stops touching you, is super protective of you. And he told Nick weeks ago that he intends to convince you to become part of our pack permanently—which I fully support, by the way. Derren's not reckless or impulsive. He thinks things through. If he's made this choice to keep you, then he's one hundred percent sure he means to imprint with you."

Derren hadn't mentioned imprinting to Ally, but for their relationship to be permanent they would need to eventually imprint on each other. Sure, there were shifter couples that didn't go down the imprinting route. But such a relationship never lasted, because their inner wolves would only be satisfied with total commitment on every level—physically, sexually, and emotionally. If they didn't get it, their wolves would sooner or later withdraw from the weak relationship and fight their human side for more.

Shaya crossed one leg over the other. "How do you feel about Derren?"

"Look, I'm a very self-aware person. I know I have plenty of flaws. I know I'm not very forthcoming when it comes to feelings or my past. I have constant nightmares and prefer sleeping outside in my hammock. I cook when I'm stressed—even if I'm not hungry or it's three o'clock in the morning. Being a Seer, feeling people's emotions all the time, means I sometimes get struck by a sensory overload, and so I'll have my days when I need space, time, and privacy.

"Derren is a very dominant, forceful, intrusive male who thinks my business is his and who is determined to have his own way all the time. But even though he pushes me to tell him things, he never pushes too hard—he shares with me so that I'll share with him. Even though he doesn't like any distance between us, he lets me have my space and privacy when I need it. And even though he very rarely gets a peaceful night's sleep because of me, he never complains or sleeps anywhere but beside me. How can I not care about the fucker?"

Shaya smiled. "It annoys you that he's dug deep and made a place for himself in your life, doesn't it?"

"Yes, because I didn't see it coming. I didn't think I even had the ability to let someone get that close to me again. Not after what happened with Zeke. But Derren wormed his way in."

"Derren can be sneaky and subtle in working to get what he wants."

Ally handed Willow one of her plush bears. "When Zeke set me aside, it stung even though I respected his mating. I think the worst part of it was that the rest of the pack set me aside too. I lost everything all at once. But I know that if Derren set me aside, it would hurt me more than *all* of that did. I don't think I'd recover."

"Aw, sweetie, you don't see it, do you?" Shaya came to sit next to Ally on the rug. "Derren's typically a hard person to understand. I'm not sure that anyone other than Nick and you can claim to really *know* him. But I do know that trusting others is something Derren finds extremely difficult to do. Trust is a lot more important to him than any other feelings. And he trusts you. That's huge for him. You've become important to him. Important enough that he's chosen you over his true mate. Don't run from that. Hold tight to it."

Shaya's advice stayed with Ally all day. And as Ally ate her evening meal she had to admit, even if only to herself, that she *couldn't* run from this thing she had with Derren. She didn't even want to. She cared too much for this person who trusted, respected, protected—though she didn't need it—and accepted her despite all her faults.

Walking away from him, pissing all over what they had, would not only hurt both of them but make her a coward. She'd never been a coward. Just because he might not care for her now didn't mean he couldn't grow to feel that way, did it?

"Where are you, baby?"

Pulled out of her thoughts by Derren's voice, Ally blinked at him. "Woolgathering."

His expression called her a liar. "Ready to leave?"

She blinked. "Already?" They hadn't had dessert yet.

"Yes, already."

Figuring he must want to talk about something without an audience, she rose from her seat. Having said their good-byes, they walked out into the warm evening. Without breaking stride he gripped her wrist, twirled her to face him, and yanked her against his body—forcing her to walk backward. "What's wrong?" she asked. He seemed surprised by the question.

"Nothing at all."

Ally slipped her arms under his and grabbed the back of his shoulders. "Then why did you want to get me out of there so fast?"

"I've hardly seen you today. I wanted to be alone with you. And I was close to hitting Bracken for flirting with you." Of course Derren knew that the enforcer would never poach. Unlike Dominic, he didn't take the flirting too far. But it was still irritating at times. "I don't share."

"Really? But you're not in the least bit possessive," she mocked.

"Such a little smart-ass."

A very un-Ally-like squeal left her as he abruptly slung her over his shoulder. "Hey! Put me down!"

Derren spanked her ass before giving it a firm squeeze. "No."

"Stop spanking my ass!"

"It's *my* ass. You should know that by now." He'd bitten and marked it enough times.

"I mean it!" It was impossible to sound firm and outraged when she was laughing. She smacked his own ass, but he didn't seem to care. "Derren, *put me down!*"

"I don't want to." Hearing a familiar chime, he dug his cell out of his pocket. "Shush, baby, while I take this call." Seeing "Unknown Number" flashing on the screen, Derren frowned. "Hello."

"Derren, it's me."

Derren halted abruptly. *Cain.* Not a voice Derren wanted to hear. His good humor literally fled his body, and his wolf snarled—as far as the animal was concerned, Cain was a rival. "Hey." The word came out guttural.

"I heard your pack's still having trouble." Danger dripped from every syllable.

Putting Ally on her feet, Derren met her knowing gaze—her shifter hearing had obviously picked up Cain's voice. "We know who the culprit is. It's only a matter of time before we have them."

"Good. How's my Ally?"

His wolf's ears flattened as a loud growl rumbled out of him. The animal did not at all like Cain's use of the word "my." Derren didn't like it much either. "Fine."

"Is she close?"

Close? She couldn't get much closer. "Yeah."

"Put her on."

Without a word, Derren held out the phone.

Taking it, Ally tucked her hair behind her ear. "Hello."

"How are you, sweetheart?"

A low but fierce growl built in Derren's chest at the endearment. His wolf curled back his upper lip, his anger almost palpable as his vicious temper threatened to take over.

Ally swallowed hard. "Good."

"Have the Collingwood wolves bothered you since you left their pack?"

"No. No, they've left me alone." Ally ignored the way Derren's brows lifted at the lie.

"How are things at the Mercury Pack? Is Derren taking good care of you?"

That was one way to put it. "I don't need protecting."

Cain laughed. "How did I know you'd say that? I can't talk long, sweetheart. But I'll be out of here very soon. Then we'll talk more."

"Okay."

"Put Derren back on."

Retrieving the cell, Derren gritted out, "Yeah?" With jealousy riding him, it took all of his control not to tell his friend to fuck off.

"She's lying to me," growled Cain. "The Collingwood fuckers have been bothering her."

"Yes," Derren confirmed, watching her wince at Cain's words.

"Don't let any of them harm her."

"I won't." Derren would kill them before he allowed that to happen. Not for Cain, but to protect Ally.

"I'm trusting you with her, Derren. Don't let me down." The line went dead.

Let him down? Derren was pretty sure he'd let Cain down the moment he first thrust his tongue inside her mouth. Didn't matter to him, though. It should, he knew that. But Derren *needed* her in a way that probably should have freaked him out. But he'd accepted it.

Ally cleared her throat and offered Derren a weak smile. *Well, that was awkward.* Of course, it wouldn't have been awkward if Derren weren't under the impression that Cain was her mate. Trying to keep her body language casual, she proceeded toward the lodge. His words almost made her trip over her own feet.

"Why hasn't Cain claimed you?" There was affection in Cain's tone as he spoke of and to her. It was obvious to Derren that the guy cared a lot for her—or, at least, as much as a sociopath was capable of caring for someone. She was a female that any male would be proud to have as his mate. Why the fuck would Cain decide against claiming her?

Ally flinched as flickers of jealousy, indignation, uncertainty, and possessiveness lashed at her, making her break out in a cold sweat. Derren might look the image of composure, but his emotions were in turmoil. *All right, truth time.*

She inhaled deeply as she spun to face him. "You want to talk about Cain? Good. Because I can finally make you hear what I've been trying to tell you all this time." Her next words tumbled out in a rush. "He's not my mate. When I first got here, I didn't feel safe—everyone but Shaya seemed to hate me. I figured I'd be safer if I didn't correct your assumption that I was Cain's mate. So go on, yell at me for not correcting you in the beginning."

She closed her eyes, not wanting to see the betrayal and hurt that would surely glimmer from his dark gaze. The flickers of his emotions suddenly cut off . . . it wasn't like he was numb, but as if he were so shocked that his emotions were on hold.

200

Peeking out of one eye, she found him staring at her, his expression completely blank. His eyes, though . . . they weren't so blank. There was something in them that told her to run. Not out of fear. No, she wasn't scared. But the primal instinct to run was there nonetheless, and her wolf was backing it up. Like the animal wanted Ally to challenge him, to make him work for . . . something.

Never one to ignore her wolf, Ally took off.

Thank God she was fast, because he gave chase. She rocketed through the trees, ignoring how the branches that fluttered with the breeze abraded the skin of her cheeks and her bare arms. Wildlife scrambled as it sensed two predators coming.

Ally knew Derren was gaining on her, knew he'd catch her soon. But it still seemed important to not make it easy for him, though she didn't understand why. She just knew that—

Motherfucker. A body clamped around her, taking her to the ground but rolling to cushion her fall. Derren positioned her flat on her back on the grass as his body pinned her in place. This time, she could sense his emotions. They didn't hurt her, they *lapped* at her—which was just weird, despite being a welcome change. The possessiveness was still there, and much more strongly than before. There was also determination, surety, surprise, and greed.

His dark-velvet eyes glittered down at her, filled with purpose and resolve. "You're not his," Derren rumbled. "Never were."

He bit her. Just leaned down and sank his teeth into the crook of her neck, making Ally gasp in shock and pleasure. At the same time, his hand snaked under her T-shirt and closed around her breast; it was a hold so possessive, she reflexively growled in warning despite how good it felt. He released a growl of his own, rebelliously gripping her tighter.

He licked over his mark before returning his gaze, now glinting with satisfaction, to hers. "I should have seen it. The truth of who you are to me was right in fucking front of me, but I didn't see it."

Ally shook her head a little. "What are you talking about?"

201

"You know. You're my mate, Ally." He went nose to nose with her. "And you're about to get claimed."

She shoved him hard, but he didn't move . . . except to nip punishingly at her earlobe. "Wait, hold on a minute."

"Are you going to deny it?" His eyes blazed down at her with fury. "Try. Fucking try."

She opened her mouth, ready to do just that. But she found that she couldn't. Something deep inside her wouldn't allow her to repudiate him. It made no sense. "We'd have known before now."

"Not while I believed you were meant for Cain." The moment she'd told him that Cain wasn't her mate, a *knowing* had hit Derren so hard his entire equilibrium had faltered. It was as if now that the truth was clear, the mating frequency was no longer jammed. Just as sure as he knew he needed food to survive, he knew she was his mate.

At first, he'd felt too shocked to emotionally process her words. Then she'd ran from him, snapping him out of his daze as she triggered every primal instinct he had to *take* what belonged to him and only him.

With confusion etched in every line of her face, she looked so vulnerable right then that his chest ached. "It's true, Ally. Part of you already knows it. You were meant for me." He saw the smallest glimmer of hope in her eyes, and he realized she wasn't fighting this because he wasn't what she wanted. She was battling it because she feared being wrong; she'd stopped trusting her own judgment. "Stop looking at the world through guarded glasses for just one minute, baby. Listen to your instincts. Don't *think*, Ally. *Feel*."

Ally might have tried once more to refute his belief, but her wolf was riding her so hard to claim him that it had to mean something, right? So she pushed aside her distrust in herself and the world around her . . . and there was the truth. That was when the mating urge kicked in—fast, furious, and leaving no room for thought.

Startling the shit out of Derren, she reared up and bit him. Not lightly, not even seductively. Her teeth abruptly pierced the skin, making it sting and throb and bleed. Then she sucked hard, and he realized something: she wasn't just biting him, she was claiming him. "*Fuck.*"

His control splintered. Using his claws, he slashed away her clothes, baring every inch of the body that belonged to *him*. He cupped her pussy, sliding one finger through her slick folds. "Already wet for me. Know why? Because your body knows it's mine."

It was instinctive for Ally and her wolf to snarl, to challenge his dominance. "No one owns me." She'd never admit it aloud, but the weight of his solid, powerful body on hers was somehow a turn-on. His face was a mask of utter determination, and his eyes were aflame with a savage need that thrilled her wolf. A claiming between true mates was reported to be wild, merciless, explosive, and no-holds-barred. Ally knew from just the look on his face that this one would be no exception.

"Wrong. I own every part of you." Hissing through his teeth as her claws raked down his back in warning, he drove two fingers inside her.

Ally gasped, curling her legs around him and grinding against his cock through his jeans. His mouth was hot on hers. Greedy. Consuming. She clawed off his T-shirt and skimmed her hands over his warm, defined chest; he grunted as the tips of her claws pricked his abs. Her need for him was a raw, blistering ache that was made all the worse by the fierce and violent urge to take, own, and claim. "Fuck me," she rasped against his mouth.

Derren wanted to be in her so badly he could taste it. Her delicious scent was now spiced with her arousal and twining around him, tempting and torturing him. In the confines of his jeans, his hard cock throbbed painfully. But he shook his head. "I'm not done with you yet."

"Then make me come."

"No."

Ally and her wolf stilled. *"What?"*

"You can come when you admit that you're mine."

The words were a taunt, a challenge, and a demand all rolled into one—and they pissed her off. She repeatedly punched at his chest. "Motherfucking piece of fucked-up shit!" In seconds, he had her wrists clasped above her head in one hand; his free hand was still finger-fucking her, and his rhythm hadn't even slightly faltered. "Let me fucking go!"

Ignoring that order, he drew her nipple into his mouth. Determined to torture her with pleasure, he sucked hard the way she liked it while plunging his fingers faster and deeper. She twisted and arched beneath him, alternating between moaning and cursing him.

When her pussy began to flutter around his fingers, he sent her a warning glance. "Don't come." Defiance flashed in her eyes, and he knew she didn't plan to fight her climax. He withdrew his fingers, which made her growl a string of profanities at him. He brought his face close to hers, pinning her gaze. "I warned you."

That rumble coated in dominance made her pussy quiver. "You're being a bastard!"

Call him crazy, but he fully approved that she was making him battle for dominance and the right to claim her. His wolf loved her strength, loved the fight in her. "Give me what I want, and I'll give you what you want. That's how this will work, baby."

As the asshole blew over both nipples, they tightened painfully. "I'm going to gut you."

"No, you're going to get ruthlessly fucked." He sank his fingers inside her again. "But there's a little something you have to do for me first." He sucked at a patch of skin on her neck. "This is where I'm going to mark you." His teeth nipped her skin, teasing her with what he'd soon give her.

She moaned as he licked over the imprint of his teeth. The warmth of his breath, the weight of his body, the graze of his chest against her tight nipples, and the feel of his fingers pumping inside her—it was all too much. Her release began to creep up on her again, and she did her best to hide it, but the irritating fucker sensed it.

"Say it, Ally. Say it or you don't get to come." He pulled out his fingers when she didn't speak. Of course, the luscious legs that were wrapped around his body then began to kick the shit out of him. So he bucked his hips, sharply grinding his cock against her clit. The move was enough to make her still with a gasp. "You know you're mine, Ally. You know it. All you have to do is say it. Is that so hard?" She squeezed her eyes shut and her mouth set in a grim line. Apparently his little Seer did in fact find it too hard to yield.

Derren sucked his fingers clean, groaning as her taste burst on his tongue. "Don't you want my cock in you? Don't you want me to give us what we both want?" No response. Releasing her wrists, he got to his knees and ripped open his fly. Her eyelids flipped open. Ah, that got her attention. She tilted her hips, offering herself. He fit the head of his cock in her opening, but he didn't push inside. "If you're not mine, I'm not yours." He smiled at her growl. "The claiming mark on my neck—it means nothing."

That pissed her wolf motherfucking off. Admittedly, Ally was just as infuriated by that comment. The bastard was hers. "You're such a fucking asshole." She was about to rear up and bite his shoulder punishingly, but he leaned forward and collared her throat, pinning her lower body to the ground. It didn't hurt, but his hold was firm and sure. That assertive display of dominance made her wolf settle rather than bristle.

"The only way I belong to you is if you belong to me." Derren fed her an inch of his cock but then quickly pulled out. "And you do. You're meant for me. Aren't you?"

Ally licked her lips and nodded once. It galled her to yield, but he'd outlasted her, earned the right to claim her.

"Good girl. But I need to hear you say the words. Tell me."

Awkward, demanding fucker. "I'm meant for you." Her back bowed as he slammed home, burying himself balls deep in her. He groaned as her pussy contracted around him, holding him there. Then he was punching his cock in and out of her. The muscles in his back bunched and flexed beneath her hands. His thrusts were so deep, rough, and hard that they hurt. But she didn't care; she wanted this, wanted to feel his vicious, frenzied need to claim her. She burned hotter and hotter, wound tighter and tighter.

His hand flexed around her throat. "This body and this sweet little pussy belongs to me. Always has, always will. Do you understand?" The claws pricking his back dug deep enough to break the skin, and he snarled in the back of his throat. *"Do you understand?"*

"Yes," she hissed.

"That's good." Releasing her throat, he threw her legs over his shoulders and powered into her. "All. Mine." Tangling his fingers in her hair, he snatched her head to the side and sank his teeth down hard into her neck, sucking, marking, and claiming. Her body bowed and then locked in place as a scream tore out of her throat and her pussy clutched and milked him. He slammed into her once, twice, three times, and then exploded deep inside her—marking her with his come just as he'd marked her with his teeth.

Then the world seemed to fucking tilt as pain sliced through his head only to be quickly replaced by warm, fuzzy feelings he wasn't interested in, because there was one other thing he could feel: *Ally.* He could feel her inside him, *outside* him; she lived in him now just as he lived in her. As expected, their bond wasn't fully formed yet. It took emotional "steps" to make that happen. But their link was still strong and distinct.

He rolled onto his back, taking her with him, watching the series of emotions that played across her face—emotions he could also feel through their bond. She was content, sated, and satisfied . . . and a little annoyed. "What is it?"

"We're so fucking stupid."

He chuckled, knowing what she meant. "We didn't have a hope in hell of sensing the truth any sooner."

He was right, Ally knew. They had both been too messed up by other things to sense it. The mating bond was . . . comforting. The brief pain had been quickly smoothed away by the tranquility and peace that had both calmed and gratified Ally and her wolf. And Derren . . . it felt like he was part of her, like he both filled and surrounded her.

Best of all, she could sense something she'd worried over for some time. "You care about me."

"Of course I care about you." Derren circled her claiming mark with his finger, loving to look at it and know she was irrevocably his. "I already made that clear weeks ago when I told you I was keeping you."

She frowned, sitting up to straddle him; his hands curved around her hips. "No, you didn't."

"Yes, I did."

"No, you said I was your obsession. That's not 'caring.'"

"I also said you were mine. I don't claim things or people, Ally. I'm protective of what's important to me. But I'm not a possessive person." He traced her hip bones with his thumbs. "But if you really need me to say the words, fine, I care about you." He knew the smile that curved his mouth was smug. "And you care for me." He could *feel* it.

Sensing an element of surprise mingled in with all that masculine satisfaction, Ally cocked her head. "You thought I didn't?"

"I thought it would take a lot of work on my part before you did. It was bad enough that I was a shit to you in the beginning. Add in that I'm pretty much an asshole, have an underdeveloped conscience, and I'm fucked up in too many ways to count, and I'm not exactly easy to care for."

"You're not an asshole"—she smiled—"all the time." His mock scowl made her smile widen. "It's true that you're an awful cook, have little room for error in your world, can be somewhat judgmental, and are a little too serious. *But* you're also extremely supportive, your word is as good as gold, and you own your shit to the extent that you actually verbally admit you're wrong—do you know how rare that is for a dominant male wolf?"

Sitting upright, he pressed a kiss to his claiming mark. In his opinion, he didn't deserve her glossy view of him. He was a selfish, aggressive bastard with a serious amount of baggage. But it didn't change anything; she was his mate, and he was keeping her. Would have kept her even if she hadn't been his true mate. "I know you find it hard to settle in places, baby. But you belong with me, which means you belong here. Now that I've marked and claimed you, you can't leave."

That commanding tone never failed to make her bristle. "Well, I *could*. But I won't leave, because I don't want to."

"Have you always had such a serious issue with authority?"

"Let's get something straight right now." She pointed hard at him. "You're Beta male here, yes. But you're not *my* Beta. You're my mate." He couldn't be both at once. Their relationship would never be peaceful if he tried.

Gratified by the latter fact, he smiled. "It's cute when you get all assertive." She'd make a perfect Beta female with her strength, dependability, and way of inspiring loyalty in people.

"Do you think the pack will be as shocked as we are?"

"I don't know. We'll find out tomorrow morning. For tonight, I want to be alone with my mate." He lifted her and poised her above his cock. "Ride me."

"Ooh, I like this plan."

CHAPTER FOURTEEN

The next morning at breakfast, their news was met with a stunned silence. Only one person claimed to have suspected that Derren and Ally were mates.

Draping his arm over the back of Ally's chair, Derren asked Kathy, "What made you suspect it?" The fact that *he* hadn't suspected it continued to gall him, even though he understood why.

At the stove, Kathy shook her head in exasperation. "Derren, I've known you a long time. I've seen how you relate to people, how you keep females you're dating at a distance. Though I suppose 'dating' is a generous word." She gave a disapproving huff at his past of casual hookups. "You treated Ally differently. You were protective and possessive, and when placed in a dangerous situation, your first thought was for Ally's safety. Your instinct was to protect her. Not Nick—your Alpha, friend, and pack mate—but a wolf who was technically an outsider until now."

"If I hadn't believed Cain was her mate," began Eli, "I would have suspected it."

An excited Shaya smiled at Ally. "I did start to wonder about it after our little chat yesterday morning."

Bracken looked at Derren. "I noticed you were pretty heavy with Ally, but I just figured you were pussy whipped." At Derren's growl, he shrugged innocently. "What? Just sayin'."

Stone, Shaya's human father and ex–Navy SEAL, who took utter delight in torturing Nick, laughed. "A little like my daughter's mate." He'd arrived for a visit early that morning and was extremely annoyed with Shaya for not alerting him to the danger the pack had been in.

"Well," drawled Nick, ignoring Stone's comment, "congratulations to you both. And welcome to the pack, Ally."

Shaya clapped. "I already considered you one of us, Ally, but now you're an official member."

That comment felt like sunshine on Ally's skin. She smiled. "Thanks." The warmth increased as everyone offered their congratulations. Her wolf was more than content with their acceptance.

Shaya grinned at Derren. "*Now* aren't you glad I argued to have Ally come here?"

Nick rolled his eyes. "Yes, baby, he owes his happiness to you."

"Damn right, he does," Shaya stated smugly before taking a sip of her coffee. "Roni will be glad to hear the news. She and Marcus have gone to Phoenix Pack territory."

"I didn't want them to leave," said Nick. "But Marcus hasn't seen them for a while, and they're family to him. It's difficult for him and his wolf to be separated from them for too long."

"It has to be hard to be caught between packs like that," mused Stone, feeding Bruce a slice of bacon. "I'm surprised he didn't insist that Roni remain here."

"Oh, he tried." Eli smiled. "In fact, he ranted at her to 'stay inside the main lodge where she'll be safe.' Roni just stared at him until he started squirming and gave in."

"She reminds me of Kye when she does that," chuckled Shaya, referring to Taryn and Trey's infant son, who was also her godson. "He never cries or shouts if you say no to him. He just stares at you until you give him what he wants."

Kathy took a seat, grinning. "It even works on Nick."

Affronted, Nick scowled. "No, it doesn't." But Shaya, Kathy, and Stone continued to tease him about it while they all ate, much to Ally's amusement. He looked close to strangling all three of his tormentors when his cell phone rang. He left the room to take the call. When he returned, both surprise and suspiciousness were wafting from him . . . acting like pinpricks to her skin.

"That was Donovan," Nick announced, garnering everyone's attention. "The hit on us and the Phoenix Pack has been canceled."

"Canceled?" echoed Bracken.

The Alpha male nodded. "Someone removed the bounty two days ago."

"You don't look relieved," noted Stone.

"It just seems too . . . easy."

"Well, I don't find it so shocking." Kathy stood and began collecting the empty plates. "Kerrie didn't seem to be having any luck getting people to cash in on the hit."

"I find it hard to believe she'd just give up." Derren toyed with his mate's hair, unable to stop touching her.

"Maybe she's decided to cut her losses." But Eli didn't sound particularly convinced.

Shaya sighed. "Whatever the case, at least there's no longer a bounty. That's something."

"We should still remain on guard," advised Derren.

"I agree," said Nick. "Now I'll pass on the news to the Phoenix Pack."

Once breakfast was over and she and Derren were strolling out of the kitchen, Ally said, "I guess we'd better get to work, huh." At the blank incomprehension on his face, she rolled her eyes. "I'm Beta female now. That means I have responsibilities to the pack, just like you." And she was hoping to ease Derren's load a little.

Surprised by her statement, it took Derren a moment to respond. "You don't need to help, baby. Not all Beta females take on responsibilities." Many did, but not all, because it wasn't an easy position to fill. "You already have a tough job." There was no one else in the pack who possessed any healing skills, which meant that not only did they rely on Ally for warnings of danger but also for her ability to heal. As that effectively made her their healer, she basically needed to be on call at all times. "I'd rather you saved your energy in case someone needs your healing skills."

Ally fisted her hands in his T-shirt. "You listen to me, Derren Hudson. I'm Beta female of this pack now, and I *am* going to take on the duties that come with that. Not just because I should, but because I want to." She pressed a light kiss to his mouth. "You're right that I can't afford to be tired when I might be needed to heal someone. But I can still help in some ways."

Pride filled Derren—his mate didn't resent his status; she accepted it and embraced the fact that it was a status she now shared. It deeply satisfied his wolf, who needed that acceptance of who he was. Derren cupped her face. "You'll make a good Beta female, you know."

She smiled winningly. "Of course I will. I'm awesome." He chuckled. Turning serious, she said, "I don't mind doing paperwork and monitoring the pack web, but I won't be able to work in an office without going stir crazy."

Pack webs were social networks and, just as a person's Facebook page might be exclusive to their friends—permitting only said friends to post on their "wall"—a pack's web page was exclusive to pack members. Packs were allowed to check out the profiles of other packs through the webs just like people could look at others' Facebook profiles.

"Can I work from our lodge?"

Derren licked over his claiming mark. "If that's what you want."

"If anyone from the pack has any problems, send them to me." Her voice turned embarrassingly husky and breathy as he sucked on the mark. "I'll deal with that."

She'd probably be a lot better at that than he would, he thought. He bit her lip and then licked over it to soothe the sting. "All right." He smacked her ass. "Let's get started."

Despite knowing how capable his mate was, Derren had wondered if she'd cope well with the duties she'd decided to take on, wondered if she'd still feel so strongly about them once she realized how mind-numbingly boring they could be. But each time he went to the lodge to check on her, she offered him a bright smile. She finished the paperwork in record time, updated and spruced up their pack web, and helped Caleb deal with a few minor issues he'd been too nervous to bring up to Nick.

When Derren finally returned to her at the end of a long day, they ate an evening meal together before going on a run in their wolf forms. For hours, the black wolf and the white wolf played, tussled, and lunged. On arriving back at the lodge, they returned to their human forms.

Later, lounging side by side in the hammock, Ally said, "I have a question. Since I'm part of the pack now, will I have to give up this place to move into your lodge?"

Although there was no reluctance in her voice, Derren knew that it would hurt Ally to give up this lodge that she'd made her home. She was relaxed here, considered it her haven. Although he'd miss his own lodge, he couldn't bring himself to ask her to give this place up. Besides, the only thing he needed was his mate—he'd go wherever she was happiest. "I was thinking I could move in here permanently, and we could make this our home."

Shocked, she asked, "Really?"

"I know how attached you are to it. Well, to the porch and hammock."

She laughed. "Thank you."

He took her mouth softly but still as possessively as always. "I have an ulterior motive."

His playful tone made Ally smile, since he wasn't a particularly playful person. She liked that he let his guard down for her. "Oh? What's that?"

"As much as your prickly nature amuses me, I like it better when you're happy, because then you're much easier to seduce."

She snorted softly. "You don't seduce, you take."

"I take what belongs to me." When she rolled her eyes, he chuckled and pressed a kiss to her temple. "Sleep."

Exhausted after a hectic day, she cuddled into him, closed her eyes, and drifted off.

Derren was in the middle of a dream about Ally covered in whipped cream when he woke up with a jerk as the hammock began to bounce. That was when he saw Ally darting inside the lodge like the hounds of hell were on her heels. Following her, he found her in the living area dialing a number on her cell phone. "Baby, what is it?"

She held up one finger as she put the phone to her ear. Knowing that something was very, very wrong, it took everything he had not to prod her for answers. Right now, she was in her "let me do this" zone. His wolf was on high alert, sensing her fear and wanting to protect her from whatever was causing it.

"Come on, Roni, answer," she groused as she paced. But Roni didn't. Ally dialed another number. Within moments, a voice greeted her on the other end of the line. "Jaime, has a red Chevy appeared at your gate?" asked Ally, frantic.

Derren could easily hear Jaime's response: "Yeah, it's an old contact of Trey's. He's on his way to the caves now. He says he's got information on Kerrie's whereabouts."

"Stop the car before it reaches you, Jaime! It's got a fucking bomb in it!"

Derren advanced on Ally, alarmed. *"A bomb?"* His wolf froze before releasing a low growl.

"I had a vision," Ally told a rapidly talking Jaime. "I'll explain all of it to you, I promise, *but first you need to stop that car.*" She ended the call to allow Jaime to do just that.

"Ally, what the fuck is going on?" demanded Derren.

Sensing that her mate was going to explode if she didn't quickly explain, Ally told him, "I had a vision in my sleep. I saw Roni, Marcus, and some of the Phoenix wolves in an underground parking lot. Roni and Marcus are on Phoenix Pack territory, so my immediate guess was that that is where it will happen. The wolves were all watching as a red Chevy pulled up. Instead of getting out of the car, the driver mouthed, 'I'm sorry.' Then he lifted a remote, pressed a button, and *boom.*"

"Fuck." Derren had visited Phoenix Pack territory many times, knew the parking lot was at the base of the caves and full of vehicles. If a bomb went off there, it could make the foundations of the caves crumble. One thing was for sure: it would have killed the wolves in the parking lot, which included Roni and Marcus.

Noticing that his mate was shaking, and *feeling* her distress, Derren cupped the back of her head and pulled her close. She locked her arms so tightly around him, it almost hurt. "It's okay, baby." He used his free hand to soothingly rub circles on her lower back. "It's okay."

"It felt so real." She buried her face in his chest, unable to spit the sickening death-filled images from her head. "I watched them fucking explode. Heard Roni scream. The fire . . ."

Derren rubbed his cheek against hers, sharing his wolf's need to calm and soothe her. "You saved them." Pulling back, he said, "Look at me, Ally." Her emerald-green eyes were clouded with the anxiety flooding her veins. "They're going to be fine."

She nodded, taking a calming breath, knowing she needed to pull herself together. "We should go tell Nick."

After washing and dressing in record time, they headed for the main lodge. Inside the kitchen, Ally had barely finished retelling her vision to the pack and Stone when Nick's cell phone rang.

215

"It's Trey," Nick told them after a glance at the screen. Putting the Phoenix Alpha on speakerphone, Nick immediately said, "Tell me my sister's unharmed."

"She's fine." Trey's voice contained a simmering anger that they all knew was directed at the bomber. "We stopped the Chevy before it got even halfway to the caves. To our surprise, the driver got out with his hands held up in surrender. He said his family's been kidnapped, that he received a call to say that if he didn't do as instructed, they would be killed."

There was no sympathy in Trey's tone. Clearly the Alpha was too enraged at the thought of his mate, son, and pack being blown to fucking pieces to feel anything but contempt for the male who had not only crossed into his territory under false pretenses but would have caused the deaths of so many.

Nick's brows drew together. "Wait, you're telling me the guy was a suicide bomber?"

"Shockingly, yes."

"That's some fucked-up shit," muttered Bracken.

"Was Kerrie behind this?" asked Derren, suspecting that she had decided to take matters into her own hands since her previous plan hadn't worked.

"He doesn't recognize her name," replied Trey. "He says that the voice on the phone was distorted but sounded male. Even if Kerrie hadn't made the call, she could be the mastermind behind it; she could have hired people to help her. We've no way of tracking his family before anything can happen to them."

Stone sighed. "I doubt they would have been allowed to live in any case—they're witnesses who could identify their kidnappers."

Derren was thinking the same thing.

"On one hand, I feel sorry for him," began Shaya, cuddling Willow close. "On another, I want to rip him apart for putting so many lives in danger."

Taryn's voice came on the phone next. "Hey, sweetie. I'm feeling the same. A part of me wants to force him to choke on his own testicles. But I know I'd do whatever I had to do to keep my family safe, no matter what it was. And it's hard not to feel a *little* sorry for him; he's so petrified of what will happen to his family that he's shaking."

"Thank your Seer for us," said Trey. "We owe her big-time. That bomb could have killed us all."

Derren blinked. "Wow, that 'thanks' didn't even sound begrudging." The Mercury wolves and Taryn chuckled.

Trey snorted. "Don't be an asshole all your life, Derren."

"He's just defending his mate," Nick told the other Alpha male with a smile.

There was a short silence. "They've imprinted?" asked Taryn.

It was Shaya who answered, her voice excited. "No, it turns out they're true mates."

"Really?" Taryn's smile was in her voice. "But I thought Cain—"

"Yeah, it's best if we don't talk about him right now," Nick interrupted on hearing Derren's growl.

Trey chuckled. "Congratulations, Derren, to you and your Seer."

"Yes, congrats!" added Taryn. "I know this is totally selfish, but could you wait until after all this shit is over before you have your mating ceremony? I really, really want to go."

Ally smiled. "We'll wait."

After thanking Ally and Derren profusely for being willing to hold off the ceremony, Taryn ended the call.

Eli turned to Nick. "It's doubtful that Kerrie could have kidnapped an entire shifter family on her own. My guess is she either hired people to help her or the kidnappers are friends of hers. Either way, it means there are people who know where she is."

"If no one's willing to give up her location for the reward, the person hiding her has to be someone she's close to," said Caleb. "A family member or boyfriend."

"Marcus said that, according to her family and pack mates, she doesn't have a boyfriend," Kent reminded him. "And both Donovan and Rhett confirmed that through their research."

"All I'm saying is that *someone* has to know *something*," said Caleb.

"But if it's someone who owes her, they might be willing to keep hiding her." Derren knew from his experience with Cain that owing someone could mean agreeing to a favor you might not agree with. "As a Seer, she'll have had visions that saved lives. They might feel indebted to her."

Hearing her cell phone ring, Ally retrieved it from her pocket. It was Roni, which brought a smile to her face. "Hey."

"*Why am I hearing from Taryn that you and Derren mated?*" demanded Roni, sounding a little hurt.

Ally winced. "I didn't mean for you to find out from someone else. I wanted to tell you in person."

When Ally left the room as she continued to attempt to placate Roni, Derren looked at Nick. "We need to find Kerrie fast. If she's behind that bomb, she'll send someone after us next."

Nick's jaw hardened. "But we'll be ready when they come. And we'll destroy them."

Shaya nodded. "And then we'll find and destroy *her*—and we'll enjoy it."

CHAPTER FIFTEEN

F ive days later, after unpacking the rest of his things in what was now his and Ally's lodge, Derren followed the smell of coffee downstairs and into the kitchen . . . just in time to watch his mate do a very feline stretch that made him want to slam her against the wall and thrust deep inside her.

His mate.

The shock of finding her still hadn't left him. He hadn't had many good things in his life, and he hadn't expected that to change. And he definitely hadn't expected the gift of finding his mate, particularly since he could be a broody, aggressive son of a bitch. He couldn't be prouder or more satisfied to discover that his mate was Ally—the female who'd showed him how to *live* when he'd forgotten what that was like. She made him play with her, swim with her, chase her, argue with her. It all invigorated him.

She accepted the dark places inside him, accepted his scars and his past. Moreover, she forced *him* to accept it all too. She had faith in him, saw a goodness in him that he wasn't sure was truly there. Despite the dark stories he'd told her about juvie, about the things he'd done to survive that place, she'd never once pulled away from him. Hadn't condemned him for going after Neil, for killing him, or for the fact that he'd never regret it.

There was never any judgment or horror with Ally. Never anything except total acceptance—so much so that she'd not only accepted him as he was but the position of Beta female as well. She'd fully embraced it, happily took on the responsibilities, and even trained with him, Eli, and the other enforcers every day to keep fit and sharp.

He wasn't sure he deserved the acceptance she offered, but he selfishly wanted it anyway.

The truth was that, even if she had tried to pull away from him, Derren wouldn't have let it happen. Even though he'd have understood it, he wouldn't have let her go. He couldn't—not now, not ever. She was too much a part of him, too vital to him; an anchor he hadn't known he needed but now knew that he couldn't exist without.

His wolf too was a total goner—he adored Ally. She was theirs, and God help anyone who ever attempted to cause her harm. Derren would slaughter them without blinking, and he wouldn't miss a second of sleep over it.

He understood now what his Alpha had meant when he once said that every emotion was magnified when it came to mates. Adoration, protectiveness, respect, tenderness, hunger, jealousy, possessiveness—they were all tied up in what he felt for Ally and were so unbelievably intense, because the mating bond amplified everything. And Derren knew there wasn't a damn thing he wouldn't do to protect that bond, to keep this person who was and always would be more important to him than anything else.

Spotting him, she gave him a smile that never failed to make his cock begin to stand to attention. "Coffee?"

"Do you really need to ask?" Pulling her close, Derren gently mashed his lips with hers. He thrust his tongue inside, tasting and teasing. Wanting that unique scent that was all Ally settled in his system, he buried his face in the crook of her neck. "You smell too good. Exotic and tasty and mine." Her blush made him smile. She could take an insult with a bored snort, could take a hit without a flinch, but a compliment? Too much for his little Seer to process.

"You smell better. Like oak bark, Brazilian coffee beans, and seriously hot sex."

Chuckling, he slid his hands down to cup that ass he loved. "Perfect." She winced slightly. "A little sore?" When he'd bent her over the sofa the night before, he'd spanked her a couple of times. Of course, his little Seer hadn't been too pleased about that—she'd cursed and clawed him. So he'd spanked her again.

She narrowed eyes that were glinting with amusement. "No need to look smug. And get your hands off my ass."

"How many times have I gotta tell you, baby? It's *my* ass." He let one finger slip gently between her ass cheeks, hating that her jeans acted as a barrier. "Has anyone had you here, baby?"

The question had a whisper of menace in it, and Ally knew it would have pissed him off big-time if she hadn't saved that for her mate like most shifters did. As it was, she *had* saved it for him. "No, they haven't."

Gratified, Derren swiped his tongue over her bottom lip. "Good girl. One day, I'm going to take this ass." He was rock hard just imagining it.

Ally wasn't afraid to admit to herself that she wanted him to do it. She was curious, and, like her wolf, she wanted him to claim her every way a shifter could. But Ally would still make him work for it. She sniffed. "Maybe."

Hearing the challenge in that one word, Derren smiled, rubbing his nose against hers. "You are the most—" Cutting himself off when he heard his cell chiming, he gave her ass a gentle pat before going to retrieve the phone from the coffee table in the den. Seeing that it was Marcus, he answered, "Yeah?"

"We have ourselves some visitors," drawled Marcus.

Derren stiffened. "Who?" If it was any of the Collingwood wolves, he was going to—

"Miranda and two of her enforcers." There was a wealth of

agitation in Marcus's voice. "They've all been checked for weapons and bombs, although she didn't like it much. They're all clear."

"Okay, well, call me when she's gone. I have no desire whatsoever to be in her company." Derren's comment made Ally shoot him a quizzical look from the kitchen. He held up one finger.

"She wants you to come. According to her, you're going to want to hear this." The line went dead.

Growling low in his throat, Derren looked at his mate, who, mug in hand, was crossing the room. "I have to go to the main lodge. I won't be long."

"Who's here?"

"Miranda and two of her enforcers."

"Huh." Ally placed the mug on the table. "Let's go then."

Not liking that idea at all, Derren scowled as his hand involuntarily tightened around the phone. For as long as the mating bond was incomplete, he would find it difficult to have others around Ally—particularly outsiders—as it created a lingering insecurity, making him more possessive and protective than ever. He wouldn't, couldn't, take any chances with her safety.

In honesty, he didn't believe Miranda was actually a real physical threat to Ally. After all, to attack Ally here would be the height of stupidity. Miranda was many things, but stupid wasn't one of them. Still, Derren didn't want outsiders around his mate right now. If that meant he was being irrational and paranoid due to their mating bond not being fully developed, fine. "Baby, you don't need to come."

"Probably not. But I am."

"*Ally.*"

"*Derren.*"

"I want you to stay here."

That Beta tone made Ally bristle, as usual. "And I want Rachelle to die a slow, horrible, excruciating death—preferably soon and in full view of me. Unfortunately, life doesn't always give us what we want." She almost smiled at Derren's exasperated growl.

"Miranda's a sly, cunning bitch, Ally."

"Of course she is. But she won't hurt me, and you know that, so stop being so dramatic." She cocked her head, her smile one of pity. "You know, you'd be a lot less stressed if you just accepted that I don't need you to protect me, since I'm no damsel in distress and all."

Derren cupped her jaw, his eyes flashing wolf as the animal wanted to make his simmering anger clear. "I know it pisses you off that I'm trying to protect you. I get it. You can protect yourself. I know that too. But, baby, there's been a lot of danger around our pack recently, and our mating bond is only partially developed. Give me a little room to be paranoid here."

Feeling her irritation slip away at his anxiety, Ally pressed a kiss to his chin, wanting to soothe both Derren and his wolf. "I'm glad you care so much, and I understand why you're worried. But don't you think I'm worried too? I know exactly how sneaky that bitch is, I know how much she wants you, and I know she thinks she's therefore entitled to have you. But both me and my wolf need her to understand that it isn't gonna happen." The bitch needed to see he was mated and off-limits. "You'd do the same thing in my position."

Unable to deny that, he ground his teeth. "I just want you safe."

"So do I, so I'm hardly going to put myself in danger, am I?"

Derren sighed, still opposed to the idea of her accompanying him but knowing she wasn't going to back down from this. Backing down was one thing Ally never did. That strength of will he admired and adored could also be a pain in his ass at times. "Fine. Let's go." His wolf raked his claws at Derren, unhappy with his capitulation even as the animal understood it.

Entering the living area of the main lodge a few minutes later, they found the Alpha pair and Eli, Roni, Marcus, and Zander scattered around the room. Miranda was lounging in an armchair, her two enforcers standing behind her. She smiled at Derren. "Glad you could join us, Derren."

She didn't acknowledge Ally, effectively dismissing her as unimportant—which wasn't at all surprising. Her jealousy and contempt scalded Ally's skin, almost causing a hiss of pain to slip through her gritted teeth. Seemingly just the mere fact that Ally *breathed* was enough to piss off Miranda. It was rather satisfying.

Derren led Ally to the spare spot at the end of a sofa and then stood alert beside her, his stance protective—a stance Miranda didn't appear to like. "What's this about?"

Nick replied, "Our neighbor says she has some info we should hear."

Derren arched a brow. "Really?" He wouldn't have expected Miranda, of all people, to have sought out information about Kerrie on their behalf. She wasn't the type to give a shit about other people's problems. Of course, it was highly likely that she wanted something in return.

"She believes you should be present for this, Derren," added Shaya, her suspicious gaze locked on the other Alpha female. He could understand Shaya's apprehension. There was just something not quite right here. His wolf was similarly uneasy, wanting this female away from his mate, despite his confidence that Ally could take her in a fight.

"Would you not prefer outsiders to be excluded from the conversation?" Miranda asked Shaya, shooting a meaningful—and disdainful—glance at Ally.

"Miranda, get on with it," urged Nick, waving his hand impatiently.

Bristling, she objected, "But it's your pack's business and—"

"You're trying my patience in a *big* way," Nick growled. "You asked for permission to cross the border, I granted it. You asked me to summon Derren, and I have. He's here. Now *talk.*"

Miranda straightened, her flawless face hardening. "As you wish. I appreciate that what happens within your pack and on your territory is of no one's concern but your own. However, I discovered a shocking fact and felt it was something you should know. Especially since there were attacks on your pack not so long ago. As neighbors, we should always look out for each other."

Nick narrowed his eyes. "And what is this discovery of yours?"

"You have no idea who you have in your midst. But I do." Again Miranda fleetingly glanced at Ally. "If you knew who *she* was, you wouldn't have her on your territory."

Wait, what? That was pretty much the last thing Derren had expected her to say. No, it was something that Derren hadn't *at all* expected her to say. His pacing wolf halted, peeling back his upper lip to expose his teeth and gums. Miranda was a hot button to the animal's vicious temper.

Miranda looked at Derren, eyes diamond hard. "And *you* certainly wouldn't have her in your bed if you knew the truth."

Derren couldn't help but growl at the insult, which made Miranda flinch in surprise. Through his mating link with Ally, he could sense that she was just as taken aback by Miranda's words, but her expression gave nothing away.

Miranda spoke to Ally then. "When we met here, I knew I'd seen you somewhere before, but I couldn't place you. It was only later that I remembered. You're the Holts' foster pup, aren't you?" Miranda nodded a few times, an ugly smile growing with each nod. "That's right, I know who you are."

The scorn coating every word pissed off Ally's wolf, who unsheathed her claws and took a swipe at Miranda. She wanted at the bitch who not only offended her but coveted her mate. Even though Ally didn't think it was a bad idea at all, she didn't give in to the urge to lunge at her. No, Ally wanted to see where the Alpha female was going with this.

When Ally gave her no reaction, Miranda turned back to Nick. "She may go by a different name, but she is—for all intents and purposes—a Holt, a Brookwell wolf. And we all know what that means. So, out of concern for your pack, I did some digging. Since becoming an adult, she's gone from pack to pack. Most likely acting as a spy, getting inside information to pass on to her criminal family. And now she has inside information about *your* pack. I'm sorry to say it, to be the one to tell you, but it's true. She's been fooling you all."

Miranda shot Derren a particularly sympathetic smile, though there was an element of smugness to it. And going by the expression on her face, she expected eternal gratitude from the Mercury wolves for her big reveal. Clearly she was under the impression that they now wouldn't want Ally here.

For a moment, there was complete silence. Derren broke it, his voice dry and cold. "Are you done?"

Miranda's face went slack. "You don't believe me? Or perhaps you haven't heard of the Holts, is that it?"

Shaya sighed, flicking her hand in a very regal movement. "You can go now, Miranda."

The other Alpha female shook her head. "You don't under-stand—"

"You're right, I don't understand," said Shaya. "I don't understand why you're trying to make trouble."

"Make trouble? That is the last thing I want. We're neighbors, not enemies. I have no wish to change that."

"Then why come here today?" demanded Nick, having gone from bored to angry. The male would take offense to anyone, even a close neighbor, insulting one of his wolves.

"Because the Holts cannot be trusted. Add in that she's a Seer, and, well, this female is naturally untrustworthy." Miranda's distaste clawed its way down Ally's arms. "I'm simply concerned about what this means for your pack."

"Well, your concerns have all been noted. And dismissed." Shaya turned to Roni, Marcus, and Zander. "Please escort our visitors to the border."

The three Mercury enforcers rose, but Miranda didn't move. "She could be a plant, learning your weaknesses!" Realization suddenly dawned on her. "You already knew who she was, didn't you? Does she have you fooled into believing she's not like the Holts?" Miranda looked to Derren. "You cannot possibly wish to have one of *them* in your bed!"

Before Ally could jump to her defense, Derren was talking—well, growling—with his eyes flashing wolf.

"Watch how you speak of my mate." His sentence ended with a snap of his teeth. His wolf backed him up with a lengthy growl.

Miranda gaped. "Your mate?"

"My mate," he confirmed proudly, possessively playing with Ally's hair.

"You know, Miranda," began Ally, "I don't think you're really in a position to judge Derren, considering you once did all you could to get into my uncle's bed."

A smile curved Shaya's mouth. "Really?"

Ally nodded. "Dan told me." Dan was the playboy of the family, and a guy known for having no standards whatsoever when it came to women. But he turned Miranda down, recognizing her for the twisted puppeteer of males that she was. The female retaliated by spreading false, insulting rumors about him.

"You think I wanted Dan?" Miranda scoffed. "It was the other way around. I have more pride than to jump into the bed of a Holt."

"Insulting my family really isn't wise. Unless, of course, you're trying to goad me into challenging you. I guess dueling with you could be fun." Ally's wolf *seriously* loved that idea.

Miranda laughed. "I'm an Alpha. You're a Beta."

"Do you have a point?"

"I can easily take you," sneered Miranda.

"You *could* if you were a born alpha. But you're not. I'd wipe the floor with you, and we both know it."

Miranda's eyes narrowed. "Are you threatening me?"

"I don't make threats. They're boring. I'm stating a fact. If you wish to challenge my belief, feel free to do so." Ally felt Derren tense beside her, and she understood that he wouldn't want her fighting with anyone whether he believed she could take them or not. Even though his unnecessary protectiveness annoyed her, it was nice to have someone who cared so much.

"You'd love that, wouldn't you? You'd love it if I challenged you here and now. Because then I'd have made an enemy of my closest neighbor." She shook her finger. "I'm not falling for that."

"Nice way to save face."

Roni nodded at Ally. "It is, isn't it?"

Casting a withering glance at Ally, Miranda turned her attention to Derren. "You have no idea what you've done, do you? You've sentenced your entire pack to death. Once the Holts' enemies realize their foster pup is here, they'll come for her. They'll use her against them—and if that means fighting their way through all of you to reach her, that's exactly what they'll do."

And Ally would bet that Miranda would take delight in ensuring those enemies became aware of her whereabouts. But there was something Miranda hadn't considered. Ally smiled at her. "You won't tell."

One overplucked brow slid up. "I won't? And why is that?"

Ally shrugged as she said simply, "Because you'll die if you do. I have a mate and a pack that will avenge anything done to me. Of course . . . that's assuming my family doesn't beat them to it."

Eyes flaring, Miranda made a derisive sound. "You think I'm scared of the Holts?"

"Yes, I do. And you should be. Because Cain would do everything he could to get to you first." That comment put a tint of fear in Miranda's eyes, just as Ally had expected. "If you think your pack could protect you from him, you're wrong. He wouldn't attack your wolves, because it would be *you* he wanted. You wouldn't even know he was there until his hand wrapped around your throat and snapped your neck."

Face flushed with rage, Miranda shot to her feet and glanced at her enforcers over her shoulder. "I think it's time we left."

"I think it's *long* past the time you should have left," said Roni, earning her a smile from her mate.

Spine straight, Miranda spoke to Nick and Shaya. "If you wish to have her as part of your pack, that's your business and I shall respect it. But I still believe you're making a grave mistake." Then she and her enforcers marched out while Zander, Roni, and Marcus acted as escorts.

Eli scratched the back of his head. "Well . . . I didn't see that coming."

"Do you truly think she won't tell anyone where you are?" Shaya asked Ally.

"I think Miranda loves her throne, and she won't do anything to risk losing it," replied Ally.

"That's a good point," conceded Eli.

Standing, Ally turned to Derren. "Come on, we've got Beta stuff to do."

"Actually," began Nick, "we were all thinking of going on a pack run. You game?"

Derren nodded, rolling his shoulders back to shake away his tension. "My wolf could do with a run."

"My dad will stay here and keep a look out for intruders," said Shaya. Stone was refusing to leave until all the danger to the pack was over. "If he sees anyone, he'll shoot once to signal."

As a thought occurred to her, Ally told Derren, "I doubt it's a good idea if I shift."

"Why?" he asked as he curled his arms loosely around her.

"Your wolf's even more possessive than you. I'm not sure he'd be rational seeing my wolf around the other males of the pack."

Derren sighed as he realized she could have a point. Rubbing his nose against hers, he coaxed, "At least come with us." If she stayed behind, he'd remain with her.

She thought about it for a moment. "All right. I'll carry Willow around so she can come along too."

After walking deep into their territory, the pack—with the exception of Ally and Willow, who wouldn't be able to shift until puberty—shifted into their wolf forms. Holding Willow in her arms, Ally kept pace with the wolves as they loped around, both playful and watchful. Her mate stayed close to her, repeatedly rubbing against her or licking her hand. His power, strength, and level of dominance were evident in his stature and the vibes he exuded.

Finally, the wolves all settled in a clearing. Some lay sprawled on the ground while others played and tussled. Ally sat with Willow between her legs, but the infant apparently had no intention of staying in place. She crawled away and was quickly circled by a red she-wolf and a large gray wolf—Shaya and Nick. She giggled each time the wolves gently nuzzled her.

A black wolf—Derren—alternated between wrestling with the enforcers and lying at Ally's side while she sank her fingers into his thick fur. The animal released a feral growl if any of the males, even his Alpha, got too close to Ally.

"I was right to stay in my human form then, huh," Ally said to the black wolf, knowing Derren would understand the words. "Next time, I'm shifting." Although going along on the run was satisfying for her and her wolf, it didn't soothe them the way it would if she were in her wolf form. The black wolf trotted behind her, disappearing from view . . . and then suddenly a naked male was wrapped around her, his front to her back. *Well, now.*

"Yes, you were right," Derren admitted, lapping at her claiming mark. "My wolf sees each of the males here as threats to our bond—even the mated ones." His wolf's jealousy was now worse than ever, which meant his mood was more temperamental than usual. Barely resisting the urge to clutch the breasts that were crushed beneath his arms, Derren told her, "He even gets jealous of the attention you pay to Bruce."

Ally chuckled, tilting her head to give him better access. He nuzzled her and inhaled deeply. "My wolf can get just as jealous."

"But at least she's rational."

"Well, there is that." She hooked one arm over his nape to thread her fingers through his hair. Ally relaxed into him as he practically enfolded his body around hers, touching and kissing her both soothingly and reverently. She closed her eyes, enjoying the sensations: A kiss to her jaw. Fingers playing along her collarbone. A kiss to her neck. A stroke of his hand down her arm. A nip to her earlobe. A lick to her claiming mark. A kiss to the hollow beneath her ear.

As he brushed aside her hair to nip and lick her nape, she said, "I don't think you're in a position to judge your wolf."

"What do you mean?"

She snorted at the innocence in his tone. "Don't think I don't know what you're doing."

"What?"

"You're making sure I'm wearing your scent."

Smiling against her nape, he admitted with no repentance whatsoever, "Fine, so I want you to smell of me." Just the same, he wanted his skin to smell of her. He brushed his cheek against hers. "Although I love your scent exactly how it is, there's one thing that would make it better: if it was mixed with mine." When the mating bond progressed a step, it would happen; their scents would twine and form a unique scent that would declare they were mated.

He wanted that, but he wasn't sure how to make it happen. The bond wouldn't fully snap into place until he and Ally were completely naked to each other—it was a form of surrender on both parts. For most couples, that often meant overcoming fears, accepting hard or painful truths, and exposing and moving past their personal scars.

Although he and Ally were working toward it, the progression of the bond wasn't something that could be forced or hurried. That pissed him off, because Derren wasn't a patient guy when it came to Ally—he wanted everything, and he wanted it now.

"Maybe your wolf will settle a little when he knows a single sniff will tell other males I'm claimed and off the market."

He doubted it, but one could hope.

"Maybe you'll be calmer too."

"I'm always going to be very possessive, Ally," he warned her, his hand cupping and shaping one luscious breast while no one was looking, loving her sharp inhale. "It's not part of my personality,

231

but it's who I am with you. You don't have to tell me it's not healthy to want to own you—mind, body, and soul. I already know that. And I already know it's not good to want to possess every part of you, to be all you need and want. But I do anyway." He narrowed his eyes at the large wolf that wandered too close. "Fuck off, Brack."

With a playful snap of his teeth that made Ally smile, the wolf bounded away—crashing into Jesse's wolf and then flopping onto the ground.

"Don't," she moaned quietly when Derren licked and nipped a particularly sensitive spot on her throat. "Not unless you want me to have an orgasm in front of all these people." As his arousal trickled over her and fed her own, she gasped. "Oh my God, a part of you likes that idea."

Derren laughed. "Like the idea that everyone can see how hard you come for me? Yeah, part of me does. But it's not something I'd ever let happen." He spoke into her ear as he discreetly pinched her nipple just shy of pain. "No one gets to see what you look like when you come but *me*." He punctuated that with a sharp tug on her neglected nipple.

She moaned inwardly when his mouth latched onto her pulse and sucked. "That'll change fast if you don't stop touching and teasing me right now."

"I'll stop before you can come."

Little bastard. "If you do that I'll fake an orgasm in front of all these people so they can see just what I look like when I have one."

He bit her jaw. "Hey, don't you ever fake orgasms with me."

She huffed. "I don't get why guys get so pissed when girls do that. Hell, your gender can fake an actual relationship."

His mouth twitched into a smile. "Oh, you're getting all huffy and snippy."

"I'm snippy pretty often."

"It's true that, emotionally, that's your basic setting."

"Why are you saying that with approval?"

"I like that you're prickly, because you're hot when you get all flustered. Even more so when you're angry." Seeing her worked up just made him want to fuck her until she was boneless and relaxed in his arms—and he often did. "I also like that I know what's under that testy, impatient exterior."

He would bet that many people would be surprised to find a great deal of softness and emotional insecurity under Ally's tough surface. The fact that he saw sides of her no one else saw, that she let herself be open and, in effect, vulnerable around him . . . it gratified and humbled him and his wolf.

"Just like I know what's under your serious, secretive, and relatively intolerant exterior."

"Yeah?" He arched a brow. "And what's that?"

"You have an unexpected playful streak." He fussed over Willow sometimes but never enough so that people could see past his solemn surface. "You can be quite a relaxing person to be around when you haven't got your guard up. *And* you've got an amazing singing voice. But don't worry, I won't tell anyone."

"It's not amazing."

"Oh, and there's that too."

"What?"

"You're quite shy when it comes to revealing your talents."

Derren nipped the tip of her ear, making her release a low yelp. "You really shouldn't tease me, baby. Not unless you want a repeat of last night."

Quietly, she hissed. "You spank my ass ever again and I'll—"

"Love it, just like you did last night." He chuckled at her snarl. "Hmm. It seems I have to prove it." And he did exactly that later that evening . . . which earned him a rake of her claws to his chest. The brand did nothing but satisfy him.

CHAPTER SIXTEEN

Y ou son of a bitch!"

Derren's eyes snapped open. Looming over the hammock, his face twisted with incredulity and anger, was a very familiar male wolf—and the last person Derren would have expected to see. Three other faces stared down at Derren, curious and grim.

Ally shot upright, almost tipping over the hammock. "Fuck. What are you all doing here?"

"What's *he* doing wrapped around you?" demanded Cain, fists clenched, his chest rising and falling with uneven breaths. This was going to be bad, Derren knew. A battle between him and Cain was inevitable, since the fact that he and Ally were mated wouldn't placate Cain much.

She raised her hands as she said softly, "Let's just all stay calm."

"Calm?" echoed Cain disbelievingly. *"Calm?"*

"Yeah, that would be good. Why didn't you call ahead of time to let us know you were coming? Uncle Wyatt," she growled at a shifter who clearly went for the cowboy look, "stop snarling at Derren."

"This is the guy you asked to protect her?" Wyatt asked Cain, his voice bland. "Hmm. I think he might have taken the bodyguard role a little too literally."

The second male, looking like he belonged on a *GQ* cover with his Armani suit and gelled hair, regarded Ally curiously. "You have a thing for Betas or something? I mean, you were with the Collingwood Beta not so long ago. And now you're involved with this asshole."

"Dan has a point, Ally," said the third—and seriously muscular—male. Hell, he was even bigger than Dante. "Well, Cain, your worry about this guy's bias against Seers was unnecessary. He seems very . . . *close* to our Ally."

"Don't make this worse," Ally hissed at the mountain of muscle.

Wyatt nodded. "She's right, Brad. We don't want Cain getting more worked up than he already is. Besides, Ally's a grown woman—if she wants to get involved with a wolf who took advantage of his friend's trust, that's her business."

Oh, these males were good. Derren could tell that they obviously wanted Cain to be totally riled and were doing their best to get him all worked up. And that was exactly what he was.

Cain glared at Derren, his eyes glittering with rage. "*You.* Get up." Then he backed off the porch and took a position on the grass, rolling his shoulders. "I'm going to shatter every fucking bone in your body!"

Ally placed her hand on Derren's leg, encouraging him to stay in place. "No, Cain, you have to listen to me." But Cain wasn't paying any attention to her; he only had eyes for her mate. Worse, Derren had hopped out of the hammock and was striding off the porch before she could stop him. Leaping to her feet, she got between them. "Cain, you need to hear me out!"

"In a minute, Ally. I want to deal with this motherfucker first."

"No, listen to me *now* before you do something you regret."

"I won't regret kicking the ass of this devious piece of shit, sweetheart." At Derren's growl, Cain arched a brow tauntingly. "Oh, you don't like it when I call her that?"

No, Derren didn't—and neither did his wolf; the animal raked his claws at this male who he perceived to be a threat to his bond with Ally. Derren found himself just as pissed. *No one would ever take Ally from him. She was his.* And he'd fight God himself for her if he had to. "She's not your 'sweetheart,' asshole."

Her mate's provocative tone had her spinning to face him. "Derren, what are you doing? I'm trying to keep this situation calm *and you're not helping.*"

Cain growled at Derren. "*I'm* an asshole? You were supposed to look out for her! Not use her!"

"Wait," Ally snapped at Cain, "it's not like that, he's my—"

"Dan, get her!" Cain signaled to his uncle.

Dan raised his hands. "Oh no, I'd like to keep my ball sack. You taught her too many dirty moves."

"I trusted you with her safety!" Cain shouted at Derren, baring his teeth.

Derren shrugged carelessly. "She's alive, isn't she?"

"You goddamn bastard!" Cain bypassed Ally and launched himself at Derren.

They met in a furious clash of fists, growling and snarling. Ally flinched at the sounds of fists meeting flesh, at each pain-filled grunt. Her anxious wolf paced within her, worried for her mate but also concerned for a wolf who had been her friend since they were pups.

"I don't think I've ever seen anyone bait Cain before," mused Brad, turning to Ally. "You couldn't have chosen someone who's, I don't know . . . sane?"

When Ally moved to part the brawling males, Wyatt blocked her path with his arm. "You know better than that."

She did. When two male wolves locked on each other like that, there was no separating them until they were ready. So she could only watch as they punched, shoved, head-butted, and charged at each other. She winced as Cain's claws sliced into Derren's bare chest, drawing blood. Her mate's eyes flashed wolf, and then the two males went at each other even more furiously than before.

It was only moments later that the Alpha pair, Eli, and the enforcers arrived, but a signal from Derren made them resist interfering. None of them looked worried on Derren's behalf as they stood back and watched—or surprised that a fight had commenced between the two males.

Shaya dashed over to Ally. "We didn't even know they were on our territory." She nodded in greeting at Dan, Brad, and Wyatt as she said begrudgingly, "You guys are good."

"Why, thank you," drawled Dan with a charming smile.

"I take it Cain doesn't have all the facts yet," Shaya said to Ally, sighing.

Shaking her head, Ally replied, "Cain's too worked up to listen. And Derren seems happy to fight him."

It pissed her off that Derren was fighting back rather than explaining the truth, but she had to wonder if her mate thought Cain deserved to get a few shots in, considering that Derren had pursued her before knowing they were true mates. Dumb but understandable for someone like Derren to whom loyalty was extremely important.

Or maybe Derren was fighting with Cain since he viewed the male as a potential threat to their mating and wanted to make his point that no one could come between them. She knew from her experience with Miranda that the need to ensure rivals understood a mate was off-limits was too strong for anyone to ignore.

Spitting out blood after a particularly hard uppercut from Derren, Cain pointed hard at him. "You shouldn't have touched her."

"Jealous?" taunted Derren, swiping the back of his hand over his bleeding brow.

Cain jerked back in abject horror. "What? *No.*" His tone said that being with Ally in a sexual sense would be like incest, but that only slightly mollified Derren's jealous wolf.

Derren shrugged. "Then I don't see how this is any of your concern."

"Ally is family to me. That makes her, and this, my concern." Then Cain was rushing at him again, his face a mask of anger.

Ally yelled, "Stop before one of you gets seriously hurt!" They didn't. They continued to brawl like two drunken bikers in a bar fight. The only difference was that they were also clawing and biting each other—and they weren't dressed in leather.

Pausing to snap his nose back into place, Cain grunted. "After today, I don't ever want to see your ass again, you two-faced fucker. And you'll stay away from Ally. I'm taking her away from here—"

Panting and sweating, Derren shook his head. "I can't let you do that."

Cain stilled. "What did you just say?" It was a menacing dare for Derren to repeat himself. It made her uncles wince.

"I'll rephrase. I *won't* let you do that. Ally stays with me."

"Do you want me to kill you, is that it?"

"You could give it a shot."

"Don't think you can stop me from leaving with—"

"*You* can go wherever the hell you like, I really couldn't give a fuck. But Ally stays. She's mine." It was a possessive rumble that seemed to surprise Cain with its intensity.

Still, the male scoffed. "Yours?"

"We're mates, Cain!" shouted Ally, her stomach hurting at the sight of Derren's busted lip, swollen jaw, clawed chest, and the gash on his brow.

Cain completely froze, falling silent for a moment. "Mates?" The eye that wasn't swollen shut darted repeatedly from her to Derren. Then Cain tipped his bleeding chin at Ally's neck. "Show me."

When she tugged at the collar of her T-shirt to reveal her claiming mark, she said, "There. See? He wasn't betraying your trust or disrespecting your friendship. This isn't some casual fling."

"You're mates?" He looked at Derren. "You aren't using her?"

"We're mates," confirmed Derren. "That's as far from casual as you can get."

"So you didn't touch her until you realized you were mates?" When Derren didn't answer, Cain lunged at him again.

"Cain!" growled Ally. As the males wrestled each other to the floor, she threw her hands up in the air. "Goddammit!" She marched into the lodge, reappearing only moments later with a bucket. As she slung the contents over the two males, they both jumped apart and got to their feet.

"You drowned me in ice-fucking-cold water," said Cain in pure disbelief.

"Yes, I did." Ally strode over to him and forced herself to speak calmly. "Now listen to me, hear me out. I know you're just looking out for me. I know you don't want to see me used or disrespected. I appreciate all that, I do. But . . . you can't hit him again."

"Why not? I like it." He sounded like a child sulking over his toy being taken away.

Smiling a little, Ally replied, "Because I kind of like him in one piece. Not bleeding and bruised."

"He broke my trust."

"Probably because on some level he knew I was his mate and the draw was there." She'd felt the draw from moment one; she simply hadn't understood the source of it.

It was clear to Derren that her attempts to placate Cain weren't working well; he looked eager to pounce on Derren once more. "Come at me again if you want. But it won't change anything. She's mine and I'm keeping her. I'll never let anyone take her from me."

A muscle in Cain's bruised jaw ticked. "She can do better than you."

"I won't dispute that."

"Hey!" complained Ally, not liking Derren putting himself down in any way. A silence descended as both males stared at each other, their expressions inscrutable.

Cain spoke first, pointing his finger hard at Derren. "If you ever hurt her, I'll shove a pole so far up your ass you'll feel it in your throat. You got me?"

Frowning thoughtfully, Derren tilted his head. "Not really, since that's physically impossible." As expected, Cain snapped with a roar and charged at him again.

Ally yelled, "Cain, not his nose!"

Half an hour later, Derren was wincing as Ally none too gently placed her hands on his wounded chest. His mate had *ordered* him into their lodge, and everyone had followed them inside and were now scattered around. After giving both him and Cain towels to dry off with as best they could, she'd ordered them to sit at the table.

Cain was opposite him, in no better shape than Derren. She'd delayed healing both of them, pissed at Cain for not listening to her and pissed at Derren for provoking Cain rather than aiding her in keeping the situation calm. Basically, she blamed Derren for his own injuries.

Even as her healing energy hummed through his bones, reaching each of his wounds as her hands slid over him, he could feel her anger. The last thing he wanted was for her to be upset in any way. Cupping her nape, he pulled her down for a brief kiss that was both possessive and apologetic. Her taste calmed him and his wolf. "Now I feel better."

Ally just humphed, not ready to forgive him yet. Although she understood that Derren wasn't someone who backed down from a challenge, no matter the circumstances, she didn't have to be okay with it. Once her mate was healed, she moved to Cain, pretty much slapping her hands over the deep slashes on his arm. He barely winced, which pissed her off even more. "When were you released?"

Cain glanced at her sideways before going back to glaring at Derren. "Yesterday. We slipped away last night to come for you and take you someplace safe."

"Ally stays with me," Derren stated firmly yet again. Cain growled his displeasure, but he didn't contest Derren's claim this time.

"Were you followed here by the humans?" Nick asked Cain, his arm draped over the back of Shaya's chair.

Cain grimaced at the Alpha. "Don't insult me."

Tapping her fingers on the table, Shaya asked, "Why sneak onto our territory? We wouldn't have turned you away. You're Ally's family."

"We like the challenge," Brad told her.

Shaya leaned back in the seat, running her gaze along the uncles. "If you three think of Ally as family, why was it only Cain who reacted so badly to seeing Derren with her? My father would have torn apart any guy who touched me."

It was Wyatt who answered, shrugging. "She's mated."

"But you didn't know that at first," said Shaya.

"Sure I did. From where I was standing, his claiming mark was easy to see." Brad and Dan nodded, indicating they'd also seen it.

Ally gaped at them. "And you didn't think to help me explain this to Cain and stop these two idiots from fighting?"

"Just because we can accept that you're mates doesn't mean we like the look of any male wrapped around you like a clinging vine," said Brad.

Dan nodded. "He needed to fight for you, prove he could protect you."

Ally sighed, turning to Shaya as she pulled away from a fully healed Cain. "I don't understand men."

Shaya patted her hand. "I'm not sure we're supposed to, sweetie."

"You might be right." Wetting two cloths, she gave one to Derren and the other to Cain so that they could wash away any blood or dirt. Each male then slipped on one of Derren's clean shirts, though Cain wasn't too happy about it.

"Be fair," Cain said to Ally. "He didn't exactly try to explain the facts to me. He seemed pretty damn happy to fight with me. Some of the shit he said was like waving a red flag at a bull."

Roni cocked her head, her irritated gaze on Cain. "Did you know that bulls are actually color blind? It basically means they'll charge at any cape, no matter the color."

"*Roni.*" As usual, Marcus's rebuke was filled with amusement.

She blinked innocently. "What? What did I say?"

Derren smiled, understanding that Roni, being protective of Derren, was annoying Cain on his behalf. "But you forgive me for baiting him, don't you, baby?" he asked Ally.

Not really, but she'd have him make it up to her later with multiple orgasms. Hearing Cain and her uncles growl, Ally smiled weakly at Derren. "I said that out loud, didn't I?" He just chuckled.

Sighing, Cain turned back to Ally. "Okay, now that you've healed us, why don't you tell me everything that happened between you and the Collingwood wolves? I want the whole story."

She took the seat on Derren's left, and he immediately threaded his fingers through hers. "It's resolved now. Forget it."

Cain snorted. "You know better than to think I'll even consider letting this go. Tell me."

"I don't want you to lose your shit and do something drastic."

"You know I'd never assassinate an entire pack in retaliation for something a couple of wolves did."

That was the thing, though. The entire pack had turned on her. Although their betrayal hurt, she didn't think buying a skank's lies warranted death. "I'm away from there now. It doesn't matter anymore."

"They don't deserve your protection, Ally," insisted Roni, unwrapping a lollipop.

Derren looked at his mate, understanding why she was reluctant to share the tale but knowing it was important that her family knew. The Holts might not be her biological relatives, but DNA didn't make family. "Either you tell them or I tell them."

She gaped. "Thanks, Judas."

"I get that you don't want the Collingwood Pack to be under a mass attack, but your safety is more important to me than theirs. That's what it boils down to." Derren wished he could be sure that Rachelle would quit bothering Ally, but the kind of hatred that female harbored for his mate didn't just evaporate.

With a resigned sigh, Ally nodded. She told them everything, from Rachelle's very first accusation to the visit the skank had made with Zeke and Matt to Mercury Pack territory a little while ago.

When she was done, all four Holt males were scowling. "What a fucking bitch," spat Cain. "And this Zeke guy is no better."

"The Alpha's a shithead too," stated Dan. "He should have protected you."

"They need to pay," growled Brad. "All of them."

Ally waved a nonchalant hand. "They're not important compared to the whole 'having a bounty over the pack's head' business." When her uncles and Cain looked at her, puzzled, she smiled wanly. "You didn't know about that, huh."

"A bounty?" echoed Brad.

Derren explained everything before adding, "The bounty has been lifted, but we don't believe the female who put out the hit on us is done."

After a moment of pensive silence, Wyatt declared, "We'll stay until this is all resolved."

"We don't know how long it will take for that to happen," Ally told him.

Wyatt seemed unmoved. "Holts protect their own, Ally. You're our family. We're here for you until you're safe." Brad, Dan, and Cain nodded.

"Then I guess we'd better set you all up in one of the guest lodges," said Shaya.

Within minutes, the Alpha female was ushering everyone out of Ally and Derren's lodge, intending to lead the Brookwell wolves to their temporary accommodation. Although Cain had left without delivering any more insults to Derren, he still hadn't looked any happier about Derren's claim on Ally.

Surprisingly, it had been the elegant-looking, cultured Dan who had growled a warning at Derren before leaving: "You *will* be good to her. Or I'll come for you. Believe me, you don't want that." Derren had a feeling that Dan was much more dangerous than he looked.

Closing the door behind everyone, Derren pulled Ally to him and pressed a kiss to her throat. "Still mad at me?"

"Maybe a little." But she was sliding her hands up his solid chest to curl them around his neck. "I get that it's instinctual for you to protect our mating and that you don't back down from a challenge—"

"It wasn't just about that, baby. I had to make Cain understand that things will be different from here on out." He nipped her lower lip and then laved it soothingly. "He's been your protector all his life. He thinks he has rights to you. I need him to understand that *I'm* your protector now, that you belong to me and I have no intention of giving you up. If I hadn't stood up and fought him today, if I hadn't made my place in your life and my claim on you very clear, he would have tried to take you."

Unable to deny the truth of that, Ally inclined her head. "Fine. But no more fighting with him. I don't want either of you hurt."

Derren might have been jealous of her regard for Cain, but he and his wolf had come to understand something after watching their interactions today. "He's like a brother to you, isn't he?"

"Yes. He's always looked out for me the way a brother would."

"You sort of anchor him, bring out a little of the old Cain."

"He'll always be part of my life to some extent," she warned Derren. "Always feel he has some rights where I'm concerned because, well, he isn't normal."

"As long as he understands you belong to me, I can accept that." It was only today he'd realized that somewhere in the back of his mind he'd worried about her relationship with Cain. Not that Derren believed there was even the slightest possibility that the guy was her mate. No, but Derren knew she and Cain were close. She'd known him since childhood, had gone through a horrific event with him, and had had him as her protector all these years. Something like that could form a very strong bond, and Derren had worried that said bond was stronger than what he had with Ally, given that their mating link wasn't yet complete.

But Derren no longer had that concern. She'd tried to protect him from Cain's anger, had defended his honor, and had *proudly* declared they were mated. Even the mere fact that she'd healed Derren before she'd healed Cain indicated that he came first to her. Derren needed to know that he was as important to her as she was to him, that their bond, despite being incomplete, was still stronger than any she might have with anyone else.

He cupped her face, staring into those almond eyes he loved. "I didn't think anything could be this essential to me." Intellectually, he'd known his mate—if he ever found her—would be important to him in every way. But he hadn't imagined that such an incredible *depth* of emotion was possible for anyone to feel, particularly him. There was something else he'd been wrong about. "I always figured that love was sappy and gooey. But it's not." What he felt for Ally was a feral, hissing, clawing, boundless emotion that probably should have scared him but didn't.

Her features softened, turning vulnerable. "You love me?"

He smiled. "Fuck yeah."

"I'm glad, because it's rare for one-sided relationships to work out well."

His smile widened. "Is that your very poor way of telling me you love me?"

"It *was* pretty poor, wasn't it?" Rubbing her nose against his, she said, "I love you." With a rough groan, he brought his mouth down hard on hers. Fingers digging into her hips, he held her flush against him as he dominated and consumed her mouth with every stroke of his tongue and every nip of his teeth. Need unfurled, inflamed, and fired through her body fast and furiously.

Shoving his hand under her T-shirt, Derren tugged down her bra and cupped one firm breast. It fit perfectly in his hand, reminding him that she was made for him. She was his. Would always belong to him. And he knew he would never have been whole without her.

He tasted her, caressed her, and breathed her in—igniting and filling his senses with her. His body tightened with the molten lust that was ripping through him, making him need more. "I want you slick for me."

The breath rushed out of Ally's lungs as he backed her into the wall, caging her there with his broad, powerful body. Literally clawing away her jeans and panties, he then clamped his hand around her pussy, pushing up against her with his palm.

"You're already wet," he rumbled. "But I want you even slicker." He slipped one finger inside her, loving how hot she was. "Take off the T-shirt and bra, Ally." She obeyed without hesitation. "That's my girl." Swooping down, he flicked her nipple with his tongue. Threading her hands through his hair, she arched toward him, hinting for more. He gave her what she wanted.

Ally groaned as his hot mouth latched onto her nipple, and he drove another finger inside her. Thrust. Suck. Thrust. Suck. Thrust. Suck. The rhythm was torture. And when that rhythm sped up, a relentless, raw ache began to build deep inside her pussy. Wanting his skin against hers, she bit out, "Shirt. Off." She jolted as he scored her nipple with the edge of his teeth.

"I'm busy, baby."

"Take it off or I'll rip it off." Two dark brooding eyes met hers; both were alive with heat, hunger, and caution—he didn't like her issuing an order.

Refusing to be intimidated, she bit his lower lip. "I want to touch you." His eyes flared, and she knew she had him. Withdrawing his fingers, he whipped off his T-shirt. But before she even had the chance to experience a moment of triumph, a strong hand roughly tangled in her hair hard enough to make her scalp prickle.

"You know I don't like it when you give me orders." He also knew that was exactly why the little minx did it. Holding her head in place, he tugged her bottom lip with his teeth and then drove his tongue inside her mouth to stroke hers. He licked, sipped, and bit. She tasted of everything he wanted and needed, of sin and sex.

A growl rumbled out of him when she sucked on his tongue, conjuring images and fantasies in his mind. She knew damn well what she was doing. Pulling back, he tore open his fly. "I need your mouth."

Ally licked over his lower lip. "You have it."

"I need it on my cock." She hadn't yet sucked him off, since dominant females did oral sex on their own terms and in their own sweet time. She'd licked him a few times, teasing him with what she would one day give him, and he'd known she wanted him to be so desperate for it that he'd eventually do exactly what he was doing now—lose control.

"Oh, you do?" she drawled, not at all liking the expectancy of obedience in his expression. Her wolf wasn't too pleased about it either.

"Yes. I want your mouth." The words came out harshly through clenched teeth, and her mesmerizing eyes narrowed dangerously.

"Yeah? Well, I want to fuck."

"And you'll get fucked . . . when I've had what I want. You're mine. This gorgeous mouth is mine. And I want it." Using the hand bunched in her hair, he pushed down, urging her to drop to her knees. She didn't. "*Now*, Ally." He felt like he'd go out of his goddamn mind if he didn't feel that plush mouth around him right then.

Ally arched an imperious brow. "Or what?"

"Or you don't get fucked." When she would have objected, he growled. "This is what you wanted, baby. You wanted me to need this so bad I couldn't take it anymore."

He was right, she had. And the dangerous glint in his dark gaze told her she'd teased him past the point of endurance.

"On your knees." She did nothing other than stare at him defiantly. He growled, "Do it." Ever so slowly, she dropped to her knees. The defiance didn't leave her gaze, and *fuck*, that just made it a million times better. "Very good." Rewardingly, he brushed his thumb across her lower lip. "Open up, baby."

Fisting the base of his long, thick cock, Ally opened her mouth . . . but only enough to deliver a catlike flick of her tongue to the head. His warning growl made her smile. Although she opened her mouth a little wider, she only lazily laved the head before lapping up the pearl of pre-come there. And apparently her mate had had enough, because she sensed the feverish tension that had tautened his body simply *snap*.

Tightening his grip on her hair, Derren snatched her head back. "*Don't* tease. I want those lips wrapped around me, so do what I fucking told you and *open up*."

That order, which rang with dominance and authority, should have pissed her off. But knowing she'd driven him past the edge of his control made self-satisfaction settle low in her stomach. Her wolf kind of liked it too. The moment she opened her mouth wide, he surged inside.

Derren groaned as the burning heat of her mouth finally enveloped his cock. It felt too fucking good. Seeing her there on her knees, his cock in her mouth, her nipples hard, and her defiant stare boldly meeting his while the scent of her need cocooned him . . . it was all enough to make him almost explode right then. "Suck." She swirled her tongue under and around him as her head bobbed up and down his cock. "That's it, baby. Fuck, that's good. Take more." He used the hand in her hair to guide her movements, urge her to move faster and suck him deeper.

Another groan was wrenched out of him as the head of his cock bumped the back of her throat. Instead of panicking as he'd expected, she relaxed her jaw and swallowed. "Good girl." As her throat contracted around him, he felt the telling tingle at the base of his spine and knew he wouldn't hold out much longer.

Then she glided the edges of her teeth along his length, trailing it with her tongue, and Derren's release barreled into him. Just as he was about to burst, she tugged on his balls. *"Son of a bitch."* He erupted into her mouth, watching with utter bliss as she continued to suck and swallowed every last drop—it was yet another way to mark her as his, and it made his wolf release a satisfied growl.

Gently pulling her to her feet, Derren brushed her hair aside. "Thank you, baby. You definitely deserve a reward for that." He kissed her, capturing her breathy, needy little moans as she rubbed against him almost frantically, desperate for relief. "Shush. I'll give you what you need." Cupping her ass, he lifted her. She curled her limbs around him as he carried her to the bedroom, where he gently laid her on the bed.

Ally watched as he quickly took off his shoes and jeans, his eyes on her pussy. When his hands slid down her thighs, she shook her head. "No tongue, no fingers—I want your cock." A cock that was quickly reviving, most likely directly in response to the scent of her unanswered arousal. "You said I'd get what I want when you got what you want."

"But I want your taste on my tongue."

Spoiled motherfucker. Ally swiped a finger through her slick folds and then offered it to him. A wicked smile curving his mouth, he sucked her finger clean. "Now you have it." She shot her hand out and curled it around his cock. Again and again, she stroked him with a firm, possessive grip, knowing exactly how he liked it.

Thick, hard, and aching with the need to be in her, Derren tugged her hand away and flipped her onto her stomach. Grasping her hips, he pulled her onto her knees. "Keep your head down, baby."

Ally jerked forward as he slammed into her, burying every inch of himself in one swift, smooth thrust—no warning, no finesse, no preamble. It was exactly what she wanted. His pace was frenzied as he pounded into her with deep, powerful, branding thrusts that drove every thought from her mind and sent pleasure whipping through her.

She tensed as his hands parted her ass cheeks and one wet finger circled the ring. "Derren . . ." That finger then gently pushed inside, causing a burn that was somehow both pleasure and pain.

"I'm going to take you here, Ally." He punctuated that by thrusting his finger in and out.

Of course, it was pure reflex for Ally and her wolf to challenge that dominant tone. He must have sensed that, because one strong hand slipped around her throat in a very possessive and cautioning grip.

"You're mine, Ally," he ground out, still hammering into her. "That means this mouth, pussy, and ass are mine to fuck." Her pussy was so hot and slick around him, squeezing and quivering—nothing had ever felt better. "I'm going to come in your ass, claim it. And you're going to love it, baby, I promise you that. I just need you to relax for me, okay? You want this."

She did want this, so she forced her body to relax as he inserted a second finger into her ass. At first it stung, but then the burn spread and became pure pleasure, making her pussy throb—much like when he spanked her. By the time he added a third finger, she was so far gone the pain barely registered.

As the thumb of his free hand found her clit, Ally moaned. With his cock pounding into her pussy, his fingers thrusting into her ass, and his thumb circling her clit, she was more than ready to come. Then it happened. Bliss flooded her veins, making her pussy ripple and spasm as she plummeted hard into an almost painful release. It was right then that he snatched his fingers out of her ass and replaced them with the head of his cock.

"Relax, baby." Derren rubbed her lower back. "Push out as I push in. Remember, you were made to take me." Little by little, his cock slid into her ass, and he loved the feel of it stretching around him. He was so damn close to coming it wasn't even funny. When he was finally balls deep inside, he groaned. "So fucking hot and tight. You okay, baby?"

"I'm fine." It wasn't a lie. Sure, it hurt. But not enough to make her want to stop. "Get moving."

Very slowly, Derren reared back and then smoothly slid back inside. Over and over, he did that, determined not to cause her any pain. Through their bond, he could feel that, although there was a slight sting of discomfort, she was enjoying it. When she tried throwing her hips back at him, he upped his pace. Soon she was moaning and squirming, and he began pumping his hips, giving her what he sensed she wanted. His cock was pulsing and throbbing with the need to explode, to give over to the pleasure it promised.

Draping himself over her, he spoke into her ear as he returned his thumb to her clit. "I want you to come for me, Ally. Let me feel it, baby." He slammed in and out of her ass as he circled her clit, wrenching groans and gasps of his name from her throat. "Now, Ally, I need it."

Sinking his teeth into her nape and pressing down hard on her clit with his thumb, Derren threw her into her second release, and her mouth opened in a silent scream. Her ass clenched so tight around him it almost fucking hurt. He rammed into her one last time, groaning as his cock shot jet after jet of come into her ass, claiming and marking it as his.

When his brain finally rebooted, he carefully slipped out of her body and crashed on the bed beside her. For a while, neither of them spoke as tremors rocked them. Derren kissed her shoulder. "You okay?" One eye slowly flipped open, and she nodded. He smiled at the sight of his mate, boneless and fully sated.

Something made his smile widen in both wonder and surprise. "Baby, what can you smell?"

Frowning at the odd question, she shrugged a little as she mumbled, "Sex."

"What else?"

Inhaling deeply, she stilled. Opening her eyes, she returned his smile. "Our scents have mixed." Her wolf stretched out inside her, content and a little smug.

"At fucking last." He pressed another kiss to her shoulder, sharing his wolf's intense gratification. "Now you'll always smell of me, and everyone will know you belong to me."

She rolled her eyes. "Like you'd ever let them forget."

He chuckled. "I did warn you the possessiveness probably wouldn't fade."

"The bond's a little stronger now. More vibrant."

"Good." Dragging himself to his feet, he scooped her up. "Shower."

"I don't think I can stand."

"Yeah, I'm sensing that." So he kept her cradled against him as he turned on the spray and stepped into the stall. "I love you, baby." It was a lot easier to say than he'd expected. She gave him a shy smile that plucked at a heart he hadn't been sure he had.

"And I love you. For a while, I had a hard time believing I'd ever say that to anyone. That I'd ever feel that way."

He'd had the same doubts. He still doubted his ability to make her happy. "I'm going to piss you off a lot, Ally. I'm going to mess up, say the wrong things, be crazy jealous, and annoy the shit out of you with how overprotective and interfering I can be. But I'll never take you for granted, never purposely hurt you, and never betray you in any sense of the word—I swear that to you."

Melting at that statement, which was about as romantic as her mate was ever capable of being, she smiled. "Same here. Please note that I'm going to drive you equally insane. We'll clash and we'll argue sometimes. But that doesn't mean I'll ever care about you any less."

"That's good, since you're stuck with me." At her chuckle, he added, "I'm serious, Ally. You're mine. Everything you are belongs to me. I'll never give you up."

She arched a brow at his dominant tone. "If I wanted to leave, I totally could."

"You're always going to challenge me, aren't you?"

"I'm so thrilled we got that cleared up."

CHAPTER SEVENTEEN

W hy can't we find her?" Nick paced up and down in front of
the sofa, his frustration drumming at Ally's skin. Derren,
who had positioned her between the *V* of his legs on one of the
armchairs of the living area, curved his body protectively over
hers—as if he could feel her discomfort through their bond.

Nick's mood was understandable. A week had gone by and
still no one had come forward with any information regarding Kerrie's location. It was wearing on everybody. Other than
Zander and Jesse, who were on patrol, the whole pack had con-
gregated in the main lodge to discuss the matter and hopefully
come up with fresh ideas.

"You offered a reward for her capture or any information on
her whereabouts." Cain sliced off another piece of the apple in his
hand with a small knife. "So if no one's given her up, she's being
hidden by someone who's either family or who owes her."

"That's what Derren said." Nick scrubbed a hand over his
face. "But her relatives claim they haven't seen her. According to
Marcus's sister, who belongs in the same pack as Kerrie, the Seer
has saved their pack from conflict many times. A lot of people will

feel they owe her for saving their lives and those of their children or mates."

Lounging on the sofa, Bracken spread out his long legs. "What I find odd is that she hasn't issued a personal attack on us. She sent a suicide bomber to the Phoenix Pack, but she's left us alone."

"It could be that she's trying to make us think it's all over, wants to lure us into a false sense of security so she can take us off guard," suggested Caleb.

Kent tilted his head, his expression thoughtful. "Or maybe she really has given up. Maybe her failure to bring down the Phoenix Pack has made her totally back off."

"I seriously doubt it," said Stone, scratching Bruce behind the ear. "To go as far as to put a hit out on this pack *and* the Phoenix Pack indicates a *lot* of rage—and a huge grudge. That depth of emotion doesn't just disappear. In fact, I'd say her failure has fed that rage and made her more determined to see her plans through to the end."

Derren nodded, skimming his fingers up and down Ally's arm. "Her plan to keep Marcus from recognizing Roni as his mate ultimately failed. Her plot to make Roni leave Marcus before they could mate also failed. Her current aim to destroy Roni and Marcus hasn't worked out so well either, and I get the feeling that someone like Kerrie wouldn't be prepared to fail again."

On the sofa, Marcus massaged Roni's nape. "In her warped mind, Roni and I need to be punished. Her rage is *our* fault."

"I really should have killed that bitch when I had the chance," said Roni.

Marcus kissed her cheek, a slight smile curving his mouth. "I love that little vengeful streak you have." His mate just rolled her eyes.

The sound of the kitchen door opening was quickly followed by the entrance of Jesse. "We have visitors. Miranda and two of her enforcers are heading toward the border."

Shaya, who was cradling a sleeping Willow, sighed in annoyance. "Great, we can look forward to the company of yet another woman who has a big issue dealing with rejection."

"After how her last visit ended, I'm surprised she's come back," said Jesse.

Shaya looked at Kathy. "Could you take Willow upstairs, away from this vile woman?"

Happily taking her granddaughter, Kathy said, "Of course." She promptly disappeared, obviously not wanting Willow around Miranda any more than Shaya did.

Ally turned to Dan with a smile. "This should be fun for you. You remember Miranda Whitney, right?"

His brows pinched together. "Miranda Whitney?"

"Yeah, the female wolf who spread shitty rumors about you when you rejected her. She recognized me as part of your family, told the Mercury wolves that they should kick me out."

Realization flashed in his eyes. "Oh, you mean Miranda Moore. She's Alpha female of her own pack now, right?"

Ally frowned, glancing over her shoulder at Derren. "I thought it was Whitney."

"It is," Derren confirmed.

Dan held up a finger. "It *was*. But after she had a huge fallout with her parents, she left her pack and changed her surname as a sort of 'fuck you' to them."

Disowning and rejecting them before they could disown and reject her; Ally understood.

"What's wrong?" Roni asked Marcus, who Ally then noticed was stiff as a board.

As his body seemed to lose a little of its tension, Marcus clasped his hand around Roni's nape. "This could be purely a coincidence . . . except I don't believe in coincidences."

"What?" Derren prodded.

"Kerrie's surname is Moore." Marcus's revelation was followed by a bemused silence.

Stone spoke first, his focus on Marcus. "You think she could be related to Miranda?"

"Derren, call Donovan," ordered Nick. "He'll find out within seconds."

When Ally stood to allow him to rise, Derren kissed her temple. "I'll be back in a minute, baby."

Once Derren had left the room to make the call, Nick began pacing again. "If Miranda's related to Kerrie, she could be protecting her."

"Not necessarily," said Shaya. "Miranda doesn't have a relationship with her parents anymore, which means it's possible she isn't in contact with any of her extended family either."

Stone told Nick, "Shaya's right." But the Alpha male didn't appear convinced.

When Derren reentered less than a minute later, Nick immediately pressed, "Well?"

Derren clenched his fists. "Kerrie and Miranda are cousins." Curses rang throughout the room, and Nick resumed his pacing

"That doesn't mean they have a relationship," Shaya maintained. "I'm not saying I think they don't, I'm just saying we shouldn't act on this until we know for certain."

Raising one finger to signal for silence, Marcus dialed a number on his cell phone. "Hey, Teagan, did Kerrie ever mention a Miranda Moore to you? Okay, thanks. Possibly. I'll call you again later." Returning his cell to his pocket, Marcus spoke, his tone hard. "According to my sister, Kerrie was visited occasionally by a Miranda who's an Alpha female. That's all Teagan knows. But it's enough to tell us that our suspicions are correct."

Eli spat a curse. "She could have been hiding Kerrie on her territory all this time. *Practically right under our noses.*" He looked ready to go on a killing spree, and Nick and Roni looked ready to join him. "The night Miranda came here to ask about the grenade, it wasn't out of concern or even to fish for gossip," Eli continued. "She wanted to check just how much we knew about the attack, if we were aware of the hit, and if we suspected Kerrie."

Shaya nodded. "On her last visit, she wasn't trying to get rid of Ally because she was jealous over Ally's claim on Derren. Miranda knew that if Kerrie had our pack assassinated while Ally was part of it, the Holts would retaliate."

"And that The Movement would join us on the hunt for the culprit," added Cain. "We wouldn't have stopped until we found and destroyed Kerrie and anyone who aided her." His uncles muttered their agreement.

"So it's more than likely that Kerrie has been hiding next door all along." Nick shook his head in disbelief, a growl rumbling in his chest.

"Smart, really," conceded Ally begrudgingly. "I would never have thought she'd stick so close."

Derren retook his seat with Ally and nuzzled her neck. "It's ballsy too."

"Or just plain crazy," said Bracken with a shrug. Ally had to agree.

"Miranda's risked a lot by protecting Kerrie," pointed out Eli.

"Fucking bitch," ground out Nick. "Miranda might not have put out the hit on us, but hiding Kerrie makes her an accomplice."

"Are we sure that Miranda is hiding her? It makes sense," Caleb quickly added before Nick could oppose his comment. "And I agree it's very, very likely. But we still don't know for certain."

"We'll know for sure soon enough," Nick replied, his smile crooked and a little evil.

"Here she comes," said Kent, who had been peeking out of the window. He skipped back over to the sofa and sat next to Caleb. Moments later, Jesse and Zander escorted Miranda and her two enforcers into the living area.

Rising, Shaya flashed her a welcoming smile that held no hint of the distaste that grazed Ally's arms like a bristle sponge. "Miranda, what a pleasant surprise."

"Thank you, Shaya." Miranda's smile was just as wide. And just as forced. "I was worried there would be some ill will after my last visit." She looked from Shaya to Nick as he went to stand beside his mate. "Please understand that I was just concerned for you and your pack."

"We get it," Shaya assured her.

Miranda's friendly gaze traveled around the room but narrowed ever so slightly when she found Ally snuggled up against Derren, who was tracing her claiming mark. The female's spite coiled tight around Ally's chest. "I'll say what I should have said last time I was here: congratulations to both of you on your mating."

Neither Ally nor Derren thanked her for those so obviously insincere words. Ally's wolf was equally unhappy to see the bitch; she wanted to dive at the female and rake her claws across her face. The thought had some appeal. When Miranda's narrowed gaze landed on Dan, she froze, and a red, angry flush crept up her neck and face. "A Holt family reunion. How cozy." Settling gracefully into an armchair while her enforcers stood behind her, Miranda again forced a smile for Shaya. "As you can imagine, I'm still terribly worried for all of you. Even though the attacks on your pack have stopped, it's still disconcerting to know that the people responsible are out there."

"It's sweet of you to worry, but we have this under control."

Miranda arched a brow. "You have captured the culprits?"

"We have." Shaya leaned forward, as if about to confide something interesting and important. "It turns out, though, that the shifters who attacked us didn't actually have a *personal* problem with us. In fact, someone put a hit out on us. Can you believe that?"

Miranda stilled. "Really?"

"The hit has been canceled now, which is no doubt because anyone who attempted to attack us didn't live to tell the tale."

Alarm briefly flickered through Miranda, prickling Ally's skin, as the Alpha female asked Shaya, "Do you have any idea who is behind the hit?"

"We do. The shifters we captured knew enough to point us in the right direction. Turns out it's a scorned woman."

"A . . . scorned woman?" Miranda's alarm became full-blown panic; it smothered Ally like tropical humidity.

"A Seer," elaborated Shaya. "She doesn't like that Marcus mated our Roni. She's jealous." Ally noticed that Miranda's enforcers stiffened and suddenly looked very uneasy.

"I see." Miranda licked her lips nervously. "I'm guessing, then, that you have a name?"

"Yes. It's only a matter of time before we find her, don't you worry."

"That's good." With a brittle smile, Miranda stood. "Well, I should be going."

Shaya also rose to her feet. "So soon?"

"I have a busy afternoon ahead." Miranda turned to leave . . . and almost crashed into Eli. What she hadn't realized was that Eli and the Mercury enforcers had subtly moved to gather behind her and her own enforcers, intending to obstruct their path to the exit.

"You're not going anywhere just yet, Miss Whitney," Eli told her. "Or should I say . . . Miss Moore?"

Marcus tilted his head. "You wouldn't be related to Kerrie Moore, would you?"

"Who?" Miranda sounded appropriately confused.

"She's the Seer we're looking for," explained Shaya, her smile now gone. When Miranda turned back to face her, Shaya added, "But you already know that, don't you?"

"We always thought it was likely that a family member was giving her sanctuary," rumbled Nick. "I have to admit, I hadn't suspected that it might be you."

"You have this all wrong," Miranda claimed. "I wish I could help—"

"That's good," said Roni. "That's very, very good. Because you can help, can't you? *Where is she?*"

"I do not know any Kerrie M—"

"Cut the shit," spat Eli. "We know she's your cousin. We know you used to visit her at her pack."

Miranda sighed heavily. "That much is true," she finally admitted. "But I have no idea where you can find my cousin."

Still curved protectively around his mate, Derren told Miranda, "When you lie, you purse your lips." The bitch's mouth then set into a hard slash as she glared daggers at him.

Nick advanced on Miranda, growling. "Tell us where Kerrie is."

Swallowing hard, she lifted her chin. Despite looking like a cornered animal and being the target of an entire pack's anger, Miranda still maintained a haughty, antagonistic edge. "I'll want something in exchange."

Nick laughed at her nerve, but there was nothing pleasant about the sound. "This isn't a negotiation. You *will* tell us where Kerrie is." His voice hardened. "All this time you knew what was happening, you knew your cousin was responsible for the hit and the subsequent attacks. But you didn't warn us. You didn't aid us. By siding with your cousin and protecting her, you're against us." She didn't speak, just returned his stare defiantly.

"How many males in your pack are eager to take over your position as Alpha, Miranda?" Derren asked, playing his fingers across Ally's collarbone.

"I'll bet there are plenty," added Eli. "Hell, I'll bet even your enforcers here think themselves capable of it. They'd relish the opportunity to fight the other males for the position. And let's face it, you haven't been a great Alpha, have you?"

Miranda gasped, flushing. "How dare you!"

"You cast out every strong female, not wanting any threats to your throne," began Derren. "Any male who claimed a dominant female as his mate was forced to leave for the same reason. Those who were cast out often took their extended families with them. All of that not only meant your numbers dwindled, but that the males had to either seek sexual contact outside the pack or fall into your arms. You basically treat that pack as a stable of stallions for yourself."

"How many times did you lead on one of the males, let him believe you might make him your Alpha male, only to then cast him aside?" asked Eli. "I'm guessing it was pretty often."

Nick spoke then. "Considering you haven't been much good as an Alpha female, I don't think your pack would care all that much if you suddenly . . . disappeared."

"Do not think to threaten me," she hissed through clenched teeth. "Your submissive mate isn't a match for me." Shaya actually snorted at that, not looking at all offended.

Nick smiled. "You're right. Shay's stronger than you'll ever be—and certainly a better Alpha than you could ever hope to be." Miranda's eyes flared with a simmering anger that scalded Ally.

"But it's not Shaya you need to worry about," promised Roni. "It's me." No one wanted Kerrie caught and punished more than Roni did, and Miranda was in her way.

One of Miranda's enforcers cleared his throat to catch everyone's attention. He cast his fellow enforcer a brief look before speaking. "Clark and I can take you to Kerrie."

Miranda whirled on them. "Do not dare betray me, Jason!"

"Everything these wolves said is right," Jason said to her, looking defeated. "Our pack was strong until you took it over. We've watched friends leave because of you. I don't want to see any others leave. And I don't want to be forced to go one day just because I might have been blessed to find my mate and she turned out to be dominant."

"All that aside," began Clark, "betraying our neighbors like this . . ." He shook his head. "It's wrong."

Nick didn't appear totally convinced that their sudden willingness to cooperate was authentic. "If that's how you both truly feel, you can tell me what I want to know."

Jason nodded. "Kerrie's on our territory." Miranda gasped,

bringing her hand up to cover her mouth. Ignoring her, Jason went on. "She's been staying in one of the guest cabins."

"She's obsessed with getting vengeance," said Clark. "We thought about coming forward sooner, but . . ."

"But you'd pledged an oath, and it felt wrong to dishonor it," finished Shaya, her tone one of understanding, though her facial features were still etched with infuriation.

Jason straightened his shoulders. "We caught the foxes that shot the grenade on your territory. We . . . disposed of them."

Nick inclined his head. "It's appreciated."

Miranda went to lunge at her enforcers, but Jesse caught her and held her back as she ranted and raved at them for betraying her. She was screaming so loud that Willow woke up, at which point Shaya looked close to diving on her.

"Jesse, put this bitch in the toolshed," ordered Nick. Jesse immediately—and happily—obeyed. Miranda could still be heard screaming from outside the lodge.

"We ask that you don't punish our pack for Miranda's actions," said Jason.

For a moment, Nick remained silent. "You would need to leave this lodge without your Alpha female." It was clearly a dare. Any reluctance by them to do so would indicate that their loyalty still lay with her. "And you would need to vow that your pack will not challenge ours to avenge her."

"There will be no challenge," swore Jason, to which Clark nodded.

"And we want Kerrie," stated Roni.

Again, Clark nodded. "We'll take you to her. It was never our wish to give her sanctuary."

When Nick raised a brow at Ally, she knew he was asking if they were being truly sincere. "You can trust them on this. They're being honest," she assured him.

"All right then. Jason, Clark—wait outside while I have a quick talk with my pack." Nick didn't speak again until the enforcers shut the kitchen door behind them. "I'm not willing to rely on these guys handing Kerrie over. Not that I don't trust your judgment, Ally, I do. And I think Jason and Clark genuinely want to get rid of Miranda. But there's no saying the rest of their pack will feel the same. One of them might warn Kerrie before we can get to her. I won't risk that."

"I'll go with them," offered Marcus.

Roni sidled up to her mate. "Not alone you won't." When an odd expression crossed Nick's face, she glared at him. "Do *not* go all overprotective on me right now. I *need* to be part of this."

The Alpha male sighed at her in resignation. "Fine. You, Derren, Marcus, and I will go with Jason and Clark. We'll get Kerrie and we'll bring her back here to deal with her and Miranda together." Nick addressed everyone else as he said, "If something goes wrong, we'll howl."

It was no secret that Ally wasn't the most patient person in the world. The fact that she was also worried for the safety of Derren and her pack mates meant that she was beyond edgy as she took Bruce for a short walk through the trees near the border of Miranda's territory, waiting for them all to return. She was hoping to catch a glimpse of her mate making his way back, but she was also hoping to walk off her pent-up restless energy.

Her wolf was just as anxious, pacing and flexing her claws. She didn't like being apart from her mate at the best of times. Being apart from him while it was possible that he could be walking into danger wasn't something her wolf was handling too well. Ally had asked to go along, but Nick had said that it was important to him that Shaya and Willow were adequately protected. And Derren had backed him up. Not for Shaya and Willow's sake, she knew, but because he didn't want Ally walking with him into what could be a dangerous situation. He was being his usual over-protective self.

It was annoying, but it was also comforting to have someone who put her first like that. For so long, Ally had been close to a nomad—flitting from place to place, never putting down roots. She'd never felt "home." Until now. She felt settled, like she fit in somewhere, like she belonged. But it wasn't being part of the Mercury Pack that made her feel that way. *Derren* was home, *he* was her safe place, and *he* settled her.

Hearing a short, doglike yelp, she froze. That was when she noticed that the dog was nowhere in sight. "Bruce?" All she heard was a heavy thud. Torn between following the sound and signaling for—

Ally flinched as a sharp sting struck her neck. *Son of a bitch.* For a moment, she thought she'd been stung by a wasp or a bee. Then, as she brought her hand up to her neck, she felt it: something long, metal, and feathery. Yanking it out, she realized it was a fucking dart. She howled a warning.

Or, more specifically, she tried.

Nothing happened. She couldn't even open her mouth, let alone use her vocal cords.

Then, as if the muscles in her body lost their tone, she slumped . . . into a set of strong arms. The scent of the person holding her was male, tiger, and totally unfamiliar. Another male tiger shifter appeared in front of her, equally unfamiliar, and lifted her by her legs.

Carefully and quietly, they carried her through the trees . . . and she could do nothing but watch as paralysis set in, leaving her awake and alert but unable to move. *Fuck it all.*

Her wolf howled and lunged for the surface, fighting for supremacy so that she could defend Ally and rip the strangers apart. But Ally was just as unable to shift forms as she was to do anything else.

Soon enough, they reached a vehicle parked among the trees. Then the fuckers opened the trunk and dumped her in it. *Oh, she was going to burn shit down when she could finally fucking move again.*

"Something's wrong." Derren came to a total standstill seconds after crossing the border back onto Mercury territory.

"What?" asked Nick, spine locking. Roni and Marcus, who were dragging an unconscious Kerrie, also tensed.

"Ally," replied Derren as apprehensiveness began to build in his system and his wolf started to pace anxiously. "I could feel through our bond that she was nervous and frustrated with waiting," he explained as he dug out his cell phone. "But now . . . now she's seriously pissed and feeling sort of helpless." Which made no sense.

He called her phone. It rang. And rang. And rang. No response at all.

Every instinct he had went on high alert, and his apprehensiveness became blind fear. "Something's wrong," he repeated, adamant this time.

"I'll call Shaya. You try reaching Ally again."

Again, Derren's call went unanswered. Shaya, however, answered her call from Nick with a "Please tell me everything's okay?"

"We're fine, we have Kerrie," Nick assured her quickly. "Where's Ally?"

Through the receiver, Derren heard Shaya's answer clearly: "Ally? She went to take Bruce for a walk just outside our lodge. Why?"

With that, Derren raced through the trees, fear pumping through him. He called out her name several times as he searched the area surrounding the main lodge, but there was no answer, nor was there any sign of her.

Pausing, he spun around to face Nick, who had followed him. "I don't see her. You?" Then two scents reached his nose. Two scents that didn't belong. "Tigers."

Nick inhaled deeply, inspecting the scents. A growl trickled out of him. "Fuck."

He and Nick both followed the unfamiliar scents, continuing through the trees, while Derren's heart slammed hard against his ribs and his wolf lost his fucking shit. Nothing could happen to Ally. *Nothing.*

Derren swore loudly as he found Bruce's body slumped on the ground. Dropping to his knees, he pulled out the dart that was embedded in the animal's flank. "He's alive. But he's been drugged."

Nick frowned. "His eyes are open. Alert."

"He's been drugged with something that's paralyzed his muscles. And so has Ally." That was why she was feeling so helpless. She was basically a prisoner in her own body. "I need to keep following their scents."

To Derren's utter frustration, the strange scents disappeared abruptly at a spot farther ahead. Studying the tire tracks, he spat a string of curses. Returning to Nick, he said, "Someone took her. The Collingwood wolves are behind this." He knew it as surely as he knew that if anyone hurt Ally, they would die a long, brutal, excruciating death at his hands. "I have to get to her."

As if suspecting Derren might run around aimlessly in his panicky state, Nick grabbed his arm. "Yes, but we don't know where she is. Try calling her again." As Derren was cursing when Ally's phone went unanswered for *the third time*, Dan and Cain came rushing toward them.

"Shaya told us Ally's missing," said Cain, eyes sharp.

Nick nodded. "My guess is she was taken by tiger shifters—possibly at Rachelle's order. She has a huge hard-on for Ally."

Dan waved a hand. "She'll be fine."

Derren blinked at him, shocked at his nonchalance. *"She's been kidnapped."*

Dan actually shrugged. "It's not like it's the first time."

"Elaborate," Nick bit out.

It was Cain who replied, looking no more concerned than Dan. "When she was nine, she and a few other pups were snatched right off our territory by a rival pack. They were home within the hour."

"Ally got free and untied the others," said Dan. "Then they just jumped right on out of the vehicle and made their way back. Of course, she was totally pissed and made us buy her a goldfish. Our Ally's tough."

"Yes, she's tough," agreed Derren, infuriated by Cain and her uncle dismissing the danger she was in. "The Collingwood Beta female wants her *dead*. She'll try to kill her."

"Yes, she'll *try*. Don't worry. My niece will be fine."

"She's drugged."

"Oh." Dan looked sheepish. "Well, that complicates things a little."

"Feed her strength through your bond," Nick told Derren. "It will make the effects of the drug wear off faster."

"I can't." It was painful to speak the words, to vocalize what was tormenting him. "The bond isn't fully formed yet."

Cain frowned. "Why? You having doubts about Ally?"

"None whatsoever."

"So, what's holding you both back?"

Derren had no fucking idea. Ally had changed everything for him. He'd never believed he could be loved just the way he was, but she did. He'd always felt stifled by responsibilities, but she made him realize that they didn't have to weigh him down and that there was strength in his status and in being responsible for others.

It was only right at that moment, while fear had such a strong chokehold on him that he felt both suffocated and trapped, that he realized he surprisingly hadn't had that "trapped" feeling for a long time. He'd always worried that being mated would make him feel confined, but he'd been totally wrong. Ally made him feel balanced and important to someone. Being mated to her didn't trap him, it liberated and anchored him. She was—

Derren jolted at the sudden dual sensation of an explosion in his chest and a hammering thud to his head. The pain disappeared as fast as it came, and understanding quickly dawned. His breath caught in his throat as he realized their mating bond had snapped into place.

He could feel her heartbeat, sense her own surprise, realization, and pleasure at what was happening. Without hesitation, he *shoved* strength down that connection, forcing her to absorb and use it.

"Why do you have a dreamy look on your face?" asked Dan.

"My guess is the mating bond just fully formed," said Nick.

Derren nodded. "My strength's helping her a lot quicker than I thought it would."

Nick slapped Derren's upper arm supportively. "That's a good thing. It means she won't be helpless. Now all we have to do is find her."

Ally wasn't sure how much time went by before the paralysis started to wear off. She just knew that it would have taken a hell of a lot longer without Derren's help. She had every intention of celebrating the amazing fact that their mating bond was now fully formed. Later. Right now, she needed to focus on her little predicament.

She also needed to maintain her calm if she had any intention of getting out of the tight, uncomfortably hot space. But since her kitty kidnappers had secured her wrists together with a zip tie, escaping wasn't going to make remaining calm an easy feat.

During the journey, she'd been able to hear the tigers chatting away. Since they were playing the music loud, she hadn't made out every word, but she knew two things: one, Rachelle had hired them; two, they had been instructed to take Ally *alive* to a place of Rachelle's choice.

Well, there wasn't a chance in hell that Ally would let them get her to a secondary location. If she did, it would all be over.

Having fully shaken off the effects of the drug, Ally caught the end of the zip tie between her teeth and tugged until it was super tight. Then she rolled onto her back, raised her arms above her head and brought them down hard toward her stomach. With that, the lock mechanism snapped. Her wolf growled her approval.

Now it was just a matter of opening the damn trunk. But first . . .

She dug into the pocket of her jeans and whipped out her cell phone. The dumb fuckers should have taken it from her just in case she got free. With a few swipes of her thumb on the screen, she'd dialed the panic button to alert the pack to her exact location. Then she called Derren, who had tried calling her several times. She'd felt the phone vibrate in her pocket each time and suspected it was him. She'd hated that she couldn't talk to and reassure him, since she could feel his panic and anger through their bond.

He answered after two rings. "Baby, tell me you're okay."

His voice made her smile, despite the situation. She whispered, "I'm all right. Just pissed. I've pressed the panic button; track my location. When you get close to where I am, call me again."

"They dumped you somewhere?"

"No, but I'm planning to jump out of the trunk in, say, thirty seconds."

"What?" His sharp demanding tone made her wince. *"Are you out of your fucking mind?"*

"Possibly. Look, I have to go." She didn't have time to waste.

"Baby, please be careful," he rumbled, his anxiety and adoration evident.

"I will. Love you." She slipped the phone into her bra, worried that it would smash if she left it in her pocket when she jumped. That done, she searched for a trunk release near the latch. No such luck, apparently. She'd just have to get out the old-fashioned way.

With a brief struggle, she peeled back the carpet and located the trunk release cable. Two strong pulls later and there was the fabulous pop sound of the trunk opening. She stilled for a moment, listening hard for any sign that the tigers had heard the noise. Nothing. It would appear that the sound of the radio had drowned it out.

She waited only long enough for the vehicle to slow a little before she opened the trunk and, not giving herself the chance to worry about the fall, jumped—careful not to land on her hands or directly on her shoulder. The air whooshed out of her lungs as her body landed hard. Thinking past the pain in her back, she then rolled along the ground until she felt grass beneath her. At least she had no broken bones.

Looking up, she saw the vehicle was heading toward a residential neighborhood. Knowing it would be only moments before the tigers realized she was free, Ally forced herself to get to her feet and did the only thing she could do: she ran.

CHAPTER EIGHTEEN

H ow much farther?" Derren impatiently asked Jesse, who was on the other end of the phone.

"She's somewhere close," he replied, monitoring Ally's GPS location from their computer at the main lodge. "Call her now."

Chest tight with a cluster of emotions tormenting him, Derren ended his call to Jesse and dialed Ally's number.

She answered quickly. "I can hear the SUV. I'm coming right now." She hung up before he could speak. Then she suddenly appeared out of the trees and jogged onto the road, waving her arms. Eli brought the vehicle to a screeching halt.

Derren jumped out and dragged her to him, locking his arms tight around her. "Fuck, baby, thank God you're okay." He was trembling with fear, rage, and relief. Fisting a hand in her hair, he kissed her hard, pouring into it everything he didn't know how to say. His wolf took comfort in her touch, scent, and the feel of her skin under his hands. She was there with him. She was okay.

"I knew you'd come for me." Her happiness at seeing him was so profound Ally might have fallen to her knees if he hadn't been holding her up. Her wolf wanted to rub up against him to both comfort him and receive comfort.

When she went to pull back, Derren bit out, "Don't. I just need to hold you for a minute." He needed to reassure himself that she was fine. Safe. With him. He'd always prided himself on the fact that he didn't need anyone. But he couldn't breathe, couldn't function, without Ally. He needed her, and he wasn't even ashamed of that.

"Derren, let's go!" shouted Eli.

Bracken hopped into the passenger seat, guessing that Derren would want to sit in the back with Ally. He'd guessed right. Without easing his hold on her, Derren picked her up and slid into the backseat, sitting her on his lap. The small cuts and abrasions on her skin made him growl; she patted his chest soothingly.

Eli immediately sped off, glancing at them briefly over his shoulder. "Ally, are you hurt? Did they hurt you?"

She shook her head against Derren's chest, inhaling his scent and letting it calm her and her wolf. "I'm okay."

"What the hell happened?" demanded Cain from beside her. He tried tugging her to him to embrace her, but Derren held tight—his stare *daring* Cain to try to take Ally from him. Cain bared his teeth but didn't try again.

"I was drugged and dumped in a trunk by two fucking tigers."

"They're dead." Derren's voice was low and deadly. He'd find out who they were, and he'd kill them. "What did they look like? Have you seen them before?"

"They didn't look or smell familiar. They're both Chinese, medium height, and damn strong."

"Tigers usually are pretty strong," commented Cain. "Did you hear any names?" She shook her head.

"Here." Twisting in his seat to face her, Bracken gently chucked his cell phone to her; Ally caught it easily. "It's Shaya. I promised I'd call her when we found you. She's a mess."

As Ally put the phone to her ear, she heard Shaya's voice sobbing, "Ally, if you're not alive, I'm going to kick your ass."

"I'm alive," Ally assured her with a smile. "Is Bruce okay?"

"Yes, he's fine. The drugs have worn off. Hurry home. I need to see you with my own eyes."

"Not yet. I have somewhere to go first."

"You're going after Rachelle," guessed Shaya.

"Yes, she was behind the kidnapping."

"I want to be there!"

"No, you all need to keep an eye on Miranda and Kerrie. They need to be heavily guarded in case a few of Miranda's pack—or *previous* pack, as the situation now stands—come to help her. Some of the guys were smitten with her. Besides, I've got some backup with me."

"Make sure Rachelle feels some serious pain."

"That won't be a problem. This shit needs to be dealt with once and for all." The bitch had had the chance to leave Ally be, but she hadn't. Now Ally needed to be the one to end it. Ally handed the phone back to Bracken, whose smile was a little blood-thirsty. Apparently he was also eager to see Rachelle punished. Derren, on the other hand, didn't seem at all pleased.

He kissed her hair. "Baby, I get that this is something you need to do—"

"Then back me up on this."

"—but you were drugged not so long ago. You've got cuts and scrapes, which I'm guessing are thanks to your crazy idea to leap out of a trunk."

"They're not bad, and they're healing fast."

"That's not the point."

"Then, pray tell, what is?"

"Baby, do you have any idea how fucking terrified I was for you?" The fear still hadn't left him, still threatened to break his composure. If he hadn't known through their mating bond that she was alive, he would have lost his fucking mind long before now. "Could you not give my heartbeat a chance to get back to normal? Do you really have to walk right back into more danger?"

274

Ally met his dark, tormented gaze. "I have to do this now, Derren. The tigers were supposed to take me to a spot a few miles from here. Rachelle's intention was to join them later today. I need to get to Collingwood territory before she leaves."

"If the tigers call and tell her you got away, she'll probably flee, worried you heard them talking about their plans."

Ally shook her head. "They spoke in Mandarin. She doesn't know I speak the language. And cocky as she is, she won't believe she'll ever get caught." Rachelle had gone too long without having to face any consequences for her actions against Ally. "I have to deal with this now."

"She's right." Cain sighed. "I don't *like* that she's right, but there's no escaping the fact that she is."

"Eli, we're making a pit stop at Collingwood territory," she told him.

The Head Enforcer glanced at Derren in the rearview mirror. "I know you're not totally okay with this, but you know she has to do it, right?"

After a long sigh, Derren nodded. "If I'm lucky, Zeke will do something stupid, and then I have an excuse to tear out his throat." The thought lightened his mood a little.

When they finally crossed the boundary into Collingwood territory, Matt's enforcers nervously let them pass while one of them called Matt on his cell phone. As soon as Eli pulled up in the parking lot, Matt came strolling toward them with Zeke at his side. Matt's smile was genuine but shaky.

"You have to stay in the SUV, Cain. They won't be able to see you through the shaded windows." At his disapproving growl, Ally reminded him, "You can't be seen. Your link to me can't become common knowledge for both our sakes."

He was silent for a short moment. "Kill her, Ally. Nothing else will stop her from coming after you." Ally suspected he might be right about that. "But don't do it quickly. Make her hurt, make her

275

bleed, and make sure her pack mates see how well you can fight so they don't dare even think about avenging her death. Got it?"

Nodding, Ally said, "Got it." Only once the other males were out of the SUV, awkwardly greeting the Collingwood Alpha and Beta, did Ally hop out.

Zeke's gaze skimmed over her, taking in the dirt and healing abrasions. "Shit, Ally, what happened?" He went to move toward her.

"Not too close," warned Derren in a deceptively cool drawl. "I'm not in a tolerant mood right now."

"Come inside the house," invited Matt. "We'll talk."

"We're not here to chat," Ally told him. "Where's—" She stopped as movement caught her eye: a blonde female was jogging toward them, shock flaring in her eyes at the sight of Ally. *Rachelle.* How grand.

"What are you doing here?" Rachelle sneered at her. "You and your friends told us to stay away from you. Yet here you are."

"Yes, not where you expected me to be, I'll bet." Ally smiled inwardly when the Beta female's eyes flickered nervously. "Coming after me was by far the dumbest thing you've ever done. Seriously, even for you—someone whose elevator doesn't go to the top floor—it was stupid."

Rachelle's tired sigh was actually very convincing. "So you've come here to accuse me of something, I see."

"Did you think that if you killed me, you'd get away with it?" Ally snickered. "You would have forever been looking over your shoulder at the wolves chasing your crazy ass. You should have just stayed away."

"I did. But apparently *you* can't stay away from *me*, can you? You just can't let go of your grudge against me."

"Maybe if you opened your mouth for more than talking bullshit or giving blow jobs, we wouldn't have a problem." Ally's wolf released a satisfied growl at the angry flush on Rachelle's cheeks. "I gotta say, those tigers weren't very competent. I suppose I should pity you for your delusions of tactical brilliance."

Zeke spoke then. "Tigers? What about tigers? You're not making any sense."

"Sure I am." Ally turned back to Rachelle. "You didn't expect me to link the incident to you, huh."

"What incident?" Matt asked. By that point, they had drawn a bit of a crowd, including Clint and Greg—both of whom were scowling at Ally.

"I was drugged and kidnapped by two tiger shifters a little while ago," Ally told Matt. Surprise and dubiousness wafted from the Collingwood bystanders.

The Alpha gaped. "What?"

"You heard her," growled Derren.

Matt slid his gaze briefly to his Beta female. "And you all think Rachelle had something to do with this?"

"We *know* she did." Derren clenched his fists, barely resisting the urge to plant one in Matt's face for being so evasive.

Rachelle folded her arms across her chest, regarding Ally like she was ridiculous. "Kidnapped? Yeah, right. Oh, and they just let you go, I suppose?"

"No. I jumped out of the trunk while they were still driving." Ally rolled back one shoulder. "Hurt like a motherfucker."

"You persist in seeing me as the enemy." Rachelle dragged a hand through her hair. "You see conspiracies everywhere. I wouldn't be surprised if you faked the kidnapping." Derren's snarl made her snap her gaze to him. She sneered at him, "Or maybe it was someone trying to get at *you* through your girlfriend."

"I speak Mandarin, Rachelle. I understood every word." Ally smiled faintly as Rachelle stilled. "You hired them. You were supposed to join us in a few hours at a location you gave them. You undoubtedly meant to kill me. And I'm not down with that. So there's only one thing left for me to do." Ally straightened her shoulders. "Rachelle Lavin, I challenge you to a duel."

Zeke took one step forward, his tone desperate. "Ally, don't do this."

"Don't speak to her," Derren snapped at him. "She's no one to you."

Zeke curled back his upper lip. "Yeah? Well, *you're* just someone she's screwing."

Derren smiled. "If you were close enough to scent us, you'd know that couldn't be further from the truth."

Zeke's chest expanded as he inhaled deeply, straining to pick up their scents. His eyes widened, a hint of dejection in them. "You're mated." It was a guttural statement.

Ignoring Zeke, Ally focused on Rachelle. "Let's get this over with." Everyone stilled as they heard the sound of another vehicle nearing. Rachelle smirked, undoubtedly thinking exactly the same thing as Ally: if more Collingwood wolves were on their way, the four Mercury wolves could find themselves boxed in. "Worried you can't take me, Rachelle?"

The Beta female snorted. "I simply refuse to be baited into dueling with someone who isn't worth my time." The Mercury males snickered derisively at the idiotic excuse.

As the approaching vehicle entered the parking lot, Derren glanced over his shoulder. And smiled. It was a very familiar Chevrolet Tahoe. Within moments, six Phoenix wolves exited the vehicle—Taryn, Trey, Jaime, Dante, Dominic, and Ryan.

Taryn's smile had a feral edge to it as she sidled up to Ally. "Shaya called me and told me what happened. I figured having some allies might discourage this pack from leaping to their Beta female's defense." She arched a brow at Matt. "We can't have that, can we?"

"Otherwise things would get extremely ugly," warned Trey.

"No one will interfere," Matt assured the Phoenix Alphas, giving them a respectful nod of the head that they didn't return.

Rachelle whirled on her own Alpha. "You're sanctioning the challenge? You believe her accusations?" He didn't speak, so she turned to her mate. "You're okay with this?"

"No, I'm not." Zeke raked a hand over his face. "I know Ally's a good fighter, and I don't want you hurt. But I can't interfere."

"You're *siding* with her?"

"You came home smelling of tigers, Rachelle." His voice was low, devastated. "You're my mate, and I love you, but you're—"

"Indisputably neurotic?" supplied Ally.

"A total fucking nutcase?" offered Taryn.

Rachelle whipped her hateful gaze to Ally. "You think you're so smart? You think you've won?"

Ally seriously didn't understand this female. "What is there to win? This isn't a game. It never was."

"You have to die!" Apparently Rachelle had given up on acting like the falsely accused victim.

"Why? Because you believe I'm jealous of you?"

"Because there's no other way he'll let you go!" Rachelle's words had the crowd gasping. She raised a brow at Ally. "You think I don't know? You think I'm so stupid I can't see why my mating bond isn't complete? It's *your* fault."

"Don't be so fucking dramatic. Zeke wants you, not me."

"That's true. He doesn't want you, and he doesn't regret our mating, but a part of him still cares for you."

"Don't pin the blame on Zeke, don't act like you don't get a kick out of stirring shit for people. You're too much of an accomplished liar for me to think any differently." Ally's expression dared her to deny the truth. "You want me dead because you want me to suffer."

"Oh, I do want you to suffer. I tried everything. I tried turning him against you, but it never worked. Everyone else fell in line, but not Zeke. No. He doubted every story I told him. He didn't for one moment believe you would try to kill me. No. It didn't even make any difference that you left the pack. He just wouldn't forget you—he kept texting you, calling you—he wanted you back in the pack. He wanted you where he could see you and be near you, even though he would never have touched you." Rachelle shrugged one shoulder. "I will admit it was fun to watch as you lost everything—your friends, your status, the trust of your pack mates."

Matt groaned, covering his face with his hands, no doubt feeling dumb at how easily he'd been fooled. Zeke looked distraught but not particularly surprised, and it made Ally wonder just how long he'd suspected his mate was a lying, crazy heifer.

"Thankfully," began Ally, "your lies have been discovered. Your pack knows the truth. Your reign of bullshit is over. And now *you* have lost your status and the trust of your pack." Their disgust in Rachelle beat at Ally's head. "No more stalling. I challenged you, and no one's going to dispute my right to do so."

"Submit now, Rachelle," Zeke urged. "If you submit now, there'll be no challenge. We'll step down from our role as Betas; we'll switch to another pack and start over."

Her upper lip curled back, Rachelle looked down her nose at him. "Flee, you mean?"

"It's not fleeing when you're banished." Matt's tone was harsh, nonnegotiable.

"You're banishing me?" Rachelle actually seemed shocked— even more support to the theory that she was insane.

"You expected anything different after all that you've done?" asked Matt. "I almost banished an innocent wolf because of your lies! How can you expect me to overlook that, to trust you?" He shook his head. "You no longer have a place here."

Rachelle didn't speak; she just gawked at her Alpha. But Ally could feel her rage and resentment rising, burning Ally's skin until she thought it would blister.

Ally tilted her head. "Sucks, doesn't it? Being banished and isolated, I mean."

Rounding on her, Rachelle cracked her neck. "You want to duel? Fine. We'll duel."

"Rachelle . . ." Zeke tried to pull her away, but his mate shrugged him off.

"Don't. You don't care whether I'm hurt," Rachelle accused him. "You know you might survive my death, since we're not fully mated, so you don't even care if I die!"

"That's not true," he maintained. "I'm trying to protect you!"

"I don't want your help."

"Step aside, Zeke," ordered Matt, pulling Zeke with him as he backed away. The other Collingwood wolves followed their Alpha's lead, giving the females plenty of space to duel. "This is between Ally and Rachelle now."

Derren cupped Ally's nape as he kissed her temple. "You can take her, baby. Finish this so we can go home."

Feeling that both he and his wolf were in turmoil despite their confidence in her, Ally gave a reassuring smile. "Gladly."

"I love you," he whispered low enough for only her to hear. He backed away before she could respond, signaling for Eli, Bracken, and the Phoenix wolves to do the same.

"Don't hesitate," Taryn told her. "Do what you have to do." Ally understood what she meant: if Rachelle refused to submit, kill her.

Jaime nodded. "Smack the bitch down, Ally."

Focusing her attention on her opponent, Ally kicked off her shoes and took on a strong, stable stance: feet shoulder-width apart, knees slightly bent, claws unsheathed. She also kept her expression totally neutral, her gaze locked on Rachelle with lethal intent.

Ally planned to fight as hard and dirty as she'd been trained to do, well aware that since Rachelle was equally dominant they were well matched. Ally had seen her fight, knew the bitch had some good moves and didn't mind cheating. As such, she didn't intend to give Rachelle any openings, especially since her craziness could give her an edge.

The tension had Ally's wolf still, coiled, and raring to strike. Right then, the animal was infuriated, vengeful, and restless with the need to end this shit. For the wolf, it was all very simple. Rachelle was a threat. And any threat to Ally was a threat to Derren. Ally and her wolf would eradicate every single one, would do whatever it took to keep him safe.

Ally had never really liked dueling, but sometimes it was the only language shifters understood. Although she detested Rachelle, Ally hadn't wanted it to come to this. Not because she had any mercy for the heifer, but because she had the distinct feeling that Cain was right: Ally would have to kill her.

Taking a life wasn't something Ally had ever done before. As a Seer, she was used to trying to *save* her pack from danger and death, not fight to the death. But she was also Beta female now, and that meant being strong for her pack and doing whatever she had to do.

Standing there, so many emotions flowed over her: the worry, aggravation, and support of her allies; Rachelle's fury, bitterness, and nervousness; the shame, guilt, and anxiety belonging to both Matt and Zeke; the contrary emotions that flitted through the crowd.

The Collingwood bystanders had turned silent. Their anticipation, anger, and confusion almost made her itch. Although they couldn't deny to themselves that Rachelle was guilty, there was still an element of uncertainty there. They hadn't yet accepted what they had heard, didn't want to admit to the fact that they had been so easily fooled and had wrongfully isolated and targeted Ally.

Rachelle balled her hands up into fists. "Last chance to go home."

Go home? "You really are a nut job." Ally struck. No warning. No holding back. She rammed her elbow into Rachelle's throat at the same time as she stabbed her claws under the bitch's breastbone.

Stumbling backward, Rachelle doubled over, expelling a whoosh of air. To her credit, she didn't take a moment to recover, didn't move her eyes from Ally. Instead, the blonde straightened up, eyes shimmering with rage. She raked her claws, narrowly missing Ally's face. Apparently, Rachelle was out for blood.

Ally had long ago learned not to telegraph her moves, to give nothing away. Rachelle, on the other hand, didn't appear to have been taught any such lesson. So when the heifer dipped her chin and cocked back her arm, Ally easily ducked and slipped out of range. Again and again, Ally sidestepped her punches and kicks, allowing her opponent to tire and weaken from blood loss.

That was when Ally went at her full force. She used her claws like knives and delivered one dirty disabling shot after another, making every pitiless strike and slice count. Her anger was raw but controlled, giving her the fuel she needed.

This was for all the lies, all the insults, for turning her pack against her, for causing Ally to lose her status, and for plotting to kill her. If Ally hadn't gotten away from the tigers and had died today, Derren would most likely have died right along with her. That wasn't acceptable to Ally. Not one little bit.

Ally brought up her arm, ready to deliver a palm strike. Rachelle shoved her claws right into Ally's palm. *Motherfucker.* Snatching back her bleeding hand, Ally sliced at the tendon on her opponent's forearm, making Rachelle cry out. *Good.*

Rachelle drove her foot at Ally's knee, hitting it hard with her heel, the bitch. The impact made Ally stumble and bend slightly. That was when Rachelle wrapped Ally's ponytail around her fist and dragged Ally to her. She snapped her teeth at Ally's claiming mark, trying to mar it—pissing Derren the hell off. *Not a fucking chance.*

She dug her claws just above Rachelle's pubic bone, and the bitch instantly released her hair and backed away slightly. Feeling Derren's anger so intensely, tasting it in her mouth, it was hard for Ally not to let it feed her own ire and make her lose her shit. She fought to keep her head clear, knowing that dueling in anger would make her sloppy and careless.

She heard Derren, Taryn, and Jaime shouting their encouragement—and making many disparaging remarks about Rachelle. One insult in particular made Ally chuckle... which was when the crazy heifer swung her claws toward the juncture of Ally's thighs. *Fuck.* Ally barely intercepted the strike, retaliating with a punch to Rachelle's temple that made her take a lurching step back.

"*Rachelle, submit!*" bellowed Zeke.

If Ally hadn't been so focused on Rachelle, she would have told him that there was no point. Ally wouldn't be content with her submitting right then. She wouldn't buy it as a truthful surrender.

"Rachelle!" He took a step toward the fighting females but halted abruptly at Derren's warning growl.

"Stay the fuck out of it," Derren cautioned him in a tone that promised retribution. "Your mate deserves this. You can't save her from it. If you try to interfere again at any point, I'll be on you before you can blink. We clear?"

"She's my mate!"

"And Ally's *my* mate."

A part of Ally—small though it was—felt a little sorry for Zeke. It had to be hard watching your mate losing a fight. But that wasn't going to stop Ally from dueling the bitch. In a quick explosion of brutal hits, she almost had Rachelle on the ground. But Rachelle quickly righted herself and slammed her foot into Ally's ribs. *Son of a bitch!* Pain pulsed through her abdomen, almost making her heave with nausea.

The scents of blood, sweat, rage, and apprehension tainted the air, swirling around them and inciting Ally's wolf. The animal, despite being so eager to play a part, hadn't battled Ally for supremacy; she knew Ally wouldn't keep the wolf out of the fight. So she'd lain in wait, ready to lunge at the first opportunity. Now Ally was ready for her wolf to join in.

In a split second, she shifted into her wolf form just long enough to leap up and bite a chunk out of Rachelle's upper arm.

Then Ally was back in human form so fast her clothes barely suffered from the change. Gasps and exclamations of shock rang throughout the crowd. Rachelle appeared just as shocked, and Ally—wearing a grin that could only be called evil and clearly freaked Rachelle out—took clear advantage of it. She briefly shifted back and forth again and again as she mercilessly attacked.

Executing a pitiless punch to her opponent's throat, Ally winced. Her knuckles were chafed and swelling. Her ribs were aching, making it hurt to breathe. Her palm, chest, arm, and cheek were bleeding. She could taste Rachelle's blood in her mouth, thanks to her wolf biting the bitch repeatedly. And she was sweating and beginning to tire, but she felt Derren feeding her strength through their bond.

Rachelle wasn't in a much better state. Her jaw and nose were swollen, her face was badly bruised, one of her arms was almost limp, sweat and blood matted her hair, she was panting heavily, and her clothes were stained with blood from the many places she'd been bit, sliced, raked, and stabbed.

Flinching as she received another deep wolf bite to her side, Rachelle ground out, "Fuck this." Then, ripping her clothes, she shifted into a red wolf. Ally followed suit, giving her wolf complete control—and, as such, totally destroying her clothes.

The white wolf flattened her ears and peeled back her lips as she growled at her opponent. Hackles raised, the red wolf bared her teeth as a bold growl trickled out of her. They lunged at each other, their bodies crashing hard. Clawing deep into fur and flesh, they growled and snarled as they both viciously battled for dominance.

Yelping from a harsh bite to her flank, the red wolf sprang away. Chest heaving, she released a fierce growl, daring the white wolf to attack again. But the white wolf wasn't in the mood to toy with her prey. Didn't want a duel. Her human side had punished their opponent, and now the white wolf wanted to end it, to force their opponent—who by killing her would have killed her mate—to submit or die. There could be no middle ground.

She didn't leap at the red wolf. She barreled into her, causing her opponent to fall onto her side. The red wolf brutally swiped at the white wolf's muzzle before righting herself. In retaliation, the white wolf sunk her teeth deep into her opponent's shoulder, tearing through fur, flesh, and muscle until they grazed bone.

Bucking and clawing, the red wolf managed to get free. But she didn't manage to move far away. The white wolf slammed her body into hers hard enough to send the red wolf sprawling onto her back. The white wolf wasted no time in taking advantage of it. She straddled her opponent and pressed her forepaws onto the red wolf's shoulders to pin her flat. Then the white wolf clamped her jaws around her opponent's throat, causing the red wolf to freeze.

Freeze, but not submit.

The white wolf heard voices shouting. She didn't understand the words, nor did she care. Her attention was on the female beneath her, who attempted to struggle free. The white wolf warningly tightened the grip of her jaws slightly, feeling a little of the red wolf's blood seep into her mouth.

Again, the female froze. But again, she didn't submit.

Giving one final warning, the white wolf growled as she shook her opponent. There was more shouting from the crowd, and then the scent of the red wolf's mate as he rushed at them. The white wolf didn't panic, sensing that her own mate was holding him back, that he would protect her.

The red wolf suddenly bucked, snapping her teeth. There would be no submission, the white wolf then knew. Despite knowing that part of her human side would be sad to take a life, the white wolf didn't hesitate to act. Using her back paw, she sliced open her opponent's midsection as she twisted her neck, tearing out the red wolf's throat.

It was over.

The wolf backed away from the dead body, turning at her mate's voice. He knelt beside her, wrapping one arm around her neck and stroking her head with his free hand as he spoke words the wolf didn't understand. As Ally pushed for supremacy, the wolf rubbed her body once against his before pulling back to give her human side full control.

Breathing hard, Ally sank into Derren's arms. A hiss of pain escaped her as her injuries rubbed against his jacket. "I'm getting blood on you."

"I don't care." He kissed her forehead, disappointed that he couldn't kiss her mouth but not wanting to taste Rachelle's blood. Watching his mate battle, even though she'd been the dominant fighter throughout, had been agonizing. He'd winced at every cut, every strike, every kick, and every bite. Feeling her pain and fatigue had only made it worse.

Jaime handed Ally a bottle of water. "Here, sweetie."

Hand shaking slightly, Ally gratefully took it and practically inhaled a long swig. She allowed Derren to help her stand, surprised when her knees didn't buckle. Removing his coat, he wrapped it around her; it fell to midthigh on Ally. The pressure of the material made her scratches sting, but she gritted her teeth against the pain.

Hearing a gut-wrenching sob followed by a soul-deep cry, she looked at Zeke. He had his arm wrapped around his stomach, clearly in agony as he crouched beside the red wolf. Ally didn't know what it was like to feel a mating bond break, only knew that the more developed the bond was, the more painful it would be to break.

"I'm sorry that you've lost your mate," she told him. "I gave her the chance to submit. My wolf gave her the chance."

Standing behind him, Matt gave her a nod. "Zeke knows the rules of our culture. When Rachelle didn't submit, you had no choice but to end it the way you did." He rubbed at his nape, sighing heavily. "Ally, I'm sorry I doubted you, that I let you down so badly."

Zeke's gaze snapped to him as he exploded, "She just killed *my mate* and you're *apologizing* to her?"

Not liking that tone whatsoever, Derren interjected, "Don't blame Ally for this. You're hurt that you lost your mate—I get that." Derren wouldn't be able to function without Ally. "But part of the blame lies with you."

To Ally's total surprise, all the tension left Zeke's body as he mumbled, "I know. It took me a while to see the truth. It wasn't until we visited your territory that I finally realized that I didn't know my mate as well as I thought. That day, I felt how angry she was with Ally. I felt how badly she wanted to hurt her. I should have kept a closer eye on Rachelle, made sure she didn't go after Ally again. This is on me."

"It's on Rachelle," Matt adamantly stated, taking the words from Ally's mouth. Zeke shook his head in denial, the image of absolute devastation as he stroked his mate's flank.

Feeling like she was trespassing on what should be an extremely private moment, Ally turned to Derren. "Let's go home." She was exhausted, disheartened, and quickly heading for an adrenaline crash.

He kissed her forehead again. "Gladly," he replied, echoing her earlier sentiment.

As he went to guide her to the SUV, Taryn appeared in front of her, looking impressed. "I don't know how the fuck you switch forms like that, but you gotta teach me."

CHAPTER NINETEEN

The moment they exited the SUV, the door to the main lodge flew open and several Mercury wolves and her uncles came rushing out. Ally undoubtedly would have winced at every tight hug if Taryn hadn't ridden with them during the journey so she could heal her.

Strangely, Shaya had a pair of shears in her hand. Frowning, Ally asked, "What are they for?"

An innocent smile took over the Alpha female's face as she hid them behind her back. "Nothing." Then she exchanged a knowing look with Taryn and Jaime, both of whom now radiated an amusement that tickled Ally. With an inner shrug, Ally made her way into the lodge. The Mercury and Phoenix wolves all followed.

Inside the living area, Bracken coaxed Ally to sit on the sofa while Kathy handed her a mug of some kind of mint-smelling tea. Caleb tucked a blanket around her, and Kent offered her a cookie. Taking one, she leaned into Derren and quietly asked, "Why are they fussing?"

"They're taking care of you."

"You don't like that," she sensed.

"It's *my* job." He knew he sounded petulant. After all, this was what packs did: they looked out for their own, gave comfort and touch when it was needed. But Ally was his, and he wanted to be the one who took care of her.

"Drink it," said Kathy, pointing to the tea. "It'll get the taste of blood out of your mouth better than any toothpaste."

Saluting her, Ally did as advised. That was when she noticed that the seriously hot Phoenix enforcer, Dominic, was looking hard at her. "What? What are you staring at?"

He sighed languorously. "You, before I wake up from this dream." There were groans of annoyance and a few chuckles.

Growling, Derren would have shot up from his seat and lunged at the little shit if Ally hadn't placed a hand on his thigh to stay him. "Don't," Derren spat at him. "You're not using your cheesy lines on Ally."

Holding up his hands, laughing, Dominic said, "Seriously, I'm just messing with her." His expression turned serious yet soft as he regarded Ally a second time. "Hell, you must be tired . . . You've been running through my dreams all night."

Again, Derren went to dive at the prick, but Ally pressed her hand down harder on his thigh. That didn't mean he'd let him get away with it. "Zander!"

Standing behind Dominic, Zander whacked the enforcer over the head.

Wincing, Dominic rounded on him with a grin. "Hey, you'll mess up my hair. The others don't hit me that hard."

Casting the Phoenix enforcer an exasperated look, Nick turned to Derren. "Tell us what happened. Is Rachelle no longer an issue?"

It was actually Bracken who did most of the storytelling, praising Ally's fighting skills and making her uncles smile proudly.

Seeming satisfied, Nick said, "That's one more threat gone."

Derren arched a brow at his Alpha. "I take it no one came to rescue Miranda or Kerrie?"

"No," replied Nick. "But I can't say I'm surprised. Like you said, Miranda wasn't a good Alpha."

"Tell me they're not dead yet," said Taryn, hands clasped in prayer. "I wanted to say my good-byes to them first." There was a deadly undercurrent to that sentence.

"They're alive," Nick assured her. "Had it been *your* pack who caught them, I'd have wanted you to wait for me before you slit their throats—or something equally fun."

Trey snorted a laugh. "Good. Where are they?"

"The toolshed. Jesse, Roni, and Marcus are guarding them."

A curt nod from the Phoenix Alpha male. "Then let's do this."

Derren nuzzled his mate's cheek, not wanting to leave her while she was feeling a little raw inside and still recovering from an adrenaline crash. But he was Beta; getting rid of traitors, intruders, and enemies—in effect, doing the jobs no one else wanted to do—was one of his responsibilities. Although . . . he had a feeling Roni would want the honor of killing Kerrie. "Stay here, baby. I'll be—"

"I want to see this through." Ally wanted to see the females punished, and she wanted to be at her mate's side when he took on this heavy responsibility.

"Baby, you've had a tough enough day as it is. Sit back and relax while we deal with it."

She shook her head. "That's not me. I'm Beta too, remember? If nothing else, I should be there with you."

"I think this is something everyone here should get to see," stated Dante. "They were all targets, they all have their own share of anger toward the two females in the toolshed. They want closure as much as we do."

Nick thought on that for a minute. He addressed the whole room as he announced, "We'll take the captives into the woods behind the toolshed. If any of you wish to watch them be dealt with, meet us there."

Only Kathy, Caleb, Kent, and Willow stayed behind. The rest gathered behind Derren, Nick, Trey, and Dante as the captives were brought out by Jesse and Zander.

Nick groaned at the sight of the females and then glanced at his mate over his shoulder. "Shay, was that really necessary?" She simply shrugged, grinning. His gaze flicked to his sister. "You helped, didn't you?" It was more of an accusation than an enquiry.

"I thought you hid the shears," said Marcus, a smile playing around the edges of his mouth.

A muscle in Nick's jaw ticked. "I did."

"Not well enough," commented Roni, smirking in supreme satisfaction.

Marcus toyed with his mate's hair. "When you and Shaya went inside the shed, and I heard those two shrieking and cursing, I hadn't guessed this was why. Though I probably should have."

Jaime pouted. "I wish I'd been there. We had so much fun the time we played with the female jackal that Roni caught."

"The girls like to give their captives a makeover," Eli explained to Ally as he came to stand beside her.

She bit the inside of her cheek to stop herself from laughing—both Kerrie and Miranda had nothing but tufts left of their hair. "Well, I can see that."

Jesse and Zander shoved Miranda and Kerrie to their knees and stood behind them, on guard. Only Kerrie looked scared. If Ally hadn't been able to feel Miranda's fear scuttling across her skin like beetles, she would have thought the woman was completely indifferent to her situation.

Miranda's scowl deepened as her attention turned to Dan. "I'm sure you're enjoying this."

He pursed his lips. "Since your actions placed Ally in danger . . . yeah, this has some entertainment value."

Kerrie's fearful gaze turned ugly and malicious as it found Roni and Marcus. The couple was standing side by side, their bodies intimately close and their stances protective. Their bond was so solid and strong, it seemed to throb between them.

Roni tilted her head as she regarded Kerrie with a blank look. "All this because he rejected you?"

"He didn't reject me." Kerrie smirked. "We had a *lot* of fun together. Didn't we, Marcus?"

"Sure," allowed Roni, "for, like, two minutes. It was short and casual—nothing to write home about."

The smirk vanished from Kerrie's face. "He would have come back to me. When he was ready to commit, when he saw that other females would never know him and care about him like I do, he would have come back."

"Yeah, in an alternate reality."

Kerrie's words came out fast and furiously. "Marcus would have mated *me*. I would have become part of the Phoenix Pack, we would have been happy." Her gaze turned faraway. "He was good to me. He wasn't like the others. It didn't matter to him that I was a Seer—he wasn't prejudiced against my kind. It didn't matter to him that my father was known for being a bad drunk and an even worse mate. None of it mattered to him."

"What about your own mate?" Dante asked, "You didn't think to wait for him?"

"He died when I was fourteen. He was seven years older than me; he'd said he wouldn't touch me until I turned eighteen. He was an enforcer like Marcus."

Now Ally understood. Kerrie had wanted to create the future she should have had with her mate. She'd chosen Marcus, decided he was what she needed, and had relished his acceptance of her Seer nature. She'd made plans for their future, believing it was only a matter of time before those plans became reality.

Kerrie's eyes slid to Roni. "But then *you* came along."

Bemused, Roni snorted. "You make it sound like I'm some kind of home wrecker. He's my mate. He's mine. He was never yours."

But Ally could sense that, to Kerrie, Roni truly was the inter-loper—she'd ruined everything for Kerrie. For a second time, the female's plans for the future had collapsed as, once again, she'd lost the wolf she'd expected to mate. Kerrie's emotional state had no doubt been deteriorating for a long time, probably as a result of losing her true mate before they'd had the chance to claim each other. Many shifters lost their way after such a painful situation.

"You're not good enough for him," Kerrie sneered.

Roni snickered. "Yeah, you're a bitter, unhinged bitch, and I'm a socially challenged tomboy. Go judge me."

Trey looked at Kerrie curiously. "If you care for Marcus so much, why did you want him dead too?"

"He betrayed me," she replied, but her eyes were on Marcus. "He chose *her* over me. And he needed to know how it felt to lose a mate, to lose everything."

Looking murderous, Marcus growled low in his throat. "And that's exactly why you'll die today."

Ally's head began to badly pound as Kerrie's emotional state repeatedly swung from enraged to bitter to confused to pained to disoriented. The female was, in a word, lost. In which case, Ally had to wonder if they were looking at this from the wrong angle.

Turning her attention to the female kneeling beside Kerrie—a female who was filled with greed, ruthlessness, and naked ambi-tion—Ally said, "It wasn't Kerrie's idea to take out the hits, was it? She's eager to see Roni and Marcus dead, no doubt about that. She's been obsessing over it for some time now. But that girl ain't thinking clearly enough to have been able to arrange hits, hire people to kidnap families, and cover her tracks while doing it all. Not without a little help and advice, anyway."

Derren arched his brows. "That's a very good point."

Sure she was right, Ally continued speaking to Miranda. "You're an opportunist. You saw your cousin's pain, her need for vengeance, and you saw a way to use that for your own personal gain. I think *you* gave her the idea to take out the hits. I think you pointed her in all the right directions—always careful not to dirty your own hands. That way, if Kerrie failed, the blame wouldn't fall on you. But if Kerrie succeeded, you got yourself more land and power."

Kerrie looked at her cousin. "Miranda?" The female didn't respond—she was too busy glaring at Ally.

Taryn sighed at Kerrie. "Basically, you thought you were the mastermind behind all this, but that wasn't the case. Your cousin exploited your deteriorating emotional state for her own gain. At least you can be satisfied that it didn't work out well for her."

Kerrie shook her head. "No. Miranda wouldn't do that. She owed me."

"Owed you how?" asked Nick.

"She wouldn't have had the position of lone Alpha if it hadn't been for me. I had a vision, I told her the Alpha male would die."

Nick's gaze slid to Miranda. "And you ensured that you were in the perfect position to take over when he died, didn't you?"

Miranda snitted haughtily, but her fear was no longer hidden. It was in her eyes, her scent, and her body language. "My pack will come to free me."

Nick's smile had a cruel edge to it. "You know that won't happen. You're a malicious, traitorous, self-serving bitch—they'll be glad to be rid of you."

"They'll—"

Nick declared, "I've heard enough. Let's get this over with."

Going to her brother's side, Roni said, "Nick, you promised. You agreed she was mine."

Holding up a hand, Taryn stepped forward. "I get you want your revenge, Roni—this bitch could have cost you both your mate and your pack. But I could have lost the same. My pack needs vengeance too. We could both have the honor," proposed Taryn with a shrug. "I'll make her suffer on behalf of my entire pack. And you could do it too because, well, you'll explode inside if you don't." After a long moment, Roni nodded her agreement.

At that point, Kerrie looked ready to piss her pants. Ally would have felt sorry for her if it weren't for the danger the Mercury and Phoenix Packs had been subjected to because of this female. Many of the wolves had endured serious injuries thanks to the cougars and the grenade—including Derren, who had also been *shot*. That wasn't something Ally could ever forgive.

Nick's claws sliced out, making the female kneeling in front of him jerk. "Fine. Roni and Taryn can have Kerrie. But Miranda here is mine."

Jaime sighed in disappointment. "You guys get all the fun."

"This is what Betas are for," Derren reminded his Alpha. "I can take care of this."

"Yes, you can . . . but I *need* this." Nick's anger with the female was almost palpable. "My mate would be long dead if it wasn't for Ally's vision about the grenade, Derren. I wouldn't have survived the loss of her, which means Willow would have grown up without her parents." As Shaya's hand rubbed his back soothingly, Nick's shoulders relaxed a little.

Derren nodded. "If you're sure." He went to Ally's side and draped an arm around her shoulders.

Trey stepped aside, making it clear he had no interest in contesting Nick's desire to deal with Miranda. "Make it hurt."

Squatting in front of Kerrie, Taryn spoke in a level yet menacing tone. "Because of you, a bomb might have taken out most of my pack—*including my mate and son*—and destroyed my home. My best friend would be dead, thanks to a fucking rifle grenade. And that's not counting the other attacks on both my territory and this one. All things considered, you don't deserve to breathe."

"I couldn't have said it better myself," proclaimed Roni. Abruptly, she used her claws to slice cleanly through Kerrie's jugular. A heartbeat later, Taryn swiped out her own claws, mercilessly gutting her victim.

Miranda gasped in horror as her cousin painfully died right before her eyes. When she tried to speak, Nick cut her off.

"If you're thinking of pleading for mercy, don't bother. Your life means nothing to me. My mate and my daughter? They're everything to me. This is for them." He shoved his claws deep into Miranda's chest, shaping the heart they could all hear pumping fast with fear. Then he twisted his hand sharply and closed his open fist slightly, slashing through the organ.

It seemed to take forever for Miranda's body to finally give out, but in reality her death had been swift. It hadn't been pleasant for Ally to watch, but the executions had been necessary. Kerrie— and Miranda as an accomplice—would have been responsible for many, many deaths had Kerrie's plot worked. They knew what they were risking, knew what the punishment would be. It was how the shifter world worked.

Figuring she'd seen enough death for one day, Ally turned to Derren. "I need a shower. And clothes." She was still wearing nothing but his coat.

Derren pressed a kiss to her nose. "Yes, you do. Come on."

She tipped her chin toward the enforcers, who were preparing to move the dead bodies. "The guys might want some help with that."

"I know, but you need me right now."

She opened her mouth to deny it—dominant females dealt with things themselves, and it was what Ally had always done. But she didn't *have* to go it alone anymore. "Yeah, I do." Her admittance made his eyes gleam with approval.

Back at their lodge, Derren held her close as they stood under the hot spray. "You okay?" he asked gently.

"Rachelle deserved what she got, I know that. But I still wish it hadn't had to end that way." She never would have admitted that softness to anyone else, but she trusted Derren with every secret and every vulnerability that existed inside her.

"You had no choice."

"I'm used to saving people. It's all I've ever done. Killing was a first."

"It might not be the last," he warned her, gently massaging shampoo through her hair. "Being Beta female means you'll be part of any battles that occur, baby."

Sensing his worry that today's events had affected her acceptance of the role, she kissed his chin. "I'm not going to ask for us to step down." She smiled, gently prodding his chest with her finger. "You *like* being Beta."

"No, I don't."

Her smile widened at his petulant tone. "Yes, you do. Admit it, the position suits you. And let's face it, you couldn't handle anyone else having a Beta level of authority over you. Even Nick doesn't have your total compliance."

"He doesn't want people to follow him blindly."

"Admit it," she repeated.

He sighed. "Fine. I like being Beta." Tipping her head back under the water, he rinsed the shampoo out of her hair. "I'm proud of you."

Meeting his gaze again, she cocked her head. "Why?"

"Because you did what you had to do. It sounds simple, but not everyone does it. It's not bad that you didn't find it easy. Killing someone shouldn't be easy." But it was easier for some—including him—than others. Derren wasn't sorry she'd killed Rachelle. Nor did he feel that the female had deserved to be spared. Hell, if he could have, he'd have dealt with Rachelle himself—both to get vengeance and to spare Ally the pain of doing it herself.

He loved that Ally had the capacity to feel some regret, loved the softness to her that most didn't see. "Are you relieved that the truth is finally out? The Collingwood wolves all know what really happened now. They know who the real liar was. Know how badly they fucked up."

"Yes. I feel . . . lighter. It shouldn't have bothered me that they all thought a load of crap about me. I'm not part of their pack anymore, and I don't want to be. But all the same, I wanted my name clear."

"I get it."

"I want your name clear too." She hated the stains he wrongfully carried on his name.

"Maybe one day it'll happen, but I doubt it. It's enough that you believe I'm innocent of the accusations. That you've never doubted me. Not even once." He kissed her gently but hungrily. When she reached for his cock—which was hard, of course, since she was naked—he closed his hand around her wrist. "Later. As soon as we're done here, I'm going to get you out of the shower, dry you off, get you dressed into your sweats, brush your hair, and then lay with you."

"Uh . . . why?" His plan didn't sound even half as good as what she had in mind.

"Because you're mine, and it's my job to take care of you."

Looking into that implacable gaze, she knew he wouldn't back down. While she was disappointed that there would be no sex, she also felt cherished that he would treat her this way. "Fine. But I expect multiple orgasms later."

He smiled. "I love a woman who knows what she wants."

CHAPTER TWENTY

I t wasn't every day that you saw a grown Alpha male having a stare down with a toddler. But going by the concentration and resolve on Nick's face, Ally suspected he would be damned if he'd look away first. The twinkling of the colored fairy lights that hung on the trees surrounding the tables and dance floor reflected in Nick's and Kye's eyes, making the whole staring-down scene seem eerie. Roni, Marcus, Bracken, Zander, and Jesse were all doing their best to stifle grins of amusement.

Pausing at their table, Ally smiled. "Why are you snarling at Kye?" The little boy, who greatly resembled Trey, was sitting on Roni's lap.

Without looking at her, Nick replied, "I'll stop when *he* stops."

"He's a baby alpha." Bracken took a swig of his beer. "Every instinct he has tells him there's a dangerous predator in front of him and that he must battle for dominance."

Jesse glanced around before asking Ally, "Where's your mate?"

"I left him with Shaya while I came to get more cake." Ally gestured to the plate she was holding. The huge cake had been specially made for the mating ceremony. Everywhere, people were laughing, dancing, eating, and drinking. They were also still enjoying the freedom to come and go from their territories as they pleased.

"The cake is gorgeous, isn't it," said Roni. "I ate so much of it, I'm surprised there's any left."

Marcus gave his mate a mock scowl. "Let's not forget you ate mine too."

"And mine," added Zander. Roni just sniffed.

Hearing a string of curses, Ally looked to see that Bruce was stealing food from the buffet. Kathy and Grace—a Phoenix mated female—had been good enough to cook all of it and had also tried outdoing each other in the process. Both females attempted to shoo him away from the table.

Having no success, Kathy glared at her daughter. "Roni!"

Blinking in surprise, Roni demanded, "How is this my fault? God, you'd blame me for the fall of Eve if you damn well could." Roni was probably right, though Ally was coming to suspect that Kathy only used her daughter as a scapegoat to keep her on her toes.

Suddenly Eli came storming over, pointing his cell phone at his sister. "Oh my God! I can't believe you did that!"

Leaving the siblings to argue over whatever prank was now being played, Ally headed to her mate. She had to smile at the sight of him holding a chuckling Willow, who was tugging hard on his hair. "Everything okay over here?" Damn, he looked edible in that gray shirt and those dark pants.

Derren tickled the little girl under her arm, making her release him with another chuckle. "She likes to see me in pain. She's a sadist."

"My daughter is *not* a sadist." Shaya took her daughter with a playful huff.

"She shoved a breadstick up Greta's nose."

"Because she senses evil."

Derren blinked. "I can't argue with that." With another huff, Shaya walked away to join Stone, Brad, and Wyatt. Glad to be alone with his mate, Derren yanked her against him and took a moment to sip and nip at her lips. "I missed you."

"I was gone five minutes."

"And in those five minutes, I was repeatedly assaulted by an infant. You weren't here to protect me." He hungrily devoured his mate with his eyes as she scooped some of the chocolate cake into her mouth. She looked truly amazing in that silk, midthigh coral dress with her hair slightly curled and hanging loose around her shoulders. He just wanted to lick every inch of her. His wolf wanted to take a big bite.

"At least I didn't leave you with my uncle Chase." Cain and her uncles had returned home the day after Kerrie and Miranda's execution, but they had come back to—or, more accurately, snuck back onto—Mercury territory the previous night with two of her other foster uncles. Whereas Sam seemed to like her mate, Chase did nothing but grunt and scowl at him . . . purely to fuck with him.

"No amount of animosity could make me hate your uncles." The news they had brought on their arrival had shocked the shit out of Derren. At Ally's request, the males had done some investigating and meddling, and they'd managed to achieve something Derren hadn't ever imagined would occur: they'd cleared his name.

In Cain's words, *"It was just a matter of putting the right pressure on the right people."* And since the sociopath had also had The Movement backing him, he'd done it quickly too. Despite the false accusation no longer hanging over Derren, he'd had very few apologies from his old pack. His sister had been one of those to contact him, despite her mate's disbelief. Derren was simply glad to no longer feel the weight of a guilt that didn't belong to him.

"Oh, look out, here comes the old dragon." Ally smiled as Jaime, Dante, Dominic, Trick, Ryan, Tao, and Greta approached. Other than the dragon, they all once again congratulated Ally and Derren, making complimentary comments about the ceremony.

Well . . . Ryan merely grunted his agreement to the others' compliments, but still.

Noticing that Trey's grandmother was sneering at her, Ally arched a brow. "You do realize you can't kill me with your glare, right?"

Greta narrowed her eyes. "You might have healed my Roni after she was shot, but I still don't trust you. I'll never like Seers." Tao and Trick rolled their eyes.

Tilting her head, Ally studied the woman from head to toe. "I guess Satan appears in all sorts of packages."

When Jaime laughed, Greta huffed at the Phoenix Beta female. "You find *her* funny, do you?"

Jaime wagged her finger, leaning back into her mate, who wrapped his arms around her. "Now, now . . . Just because you're so old the Three Wise Men helped you with your homework doesn't mean you need to take it out on me."

Dominic smiled at Ally. "If you were my homework, I'd do you on the table." Trick yanked him aside before Derren's fist could connect with the prick's face.

Tao shook his head at the enforcer. "Dom, why do you want to die?"

"We should get him away before Derren breaks his nose again," proposed Trick. Grunting, Ryan—who seemed to mostly communicate in grunts—grabbed a laughing Dominic by the back of his shirt while Trick and Tao followed.

Derren was about to suggest to Ally that they leave . . . but then Taryn, Trey, Marcus, and Roni—who had Kye wrapped around her like a boa constrictor—approached.

Greta gazed at Roni adoringly and kissed her on the cheek. "Hi, sweetheart."

Tightening his grip possessively on Roni's neck, Kye frowned at his great-grandmother as he firmly stated, "Mine." The kid loved Roni.

"We know, we know," Greta gently assured him. "Roni, you look beautiful tonight. Doesn't she, Marcus?"

Looking awed, Taryn leaned into Roni's other side and whispered, "Roni, once again I have to ask: *How did you do it? How did you get her to like you?*"

Planting one hand on her hip, Greta turned a glower on Taryn. "Whispering again? You're no better than Dante's sorry excuse for a mate." Jaime smiled at that while Dante groaned into his mate's neck.

Taryn sniffed at the dragon. "Easy there, Old Mother Hubbard. You're just mad because the Wrinkle Fairy did a tap dance on your face again."

As an argument between Taryn and Greta then commenced, Trey sighed tiredly. He spoke to both Derren and Ally as he said, "You won't believe it, but my mate and Greta actually like each other."

Derren cocked his head. "Yeah . . . I don't believe it." Done with these crazy people, he whispered into his mate's ear, "Let's go home. I want to be alone with you."

Just as quietly, Ally replied, "We shouldn't. It's our party." But then she smiled. "Yeah, let's go."

They kissed, fondled, and laughed all the way back to their lodge. Closing the door behind them, Derren grazed his teeth over his claiming mark. "Finally I have you all to myself." He doubted he'd ever be okay with sharing her, even as he knew it was both childish and selfish. But he figured he had a right to be at least a little selfish about his mate. "Tonight, I want to take you in our bed. For a change."

It was true that since they both seemed to have instant-gratification issues when it came to sex, they often didn't make it to the bed. "Then you'd better let me go."

His hands flexed on her ass. "I don't want to." But he released her. "Upstairs." The little minx stripped as she walked, so that she was wearing only her black lacy thong by the time she reached the bedroom. Apparently wanting to tease him, she did a little feline stretch that pushed out her ass and pulled a growl from his wolf.

Taking off his shirt, Derren came up behind her and splayed his hand on her stomach, looming over her as he spoke slowly into her ear, enunciating every word. "When I saw you walking toward me to begin the mating ceremony, all I wanted to do was flip up your little dress and fuck you right there in front of everybody." His hand snaked up to span her throat. "But we both know I'm much too possessive to let anyone else see what you look like when you come. Because you're mine and only mine," he added with a low growl. "Aren't you?"

Ally shivered as his hand squeezed her throat—a clear caution not to defy him. His tone was calm, even, confident, and assertive. He was seemingly in the mood to dominate her. Yeah, well, she was in the mood to fight him. "I won't deny that I'm your mate. I'll even concede that—"

"There's no conceding, baby. The situation is what it is. You belong to me." Releasing her throat, he whispered into her ear, "Turn around." She did it very, very slowly—a rebellious gesture that was all Ally and made him smile. Sliding a hand to the back of her head, he fisted her hair and tilted her head back. "Always so defiant. Just how I like you." He licked and kissed her neck, groaning as the scent of her need assaulted his senses. "It's not going to be soft and slow tonight, baby." He needed her too much. "It's going to be fast, and hard, and deep."

"Feel free to get started any minute now."

"Not yet." Using his grip on her hair, Derren brought her face to his and took her mouth with a kiss that was dominant, consuming, and demanding—needing to taste and feast on his mate. But he wanted another taste on his tongue too. He pushed her back onto the bed, shoved aside her thong, and thrust a finger inside her. "So fucking wet already." He loved that.

Bending over her delectable body, he raked his teeth over her nipple. "You're the most gorgeous thing I've ever seen." His tongue

swirled and licked its way down her body, pausing to deliver suckling bites here and there and renewing any fading marks. At the
same time, he teasingly danced the tips of his fingers along her
soft skin. When she bucked demandingly, he pinned her flat with
a grip on her hip. "I know what you want, but I'm not done here.
Now be still and let me make you come."

Heat and need raged through Ally as his talented mouth
lapped, sipped, and licked at her pussy. It was more leisurely than
seductive, like this was for him, not her; like he just wanted to
taste her, feel her come on his tongue. Still, Ally's pussy began to
spasm, making her feel so much emptier than she already did—a
taunting reminder by her body that she didn't have what she
wanted most right then.

"Derren . . ." It was something between a warning and a plea.
It was ignored. He continued to feast and gorge, until her body
was being tormented by an unrelenting, savage ache; screaming
to be filled and fucked. At this point, she was literally burning
for him. "Derren, no more." To her surprise, he didn't ignore her
again. Instead, he plunged two fingers inside her and suckled on
her clit, throwing her into a release so intense it stole her breath.

Having shed the rest of his clothes, Derren covered her trem-
oring body with his. Fuck, her taste drove him as crazy as the scent
and feel of her did. His cock hurt and throbbed, wanting to slake
its need on the female beneath him. "Ready for me, baby?" He
didn't give her time to answer, just grabbed her hips and lunged.
Her pussy was swollen from her orgasm, but he thrust hard and
deep until his balls slapped against her. Her slick pussy was blazing hot as it tightened around him almost possessively. He rolled
them so he was flat on his back with her straddling him. "Ride me."

Any other time, Ally might have teased him with slow, easy
downward thrusts. But right now, she felt like she'd lose her freaking mind if she didn't come soon. Digging the tips of her claws
into his solid abs, she impaled herself on him over and over. Her

pace was fast and relentless, her body *hurting* with the need to rid herself of the burning ache inside her.

"That's it, Ally. Fuck yourself on me." Tangling a hand in her hair, Derren pulled her down so he could bite and suck at her neck. Her movements became even more frantic, and her soft little moans turned into desperate whimpers. He could feel how badly she needed to come, could sense her frustration at being unable to reach that peak. He flipped them over and rode her hard. His cock plunged in and out of her pussy as he took, owned, and possessed her.

Ally's back arched as she went plummeting into her second orgasm, but he didn't stop, didn't even falter in his pace. His dark eyes gleamed with raw unadulterated hunger, looked at her like he believed he had every right to touch and take her as and when he pleased. But there was also total adoration burning there a love she could feel through their bond.

"Get ready to come again," he growled into her ear. Withdrawing from her body, he got to his knees, gripped her hips, and yanked her toward him as he thrust as deep as he could go. Each time he slammed into her, he jerked her to him, hitting her sweet spot with every thrust. He knew he'd never get enough of her, that nothing would ever be more important to him than her. Knew he'd always need her, always crave her. Not just her body, but everything about her—her smile, her eyes, her laugh, her prickly nature. She was burrowed deep inside him, exactly where she belonged.

"Fucking come. Now." Then she said three little words, and he lost all hold on the little control he had left. "Jesus, baby." He pounded into her so hard he knew it had to hurt, but he couldn't stop. Her body bowed as she screamed, and her lusciously hot pussy tightened, quivered, and contracted around him—milking him, making him come so fucking hard, and dragging every ounce of come from his cock.

Sated and drained, he collapsed on top of his mate. Her eyes were closed, and her body had practically melted into the mattress, shaking with aftershocks. He kissed her forehead before rolling onto his side, keeping her locked against him. She fit there perfectly. "Love you, baby." All he got in response was a dreamy smile. "You okay?"

She didn't open her eyes. "Best. Day. Ever."

He laughed. Considering it had been their mating ceremony, followed by some seriously hot sex, he'd have to agree. He inhaled deeply, taking her warm, sex-spiced scent inside his lungs. "I love how you smell after we have sex." It made him want to fuck her all over again.

She released a soft, happy sigh as his tongue lapped idly at her neck. Her wolf basked in his attention and reverence. "Is that your cell beeping?"

It was. Reaching over the bed, he pulled the phone out of the pocket of his discarded jeans. And growled at what he saw.

"What's wrong?"

"Dominic," he bit out, going back to cuddling his mate. "The little shit sent me a message with some tips on how to give multiple orgasms."

"That's not too bad." For Dominic.

"*And* asked if I want him to join us."

Her chuckle made Derren growl again. She play-punched his shoulder. "Lighten up, learn to laugh a little. He's not serious. He just does it to needle you. Instead of always reacting violently, you should try ignoring him."

Yeah, but . . . "I don't want to." What Derren wanted was to lunge at the prick again, then ensure Ally didn't heal him this time.

"You know, you could try being a little remorseful for your earlier actions. You broke his nose. Twice."

"*Now* who needs to lighten up?"

"Derren."

He sighed. "Okay, I'm sorry."

She snorted. "No, you're not."

"I'll ignore him next time."

"No, you won't."

"Which is exactly why this conversation is pointless." Nuzzling her, he smoothed a hand down her back to softly shape her ass. "We should talk about how much you love me instead."

"We should?" She smiled, teasing, "I don't know if I should risk it. I mean, those three words tend to get me fucked a lot, and I need a little time to recover."

He bit her neck. "Say it."

"Fine. I love you, even if you are a pushy, interfering fucker at times."

"And I love you, even if I do keep catching you using my razor to shave your legs."

"One time. That happened *one time*."

He chuckled. "So easy to rile up." Toppling her onto her back, he smoothly drove his cock back inside her. "I still don't know why I like that."

Curling her limbs around him, she smiled. "Let's just be glad that you do."

ACKNOWLEDGMENTS

Thank you so very, very much to my family for all your endless support, patience, and acceptance of my social ineptness. I apologize for all the times I nod along to what you're saying when, really, I've zoned out because I'm stuck in my book.

Massive thanks to my editor, JoVon Sotak, and the rest of the Montlake Team—including Jessica Poore, who's always ready to help, and Melody Guy, who always has the best ideas and advice. You're all amazing.

Lastly, an enormous thanks to anyone who has taken a chance on this book. I sincerely hope you enjoyed it! If for any reason you would like to contact me, please feel free to e-mail me at suzanne_e_wright@live.co.uk. I can also be reached on Facebook, Twitter, and my blog.

Take care!

ABOUT THE AUTHOR

Author Suzanne Wright, a native of England, can't remember a time when she wasn't creating characters and telling their tales. Even as a child, she loved writing poems, plays, and stories; as an adult, Wright has published ten novels: *From Rags*, *Burn*, three Deep in Your Veins novels, four books in the Phoenix Pack series, and this, the first book in the Mercury Pack series. Wright, who lives in Liverpool with her husband and two children, freely admits she hates housecleaning and can't cook, but that she always shares chocolate.

Website: www.suzannewright.co.uk
Blog: www.suzannewrightsblog.blogspot.co.uk
Twitter: www.twitter.com/suz_wright
Facebook: www.facebook.com/suzannewrightfanpage